Praise for Lucy Monroe

"*The Sicilian's Marriage Arrangement* is one of those stories that I couldn't wait to finish, but already started to miss when I turned the last page."
—*www.romancejunkies.com*

"If you are a fan of Diana Palmer's, like I am, you definitely need to give Lucy Monroe a try."
—*www.thebestreviews.com*

Praise for Julia James

"A very engaging read. The story is not only very sensuous, it offers a lot of emotional depth."
—*RT Book Reviews* on *The Greek's Virgin Bride*

"This entertaining book boasts powerful chemistry, a great plot and high-energy characters."
—*RT Book Reviews* on *The Greek Tycoon's Mistress*

Award-winning and bestselling author **Lucy Monroe** sold her first book in September of 2002 to the Harlequin Presents line. That book represented a dream that had been burning in her heart for years...the dream to share her stories with readers who love romance as much as she does. Since then she has sold more than thirty books and has hit national bestseller lists in the U.S. and England.

She really does love to hear from readers and responds to every e-mail. You can reach her by e-mailing lucymonroe@lucymonroe.com.

Julia James lives in England with her family. Harlequin novels were the first "grown-up" books Julia read as a teenager, alongside Georgette Heyer and Daphne du Maurier, and she's been reading them ever since.

When she's not writing, Julia enjoys walking, gardening, needlework, baking "extremely gooey chocolate cakes" and trying to stay fit!

LUCY MONROE

The Sicilian's Marriage Arrangement

JULIA JAMES

The Greek's Virgin Bride

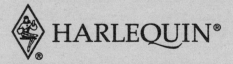 **HARLEQUIN**®

TORONTO • NEW YORK • LONDON
AMSTERDAM • PARIS • SYDNEY • HAMBURG
STOCKHOLM • ATHENS • TOKYO • MILAN • MADRID
PRAGUE • WARSAW • BUDAPEST • AUCKLAND

Recycling programs
for this product may
not exist in your area.

ISBN-13: 978-0-373-68802-9

THE SICILIAN'S MARRIAGE ARRANGEMENT &
THE GREEK'S VIRGIN BRIDE

Copyright © 2010 by Harlequin Books S.A.

The publisher acknowledges the copyright holder of the individual works
as follows:

THE SICILIAN'S MARRIAGE ARRANGEMENT
Copyright © 2004 by Lucy Monroe

THE GREEK'S VIRGIN BRIDE
Copyright © 2003 by Julia James

This edition published by arrangement with Harlequin Books S.A.

For questions and comments about the quality of this book
please contact us at Customer_eCare@Harlequin.ca.

® and TM are trademarks of the publisher. Trademarks indicated with
® are registered in the United States Patent and Trademark Office, the
Canadian Trade Marks Office and in other countries.

www.eHarlequin.com

Printed in U.S.A.

CONTENTS

With thanks to Serena for her help
with Italian phrases and perspective, but most of all
for the warmth of her friendship!

THE SICILIAN'S
MARRIAGE ARRANGEMENT

Lucy Monroe

CHAPTER ONE

"HAVE you heard? He's trying to buy her a husband."
Feminine laughter trilled mockingly.

"With his millions, it shouldn't be hard."

"The old man will live to see a hundred and five and keep
control of his company right up until he dies," the woman
said. "That means over thirty years married to a woman who
is *hope*lessly introverted, *hope*lessly ordinary and probably
*hope*less in bed, to boot. Practically a lifetime before her
future husband will see any fruit for his labor."

"Put in that light," the man drawled sardonically, "the
return on investment does seem pretty low."

"Why, darling, were you thinking of applying for the job?"
Scornful disbelief laced the woman's too knowing voice.

The masculine laughter that came in reply grated on
Luciano's nerves. He had arrived late to the New Year's Eve
party hosted by the Boston based multimillionaire, Joshua
Reynolds. Nevertheless, he knew exactly whom the cynical
woman and her male cohort were discussing: Hope Bishop—
an extremely sweet and *sì*, very shy, young woman. She was
also the granddaughter of their host.

Luciano hadn't realized the old man had decided to procure
her a husband. It should come as no surprise. While she had
the innocence of an eighteen-year-old, she must be twenty-

three or four, having completed her degree at university two years ago. He remembered attending a formal dinner to celebrate.

The dinner, like any other social gathering hosted by Reynolds, had turned into a business discussion and the guest of honor had disappeared long before the evening was over. He had thought at the time he might be the only person to have noticed. Certainly her grandfather had not, nor had any of the other businessmen present remarked upon Hope's absence.

Luciano turned away from the gossiping couple and stepped around a potted plant easily as tall as most men. Its bushy foliage obstructed his view of what was behind it, which was why he didn't realize Hope Bishop was standing there in frozen mortification until he had all but stepped on her.

She gasped and moved backward, her corkscrew curls catching on the leaves behind her, their chestnut color a startling contrast to the plant's bright green shrubbery. "*Signor di Valerio!*"

He reached out to stop her from landing on her bottom in the big Chinese pot housing the plant.

Wide violet eyes blinked in attempt to dispel suspicious moisture. "Oh, I'm sorry. How clumsy I am."

"Not at all, *signorina.*" The skin beneath his fingers was soft and warm. "I am the one who must apologize. I walked without looking ahead of myself and am at your feet in regret for my precipitous behavior."

As he had hoped it would, his overly formal, old-fashioned apology brought a small smile to tilt the generous lips that had a moment before been trembling. "You are very kind, *signor.*"

She was one of the few people who believed this to be so. He let go of her arms, finding it surprisingly difficult to make his fingers release their captive. "And you are very lovely tonight."

It had been the wrong thing to say. Her gaze flitted to the shrub and the still gossiping couple beyond, her expression turning pained. Their voices carried quite clearly, now discussing an adulterous affair between two of their acquaintances. No doubt Hope had heard their earlier words.

She affirmed his thoughts when she softly said, "Not lovely, I think, but *hope*lessly average," telling him too that she knew he had heard the unflattering comments.

He did not like the sadness in her eyes and he once again took her arm, leading her toward the library. It was the one room unlikely to have a lot of New Year's Eve guests milling about. "Come, *piccola.*"

Little one. It suited her.

She did not demur. That was one of the things he had always liked about the girl. She did not argue for the sake of it, not even with her overbearing and often neglectful grandfather. She was a peaceful sort of person.

They reached the library. He guided her inside, quickly ascertaining he had been right and no one else was present. He shut the door to keep it that way. She needed a few moments to collect herself.

Once again he was surprised by a desire to maintain his hold on her, but she tugged slightly on her arm and he released her. She faced him, her tiny stature accentuated by her three-inch heels, not diminished as he was sure she had hoped.

She really did look lovely in her formal gown of deep purple. The bodice outlined small, but perfectly proportioned curves while the shimmery fabric of the full skirt floated around her ankles in a very feminine way. She was not ravishingly sexy like the women he dated, but pretty in a very innocent and startlingly tantalizing way.

"I don't think he's trying to buy me a husband, you know." She tucked a reddish-brown curl behind her ear. "He's tried to buy me pretty much everything else since his heart attack, but I think even Grandfather would draw the line at buying a husband."

He wouldn't put anything past the wily old man, but forbore saying so. "It is natural for him to want to buy you things."

She grimaced. "Yes, I suppose so, but in the past he's always been impersonal with it."

A husband would be a pretty personal purchase, Luciano had to admit. "What do you mean, *signorina?*"

"Oh please, you must call me Hope. We've known each other for five years after all."

Had it been that long? "Hope then." He smiled and watched in some fascination as her skin took on a distinctly rosy hue.

She averted her face, so she was looking at the overfull bookcase on her left. "Grandfather has raised me since I was five."

"I did not know this."

She nodded. "But I don't think he noticed I even lived in his house except to instruct the servants to buy me what I needed, clothes when I grew out of them, books when I wanted them, an education, that sort of thing."

It was as he had always surmised. Hope had been relegated to the background of Reynolds' life and she had known it.

"But just lately, he's been buying things for me himself. My birthday was a month ago and he bought me a car." She sounded shocked by the fact. "I mean he went to the car dealership and picked it out himself. The housekeeper told me."

"This bothers you?" Most women of his acquaintance would find a car a very appropriate birthday gift.

Her pansy eyes focused back on him. "No. Not really.

Well, except that I don't drive, but that's not the point. It's just that I think he's trying to make up for something."

"Perhaps he regrets spending so little time with you through your formative years."

Her soft, feminine laughter affected his libido in a most unexpected way. "He had the housekeeper take me out to dinner for my birthday after having the Porsche delivered by the dealership."

"He bought you a Porsche?" That was hardly a suitable gift for a young woman who did not even know how to drive. *Porca miseria!* She could kill herself her first time behind the wheel with such a powerful car. He would have to speak to Reynolds about making sure she had received proper driving instruction before she was allowed onto the roads alone.

"Yes. He also bought me a mink coat. Not a fake one, but the real thing." She sighed and sat down in one of the burgundy leather reading chairs. "I'm, um…a vegetarian." She peeked up at him through her lashes. "The thought of killing animals makes me nauseous."

He shook his head and leaned back against the desk. "Your grandfather does not know you very well, does he, *piccola?*"

"I suppose not. I'm really excited about the six-week European tour he gave me for Christmas, though. Even if I won't be leaving for six months. He booked it for early summer." Her eyes shone with undisguised delight at the prospect. "I'll be traveling with a group of college students and a tour guide."

"How many other young women will there be?"

She shrugged. "I don't know. There will be ten of us in all, not including the guide of course." She crossed one leg over the other and started to swing the ankle back and forth, making her dress swish with each movement. "I don't know what the ratio of men to women will be."

"You are traveling with men?"

"Oh, yes. It's all coed. Something I would have loved to do in college, but better late than never, don't they say?"

He didn't know about that, but the idea of this naive creature spending six weeks with a group of libidinous, college age men did not please him. Why he should care, he did not stop to analyze. It was his nature to act on not only his behalf, but that of others as well.

"I do not think it is wise for you to go on such a trip. Surely a wholly female group would be more enjoyable for you."

Her leg stopped its swinging and she stared at him, clearly dumbfounded. "You're kidding, right? Half the reason for going on the trip is to spend some time with men close to my own age."

"Are you saying you object to Joshua buying you a husband, but not when it comes to him buying you a lover?" He didn't know what had made him say it. Only that he had been angry, an inexplicable reaction to the news she was interested in *male companionship*.

She blanched and sat back in her chair as if trying to put distance between them. "I didn't say that. I'm not looking for a...a lover." Then in a whirl of purple chiffon, she jumped up. "I'll just get back to the party." She eased around him toward the door as if he were an angry animal threatening to pounce.

He cursed himself in his native tongue as she opened the door and fled. There had been tears in her lavender eyes. What the gossiping duo had not been able to do with their nasty commentary, he had managed with one sentence.

He had made her cry.

Two now familiar hands grabbed her shoulders from behind. "Please, *piccola,* you must allow me to once again apologize."

She said nothing, but she didn't try to get away. How

could she? The moment he touched her, she lost all sense of self-will. And he did not have a clue, but then why should he? Sicilian business tycoons did not look to hopelessly average, twenty-three-year-old virgins for an alliance...of any sort.

She blinked furiously at the wetness that had already trickled down to her cheeks. Wasn't it enough that she had been forced to overhear her shortcomings cataloged by two of her grandfather's guests? That Luciano of all people should have heard as well had increased the hurt exponentially. Then to have him accuse her of wanting her grandfather to buy her a lover! As if the idea that any man would desire her for herself was too impossible to contemplate.

"Let me go," she whispered. "I need to check on Grandfather."

"Joshua has an entire household of servants to see to his needs. I have only you."

"You don't *need* me."

He turned her to face him. Then keeping one restraining hand on her shoulder, he tipped her chin up with his forefinger. His eyes were dark with remorse. "I did not mean it, *piccola.*"

She just shook her head, not wanting to speak and betray how much his careless words had hurt. She was not blasé enough to take the type of sophisticated joking he had been indulging in with equanimity.

He said something low in Italian and wiped at her cheeks with a black silk handkerchief he had pulled from his pocket. "Do not distress yourself so. It was nothing more than a poorly worded jest. Not something for which you should upset yourself."

"I'm sorry. I'm being stupidly emotional."

His gorgeous brown eyes narrowed. "You are not stupid, *piccola,* merely easily hurt. You must learn to control this or others will take advantage of your weakness."

"I—"

"Consider… The words of that gossiping pair distressed you and yet you know them to be false. Your grandfather has no *need* to buy you either a husband or a lover." He accentuated his words with a small squeeze of her shoulder. "You are lovely and gentle, a woman any man would be lucky to claim."

Now she'd forced him to fabrication to get out of the sticky situation.

She made herself smile. "Thank you."

The stunning angles of his face relaxed in relief and he returned the smile.

Good. If she could convince him she was fine, he would let her leave and she could find someplace to lick her wounds in private.

No one else would notice if she disappeared from the party. Well, perhaps Edward, her colleague from the women's shelter would notice. Only she had left him thoroughly engrossed in a debate over archeological method with one of her grandfather's colleagues and doubted he would surface before the party ended.

She stepped back from Luciano's touch, as much out of self-preservation as her need to get away completely. His proximity affected her to a frightening degree.

"I'm sure there are other guests you would like to talk to." Again the small polite smile. "If you're anything like Grandfather, you see every social occasion as an opportunity to advance your business interests. Most of the guests are his business contacts."

"You are a poor prevaricator, Hope." He stepped toward her, invading her space with his presence and the scent of his expensive cologne. She wondered if he had it mixed especially for him because she'd never smelled anything as wonderful on another man.

"P-prevaricator?" she asked, stumbling over the word because he was so close.

"It means one who deviates from the truth." His mouth firmed with grim resolve that warned her she would not get away so easily. "Rather than discuss business with men I can see any day of the week, I would prefer you to show me to the buffet table. I came late and did not eat dinner tonight."

She'd already known he had come late. Actually, she had thought he was not coming at all. The first she had known of his arrival had been the debacle by the banana tree. "Then, by all means, allow me to show you to the food table."

It was her duty as hostess, after all.

She turned to lead the way and almost stopped in shock as she felt his hand rest lightly against her waist. By the time they reached the buffet, her emotions and heart rate were both chaotic.

"The food," she croaked out and waved her hand toward the table.

"Will you sit with me while I eat? I prefer not to do so alone."

What choice had she? To refuse would be churlish. "Yes, of course."

She stifled a sigh. She had thought he would let her escape once they arrived in the reception room of the old Boston mansion, but she'd been wrong. The only thing that equaled Sicilian revenge was Sicilian guilt. She wondered how much penance Luciano's guilt would require before he would feel comfortable relegating her to the background once more.

Usually, she would be rejoicing at the opportunity to spend time in his company. He had fascinated her since their first meeting five years ago. She had seen him two or three times a year since as he and her grandfather had many business interests in common. Even now, she found being the focus of his attention a heady experience, no matter that compassion and guilt were the reasons for it.

She waited until he had filled a plate and then led him to one of the many small duet tables surrounding the room. There were larger tables where someone else would undoubtedly join them, but selfishly she thought that if these few moments were all she would have of him, she wanted them private.

"Are you still working as a bookkeeper at the women's shelter?"

Surprised he had remembered, she said, "Yes. We're opening another facility outside of Boston in a few weeks."

He asked her about it and then spent the next twenty minutes listening to her talk about the women's shelter and the work they were doing. They catered to victims of domestic violence, but did a great deal for single mothers down on their luck as well. Hope loved her job and could talk about the shelter for hours.

"I suppose they can always use donations?" Luciano asked.

So, that was how he planned to finish mitigating his guilt for making her cry. Not that it was really his fault. He could not be blamed for her lack of urbanity, but she wouldn't refuse him regardless.

He had plenty of money to donate to such a worthy cause. He was so rich, he traveled with not simply a bodyguard, but a whole security team. The only reason he was alone now was because Grandfather's security was known to be some of the most stringent in the East Coast big business community.

"Yes. They bought the furniture for the upstairs with my fur coat, but there's still the downstairs to furnish."

He smiled and her insides did that imitation of melting Godiva chocolate they always did when those sensual lips curved in humor. "So, you sold the mink, hmm?"

"Oh no. That wouldn't be right. It was a gift after all. I gave it to the shelter." She winked and then felt herself blushing at her own temerity. "They sold it."

"You've got a streak of minx in you I think."

"Perhaps, *signor.* Perhaps."

"Do you have contact information for the shelter?"

"Naturally."

"I should like to give it to my P.A., and instruct that a donation large enough to furnish several rooms is made on my behalf."

"I've got a business card upstairs in my room, if you'll wait a moment while I get it?" What she would never do on her own behalf, she did for the shelter with total equanimity.

"I will wait."

Hope pulled a white business card for the women's shelter from the top drawer of the escritoire in the small study attached to her suite of rooms. As she turned to head back downstairs, she realized it was less than ten minutes before midnight. She stopped and stared at the ornamental desk clock, biting her lip. If she waited just a few minutes to return downstairs, she could avoid the ritual of kissing someone on the stroke of midnight.

She didn't fear being accosted by one of the many male guests at her grandfather's party. She was aware that the most likely scenario would be her standing alone and watching others kiss. Her stomach tightened at the thought of watching Luciano locking lips with some gorgeous woman. And there were plenty of them downstairs.

Rich businessmen attracted beautiful women who had a chic she envied and could not hope to emulate.

She wasn't worried about leaving Luciano to his own devices. Even now, she had no doubt he was no longer sitting alone while he waited for her. He might not even wait at the table, but expect her to come find him once she returned downstairs. Now that his guilt had been appeased, she would no longer qualify for his undivided attention.

Going back downstairs at this moment in time would serve

no purpose other than to further underscore the humiliating fact that she did not fit amidst her grandfather's guests. She might have been born to his world, but she could never feel like she belonged in it. Perhaps because she had never felt like she belonged anywhere.

From the clock, her gaze shifted to the plaque hanging on the wall. It was a saying by Eleanor Roosevelt and it reminded her that she might not be able to help her shyness, but she did not have to be craven as well.

Luciano became aware of Hope instantly when she arrived once again in the periphery of his vision. She said and did nothing, but the sweet scent he associated with her reached out to surround him. He turned from the Scandinavian cover model who had approached him within seconds of Hope's disappearance from their table.

"You're back."

Her gaze flicked to the model and back to him. "Yes." She reached her hand out, a small white card between her delicate thumb and forefinger. "Here's the contact information for the shelter."

He took it and tucked it into the inner pocket of his formal dinner jacket. *"Grazie."*

"You're welcome."

Suddenly noisemakers started blaring around them and a ten second count down began in the other room. The model joined in as did the other guests surrounding him and Hope. Hope did as well, but an expression he did not understand crossed her features. Why should it make her sad to ring in the New Year?

He could not look away from the almost tragic apprehension turning her lavender eyes so dark, they appeared black. The blonde put her hand on his arm and he realized that men and women were pairing off. Ah, the traditional kiss to bring in the New Year with luck. And in a split second of clarity he understood Hope's sadness and that he had a choice. He could kiss the sexy, extremely world savvy woman to his left, or he could kiss Hope.

Her expression was carefully guarded, but he could tell that she expected him to kiss the model. She had grown accustomed to neglect and although she seemed more than willing to talk to him, she was terribly shy around others. She expected to kiss no one. And the expectation had put that sadness in her eyes. It was not right.

She was gentle and generous. What was the matter with the men of Boston that they overlooked this delicate but exotic bloom?

He shook off the blonde's hold and stepped toward Hope. Her eyes grew wide and her mouth stopped moving in the countdown, freezing in a perfect little *O*. Placing his hands on both sides of her face, he tilted it up for his kiss. A cacophony of *Ones* sounded around him and then he lowered his mouth to hers. He would kiss her gently, nothing too involved.

He did not want to frighten her, but he owed her this small concession for having made her cry. Buying furniture for her women's shelter would not cut it. That was money, but the insult had been personal and this was personal atonement.

His lips touched hers and she trembled. He gently tasted her with his tongue. She was sweet and her lips were soft. They were still parted and he decided to go a step further. He wanted to taste the warmth and wetness of her mouth. So he did.

And it was good, better than he would have thought possible.

Her tongue tentatively brushed against his and heat surged through his male flesh. He wanted more, so he took it, moving one hand to her back and pressing her into him. She went completely pliant against him, molding her body to his like molten metal over a cast figure. Using the hand on her back, he lifted her off the floor until her face was even with his own and he could kiss her as urgently as he wanted to do.

She wrapped her arms around his neck and moaned, kissing him back with a passion that more than matched his own.

The small noises emanating from her drove him on.

He deepened the kiss further, oblivious now to his surroundings.

He wanted to do more than kiss her. He wanted to strip her naked and taste every centimeter of her delectable little body. The library. He could take her back to the library.

His hand was actually moving to catch her knees so he could carry her off when a booming voice broke through the daze of his lascivious thoughts.

"With a kiss like that, you're both bound to have more good luck than a Chinese dragon."

CHAPTER TWO

LUCIANO'S head snapped up at the sound of Joshua Reynolds' humor-filled voice and reality came back with a painful thud. Hope was still clinging to him, her expression dazed, but the rest of the room was very much aware. And what they were aware of was that he'd been caught kissing the host's grand-daughter like a horny teenager on his first date with an older woman.

He set Hope down with more speed than finesse, putting her away from him with a brusque movement.

She stared up at him, eyes darkened with passion and still unfocused. "Luciano?"

"Didn't know you two knew each other so well." A crafty expression entered Reynolds' eyes that Luciano did not like.

"It is not a requirement to know someone well to share a New Year's kiss," he replied firmly, wanting to immediately squelch any ideas the old man might have regarding Luciano and Hope as anything other than passing acquaintances.

"Is that right?" Reynolds turned to Hope. "What do you say, little girl?"

Hope stared at her grandfather as if she did not recognize him. Then her eyes sought out Luciano once again, the question in them making him defensive.

He frowned at her. "She is your granddaughter. You know

as well as anyone how little I have seen of her over the years." His eyes willed Hope to snap out of her reverie and affirm his stand to her grandfather.

At first, she just looked confused, but then her expression seemed to transform with the speed of light. She went from dazed to hurt to horrified, but within a second she was doing her best to look unaffected.

It was not a completely successful effort with her generous lips swollen from the consuming kiss.

She forced a smile that hurt him to see because it was so obviously not the direction those lips wanted to go. "It wasn't anything, Grandfather. Less than nothing." She spun on her heel without looking back at Luciano. "I've got to check on the champagne." And she was gone.

He watched her go, feeling he should have handled that situation better and wishing he'd never come to the party in the first place.

"It didn't look like less than nothing to me, but I'm an old man. What do I know?"

The speculative tone of Joshua Reynolds' voice sent an arrow of wariness arcing through Luciano. He remembered the gossip he had overheard earlier. Rumors often started from a kernel of truth. The old man could forget trying to buy him as a husband for his shy granddaughter.

She might kiss with more passion than many women made love, but Luciano Ignazio di Valerio was not for sale.

He had no intention of marrying for years yet and when he did, it wouldn't be to an American woman with her culture's typically overinflated views on personal independence. He wanted a nice traditional Sicilian wife.

His family expected it.

Even if kissing Hope Bishop was as close to making love with his clothes on as he'd ever come.

* * *

Hope slammed the door of her bedroom behind her and then spun around to lock it for good measure.

It was after three o'clock and the last guest had finally departed. She'd made herself stay downstairs for the remainder of the party because she was guiltily aware her grandfather had arranged it for her benefit rather than business. He'd said as much when he told her he planned to have a New Year's Eve bash at the Boston mansion.

She wished he had not bothered. At least part of her did. The other part, the sensual woman that lurked inside her was reveling in her first taste of passion.

Luciano had kissed her. Like he meant it. She was fairly certain the whole thing had started as a pity kiss, but somewhere along the way, he'd actually gotten involved. So had she, but that was not so surprising.

She'd wanted to kiss the Sicilian tycoon for the better part of five years. It had been an impossible fantasy...until tonight. Then a combination of events had led to a kiss so devastating, it would haunt her dreams for years to come.

She plopped down onto the side of her bed and grabbed a throw pillow, hugging it to herself.

He had tasted wonderful.

Had felt hard and infinitely masculine against her.

Had smelled like the lover she desired above all others.

And then he had thrust her from him like a disease ridden rodent. She punched the cushion in her lap. He had been enjoying the kiss. She was sure of it, but then her grandfather had interrupted and Luciano had acted *embarrassed* to be caught kissing her.

Okay, maybe it did nothing for his sophisticated image to be caught taking pleasure in the kiss of an awkward twenty-three-year-old virgin who never dated. But surely it wasn't such a tragedy either. Not so bad that he had to shove her away like something he'd found under his shoe in a cow pasture.

The tears that had seemed to plague her for one reason or another all evening once again welled hot and stinging in her eyes. He'd made her look like a complete fool. She'd been forced to smile while cringing inside at the teasing and downright ribald comments tossed her way for the last three hours.

People were saying that she'd thrown herself at him. That he'd had to practically manhandle her to get her off of him. That as desperate spinsters went, she had won the golden cup.

Wetness splashed down her cheeks.

She'd heard it all while circulating among the guests. People had gone out of their way to speak loudly enough so she could not help overhearing. Some had made jokes to her face. A few of the male guests had offered to take on where Luciano had left off.

Grandfather remained blissfully ignorant, having closeted himself in the study with a businessman from Japan after the official New Year's toast. If she had anything to say about it, he would remain that way.

Luciano, the rat, had left the party within minutes of his humiliating rejection of her.

Even the joy of being kissed with such heady abandon by the one man she had ever wanted could not overshadow her degradation at his hands in front of a room filled with her grandfather's guests. She hated Luciano di Valerio. She really did.

She hoped she never saw him again.

"The shares are not for sale."

Luciano studied the man who had just spoken, looking for a chink in the old man's business armor, but Reynolds was a wily campaigner and not a speck of interest or emotion reflected in his gray eyes.

"I will pay you double what you gave my uncle for them." He'd already offered a fifty-percent return on investment. To no avail.

Reynolds shook his head. "I don't need more money."

The words were said with just enough emphasis to make a very pertinent point. Whatever Joshua Reynolds wanted in exchange for those shares, it wasn't money and he could afford to turn down Luciano's best offer.

"Then, *signor*, what is that you do need?" he asked, taking the bait.

"A husband for my granddaughter."

Impossible! *"Che cosa?"*

Joshua leaned back in his chair, his hands resting lightly on his oversize executive desk. "I'm getting on in years. I want to make sure I leave Hope taken care of. Regardless of what young women these days believe, and young men when it comes to it—that means seeing her married."

"I do not think your granddaughter would agree with you."

"Getting her to agree is your job. The girl doesn't know what is best for her. She spends all her free time working for the women's shelter, or the local animal shelter, or doing things like answering phones for the annual MDA telethon. She's a worse bleeding heart than her grandmother ever was."

And it was unlikely she found the slightest understanding from the ruthless old bastard sitting across from Luciano. "Are you saying that Hope doesn't know you're trying to buy her a husband?"

"I'm not interested in discussing what my granddaughter knows or doesn't know. If you want those shares, you're going to have to marry her to get them."

The shares in question were for the original family-held Valerio Shipping, a company started by his great-grandfather and passed through each successive generation. While it rankled, having a nonfamily member holding a significant chunk of stock was not the end of the world.

He stood. "Keep the shares. I am not for sale."

"But Valerio Shipping is."

The words stopped Luciano at the door. He turned. "It is not. I would never countenance the sale of my family's company." Although his interests in Valerio Shipping represented a miniscule portion of his business holdings, his family pride would never allow him to offload it.

"You won't be able to stop me."

"My uncle did not hold majority stock in the company." But the fool had sold the large block he *had* held to Joshua Reynolds rather than approach his nephew when gambling debts had made him desperate for cash.

"No, but with the proxy of some of your distant cousins as well as the stock I have procured from those willing to sell, I do control enough shares in the company to do what I damn well please with it."

"I do not believe you." Many of those distant cousins had emigrated, but he could not believe they were so lost to family pride as to give an outsider their proxy or worse, sell their portion of Valerio Shipping to him.

His uncle he could almost believe. The man was addicted to wine, women and casinos. He had the self-discipline of a four-year-old and that was probably giving the man more credit than he deserved.

Reynolds tossed a report on the desk. "Read it."

Luciano hid his mounting fury as he crossed the room and then lifted the report to read. He did not sit down, but flipped through the pages while still standing. Outraged pride grew with each successive page and coalesced into lava like fury when he read the final page.

It was a recommendation by Joshua Reynolds to merge with Valerio Shipping's number one competitor. If that were not bad enough, it was clear that while the other company would maintain their business identity, Valerio Shipping would cease to exist.

He tossed the report onto the gleaming surface of the

walnut desk. "You are not trying to buy Hope a husband, you are trying to blackmail one."

Reynolds shrugged broad shoulders, not even slightly stooped by his more than seventy years. "Call it what you like, but if you want to keep Valerio Shipping in the di Valerio family and operating business under the Valerio name, you will marry my granddaughter."

"What is the matter with her that you have to resort to such tactics to get her a husband?"

For the first time since Luciano had entered the other man's office, Reynolds' guard dropped enough to let his reaction show. Luciano's question had surprised him.

It was in the widening of his eyes, the beetling of his steel gray brows. "There's nothing wrong with her. She's a little shy and a bleeding heart, I admit, but for all that she'll make a fine wife."

"To a husband you have to blackmail into marriage?"

In many ways, he was a traditional Sicilian male, but Joshua Reynolds made Luciano look like a modern New Man. Hope's grandfather was more than old-fashioned in his views. He was prehistoric.

"Don't tell me, you were waiting for love eternal to get married, man?" Derision laced Reynolds' voice. "You're thirty, not some young pup still dreaming of fairy tales and fantasies. And you're plenty old enough to be thinking about a wife and family. Your own father is gone, so cannot advise you, but I'm here to tell you, you don't want to leave it too late to enjoy the benefits of family life."

Not only did Luciano find the very idea of taking advice from a man trying to blackmail him offensive, but Joshua Reynolds was the last person to hand out platitudes about enjoying family life. He'd spent his seventy plus years almost completely oblivious to his own family.

"I'm offering you a straightforward business deal. Take it

or leave it." The tone of Reynolds' voice left no doubt how seriously he felt about following through on his threats.

"And if I leave it my family company ceases to exist."

The other man looked unconcerned by the reminder. "No company lasts forever."

Gritting his teeth, Luciano forced himself not to take the other man by the throat and shake him. He never lost control and he would not give his adversary the benefit of doing so now.

"I will have to think about it."

"You do that and think about this while you are at it. My granddaughter left two weeks ago for a tour of Europe in the company of four other girls, a tour guide and five young men. Her last letter mentioned one of them several times. David something or other. Apparently, they are developing quite the friendship. If you want Hope to come to the marriage bed untouched, you'd better do something about it soon."

Hope peered through the viewer of her state-of-the-art digital camera that had been a parting gift from her grandfather before her trip. She knelt down on one knee, seeking the perfect shot of the Parthenon in the distance. The waning evening light cast the ancient structure in purplish shadows she had been determined to catch on disc.

It was a fantastic sight.

"It's going to be dark before you get the shot, Hope. *Come on, honey, take your picture already.*" David's Texas drawl intruded on her concentration, making her lose the shot she'd been about to snap and it was all she could do not to ask him to take himself off.

He'd been so nice to her over the past three weeks, offering her friendship and a male escort when circumstances required it. She'd been surprised how at ease she'd felt with the group right off, but a lifetime of shyness did not dissipate overnight. Feeling comfortable had not instantly translated into her making overtures of friendship. David had approached her, his extroverted confidence and easy smile drawing her out of her shell.

Because of that, she forced back a pithy reply, despite her surge of unaccustomed impatience. "I'll just be a second. Why don't you wait for me back at the bus?"

"I can't leave my best girl all by herself. Just hurry it up, honey."

She adjusted the focus of her camera and snapped off a series of shots, then stood. Interruptions and all, she thought the pictures were going to turn out pretty well and she smiled with satisfaction.

Turning to David, she let that smile include him. "There. All done." She closed the shutter before sliding her camera into its slim black case and then she tucked that into her oversize shoulder bag.

"Okay, we can return to the bus now." She couldn't keep the regret from sliding into her voice. She didn't want to leave.

David shook his head. "We're not scheduled to go back to the hotel for another twenty minutes."

"Then why were you rushing me?" she demanded with some exasperation.

His even white teeth slashed in an engaging grin. "I wanted your attention."

She eyed the blond Texan giant askance. In some ways he reminded her of a little boy, mostly kind but with the self-centeredness of youth. "Why?"

"I thought we could go for a walk." He put his hand out for her to take, clearly assuming her acquiescence to his plan.

After only a slight hesitation, she took it and let him lead her away from the others. A walk *was* a good idea. It was their last day in Athens and she wanted this final opportunity to soak in the ambience of the Parthenon.

David's grip on her hand was a little tight and she wiggled her fingers until he relaxed his. She was unused to physical affection in any sense and it had taken her a while to grow accustomed to David's casual touching. In some ways, she still wasn't. It helped knowing that he wasn't being overly familiar, just a typical Texas male—right down to his calling her honey as often as he used her name.

She stopped and stared in awe at a particularly entrancing view of the ancient structure. "It's so amazing."

David smiled down at her. "Seeing it through your eyes is more fun than experiencing it myself. You're a sweet little thing, Hope."

She laughed. "What does that make you, a sweet *big* thing?"

"Men aren't sweet. Didn't your daddy teach you anything?"

She shrugged, not wanting to admit she couldn't even remember her father. She only knew what he looked like because of the pictures of her parents' wedding her grandfather had on display in the drawing room. The framed photos showed two smiling people whom she had had trouble identifying with as her own flesh and blood.

"I stand corrected," she said. "I won't call you sweet ever again, but am I allowed to think it?"

The easy banter continued and they were both laughing when they returned to the tour bus fifteen minutes later, their clasped hands swinging between them.

"Hope!"

She looked away from David at the sound of her name being called. The tour operator was standing near the open door of the bus. She waved at Hope to come over. A tall man in a business suit stood beside her, dwarfing her with his huge frame. The growing darkness made it difficult to discern his features and Hope could not at first identify him. However, when he moved, she had a moment of blindingly sure recognition.

No one moved like Luciano di Valerio except the man himself. He had always reminded her of a jaguar she'd once seen in a nature special when she was an adolescent, all sleek, dark predatory male.

David stopped when they were still several yards from the bus, pulling her to a halt beside him. "Is that someone you know?"

Surprised by the aggressive tone in her friend's voice, she said, "Yes. He's a business associate of my grandfather's."

"He looks more like a *don* in the Mafia to me."

"Well, he *is* Sicilian," she teased, "but he's a tycoon, not a loan shark."

"Is there a difference?" David asked.

She didn't get a chance to reply because Luciano had started walking toward them the moment David stopped and he arrived at her side just as David finished speaking. Regardless of her wish to never see the man again, her eyes hungrily took in every detail of his face, the strong squarish jaw, the enigmatic expression in his dark brown eyes and the straight line of his sensual lips.

"I have come to take you to dinner," he said without preamble or indeed even the semblance of having asked a question.

"But how in the world did you come to be here?" Bewilderment at seeing him in such a setting temporarily eclipsed her anger toward him.

"Your grandfather knew I would be in Athens. He asked me to check on you."

"Oh." Ridiculously deflated by the knowledge he was

there under her grandfather's aegis rather than his own, she didn't immediately know what else to say.

David had no such reticence. "She's fine."

The comment reminding her of not only his presence, but her manners as well. "Luciano, this is David Holton. David, meet Luciano di Valerio."

Neither man seemed inclined to acknowledge the introduction.

David eyed Luciano suspiciously while the tycoon's gaze settled on their clasped hands with unconcealed displeasure. Then those dark eyes were fixed on her and the expression in them was not pleasant. "I see you have decided to go for option two after all."

At first, she couldn't think what he meant and then their conversation in the library came back to her. Option one had been a husband, she supposed. Which meant that option two was a lover. He was implying she and David were lovers.

Feeling both wary and guilty for no reason she could discern, she snatched her hand from David's. "It's not like that," she said defensively before coming to the belated conclusion it wasn't his concern regardless.

David glared down at her as if she'd mortally offended him when she let go of his hand. "I planned to take you out this evening."

"I am sorry your plans will have to be postponed," Luciano said, sounding anything but. He inclined his head to her. "I have apprised your tour guide that I will return you to your hotel this evening."

"How nice, but a bit precipitous." She didn't bother to smile to soften the upcoming rejection. After the way he had treated her at the New Year's Eve party, he didn't deserve that kind of consideration. "It was kind of Grandfather to be concerned, but there is no need for you to give up your entire evening in what amounts to an unnecessary favor to him."

"I agreed to check on you for your grandfather's sake. I wish to spend the evening with you for my own."

She couldn't believe what she was hearing. *She refused to believe it.* She glared helplessly at him. Six months ago, he had kissed her to within an inch of her life, then thrust her away as if she were contaminated. He'd left her to face hours of humiliating comments and loudly spoken asides. *And…* she hadn't heard word one from him in all the intervening months.

David moved so that his body blocked her view of Luciano. "I thought I would take you to that restaurant you liked so much first day here, honey." The accusation in his voice implied he had exclusive rights to her time, not to mention the altogether unfamiliar inflection he gave the word *honey.*

Nothing could be further from the truth.

"You could have said something earlier," she censored him.

"I wanted it to be a surprise," he responded sullenly. "I didn't expect some arrogant Italian guy to show up and try to spirit you away."

The situation was getting more unreal by the minute. Men never noticed her and yet here were two battling for her company.

She was tempted to tell Luciano to take a flying leap, but part of her also wanted a chance to rake him over the coals for his callous treatment of her. An insidious curiosity about why he wanted to be with her after rejecting her so completely was also niggling at her.

It would probably be downright brainless to give in to that curiosity or her desire to get a little of her own back, however. She had the awful feeling that her stupidly impressionable heart would be only too ready to start pining for him again if she allowed herself the luxury of his company.

*When did you stop pining for him? Was that before or after
the ten times a day you forget what you're doing remembering how it felt to be kissed by him?* She ignored the mocking
voice of her conscience, infinitely glad mind reading was not
one of Luciano's many accomplishments.

Going with Luciano would not be a bright move.

On the other hand, she was uncomfortable with the pro-
prietary attitude David was exhibiting. It struck her suddenly
that he'd been growing increasingly possessive of her time
over the past days. She hadn't minded because it meant she
didn't have to put herself forward in unfamiliar situations, but
they were just friends. It bothered her that he thought he
could plan her time without her input.

She chewed her bottom lip, unsure what to do.

She felt wedged between two unpleasant alternatives,
neither of which was going to leave her unscathed at the end
of the evening.

CHAPTER THREE

"OUR reservations are for eight-thirty. We have to be on our way, *piccola mia*," Luciano said, completely ignoring David.

"Are all European men so arrogant?" David asked her in direct retaliation.

She shot a quick sideways glance to see how Luciano had taken her friend's insolence. His expression was unreadable. "Shall we go?" he asked her.

David expelled an angry hiss.

She laid her hand on his forearm. This was getting ridiculous and if she didn't act soon, her friend would be well on his way to making an enemy of a very powerful man. David was too young to realize the long term impact on his future business dealings such an action might have. Though she was irritated by David's behavior, she liked him too much to let him do something so stupid.

Besides, if she went with Luciano, she hoped David would get the message she wanted his friendship, but wasn't interested in anything more. She couldn't be. She might want to hate Luciano, but he remained the only man she could think of in that way.

She had no experience with brushing off a man's interest and this seemed the easiest way.

"I'm sorry. Can we make it another night?" she asked by way of atonement.

"We won't be in Athens another night," he reminded her.

"I know."

He would probably have said more, but the bus driver called the final boarding call, shouting specifically for David to get a move on.

"You'd better go," she said, relieved the confrontation could not be prolonged. "I'll see you tomorrow."

"All right, honey." He bent down and kissed her briefly on the lips.

Shocked, she stared at him speechless. He'd never even kissed her cheek before.

He smiled, not with his usual friendly grin, but with an implied intimacy that did not exist between them. "If you don't want to wait for morning, you can come by my room tonight after your grandfather's crony drops you off."

The implication that Luciano was old enough to be in her grandfather's generation was enough to make her lips quirk despite the unwelcome kiss and male posturing.

"Perhaps your young friend's dates are used to going home unsatisfied and in need of further male companionship," Luciano drawled silkily, "but I can promise you, *bella mia,* you will have no such need tonight."

She gasped, all humor fleeing, and glowered at both men. "That's enough. *Both of you.* I have no intention of letting anyone *satisfy* me." She blushed even as she said the words and was irritated with herself for doing so.

"I do not appreciate this petty male posturing either." She didn't have to choose the best of two poor options, she could make another one. "I don't think I want to have dinner out at all. I'd rather eat room service alone in my hotel room than be in the company of *any* arrogant male."

With a triumphant glare at Luciano that did not endear him

to her, David loped off toward the bus where the driver stood at the open door with obvious impatience. She started to follow him, determined to do just as she'd threatened. David might think he'd won, but he would find out differently if he tried to coax her out of her room tonight.

She'd gotten no further than a step when Luciano's hands settled on her shoulder, arresting her in midflight. "We need to discuss your regrettable tendency to leave before our conversations are finished. It is not polite, *piccola*."

He pulled her into his side and waved the bus driver off in one fluid movement.

She watched in impotent anger as the big vehicle pulled away. It was that, or scream like a madwoman for the bus driver to stop. She wasn't even sure he would hear her with the door closed and the rather noisy air-conditioning unit running full tilt. And she had absolutely no desire to make a spectacle of herself in front of the tourists milling about the parking area. His highhanded tactics had effectively left her with no choice but to stay behind with Luciano.

She didn't have to like it however and she tore away from his side with unconcealed contempt. "That was extremely discourteous, *signor*. I don't appreciate being manhandled, nor do I accept you have the right or the reason to dictate my activities."

He frowned down at her. "I may not yet have the right, but I do have the reason. I wish to spend time with you, *cara*."

"And my wishes count for nothing?" she demanded while reeling inside from such an admission from him as well as the tender endearment.

"Your wishes are of utmost importance to me, but do you really prefer ordering room service to an evening spent in my company?"

That was very much in question. It wasn't her preference, but her preservation she was concerned about. "You were insufferably rude. You implied you were going to… That we… As if I would!"

She could not make herself say the words aloud and that made her mad. Angry with him for implying he was going to take her to bed in the first place and furious with herself for still being such a backward creature she couldn't discuss sex without blushing like the virgin she was.

His laughter was the last straw as far as she was concerned. She didn't have to stick around to be made fun of. She'd suffered enough at his hands in that regard already.

She turned on her heel with every intention of finding some sort of public transport to take her back to the hotel. Once again he stopped her. This time, he wrapped his arms around her middle and pulled her back into his body with a ruthless purpose.

His lips landed on her nape in a sensual caress that sent her thoughts scattering to the four winds. "I have ached to taste you again for six long months. You must forgive me if my enthusiasm for your company makes me act without proper courtesy."

Enthusiasm did not take six months to act, but she was too busy trying not to melt into a puddle of feminine need at his feet to tell him so. "Luciano?" she finally got out.

He spun her around to face him. "Spend the evening with me, *cara*. You know you want to."

"David was right. You are arrogant."

"I am also right."

She would have argued, but he kissed her. The moment his lips touched hers, she was lost. His mouth moved on hers with expert effect, drawing forth a response she could not hide or control. She allowed his tongue inside her mouth after the first gentle pressure applied to the seam of her lips.

He tasted like she remembered. Hot. Spicy. Masculine. When he pulled away, she was too lost in her own sensual reaction to his kiss to even notice he was leading her anywhere. It wasn't until he stopped at the waiting limo and rapped out instructions to the ever-present security team, that she once again became aware of her surroundings.

Mary, mother of Joseph, it was just like at the party.

He could have done anything to her and she would have let him. She was also aware that while she'd been completely lost to reality, he had been in absolute control.

She tried to tell herself she was letting him hand her into the car because she didn't relish riding public transport alone at night in a foreign country. But she knew the truth. If she didn't sit down soon, she'd fall down. Her legs were like jelly and no way did she want him realizing that betraying fact.

Inside the car, she fiddled nervously with the strap of her brightly colored shoulder bag. It had a pattern of bright yellow and orange sunflowers all over it. She'd bought it so that it would be easily spotted among the other ladies' bags on the tour, but it looked gauche sitting on the cool leather seat of the ultra-luxurious limo.

She was also positive that her casual lemon yellow sundress and flat leather sandals were not *de rigueur* for the types of restaurants he frequented.

"I think it would be best if you took me back to my hotel," she said at the same time as he asked, "Are you enjoying your holiday?"

Her eyes met Luciano's in the well-lit interior of the car. Apparently neither one of them wanted to discuss the recent kiss.

His intense gaze mesmerized her. "I do not wish to take you back to your hotel."

"I'm not dressed for dinner out." She indicated her casual, day worn clothes with a wave of her hand.

"You look fine."

She snorted in disbelief. "Where are we eating, a hot dog stand?"

"I do not think they have those in Athens, *cara*."

"You know what I mean."

She didn't even want to think how her hair looked. She'd long ago given up trying for a chic hairstyle and wore her natural curls in an only slightly tamed riot. Most of the time it suited her, but she could imagine that after spending the day tramping the streets of Athens it probably looked like she'd never brushed her hair in her life.

"You must trust me, *piccola*. I would not embarrass you."

That was rich, coming from him.

"Now, please, won't you tell me how you are finding your holiday? I remember you looked forward to it very much."

He had closed the privacy window between them and the front seat and turned on the tiny lights that ran the entire length of the roof, giving off a surprisingly illuminating glow. A glow that cast his features in stark relief. The genuine interest reflected in his expression prompted her to answer.

"It's been wonderful."

"And what has been your favorite stop so far?"

She couldn't believe a man of his extensive experiences would truly be interested in her first taste of Europe, but she answered nonetheless. "I really can't say." She smiled, remembering all the incredible things she'd seen. "I've loved every moment. Well, maybe not the airports, but David and the others have made the waiting around in drab terminals fun."

Luciano frowned at the mention of David's name. "It is not serious between you two?"

"If it were, you put a spanner in the works tonight, didn't you?" She might have preferred that spanner, but he didn't know that and his behavior had been unreasonable.

He did not look in the least bit guilty. "He implied you

might come back to his room tonight. Are you sleeping with him?"

"That's none of your business!"

He leaned over her, the big torso of his six feet, four inch body intimidating at such close range. Suddenly he didn't remind her of just any old jaguar, but a hungry one intent on hunting his prey and moving in for the kill.

She felt like the prey.

"Tell me."

She was shy, but she wasn't a coward, or so she reminded herself frequently. "No. And if you're going to act like some kind of Neanderthal brute all evening, you may as well tell your chauffeur to take me back to my hotel right now."

She'd said it so many times now, it was beginning to sound like an impotent litany.

Amazingly, he backed off. Physically anyway.

"I am no brute, but I admit the thought you share your body with him does not predispose me to good temper."

"Why?"

"Surely after the kiss we shared only minutes ago, you do not have to ask this."

"Are you saying you give the third degree to every woman you kiss?" She didn't believe it.

"You are not every woman."

"No. I'm the hopelessly introverted, hopelessly average and probably hopeless in bed granddaughter of your business associate." The bitter memory rolled off her tongue before she became conscious what the word *probably* would reveal to him. Maybe he wouldn't notice she'd all but told him she was not sleeping with David. "I don't see where that makes me anything special to you."

It seemed he hadn't comprehended the implication of her words when he spoke. "You are not introverted with this David fellow. You were laughing with him and holding his hand."

He made it sound like she'd been caught *in flagrante delicto* with David. "He's my friend."

"I also am your friend, but you do not hold my hand."

"For Heaven's sake, you wouldn't hold a woman's hand unless it was to lead her to bed." Had she really said that?

"And are you trying to say this is not where your *friend* David was leading you?"

"Don't be ridiculous!"

"It is not ridiculous for me to think this. He looks at you with the eyes of a man who has claim to you."

"There is such thing as the claim of friendship."

"And friendship requires late night visits to his hotel room?"

"I've never been to his hotel room late at night, for goodness' sake. I'm hardly the type to carry on a brief affair, or did you miss the hopeless-in-bed description?" As the words left her mouth, she realized with chagrin she'd given Luciano what he wanted—a definite answer to whether or not she was sleeping with David.

He didn't look smug, however. He was too busy glaring at her. "Stop repeating that bitch's words as if they are gospel. She knows nothing of you or your passions. You will be a consuming fire in my bed, of that I am certain."

"Your bed?"

He sighed. "I have no plans to seduce you tonight, so you can relax."

"But you do plan to seduce me?" She pinched the inside of her elbow to make sure she was not sleeping and having some bizarre dream. Pain radiated to her wrist. She was awake.

"Perhaps you will care to tell me what restaurant so caught your approval on your first day in the city?" he asked, ignoring her question.

Certain she'd had all the seduction talk she could take for

one night, she eagerly accepted his change of subject. She told him about their visit to the nightlife of the Psiri where she'd sampled out of this world food at one of the many small cafés that did not even open until six in the evening.

"It was a lot like Soho, but I felt more comfortable in Psiri than I ever did visiting that section of New York City. Maybe that's because I went there with my roommate from college. She was from Manhattan and her friends were all very gothic." Hope could still remember how out of place she'd felt in the avant garde atmosphere.

"Psiri is fantastic and a lot more laid back. I didn't feel like I was on display, if that makes any sense." Her Boston manners and introverted ways had made her feel out of place in Soho, but the Psiri was patronized by so many different nationalities, no one person stood out.

Luciano shrugged, his broad shoulders moving fluidly in the typical European movement. "I have never been to Soho and it has been several years since I indulged in the nightlife of Athens."

"I suppose it's hard to do normal things like drink ouzo in a small bar on a busy street when you've got a security team trailing you." Like the one in the nondescript car behind the limousine.

"*Sì*, and there is the lack of time as well. I have spent the better part of the last ten years building my business holdings. My socializing has been of necessity targeted to that end."

"Just like Grandfather."

"Perhaps."

"Is that what tonight is about? Are you doing my grandfather a favor in return for which you are angling for some kind of business coup?"

Luciano went curiously still. "What makes you ask this?"

It was her turn to shrug. "I don't know. I guess it's just hard to believe you've thought about me at all over the past six months." She ignored his threatened intent to seduce her as macho posturing. It must be a Sicilian male thing. "It's not as if you'd called or anything. And I know I'm not your average date."

He might socialize for business, but the companions he chose to do it with were invariably gorgeous and terribly sophisticated. Much like the model he had turned away from on New Year's Eve to kiss Hope instead. She still found that inexplicable. One of his previous *amours* had been a dispossessed princess with a reputation for fast living. His latest was an Italian supermodel who gave sultry new meaning.

Hope was as far from such a being as Luciano was from an awkward teenager.

"Accept that it pleases me to see you."

"Why should I?"

"Because I say it is so." Exasperation laced his every word and she wanted to kick him.

"You can say anything, but it's your actions that show what you really feel."

"What is that supposed to mean?"

Their arrival at their destination prevented further conversation.

Luciano helped Hope out of the limousine. Who would believe such a shy little thing could be such a termagant as well? After her response to his kiss on New Year's Eve, he had been sure wooing her would be the easy part of the deal with Joshua Reynolds. However, she was hardly falling into his arms in gratitude for his pursuit.

By the saints, she was contrary. She melted against him when he took her in his arms, but she had the tongue of an asp.

That tongue was silent during the elevator ride to his Athens penthouse. She kept her gaze averted too. He wondered at this. He wondered also if she was enamored of that blond buffoon who had put his lips on her. A definite rapport existed between them. She said she did not sleep with him, but it was not because the man was averse. Anger still simmered beneath the surface at the memory of another man touching the woman who was to be his.

That she did not yet realize she belonged to Luciano was the only reason he had not flattened the American, but soon both she and he would know it. And then let the blond man touch her at his peril.

The elevator stopped and Hope looked up for the first time. "Where are we?"

The doors slid open and he stood back for her exit first. "This is my Athens headquarters."

They stepped through one of the two doors on the landing.

She looked around them. "It looks more like a home to me, or are you trying to tell me that a Sicilian tycoon does his business in the living room rather than the boardroom?"

He felt his lips quirk at her sassiness. This unexpected side to her nature was not altogether unpleasing. A wife without spirit would not suit him. He had yet to decide if he would let the marriage stand once he had his plans for dealing with her grandfather in place.

"The apartment is located on the top floor of the Valerio building. My office is one floor below."

If Hope was ignorant of the old man's machinations, her only guilt was by association. Tradition dictated the family held responsibility for the actions of one, but he was not such a dinosaur. If she knew nothing, he could not honorably include her in the vendetta and the marriage would have to stand.

"And the other door?" she asked.

"A company apartment."

Her brow quirked. "Not the home of your mistress?"

Ai, ai, ai. "You are a spitting kitten tonight."

She blushed and once again turned her face away from him.

He had brought her with him tonight to determine the level of her guilt as much as to woo her to marriage. Her ongoing contrariness was a point in favor of her innocence. Surely if she wanted the marriage and were in league with her grandfather, she would not be so difficult toward Luciano.

On the other hand, women had known since time memorial that to play hard to get intrigued the hunter in men, particularly Sicilian men.

"I thought you were taking me out to dinner. You said our reservations were for eight."

"And so they are. My chef has prepared a special meal to be served on the terrace. If we were late, sauces would be ruined, the vegetables overcooked."

She turned, her composure restored. "What a tragedy," she said facetiously.

"*Sì.* A great tragedy."

"We're eating on the terrace?"

"It has a magnificent view of the city. I believe you will like it."

The violet of her eyes mirrored confusion. "Why are you doing this? You can't be so hard up for a date that you must spend the evening with your business associate's granddaughter."

"I told you, it pleases me. Why do you find this so difficult to believe?" He was not used to having his word questioned and he found he did not like it, especially from her.

She made a sound of disbelief. "You date supermodels, sexy, sophisticated women. *I'm not your type.*"

For some reason her protestations on that point irritated him immensely. "A man will taste many types of fruit before finding a tree he wishes to eat from for a lifetime."

"So, you're saying you were in the mood for an apple or something instead of the more exotic fruits?" The prospect did not appear to please her.

He stepped forward until their bodies were only inches apart and reached out to cup her face. "Perhaps you are the tree that will satisfy me for a lifetime."

Hope felt herself go absolutely rigid in shock. She even stopped breathing. Her, the tree that could satisfy him for a lifetime? It was inconceivable, but why had he said it?

His hands dropped away from her face and he stepped back, giving her room to breathe. "Would you like to freshen up before dinner?"

Sucking air into her oxygen-starved lungs, she nodded. Anything to get away from his enervating presence. He led her to a guest room and stood aside for her to enter. She could see an en suite off to the left.

She paused in the doorway without looking at him. "Please don't play with me, Luciano. I'm not in your league." She didn't want to be hurt again like she had been on New Year's Eve. She didn't want to be just another fruit for his jaded palate.

Once again his hands were on her and he turned her to face him. She met his eyes, her own serious. He ran his fingertip over her bottom lip and her whole body trembled.

"I am not playing, *cara*."

She so desperately wanted to believe him, but the memory of New Year's Eve was still too fresh. "Why…" She found she could not force the rest of the question past the lump of hope and wariness in her throat.

"Why what?"

"Why did you shove me away like a disease-ridden rodent after our kiss on New Year's Eve?" The words tumbled out with all the pain and rejection she had felt that night six months ago.

He looked outraged. "I did not do this."

"Excuse me, you did. I was there."

"I too was there. Perhaps I let you go a trifle quickly. I did not wish to embarrass you with further intimacies."

"You didn't want to embarrass me?" The irony of such an excuse was too great to be born. "I don't believe it."

"Believe."

"So, to save me embarrassment, you chose to humiliate me instead?" she asked in incredulity. If that was how the male mind worked, no wonder women had such a hard time understanding them.

"To kiss Luciano di Valerio is not a humiliation."

"But to be publicly rejected by you is!"

CHAPTER FOUR

A MUSCLE ticked in his jaw. "Explain."

She was only too happy to do so. "I spent three hours as the butt of every joke in the room. Poor *hopeless* Hope, throwing herself at the gorgeous Italian," she mimicked with savage pain. "*Did you see how he had to practically tear her arms off of him? We always knew she was hopeless, but to be that desperate.*"

The cruel voices echoed in her head as if it had just happened and the painful mortification sliced her heart.

"This cannot be true. *I* kissed *you.* Surely the other guests saw that. *Porca miseria!* I rejected that tall blonde's advances to do it."

"Oh, yes, the model." Hope's body went taut with remembered emotion. "You know that old saying about a woman scorned? Well, she epitomized it. She told anyone who would listen that I pushed her out of the way to get to you."

Without the model's interference, Luciano's rejection would have remained a personal source of pain, not become a public humiliation.

"What is her name?" The chill in his voice surprised Hope.

"What difference does it make?" Did he think he could do something about it at this late date? The time for his action on her behalf was past. "Anyway, I don't know her name. I just hope I never see her again. I wish I never had to see any of them again." Impossible when so many of the party guests had been her grandfather's business associates and she often acted as his social hostess, albeit a quiet one.

He swore in Italian. She didn't recognize the word, but she knew that tone. It was the same one her grandfather reserved for certain four-letter words.

"Do you know how many of the male guests offered to give me what you supposedly wouldn't?" she asked in driven tones. "Strictly as an act of charity, mind you."

As if no man would ever *want* her enough to go after her. Well, David wanted her. He'd told her she could come to his room tonight. Maybe she would. At least he wouldn't think he was doing her some kind of favor.

"I want the names of these men." The rage in him was a palpable force and quite frightening.

She stepped back from him. "Why?"

"They insulted you." He said it as if those three words should explain everything.

They didn't. "So did you."

"Tell me their names." He totally ignored his own culpability, but the deadly tone of his voice indicated he was far from ignoring the insult offered to her by the other guests.

Why was he taking this so personally?

"I don't think I should."

"Nevertheless, you will."

"Don't try to boss me around, Luciano." She would have sounded a lot more convincing if her voice hadn't broken on his name, but suddenly he was looming too close and she felt way more intimidated than she wanted to.

"I am a bossy guy by nature, ask my sister. It is something you will have to get used to, *cara.*"

"I don't think so."

"I want the names of the men who made importunate remarks to you."

"There really weren't that many." Two to be exact, but at the time it had definitely been two too many.

"So recalling their names should not be a difficulty, *sì?*"

She sighed. "What are you going to do if I tell you?"

"I will have words with them."

"That's all? Just words."

His expression was unreadable. "Just words."

She named the two men who had gone out of their way to be so objectionable. One had even trapped her in the hallway and kissed her. After Luciano's kiss, any other man's mouth was a repugnance and she had kicked him in the shin, leaving him hopping on one leg and cursing her.

"You must believe I did not intend such a thing to happen."

"I know." At least she did now. His shock and rage were too real. "However, you have got to see that it would be better for me if you just left me alone. I know I'm introverted and my looks are nothing to speak of, but I'm a woman with feelings and I don't want to be hurt any more."

And he was the only man with the real power to hurt her. The others had caused her embarrassment, but Luciano's rejection had cut deeply into her heart and left her bleeding.

"I did not hurt you."

How could he say that? "You pushed me away like I was diseased! You left! You didn't come back. I don't know what you are up to now, but I'm not such a believer in fairy tales that I would entertain for one minute the thought I could be someone special in your life."

A charming smile tilted his lips. "So you see me as Prince Charming and yourself the frog? I assure you, I am more than willing to kiss you and turn you into a princess."

His mockery was the limit. Her eyes burned with tears she did not want to shed in front of him. "Leave me alone, Luciano. Just leave me alone." She spun on her heel and this time she made her escape good. She made it to the bathroom and slammed the door only to discover it had no lock.

She looked around wildly, but there was no escape.

She stared at the knob and willed it to stay immobile accepting she had absolutely no telekinetic powers when the knob turned.

The door opened and Luciano filled the doorway, his dark gaze probing her with tactile intensity. "You have taken me wrong, *bella mia*. It was a little joke. A poor one, but only a joke."

"Get out," she said, her voice breaking on a sob, "I want to freshen up."

He shook his head. "I cannot leave you in such distress."

"Why not? You did six months ago."

"But I did not know so at the time."

"Are you trying to say that if you had, you would have stayed? That you would not have rejected me so publicly and treated me like the kiss meant nothing to you?"

His face was tight with frustration, but he did not answer. Probably because a truthful answer would put him even further in the wrong.

"I didn't think so," she said, sounding every bit as cynical as the women who had mocked her at the party.

In a move that shocked her, he reached out and pulled her to him. "That is in the past. This is now. We begin from here, *cara*."

She hated her treacherous body that longed to melt against him. "I'm not up to your speed." Miserably aware that it was too true, she tried to pull away. "I belong with someone like David."

She stared in mesmerized fascination as his rage went nuclear. "You belong with me," he said with lethal intensity. Then his mouth crashed down on hers.

She thought the New Year's Eve kiss had been hot, but it was nothing like this. Nothing.

Luciano was branding her with his mouth. There was no other way to describe how his lips molded her own, the way his tongue forced entry into her too willing mouth. He tasted the same and yet different. No champagne to dilute the impact of the flavor that was uniquely him.

Hard masculine hands clamped to her waist and lifted. She landed plastered from lips to toe-tips against the ungiving contours of an aroused male body. He aligned her with him so that the evidence of his arousal was pressed into the apex of her thighs. Sliding one hand to her bottom, he manipulated her so that his hardness teased the sensitive flesh of her femininity right through the layers of her clothes.

She'd never known anything so intimate in her life.

She tried to put some distance between them, but she had no leverage with her feet completely off the floor. His hold was too firm to wiggle out of his arms and her efforts in that direction only increased the strange sensations arcing through her from the friction at the juncture of her thighs.

He wrapped his arm around the small of her back and pressed her firmly against him while increasing the intimacy of their kiss. And she melted. Just like she'd done before. Unlike before, however, there was no voice to interrupt and Luciano did not pull away. The urgency in his kiss grew along with the rising passion in her.

She became aware of his hand on her thigh, *under her dress.* How had it gotten there? She should protest, but that would mean breaking the kiss. Besides, his hand on her bare skin felt good. Too good to fight. Knowing fingers burned a trail of erotic caresses up the unprotected skin of her leg until they reached her bottom. He cupped her there and his mouth swallowed the sound of her shock.

Feelings so intense they frightened her coursed through her every nerve ending.

She ached to touch him. She ached for more of his touch.

She lost all sense of self-preservation in the face of such overwhelming pleasure and ran her hands over his face, his shoulders, his neck, everywhere she could reach from her position locked against him.

He groaned and moved.

She realized he'd backed up to lean against the vanity when one of her feet bumped the cabinet. He pressed her legs apart and over his thighs, pushing the hard ridge of his arousal into impossibly intimate contact with her body. She didn't have time to contemplate this because suddenly his hand was inside the silk of her panties, touching the naked flesh of her bottom. Goose bumps flashed over her flesh, accompanied by involuntary shivers that had nothing to do with being cold.

In fact, she'd never been so hot in all her life.

That devastating hand went lower to the underside of her bottom. Sliding centimeters to the left, fingers stealthily found her most intimate flesh from an unexpected direction and this time even his mouth covering hers could not stifle the shriek of shock at contact.

The feel of a man's finger pressing into flesh that had never known anyone's touch before was so alien that it shocked her out of the sensual reverie she'd sunk into with his kiss. She squirmed, trying to get away from that intimate touch, but that caused an amazing friction between Luciano's excited male flesh and her sweetest spot.

His big body shuddered.

She tore her mouth from his. "*Luciano*. Please!"

He said something in Italian and started kissing her neck, using his tongue and teeth in a form of erotic teasing that made her squirm even more, but with pleasure this time, not shock.

His head lifted and dark eyes burned her with their sensual force. "You belong to me, *bella mia*. Admit it."

She couldn't deny a truth she'd known somewhere in her

heart since she was eighteen years old. "Yes, Luciano, yes." When had she not?

"Cara!" His mouth rocked back over hers in another soul-shaking kiss.

It went on and on and she lost all touch with reality. She could feel only his body beneath hers. She could taste only his mouth. She could smell only his scent. She could hear nothing but their joined heartbeats and a ringing in her ears.

He groaned, breaking his mouth away from hers. It was the sound of a man facing Purdah when Heaven had been within his grasp.

Her head was too heavy for her neck and it dropped forward into the hollow of his neck.

A moment later a discreet cough sounded from the doorway to the guest room. *"Signor* di Valerio."

"Sì?" Luciano's voice sounded strained.

"é la vostra madre."

It is your mother. The simple Italian phrase penetrated her brain through the fog of arousal still blunting her thinking process.

He said something that sounded suspiciously like a swear-word. "I must take the call, *piccola mia.*"

She made a halfhearted attempt at a nod, still too ener-vated to speak.

He slowly withdrew his hand from intimate contact with her body as if it pained him to do so. She buried her face against him until he gently set her away from him. She kept her eyes fixed on the floor. How could she have made the same mistake twice? She hadn't just let him kiss her, she'd responded with all the wantonness of a woman who routinely shared her body with men. She didn't even know she was capable of that level of abandon to the physical.

It both scared and shamed her.

"Look at me, Hope."

She shook her head. The memory of the way she had allowed him to touch her and where she had let him touch her was sending arrows of mortification into her conscience with bull's-eye accuracy.

"You have nothing to be guilty over."

That was easy for him to say. He was just fruit tasting. She'd never done any of this before. "You would say that," she accused. "You've probably seduced enough women to populate a small town."

His laughter brought her head snapping up as nothing else could have.

She glared at him. "Don't you laugh at me, Luciano di Valerio."

He put his hands out in a gesture of surrender. "I am not the rogue you think me and I was not trying to seduce you."

"Right." What the heck had he been doing then, practicing his technique?

He brushed her hair behind her ear in a tender gesture that made her treacherous heart melt. "You belong to me as no woman has. Do not regret the passion the good God has given us as a gift."

He didn't mean it the way it sounded. He couldn't. He was implying a special relationship. After New Year's Eve and how easily he had turned away and stayed away, she could not afford to let herself read too much into his words.

"You have to answer the phone. You mustn't keep your mother waiting." Hope wanted time to regroup her defenses.

He looked at her as if contemplating saying something more, but in the end, he said only, "I will be with you as quickly as I can," before turning to leave.

Hope availed herself of the toiletries in the well-stocked guest bathroom and tried to ignore the fact they had probably been put there for the convenience of his women friends. *Like her.* How much importance could she put on his avowal she was different? Her supposed difference could stem entirely from the fact that she was a virgin, undoubtedly a rare experience in the life of a male who dated such sophisticated women.

Luciano stopped a few feet from where Hope sat surrounded by the lush greenery and night-blooming flowers in his terrace garden. Strings of small white lights illuminated the dining area giving Hope, with her burnished curls and elfin features, the appearance of a fairy in her element.

Something untamed twisted inside him at the thought she could disappear from his life like the fey wood creature she resembled, leaving nothing behind but his unsatisfied and unabated arousal. If he had been shocked by the deliciousness of her response on New Year's Eve, he was poleaxed by the living flame he'd held in his arms tonight.

He wanted her.

She wanted him too, but she didn't trust him.

Anger surfaced to mix with the desire simmering inside him as he considered her reasons for feeling the way she did. She'd been savaged by her grandfather's guests after Luciano had left the party. His clumsy response to the unexpected carnality of their kiss had been read as a repudiation of her advances, when she had made no advances at all.

How had that blonde thought she would get away with spreading such lies? Had she thought they would never reach his ears, or that he would not care? She would learn to regret the mistaken assumption. Luciano di Valerio did not tolerate being the subject of a tissue of lies. More importantly, Hope was his now and he protected his own.

His hands curled at his sides and atavistic anticipation curled through him at the thought of dealing with the two men who had propositioned her. They would repent treating an innocent, shy creature with such a lack of respect.

There was a certain amount of gratification in knowing that the marriage would redress the wrong he had done her. His pride still balked at submitting to her grandfather's blackmail, but Luciano could not deny he owed Hope for the humiliation she had suffered at his unwitting hands. Their marriage would even the scales, a very important issue for this Sicilian man.

Sì, and there was again no denying that their marriage bed would be a satisfying one. Even now, he wanted to go over there and lift her from the chair, carry her to his bed and finish what they had begun earlier.

Hope felt a prickling sensation on the back of her neck and turned in her chair. Luciano stood a few feet away, a look in his eyes that made the fine hairs on her body stand up. In an instant of primal awareness she could not anticipate or block, all the composure and self-control she had managed to gather around herself in his absence dissipated with the ease of water on an Arizona highway.

"I am sorry to have left you so long." He came toward her, the muscles in his thighs flexing under the perfectly tailored Italian suit he was wearing.

Did the guy ever wear jeans? Probably not and most likely her heart couldn't stand the sight of him in the tight-fitting denim anyway.

"Don't worry about it. I've been enjoying the view. It's incredible up here."

Luciano's terrace covered the entire portion of the top story of the Valerio building not occupied by his or the company apartments. Someone had turned it into a garden, giving the impression of being in an enchanted bower high above the streets of Athens. The view over the wall was spectacular. The moment she'd seen it she'd been glad she came with Luciano, if only for the opportunity to spend her final evening in Greece in such magical surroundings.

He sat down in the chair opposite hers. No sooner than he had done and a drink was placed in front of him by a discreet servant. The first course was served moments later. They were eating their main course, a meatless moussaka when she realized the entire meal had been vegetarian.

"You remembered I don't care to eat meat." It shocked her. She'd lived with her grandfather since she was five years old and he still couldn't remember that about her. And if he had remembered, he would never have catered to her desires.

"It is not such a big thing." His shoulders moved in a typical throw away gesture. "But tell me, does it bother you to be at the table when others eat it?"

"No, but I don't look too closely at their plates either," she admitted ruefully.

He seemed pleased by that, though she could not imagine what it had to do with him. Their conversation flowed, Luciano asking her questions about her life in Boston and answering her questions about his life in Sicily.

"So, what are you doing in Athens, or is it top-secret business stuff?" She was used to her grandfather keeping tight lips about many areas of his life.

"I make frequent trips to my headquarters here and elsewhere."

He was as driven as her grandfather. "Do you ever take time off to relax?"

His smile sent sensations quivering through her. "I am relaxing now, with you."

"But even this," she indicated their almost finished dinners, "is prompted by your business interests."

"I assure you, business has not been in the forefront of my mind since I spied you walking back toward your tour bus laughing with your companion, your hand in his." His voice had taken on the hardness of tempered steel.

She didn't want a reenactment of their earlier argument,

so she opted not to reply to his comment. She chose instead, to change the subject. "How is your mother? Your sister is twenty now, isn't she? Is she dating anyone special?"

For a moment he actually looked bemused. "You know a great deal about me."

"It is inevitable after a five-year acquaintanceship." Or rather five years of infatuation, she thought with some sadness.

"My mother is fine." He laid his fork down and leaned back against his chair. "She is pressing me to marry soon."

An irrational sense of loss suffused her at his words—irrational because you could not lose what you had never had. He would oblige his mother, she was sure. At thirty, Luciano was of an age for a Sicilian male to start making babies. The thought of another woman big with his child was enough to destroy what remained of her appetite.

"And your sister?" she asked, pushing away her half-finished plate, trying not to dwell on the prospect of him marrying soon.

Warm indulgence lit his almost black eyes. "Martina is enjoying university too much to allow any one male to seriously engage her interest."

"You allowed her to attend university in America, didn't you?" She could remember discussing the merits of different colleges with him a couple of years previously at one of her grandfather's business dinners.

"*Sì*. She enjoys it very much. Mamma worries she will not wish to return to a traditional life in Sicily though."

Hope had nothing to say in reply to that. She had no experience of daughters and mothers. Hers had died when she was much too young.

"It is understandable," Luciano brooded. "Life in Sicily is still very traditional in some ways. Mamma has never worn a pair of trousers in her whole life. If you were seen holding hands with your young blond friend in the small village in the country outside Palermo where I grew up, an engagement announcement might be expected."

Why did he keep harping on that? It had been totally innocent, unlike the kiss they had shared not too long ago. "David is from Texas," she tried to explain. "He's very affectionate, but he doesn't mean anything by it."

His brows rose in mockery. "This is why he invited you back to his room."

Oh, dear. Luciano was back to looking dangerous. "He's never done that before. He was just reacting to your arrogant claim on me. It's a guy thing, I guess."

"Are you truly so naive you do not realize this man wants you?"

"I'm not naive." Introverted did not equal stupid.

His dark eyes narrowed. "Your inexperience of men and their ways shows in your foolish belief that the touches of a man who pays you particular attention mean nothing."

He didn't need to rub in how gauche she must appear in comparison to his usual date. So, she seemed a fool to him. She must be to have allowed herself to enjoy his kisses and conversation when he thought so little of her. "If you're finished insulting me, I'd like to go back to my hotel now."

"We have not yet had dessert."

"I'm not hungry." She indicated her unfinished dinner. "And we have an early start tomorrow."

"Is it that, or is that you wish to return and keep your liaison with David?" Unbelievably, Luciano sounded jealous.

"I've already told you, I have no intention of sharing David's room tonight." She spoke slowly and through gritted teeth. "But if I did, it wouldn't be any of your business," she added for good measure.

"You can say this after the way you allowed me to touch you not an hour ago?" Outrage vibrated off of him.

Wasn't that just like an arrogant guy used to getting his own way? He'd done the kissing and now held her accountable for it. "I didn't *let* you touch me. You just did it."

"You did not protest." He was six feet, four inches of offended masculine pride. "You were with me all the way."

Heat scorched into her cheeks at the reminder. "A gentleman would not rub my face in it."

"A *lady* would not go from one man's arms to the bed of another."

She jumped up from her chair, so furious, she could barely speak. "Are you saying I'm some sort of tramp because I let you kiss me?"

He rose to tower over her. "I am saying I will not tolerate you returning to this David's company now that you belong to me."

"I don't belong to you!"

"You do and you will stay here with me."

CHAPTER FIVE

SHE couldn't believe what she was hearing.

She knew about the possessive streak in the Italian temperament, but to say she belonged to him just because they'd kissed was ludicrous. Not only was it ridiculous, it was inconsistent as anything. He certainly hadn't been singing that tune New Year's Eve.

"Then why didn't I belong to you six months ago? Why did you leave and not come back? *I'll tell you why,*" she went on before he had a chance to answer, "*because those kisses meant no more to you than eating a chocolate bar.* You found them pleasant, but not enough to buy the candy store."

"You expected marriage after one kiss?" His derision hit her on the raw.

"You're deliberately misunderstanding me. I didn't say anything of the kind. You're the one who has been rabbiting on about me belonging to you because of an inconsequential kiss."

"Hardly inconsequential. I could have had you and you would not have murmured so much as a protest."

Oh. She wanted to scream. "No doubt your skills in the area of seduction are stellar, but what does that signify? With my limited experience in the area, any man with a halfway decent knowledge of a woman's reactions could have affected me just as strongly."

She didn't believe it for a minute, but Luciano's conceit was staggering. His assertion she would not have protested him taking her to bed might be true, but it was also demeaning.

"You think this?" he demanded, his eyes terrifying in their feral intensity. "Perhaps you intend to experiment with this friend of yours, this David?"

A tactical retreat was called for. "No. I don't want to experiment with anybody, including you."

He didn't look even remotely appeased by her denial.

Good judgment required she not dwell on this particular argument. "I am merely trying to point out that kissing me didn't give you any rights over me. If all the women you kissed belonged to you, you'd have a bigger harem than any Arabian prince in history."

Instead of looking insulted by her indictment of his character, he appeared pleased by her assessment of his masculinity. The fury in his expression faded. "You are different than the other women I have known."

"Known being a discreet euphemism, I assume?" She thought of all the beautiful women he had been photographed with for scandal rags and society pages. It left a hollow place where her heart should have been beating and it made her doubly determined to deny him any claim to her loyalty. "Only you haven't *known* me and I don't belong to you."

"This crudeness is not becoming."

She couldn't deny it. Crude was not her style and she'd probably blush with embarrassment later, but right now she was fighting the effect he had on her with every weapon at her disposal. "Neither is a dog-in-the-manger possessiveness."

"What is this canine in a stable?"

She stared at him. *Canine in a stable?* Suddenly the humor of the situation overcame her. She started to laugh. Here she was arguing with Mr. Cool himself that he didn't have any hold on her when she wanted more than anything for him to claim her as his own. She was nuts, but then so was he. *And* his perfect English had a few flaws.

"You find me amusing?" He didn't look happy about the possibility.

She grabbed at her self-control and reined in her laughter, humor that had taken on a slightly hysterical twinge. "It's not you. It's this situation. Don't you think it's funny that you're standing here asserting rights over me you can't possibly want?"

"If I assert them, I want them," was his arrogant rejoinder.

All the humor fled, hysterical or otherwise, and she swallowed the words that would beg him to repeat what he'd just said. He simply could not mean it the way she wanted him to.

"This isn't about me. This is about David and your reaction to him. You acted like two dogs fighting over a bone back at the Parthenon. Now, *you* are trying to bury the bone, not because you really want it, but because you don't want him to have it. Well, I'm not going to stay buried just to please your sense of male superiority."

She'd spent most of her life in the background and she was tired of it. Why the realization should come now, she didn't know and she didn't care. Luciano didn't really want her. He wanted to one-up David. She wasn't entirely sure about David's motives, but that wasn't the issue. The issue was *her life and what she was going to do with it.*

The simple answer was live it.

On her terms.

Starting now.

"I'm going back to my hotel. You can have your chauffeur drive me or I can catch a cab, but I'm ready to leave."

Her determination must have gotten through to him

because his jaw tightened, but he nodded. "I will return you to your hotel."

"There is no need for you to accompany me."

"There is every need," he growled.

Since she was getting her way about leaving, she decided not to argue about this. If he wanted to waste his time riding in the limo with her to see her to her hotel, then let him. She was also through trying to protect everyone but herself from being put upon.

The ride back to her hotel happened in silence. Luciano was too angry to talk without giving away the state of his emotions and no way was he going to allow her to know the extent of her effect on him. Shy she might be. Innocent sexually, even. But still she was a woman and emotions were the weapons of choice for the female of the species.

He could not believe the turn the evening had taken. He had thought after their kiss, she would recognize his claim on her. Her assertion that she did not belong to him had both shocked and enraged him. His quiet little kitten had claws and an independence he would not have suspected.

He needed to rethink his campaign. The time limit her grandfather had set was fast approaching. He had to get her agreement soon in order to have sufficient weeks to plan a Sicilian wedding. Anything less would hurt Mamma.

Hope reached out to open the door the minute the car stopped. Luciano allowed her to exit the car without protest, but he followed her.

She turned, her pansy eyes widening when she realized he was right behind her rather than seated safely in the car. She would not get rid of him so easily.

She put her hand out. "Thank you for an interesting evening. The food was wonderful and you could charge admission on the view from your terrace."

She said nothing about the company and he felt the urge to smile at her spirit in spite of his anger.

He took her hand, but instead of shaking it, used it to pull her into his body, so he could walk her inside. "I will take you to your room."

Her small body was stiff in his hold. "I won't argue because it won't do me any good to tell you I would rather walk alone."

His lips twisted wryly. "You have said it."

"And it didn't do me any good."

"I would be a poor escort if I did not see you to your door."

"Cro-Magnon man has nothing on you for primitive."

"Good manners are the mark of civilization, not the lack of it."

Her response to that was a disdainful sound that could only be described as a snort.

He led her into the elevator, not displeased by the lack of other guests in the small space. He had indicated to his security team that they should wait outside, so no one was with them to witness her obvious irritation. She was staying on the fourth floor and the ride up in the elevator was charged with silence.

As the doors slid open, he asked, "Which room?"

"Four-twenty-two." She pointed the way with a flick of her hand.

As they walked to her door, he noticed another one further along the hall opening. Blond hair above glowering masculine features identified the spying neighbor as David, the man from Texas. Hope might not accept Luciano's possession, but he was determined that David would recognize the fact of it.

He pulled her to a stop just inside the door and turned her to face him.

"Good night," she said in an obvious attempt at dismissal.

"Buona notte," he replied as his head lowered toward hers.

He watched as her eyes widened and her mouth opened to protest, but his lips prevented the words from expelling. Taking advantage of her open mouth, he slid his tongue inside to taste the sweetness he had quickly learned to crave.

She blinked, her violet eyes darkening even as she tried to push away from him. He moved his hands down her back, pressing one against her ribs and using the other to cup her behind. Her eyes went unfocused and then slid shut as she surrendered to his touch. He kissed her with the intent of claiming her body even if her mind denied the truth of his possession.

He kissed her until he heard a distinct American curse and a slamming door. He kissed her until her body was totally pliant against him and her mouth moved in innocent arousal against his own.

He was tempted to push her back two feet, shut the door and make love to her until she agreed to marry him. He sensed, though, that she would be ashamed afterward, that it would hurt her to be won by such means.

He did not want to hurt her. She was not part of her grand-father's scheme. He was sure of it now.

He would treat her with the respect the future mother of his children deserved.

It was harder than anything he had done since burying his father, but he gently disengaged their bodies and set her away from him.

Her eyes opened. "What…"

He smiled and touched her lips with his forefinger. "You belong to me. Your body knows it and soon your mind will accept it as well."

"What about my heart?" she whispered, her expression dazed.

"It is only right for a woman to love her husband."

Her mouth dropped open. *"Husband?"*

Now would be a good time for a strategic withdrawal. *"Sì.* Husband. Think about it, *tesoro."*

He waited to hear the bolt slide home before he left.

As he walked by the door that had opened earlier, he thought a few words with the young Romeo would not go amiss.

Think about it.

Hope shoved her suitcase closed and zipped it shut with undue force.

The fiend.

That was all she'd been doing since last night.

He'd kissed her until her hard-won composure had melted in the heat of their mutual desire. Then he'd pushed her away and left, but not before making the disturbing announcement he intended to marry her. Well, he hadn't actually said *that.* He'd said a wife should love her husband, but they'd been talking about him and her, so didn't it follow he meant he was thinking of her as his wife?

Only what if he hadn't? What if she was reading all sorts of things into a comment he'd meant in jest. He'd admitted on New Year's Eve that his jokes didn't always come off right.

But she could have sworn he wasn't joking. What if he *had* meant it? Luciano di Valerio her husband. The mind boggled. Could she survive marriage to such a devastating man? She'd decided to stop living in the shadows, but she hadn't considered a move so close to the burning power of the sun.

What was that saying about being careful what you wished for? She'd been dreaming of Luciano for the past five years, but she had never considered those dreams could become a reality. They had been safe, a way for her to allay her loneliness. Luciano in the flesh was not safe, as he'd proven each time he had kissed her.

She lost her soul when they kissed. Or found it. Either way, they terrified her—these feelings he could evoke.

And for all his tolerance toward his sister's desire to go to university in America, he was still a traditional Sicilian male in many ways. Look how he had reacted to David holding her hand. While she was a modern, if slightly introverted, American woman. How could a marriage between them work?

She was too independent to accept the long-established role of the Sicilian wife. He was too bossy not to interfere in her life in ways that would no doubt infuriate her.

It was crazy.

She pulled her suitcase off the bed and left it outside the room for the porter to pick up and add to the tour's luggage on the bus.

Contemplating marriage with Luciano was an exercise in futility. He was probably already regretting the kisses they'd shared and the implications he had made.

She walked into the hotel dining room and seeing David at a table by the window, she went toward him. They'd been sharing breakfast since the second day of the tour, sometimes *à deux* and other times joined by their fellow tour members. This morning, he was sitting alone at a table for four.

She slid into the seat opposite him. "Good morning."

He looked up from the paper he'd been reading, *The Dallas Morning News*. He had it special delivered because he said he couldn't stand too many days without news from back home.

His usually mobile face remained impassive. "Is it?"

He was still angry about her choosing to go with Luciano instead of him the night before. "Did you end up going back to the Psiri?" she asked with a tentative smile.

"What's it to you if I did?"

She started at the belligerence in his voice. "I think I'll order my breakfast." She signaled for the waiter.

"Are you sure you want to do that?"

"Why wouldn't I?" What was the matter with him this morning?

"Your boyfriend might take offense to you eating breakfast with me."

"I don't have a boyfriend."

"That's not the way it looked last night."

She sighed. "I'm sorry if you were disappointed I didn't have dinner with you last night, but you shouldn't have taken for granted that you could schedule my time."

"I realize that now."

Good. At least that had worked out from last night's fiasco. She smiled. "No harm done."

"Not for you. It must be nice having two men fighting for your attention, but personally I think your ploy was juvenile."

"What ploy?" she demanded, getting irritated by his continued innuendo that she did not understand.

"You should have told me you belonged to someone else. You let me think you were unattached."

"I am unattached." Did all men think in terms of belonging? Perhaps only the strong, arrogant ones. "Furthermore, this is the twenty-first century for heaven's sake. I belong to myself, thank you very much."

David snorted at that. "Not according to your Italian boyfriend."

"He's not my boyfriend," she gritted out between clenched teeth.

"Right. That's why you went with him last night instead of having dinner with me."

She wasn't going to admit she'd been virtually kidnapped after making her grand declaration about eating alone. It made her seem feeble and she wasn't, but she had been out-flanked.

"Are you saying that my having dinner with a man automatically makes him my boyfriend?" He was more medieval than Luciano.

"It was a hell of lot more than dinner from where I stood."

"What are you talking about?"

"I was in my room when you returned to the hotel last night."

"So?"

"I saw him kiss you. Afterward he paid me a visit and told me in very clear terms just whose woman you are." Anger and wounded pride vibrated in David's voice.

"He had no right to do that." More importantly though was why had he? She could not wrap her mind around the concept of Luciano being so possessive of her.

David's blue eyes narrowed. "He had his hand on your butt and his tongue down your throat. If he's not your boyfriend, what does that make you?"

The offensive description of Luciano's passionate good-night kiss shocked her. Up until the night before, David had been an affable and rather mild companion.

"What exactly are you implying?"

David tossed the paper on the table and stood up. "You let him paw you in a public hallway and you've never even given me the green light to kiss you good-night. You figure it out."

She watched David walk away feeling both grief and anger. It hurt that David was willing to dismiss their friendship so easily, but his implication that she lacked morals really rankled. She was an anachronistic virgin in a world of sexual gluttony, for goodness' sake. She did not sleep around.

Had Luciano been right in his assessment of David's motives? David had not reacted as a simple friend to the events of last night. Had he been angling to share her bed?

It wouldn't be the first such relationship to develop in

their tour group, but she would have considered herself the least likely candidate for one. She didn't have any experience with men wanting her.

David certainly seemed offended this morning that she'd allowed Luciano to kiss her last night, but she still could not quite believe it was about David wanting her. More likely it was that dog fighting over a bone thing again.

However Luciano's actions weren't as easy to explain, at least not in a way that didn't seem too far-fetched. Luciano di Valerio wanting to marry Hope Bishop? Not likely. Yet, that is what he had implied. Then he had gone out of his way to warn David off.

Put together, those two items were enough to prevent relaxed slumber over the next four nights.

Hope woke up feeling cranky and out of sorts the day they were scheduled to tour Pompeii. This was their fifth day in Italy and Luciano had not made another appearance. He'd managed to find her in Greece, but now that they were in his home country…nothing. And Naples was not exactly the other side of the world from Palermo. The man was a billionaire. He had a helicopter, not to mention a jet.

If it were important for him to see her, as he'd implied, wouldn't he have used one of them?

David had gotten over his snit by the time they arrived in Rome and apologized sweetly for his accusations. They'd agreed to resume their friendship and had toured the Vatican together. Their relationship wasn't as free and easy as it had been. She was careful to avoid his casual touches, afraid Luciano had been right. In allowing it, perhaps she had encouraged David to think she wanted something from their friendship that she didn't.

She yawned behind her hand as she entered the hotel dining room. If she didn't start getting some sleep soon, she was in trouble, but her dreams were filled with a tall Sicilian man and her waking thoughts were tormented by his comment about marriage.

"You are tired, *tesoro*. This tour is perhaps not such a good thing for you."

Her head whipped around and there he stood.

"Luciano, what are you doing here?" As greetings went, it was not original. She excused herself with her fatigue and shock at seeing him right when she was thinking of him.

"Surely you are not surprised to see me."

"But I am. It's been almost a week."

His brow rose in mockery. "And you expected me to show up before this?"

"No. Well…" She didn't want to lie, but she wasn't handing it to him in his lap either.

"I was called to New York on a business emergency."

"You could have called. Grandfather has my cell phone number." He was the one, after all, who had said she was different.

"I did not think of this." He looked chagrined by the admission.

She felt a smile spreading over her face. "That's all right then, but why have you come today?"

"I desire to escort you around Pompeii."

"I'd like that." Nearly five days had been enough time for her to realize that if Luciano wanted to pursue a relationship with her, she would be the world's biggest fool to deny him.

A love that had not abated in five years was not going to go away. If she wanted a chance at a husband and a family, she accepted it would be with him, or not at all. If nothing else, her renewed friendship with David had taught her that. She had no desire to pursue anything personal with him and had not been the least bit jealous when another woman on the tour had begun flirting with him.

They were together now, at a table for two.

Luciano proved his gaze had followed hers when he said, "So, he accepted he could not have you and has transferred his interests."

"You shouldn't have gone to his room that night," she chided.

"You did not yet recognize you were mine, but I made certain he did. It was necessary to avoid complications."

She sighed. It was no use arguing with him about it. What was done was done and she couldn't say she was sorry.

"No comeback?" Dark brown eyes pinned her own gaze with probing concentration.

She shook her head.

"You are mine?"

"Are you asking me?" That was new.

"I am asking if you accept it."

If she denied it, she would be lying to both of them. He hadn't meant to hurt her with his rejection on New Year's Eve and she had to trust him not to hurt her now. She had no choice. She wanted him beyond pride or reason, so she took the plunge. "Yes."

CHAPTER SIX

LUCIANO dismissed the emotion he experienced at her acknowledgment as natural relief that his plan was back on course. The sooner Hope became his, the closer he would be to regaining control of Valerio Shipping.

"At last, we progress."

She grimaced at his choice of words, but did not demur.

Smiling, he took her arm and led her to a table. Her acquiescence now was in marked contrast to her vehement protest a week ago when he had been forced to practically kidnap her in order to secure her company for the evening. He helped her into her seat brushing a light kiss against her temple as he did so. Startled pansy eyes took him in as he crossed to sit on the other side of the intimate table for two.

Even after the intimacies they had shared, she still acted surprised when he touched her.

He liked the shyness.

He had already ordered breakfast for them, but he waved the waiter over to fill her coffee cup. "You do look tired, *piccola mia.*" Her eyes were bruised and her complexion pale from an obvious lack of sleep. "Perhaps we should put the tour of Pompeii off for another day."

She hid a yawn behind one small hand. "I can't. Today's our last day in Naples. Tomorrow we fly to Barcelona."

"I do not wish for you to leave Italy."

Her violet eyes widened, but she did not fly at him in anger as she had done before when he told her he wanted her to leave the tour. "I have two weeks left of my European visit."

"Spend them in Palermo with my family. Mamma wishes to meet you and Martina is home from university. She will enjoy the companionship of someone closer to her own age."

"You told your mother about me?"

"*Sì.*" She would have been very hurt if he had sprung a bride on her out of the blue. She was not overly pleased that Hope was American rather than Sicilian, but the prospect of grandchildren outweighed even that drawback.

"What did you tell her?" Hope was looking at him as if he'd grown donkey ears.

"Why the shock?" He had told Hope his intentions. "I told Mamma I had met a woman I wanted for *mi moglie,* my wife."

"I know what the word means." She took a gulp of coffee and then started coughing.

He was around the table in a moment, pressing a glass of water into her hands. "Are you all right?"

"Yes. It was too hot."

"Be more careful, *carina.* If you burn your mouth, how can I kiss it?"

She blushed and set the glass of water down with a trembling hand as he resumed his seat.

"I wasn't sure you were serious, about marriage I mean." Again the charming blush.

"I am."

She nodded, the soft chestnut curls around her face bouncing. "I can see that, but it's such a shock."

To him as well. He had not been anticipating marriage just yet, particularly to a shy American virgin. "Life is not so easily predicted."

"I suppose you're right."

"So, will you come to Sicily with me and stay in my home with my mother and sister?"

"I don't know."

He stifled his impatience. She was skittish, like an untried mare. He did not want to spook her when his plans were finally working out as he had originally expected. Perhaps the emergency in New York had been a gift from the good God because it had given her time to make up her mind to him.

"What makes you hesitate?" he asked, allowing none of his impatience to show in his voice. "Are you concerned for your virtue? Mamma will act as sufficient chaperone surely."

"I'm not worried about that. I'm twenty-three years old. I don't need your mother's protection."

He smiled at her feistiness. "What then?"

"Grandfather might not like it."

"I have already spoken to your grandfather."

"You have?" Once again she looked like a doe startled by an unexpected sound.

"*Sì*. It is only natural I should speak to him when I wish to marry his granddaughter." He said nothing of the fact Reynolds had been the one to instigate the meeting. That was not relevant to Luciano and Hope. He wanted to marry her. That was the only issue she need be concerned with.

"How can you say that so calmly?"

"Say what?" he asked.

"That bit about wanting to marry me. I mean we haven't even led up to it and suddenly, boom, here you are saying you want to marry me like it's a foregone conclusion. You haven't even asked me."

Nor had he courted her and a woman deserved to be courted to marriage. But… "Have we not led up to it? The kiss we shared on New Year's Eve, the kisses we shared last week, they lead to bed and bed with a virgin means marriage for this Italian male."

Her pale skin took on a fiercely rosy hue. "That's not what I meant."

"Do you still deny the way we kissed gave me claim to you?" He had thought they were past that.

"No, but marriage is not necessarily the next inevitable step."

"It is."

"Come on, Luciano. Like I've said before, you can't tell me you marry every woman you kiss passionately."

Had he ever shared a passion so volatile with another woman? He did not think so. "I have never kissed another virgin."

"Hush!" She looked around, her expression almost comical. "This is not the place to discuss my sexual experience, or lack thereof."

"I agree." It was exciting him to think of introducing her into the pleasures of the flesh. He wanted to be able to walk when they left the restaurant, but if they didn't change the subject he wasn't going to be able to.

"Come to Palermo and let me convince you."

"You mean like a courtship?"

"*Sì.* Exactly."

"I didn't think men still did that."

"It is a ritual that will continue through the millennia, whatever you choose to call it. Men will pursue their chosen mate with whatever means at their disposal."

"And your means are a couple of weeks in Palermo with your family?" She sounded bemused, shocked even.

"*Sì.*"

"All right."

Hope stretched lazily beside the pool. Rhythmic splashing told her without having to look that Luciano's sister was still swimming laps. Martina was a sweet girl. Three years Hope's junior, she was very Sicilian in some things, but the influence of her years at American university was unmistakable.

She didn't defer to her brother as if he were a deity and she had no desire to marry a man solely to secure her future.

Smart and independent, Martina had made life in the di Valerio household bearable for Hope. Not that Luciano's mother was unbearable. Quite the opposite. She was kindness itself, but she took the marriage of her son and his American girlfriend as a foregone conclusion. Just yesterday she had completely unnerved Hope by insisting she be measured for a wedding gown.

When Hope had mentioned this to Luciano, he had merely smiled and complimented his mother on her forward thinking. Evidently, neither he nor his mother had any doubt as to the outcome of Hope's time in Palermo. The prospect of a lifetime married to such a confident male was more than daunting, it was scary.

Because Hope wasn't that confident.

She should be. He made his desire to marry her very clear as well as his pleasure in her company. In short, he was doing exactly as he said he would do and courting her. While he had to work several hours each day, he spent some time each morning and the evenings with her, either taking her out or having his friends in to meet her.

None of them seemed to find it as odd as she did that he'd chosen a little peahen for his proposed bride rather than a bird of more exotic plumage. But then Italian men of Luciano's income bracket didn't always consider their wives to be the one for show-off potential. They left that job to their mistresses. Did Luciano intend to have a mistress? Did he have one now?

It was a question she had to have answered before she could marry him, but she was afraid to ask. She spent an inordinate amount of time convincing herself she didn't need to. Sometimes it worked. Why wouldn't it?

She had a room that resembled a romantic bower because of all the flowers he had given her, but flowers were the least of his offerings to convince her she wanted to marry him. He gave her gifts practically every day. The bikini she was sunbathing in had been yesterday's present.

He was spoiling her rotten with both time and gifts.

But he said nothing of love and had not kissed her again since her arrival in Palermo. He had said her virtue was safe, but she had not thought that meant all physical attention would cease.

He avoided touching her which bothered her because she'd come to see that Luciano was a tactile man. He hugged his sister frequently, kissed his mother's cheeks coming and going and was very Italian in his dealing with his friends. Only she was left out of the magical circle of his affection.

Should it be that way when a man wanted to marry a woman?

While she grew more aware of his physical perfection each day, she worried he had lost interest in her body. Yet, would a man as virile as Luciano contemplate marriage to a woman he didn't want? The answer had to be no. Unless he planned to have a mistress. But then why get married at all?

Her mind spun in now familiar patterns.

"What are you thinking about so hard that you didn't hear me calling you?" Martina stood above Hope, her Italian beauty vibrant while she toweled the wetness from her long black hair.

Hope sighed. "Guess."

"My brother."

"Got it in one."

"You are going to marry him, aren't you?" Unexpected anxiety laced Martina's voice.

"I don't know."

"How can you not know? The man is besotted. He gave you that totally naff book of Italian poetry."

"I can't read Italian."

"You're learning."

She was. Her very rudimentary knowledge of the language was growing rapidly. And because of that she was absolutely certain Luciano had never said a single word about loving her, or being besotted even, in either Italian or English.

Martina settled on the lounger next to Hope. "You love him."

"I'm not saying anything on the grounds it could incriminate me. It's the Fifth Amendment of the U.S. Constitution, you know. Even nosy little sisters can't bypass fundamental rights."

Martina laughed. "I don't need you to confirm it. Every time you look at him, you about swallow him alive with your eyes. You are too sweet, not to mention deep, to have a simple lust infatuation for my brother. With a woman like you, desire is linked to love or it wouldn't be there."

And her desire was obvious to even Luciano's sister. No wonder both Luciano and his mother were so sure of her. "A woman like me?" What made her so different? "Are you saying you're capable of wanting a man to make love to you that you don't love?"

She'd never felt free talking about this sort of stuff with her girlfriends at school. She'd always been too shy, but Martina had steamrolled right over her reticence and they had become confidantes.

Martina giggled. "Maybe not make love, but I have kissed a few."

Hope's heart twitched. She could not say the same. She'd hardly ever been kissed and never like Luciano kissed her except by him. She'd never wanted it with another man. "I suppose it must be love."

"I knew it." Martina clapped her hands. "You are going to marry him. Mamma's sure of it, you know."

"*I know.*" How could she miss it having been fitted for the wedding gown, for Heaven's sake?

"She's just dying for grandbabies."

"What if I don't want to get pregnant right away?"

"I don't think Luciano would like that," Martina said candidly, concern in her voice.

Hope secretly agreed. She was becoming more and more convinced that the reason he was considering marriage now, with her, was for those *bambini* every Italian male supposedly wanted.

"Well, it's a nonissue at the moment. Your brother hasn't actually asked me to marry him. Until he does, this is all conjecture."

"Because you're not sure he's going to or because you're still trying to convince yourself you don't know if you'll say yes?"

"*Santo cielo!* Had I known the swimsuit was so revealing I would have bought another one."

"*Ciao,* Luciano. I think Hope looks smashing in the bikini, but you're right. It shows a lot more of her than the one-piece she brought with her."

Hope looked up at Luciano and smiled. "You're both being silly. It's very conservative for a bikini."

And it was. The tank style top showed the barest hint of her cleavage and the hip-hugging short bottoms didn't reveal anything like the thongs she'd seen on the local beaches, or even the high-cut brief bottoms. On her smallish figure, it was perfectly decent.

"Not conservative enough," Luciano muttered in a driven undertone.

"If it bothers you so much—" she began to say.

"Don't offer to change it. You must start as you mean to go on," Martina exclaimed. "If you let him dictate your clothes now, it will never end."

Dark flags of color accentuated Luciano's sculpted cheekbones and warning lights blazed in his deep brown eyes.

"I was going to say, no one was forcing him to look, Miss Smarty Pants." She smiled up at Luciano. "You're back earlier than expected."

"*Sì*. We have been invited to a pool party at the DeBrecos'. My friend is celebrating the close of a business deal that has given him some trouble."

"Marco is having a pool party?" Martina's interest was definitely piqued.

"He is."

"Am I invited?"

"Of course."

She jumped up from her lounger. "I'll go get ready. When do we leave?"

"In less than an hour, *sorella picolla*. Do not make us late applying makeup and effecting an elaborate hairstyle your first dive in the pool will wash away."

Martina turned to Hope and rolled her lovely brown eyes so like her brother's. "*Men*. Don't *you* go changing your swimsuit to make him happy."

"How could I? It was a gift and it would undoubtedly offend your brother for me to reject it in favor of my old swimsuit."

"Do not bet on it," Luciano growled.

Hope laughed. Would a man who did not want her be so affected by her conservative suit? She hoped the answer was no, but she was definitely leaving the suit on. If she could tempt him, at least a little, maybe he would reveal some of his feelings regarding her.

* * *

That optimistic belief seemed in vain as Luciano treated her to yet another dose of the courteous, nontouching companion of the past few days at the DeBrecos' pool party.

Feeling desperate to provoke some kind of response, she took off her swimsuit cover and dug in her bag for a bottle of high-factor sunscreen. She turned to Luciano. Wearing only black swim shorts, every rippling muscle in his body was on display and it was all she could do not to drool.

Or trip him and beat him to the ground.

She extended the lotion to him. "Would you do my back? I think what I applied earlier is wearing off and I don't want to burn."

Luciano took the bottle, a strange expression on his face. "You cannot reach your own back, *cara?*"

It wasn't her back she found impossible to reach. It was him! She tried for a nonchalant shrug. "It's easier if you do it."

She turned and presented her back to him, pulling her curly hair from the nape of her neck.

Then two things happened.

Martina dropped gracefully on the lounger beside Hope. "Isn't this great?"

And Marco waved from the other side of the pool, catching Luciano's attention.

He dropped the sunscreen in Martina's lap with more speed than finesse. "Put some of this on Hope's back, *sorella picolla*, while I go see what it is that Marco wants."

Hope watched him go with despair. It wasn't working.

Martina looked at Hope. "Didn't you slather yourself in this stuff before we left the house?"

Hope frowned. "Yes."

"Then why does my brother want me to put more on you? Not only are you limber enough to reach your own back, but you bought the lotion that lasts for hours, even in the water."

Hope hated admitting that she'd tried one of the oldest

tricks in the book and it had failed, so she shrugged and reached for the bottle. "Let me put that away."

Martina was looking quizzically at her, then her expression cleared. "I get it. You—"

"Never mind, just hand me the bottle," she said shortly, interrupting Martina before she could put voice to Hope's idiocy.

Martina handed her the lotion, her expression curious. "You know. I noticed that Luciano never touches you."

"I am aware of that." Hope sighed and shoved the plastic bottle back in her bag. Short of making a blatant request, she wasn't going to change that state of affairs either. Even then, she had her doubts.

"That's weird for a guy who wants to marry you."

Hope didn't need the reminder. *"I know."* She glowered at Luciano where he stood talking to Marco.

"What's she doing here?" Martina sounded outraged.

Hope turned her head to look where the younger girl's gaze was directed and felt her heart skip not one, but two beats. This was just what she needed. Zia Merone. She and Luciano had been photographed together several times for the society columns and scandal rags the year before. Rumors of a relationship between the two of them had been rife. Which was a lot more understandable than his name being linked with Hope's. Zia was beautiful and blond, even if it came from a bottle. Taller than Hope by at least six inches, she had a body that was centerfold material.

A little too blousy for a *Vogue* cover, but just what a passionate Sicilian male like Luciano would find attractive.

Hope chewed on her lower lip, tasting blood and her own jealousy. A most unenviable emotion. "I guess Marco invited her."

"You're right of course, but you'd think she would have enough tact not to come." Martina turned to face her, dark brown eyes snapping with indignation. "Everyone knows you're Luciano's new girlfriend."

"Do they? Maybe she's out of the loop." Hope was watching Zia's progress toward their host and Luciano with a sinking feeling in her heart.

Marco greeted Zia with a kiss on each cheek. Luciano started to do the same, but the model turned her head and caught his lips. The kiss didn't last long and Luciano pulled back with a laugh and said something Hope could not hear from her position on the other side of the pool. The greeting was a throwaway gesture, nothing all that intimate for an Italian male, but after being treated like the untouchable woman for days, it was way too much for Hope.

She jumped up. "I'm going into the house. The sun's too bright right now."

Martina followed her. "Don't worry about it, Hope," she said as she rushed after her. "It was just a little kiss. Believe me, if Luciano had wanted her, he would have kept on kissing her." Apparently realizing that that was not the most tactful thing to say, Martina shut up.

Hope ignored her and increased her pace to warp speed. He didn't kiss *her* at all.

One of Martina's friends grabbed the younger girl and dragged her off. Much to Hope's relief. She liked Luciano's little sister, but she was afraid she was about to cry and she didn't want an audience. She was searching for a bathroom when a male voice halted her. He was speaking Italian. She didn't quite catch the rapidly delivered words and turned.

"I'm sorry, I didn't get that," she said in English, hoping he spoke it as well. Then, just in case, she told him in Italian that she didn't speak the language very well.

He smiled. "Ah, you are the American girlfriend."

"Excuse me?" He made it sound like she was an alien being.

"Luciano has brought you home to meet his Mamma."

The man speaking was about her age and beautiful. There was no other way to describe him. Curly brown hair fell in boyish appeal over his forehead, but his body was anything but boyishly proportioned. Perfectly bronzed, he had sculpted muscles and the classic beauty of a Greek statue. He wasn't nearly as tall as Luciano, but he was still taller than Hope and he was smiling at her.

Hope managed a small smile in return. "Martina said everyone knew, but I thought she was exaggerating."

The man shrugged. "Gossip like that spreads fast. I am Giuseppe, Marco's cousin, and you are Hope, Luciano's American girlfriend."

He took her hand and brought it to his lips. The kiss lingered just one second longer than strict courtesy allowed. Letting her hand lower, but not releasing it, he looked her over from head to foot in a manner that made her blush. *"Bellisima!"* And he kissed his fingertips in a gesture of obvious approval.

Most beautiful. At least someone thought she was more than a stick of furniture. She smiled again, blushing more intensely with shyness and pleasure. "Thank you."

"Ah this shy little smile, this blush, it is most charming. Combined with your loveliness, it is easy to see what has my friend so enthralled."

"Is he your friend?" she asked, not remembering any mention of a Giuseppe DeBreco. But then she hardly could have met all of Luciano's friends in a few short days.

Giuseppe's lips curved in the smile of an angel. "Of course."

Nevertheless, she tugged at her hand. He let go with a comical look of regret and she found herself grinning at him.

"You are inside the house for a reason?" he asked. "Perhaps you wish to protect such beautiful pale skin from the harsh rays of our Sicilian sun?"

"Something like that." She wasn't about to admit to a

perfect stranger that the sight of Luciano with his old girl-friend had sent her running.

"Then come, I will get you a drink and keep you company in the *sala*. You are a guest of my family. You must be entertained."

No longer feeling on the verge of tears, she more than willingly followed the attractive man who wanted *her* company, not that of some other woman. Her conscience tried to tell her that Luciano had been with Marco when Zia had approached him, but she dismissed it. She was in no mood to give him the benefit of the doubt.

Once in the *sala,* Giuseppe went to the minibar against one wall. "I will get you a drink now."

She was expecting something innocuous like lemonade, but he opened a bottle of champagne from the small fridge behind the minibar.

"We'll toast my friend's capture by the beautiful American."

"He's not exactly caught." But she took the glass of champagne he offered and sipped obediently.

Giuseppe mocked her words with his eyes. "You were measured for a wedding gown."

She choked on her champagne. When she could breathe normally, she said, "You're right. Gossip does spread fast."

He shrugged.

"Just for the record," she said, feeling more militant by the mouthful of champagne, "Luciano and I are not engaged."

"Ah, so there is still hope for me," Giuseppe said with exaggerated delight, making her giggle. "Do you wish to listen to music, perhaps watch some television?"

"Maybe some music, but you don't have to stay here and entertain me. I'm very adept at keeping my own company."

He looked scandalized by the very thought. "I am a gentleman. I would never leave a lady to her own devices in the home of my family."

He really was an outrageous flirt. "I don't suppose you play gin rummy?" She had a sudden hankering for the game she played at lunch every day with her friend and co-worker, Edward.

"I am better at poker than gin rummy," Giuseppe said with a wink.

"You know what it is?" she asked in surprise, not responding to his remark about poker.

"Yes. I have an American friend with a passion for the game. I will locate a deck of cards to amuse you if you like."

She took another sip of champagne. "I'd like that. If you play gin rummy with me, I'll play poker with you," she promised.

"So, we will both indulge our vices."

That sounded good to her. She wasn't indulging any vices with Luciano.

Giuseppe was back within a minute, a deck of cards in his hand. While he amused her with stories of Luciano's friends, they played a game of gin rummy. They had only played a couple of hands when it became apparent she would win. On her second glass of champagne, she was feeling warm and benevolent when she went out for the last time.

So, although she would much rather have played another game of rummy, when Giuseppe's frown told her he did not like to lose, she offered to play poker. "I'm terrible and you're sure to win," she said consolingly.

He laughed out loud. "You know the Sicilian male, he does not like to lose, eh?"

"This is very true. He particularly does not like to lose his woman only to find her entertaining herself with another man." The freezing tones of Luciano's voice came from the doorway to the *sala*.

CHAPTER SEVEN

GIUSEPPE looked up, his expression indolent. "Ah, it is the inattentive boyfriend. A man must accept the risks when he leaves his companion to her own devices, my friend."

Hope said nothing because she agreed. Furthermore, tipsy on champagne, she was in no mood to appease Luciano's stupid male ego when he'd been grinding hers into the dust. Memories of roses and other gifts rose to taunt her conscience and she quickly dispelled them. She didn't want to think about how kind and attentive he'd been when she could still remember the sight of his lips locking with Zia's.

Brief or not, it had been a kiss.

"You have nothing to say?" he demanded of her.

"I was just about to play a game of poker with Giuseppe, but I don't have any money." She indicated her swimsuit-clad body and lack of a bag with a negligent wave of her hand. "Can I borrow some?"

Luciano's expression went flint hard. "No."

She sighed and turned to Giuseppe. "I don't suppose you'd be willing to bet in kind, would you?"

"In kind?" he asked, looking at her as if she was a strangely fascinating creature.

"You know, let me bet something other than money?"

Giuseppe's eyes widened as a strangled sound reached her from the doorway.

She ignored it. "It can't be my clothes though. I'm too shy to play strip poker and besides you'd have the advantage." In actual fact, she was thinking more along the lines of an IOU, but why be boring and say so?

Giuseppe looked at her glass of champagne, which was almost empty and back at her. "You don't drink much, do you?"

"What? No. I don't. Has that got something to do with playing poker? I'm sure I'm not too tipsy to read the cards, if that's what's worrying you."

His gaze slid sideways to a glowering Luciano and back to her. "Not precisely, no."

"You are not playing poker."

She didn't bother to acknowledge Luciano. She smiled at Giuseppe. "So, what can I bet?"

"Luciano does not want you to play." He spoke slowly, as if she might not have gotten the message the first time around when Luciano had said it in such a bossy tone.

"I'm an American woman, you know. We're not that great at being told what to do. For that matter, I'm not sure many modern women are."

"Even the shy ones, I see." His brown eyes twinkled with a level of amusement unwarranted by the situation.

"Giuseppe," Luciano interrupted in a voice that could have razed steel, "I believe Marco would like your help entertaining his guests."

"I am sorry, Hope. I must go." The younger man stood, his angelic smile marked with overtones of real humor. "Duty calls. Perhaps we will get our game of poker another time."

She sighed. "All right. I promise to let you win."

He inclined his head toward her. "I will look forward to it." Then he left.

She picked up the deck of cards, shuffled them, and then laid out the pattern for a game of solitaire. She'd been deprived of her gin rummy partner, but that didn't mean she had to return to poolside to watch Zia fawning over Luciano.

She'd moved three times when she felt his brooding presence right behind her. "Why were you in here playing cards with Giuseppe?"

She didn't bother to turn to face him, but shrugged. "I wanted to."

"I do not like finding you alone with other men." He sounded like a guy trying really hard to hold on to his patience.

"Really?" Well, she didn't like him letting other women kiss him, so they were even. "I'll remember that."

"And not do it again?" His voice was dangerously soft, but the champagne had affected more than her willingness to let Giuseppe win at cards.

"I didn't say that. I enjoyed playing gin rummy with Giuseppe. He's a very nice man. He's really good looking too," she said with more candor than wisdom, "and not so tall that he's overwhelming to a shrimp like me."

Really, she should go for a guy like that instead of the ultra-masculine Luciano. Why weren't hearts more logical?

A sharply indrawn breath behind her told her that he had not liked the provoking answer. "You prefer his company to mine?" His voice was quiet and yet she just knew he was majorly furious at the idea.

An honest answer would be too good for his ego. "I don't know," she surprised herself by saying. Apparently she wasn't done being provoking. Maybe she should drink champagne more often. She studied her cards. "I only got to play one game of gin rummy with him before you came in and chased him off."

Masculine rage radiated from Luciano in palpable waves

that burned against her back. "Yet, you think you might, given the opportunity?"

She moved a red five onto a black six. "He touched me. You don't. Maybe." Liar. She wanted only Luciano.

"He touched you?" The deadly softness of his voice warned her that she had phrased that very badly.

She spun in her chair to face him and regretted the action at once. First and foremost because it made her dizzy, but secondly because his expression was frightening. He looked like he wanted to kill someone and she thought that person might be Giuseppe. She didn't want to cause any problems between the two men, especially when the younger one had been so nice to her.

She glared at Luciano. "Not like that. I'm not like your other girlfriend, Zia. I don't go kissing men in public places."

Luciano ignored the reference to Zia. "How did he touch you, *tesoro?* Tell me." His voice was deadly soft.

"He kissed my hand and he called me beautiful. If you want the truth, it made me feel nice." A lot nicer than having Luciano dump the suntan lotion in his sister's lap and leave with the speed of an Olympic athlete when Marco signaled for him. "Now go back to your *Playboy* Bunny and let me finish my game of solitaire in peace."

Had she really said that? She sounded like a truculent child, or a jealous woman. Which she was, she admitted.

"I have no interest in other women and I do not wish to leave you alone."

She rolled her eyes. Right. "Why not?" He had a very strange way of showing his supposed singular interest in her. "You left me alone by the pool."

"I left you with my sister." He sounded and looked driven. "Marco wanted to discuss something with me."

"So, go back and talk some more business with him. I don't care." She should be used to it by now. She'd been ignored for her grandfather's business interests all her life, but if Luciano thought she was going to marry a man who did the same thing to her, then he was a fool.

But it isn't his business interests that have you so on edge, her inner voice reminded her.

"Clearly you do care." He had that superior-male-dealing-with-a-recalcitrant-female expression on his face. "You are upset."

So, he'd noticed.

"Am I?" She turned back to the cards and saw where she could uncover an ace. She did it. She was even better at solitaire than gin rummy. She'd played a lot of it growing up.

Gentle fingers played softly over the bare skin of her shoulders. "What is it, *tesoro mio?* Are you upset by Zia's kiss? It was nothing, I assure you. All is over between us. She was joking with me."

He sounded so sincere and Hope had this really craven desire to lean back into his touch. "That's not the way it looked to me."

"So, this is about Zia's forwardness?" The masculine complacency in his voice grated on Hope's nerves. He liked the idea of her being jealous, the fiend.

"*This* is about nothing. I felt like coming inside. End of story." Was prevarication becoming a habit?

"And playing a game of cards with an inveterate rake?" The complacency was gone.

"Giuseppe is very nice."

"*Sì.* He kissed your hand and told you that you are beautiful." The fingers on her shoulders were tense now, but they weren't hurting her. "You liked this."

If he had sounded angry, she might have remained defiant, but he didn't. He sounded confused and disappointed. In her.

"I'd rather you did it," she admitted. Darn that champagne anyway. The next thing she knew she would be telling him she loved him.

He pulled her up from the chair and around to face her. She kept her eyes focused on the hair-covered bronzed skin of his chest rather than looking up. It was damaging to her breathing pattern, but better for her pride. She didn't want to see his smug reaction to her admission.

He took her smaller hand in his large, dark one. Lifting it toward him and bending at the same time, he touched his lips to the back of her knuckles. "You are very beautiful."

Then he said it in Italian. He also told her she was sweet, the woman he wanted to marry and that her skin tasted like honey.

She was entranced by the litany of praise.

But he did not stop with words. He kissed each of her fingertips with tiny biting kisses, repeating the word *bellisima* after each kiss. Her eyes slid shut as sensation washed over her and then he pulled her into his body, saying something else in Italian. It sounded like, "I knew this would happen," but that made no sense.

She stopped trying to figure it out when he tilted her head up and covered her mouth with his.

The first touch of his lips sliding against hers had the impact of a knockout drug on her willpower.

She'd been starved for the taste of him for days and flicked her tongue out to sample his lips without thought. He groaned and she found herself in his arms, their lips and bodies locked passionately together. It was like that time at his apartment in Athens, but better. She knew what to expect now, what pleasure awaited her in his arms.

She wound her arms around his neck and pulled herself up his body, standing on her very tiptoes, pressing herself as close to him as possible.

He swung her up into his arms, never breaking the kiss. She opened her mouth, inviting him inside and he took the invitation with the power of an invading army. He decimated her every defense and left her helpless against his desire and her own.

He was moving. She didn't care where he was taking her. She just wanted him to keep doing what he was doing, *showing* her he wanted her more than other women. Because he certainly hadn't responded to Zia this way when she'd tricked him into that kiss by the poolside.

Shadows played across Hope's closed eyelids as the sounds of the party faded completely from her hearing. Then there was the sound of a door closing behind them. But still he didn't lift his mouth from hers and she didn't open her eyes. Awash with sensation, her sensory receptors were inundated with pleasure.

The solid feel of a bed beneath her told her he had brought her into a guest room. The feel of his more than solid body on top of hers told her he intended to stay. Her legs instinctively parted, making room for him against her most sensitive flesh. Wearing only their swimsuits, masculine hair covered limbs slid against feminine softness. The sensitive flesh of her inner thighs thrilled to the press of hard, sculpted muscles.

The hands she'd so desperately wanted to touch her were all over her skin, leaving a trail of hot desire in their wake.

She moaned and arched up toward him, pressing her womanhood against his hardness. She trembled. Intimate in a way she could not have imagined, though he was not inside her, she felt possessed. Swollen and hotly lubricated tissues ached to be appeased with a more direct caress.

His mouth broke from hers to trail hot, openmouthed kisses down her neck and across the skin exposed above the line of her tankini top. "You are no shrimp, *cara.* You are perfect." He pressed his body into hers, sending further sensation sweeping through the core of her. "We are perfect together."

She was breathing too hard to reply, her body on fire for more of his touch, her mind an inferno of erotic thoughts.

"Admit it, Hope. I do not overwhelm you. I excite you."

Did he need the words? Wasn't her body's response enough for him to see that she'd been spouting off earlier?

He rocked into her in an exciting imitation of the mating act.

She arched her pelvis, every sliding contact between his hardness and her sensitized nerve endings sending jolt after jolt of pleasure zinging through her.

He lifted away from her, withdrawing his body from the direct contact she craved.

She gasped, trying to reconnect with his body, but strong hands held her to the bed. "You have this with no other man. *Your body wants me.* Say it."

"Yes," she practically screamed. "You're perfect for me."

It wasn't such an admission. He'd already said she was the perfect size for him, but still, she felt she'd given something away. Admitted to a need that made her vulnerable to him.

Her words had a profound impact on his self-control and without really knowing how it happened, she lost her bikini. He disposed of his black shorts. Then it really was his naked flesh moving against hers.

She cried out with the joy of it and then screamed when his mouth fit itself over one turgid nipple. He suckled and she flew apart, her body straining for a release it had never known.

"Please, Luciano. I can't stand this." She felt like she was going to die, so rapid was her heartbeat, so shallow her breathing. Her muscles locked in painful rigidity as she strained toward him and the pleasure his touches promised.

His hand fondled her intimately, as he had that night in Athens. "You belong to me, *cara.*"

She stared up at him through vision hazed by passion.

"*Yes*. But it goes both ways," she managed to pant, needing him to know this was not a one-way street.

He growled his approval as he stroked her in a tortuous pattern against her pleasure spot. Within seconds she was shuddering under him in a fulfillment that both elated and terrified her. Her body truly did not belong to her in that space of time. He owned it with the gratification he gave her, the emotions that pleasure evoked in her.

"Luciano!"

He reared up above her, his dark eyes burning with triumph and unslaked desire. Aligning his erect flesh with her pulsing wetness, his jaw went rigid with tension. "I could take you now. *Santo cielo! I want to take you now.*"

"Yes." Oh, yes. Now. She wanted to receive him, to take him as primitively as his eyes told her he wanted it to be.

"But I won't." His voice was guttural with feeling, his face tight with strain and sweat beading his temple.

"You won't?" she asked stupidly, finding his denial incomprehensible.

He was literally on the verge of joining their bodies. How could he stop now?

"I do not seduce virgins." His words came out from between gritted teeth, each one a bullet of strained sound.

"But I want you, Luciano."

His forehead dropped against hers, the heat emanating from him baking in its intensity. "I want you also, *piccola mia,* but in a marriage bed."

Her eyes were squeezed shut, her body aching for his possession. "What are you saying?"

"Agree to marry me, Hope, or go home to Boston. I cannot stand this torment of the body any longer." He shivered above her, the tip of his shaft caressing sensitized and swollen flesh.

Then he threw himself on his back away from her, the evidence of his arousal testimony to his words. The fierce grip of his fingers on the bedspread proof of just how close to the edge of control he was.

But it was marriage or nothing. No. Not nothing. Not by a long stretch. He'd fulfilled her. Taken the edge off of her need, giving her the first sexual release of her life, but without marriage, he would take nothing for himself and would not give himself completely.

"Isn't it the woman who is supposed to demand marriage?" It wasn't just a weak attempt at humor. It was also an expression of how bewildering she found her current situation.

He didn't answer.

She supposed he thought he'd said it all.

Maybe he had. She loved him. So much. She wanted him almost as much as she loved him. He wanted her too. She looked at his still erect flesh. *A lot.* He wanted her a lot. He liked her too, had respected her enough to pursue her in the traditional way. Was liking, respect and desire enough?

She sat up, curling her knees into her chest and effecting as much modesty as possible without her clothes on. His hardness had not abated, but his breathing was growing calmer. She looked away, embarrassed by the intimacy of seeing him like this. She wanted to know the miracle of being connected to him in the most personal way any woman could know a man, but she didn't doubt he would stand by his ultimatum.

Marriage, or nothing.

"Luciano," she said tentatively.

"Sì?"

"Um…" How did a woman ask this kind of question? "Do you believe in fidelity?"

He sat up and glared at her, supremely unconcerned by his nudity. "Once we are married, there will be no other man."

Was he really that dense? "I meant you. If I marry you, will I have to worry about you taking a mistress?"

"No." There was a rock-solid certainty in his expression that she could not doubt.

"Do you have a mistress now?" She had to ask.

"I told you there was no other woman."

"But some men don't consider wives and mistresses in the same class. They think having one does not preclude having the other." She'd seen it often enough among the rich compatriots of her grandfather and knew that wealthy Italian men were particularly susceptible. Or so it seemed.

"I am not these men. I want no woman but you."

"Always?" she asked, finding it very difficult to believe he wanted to cleave to her for a lifetime and forsake all other women.

He reached out and cupped her cheek. "Always. You will be my wife, the mother of my children. I will not shame you in this way."

Tears pricked her eyes and she blinked them away. "All right," she said, her voice thick with emotion.

"You will marry me?"

She nodded. "Yes."

His thumb rubbed the wetness from under her eye. "You are crying. Tell me why."

"I'm not sure. I'm scared," she admitted to both him and herself. "You don't love me, but you want to marry me."

"And you love me."

Was there any point in denying it? She'd just agreed to become his wife. "Yes."

"I am glad of this, *cara*. You have nothing to fear in giving yourself to me. I will treasure your love."

But not return it.

Was that something so different? She'd practically lived her whole life without being truly loved. Her grandfather had been duty bound to care for her, but until very recently, he hadn't even acted particularly fond of her. At least Luciano really *wanted* her. He could have anyone and he'd chosen her. That had to prove something.

She forced herself to smile. The man she loved wanted to marry her. He wanted to have children with her and he had promised her fidelity. He respected her, he liked her and he desired her, she reminded herself. Perhaps from that, within the intimacy of marriage, love would grow.

"I guess we'd better get dressed," she said, not nearly so complacent as he about their state of undress when she did not have passion to dull her normal thinking process.

He stayed her movement toward the edge of the bed. "I too want an assurance from you."

"What?"

"No more being alone with other men." He was all conquering male.

She sighed. "We were only playing cards, Luciano. You must know it wasn't anything more."

"I know this, but I did not like finding you alone with Giuseppe. He is a womanizer of the first order."

"Well, he was a gentleman with me. He may be a flirt, but I don't think he would go after a woman who was attached to someone else."

Luciano didn't look impressed by her belief. "Promise me."

"You're being ridiculous. What do you want me to do, run from the room if I'm alone and another man comes into it?"

When he looked like he might agree, she glared at him. "That's not going to happen."

"Face it, you were so busy with your *friends,* you didn't even notice I was gone." The memory of Zia's overly warm greeting still rankled. "We had time for me to beat him at gin rummy before you even came looking. I don't think you should complain too loudly about me finding my own entertainment."

"I believed you were with Martina. When she came back to the pool with other friends and without you, I immediately began looking for you."

"I wouldn't have left in the first place if you hadn't let your ex-girlfriend kiss you."

"I did not *let* her kiss me. She just did it."

Hope had to give him that. And he had pulled away very quickly. "You touched her when you wouldn't even put sunscreen on my back," she accused. "When was the last time you kissed my cheeks in greeting? You treat me like the untouchable woman."

His brow rose in mockery. "Do you wonder at this? I touch you and five minutes later, we are naked on a bed together."

"Are you saying you've been avoiding touching me because you want me that much?" It was a novel concept, one that was infinitely good for her feminine ego.

"I promised you I would not seduce you."

And the most casual touching put that promise at risk. At least that was what he was implying. Knowing he was that physically vulnerable to her assuaged some of her fear at marriage to a man who did not love her.

"And now you want a promise I won't spend time alone with other men."

"*Sì.*"

Luciano hadn't liked finding her with David that day in Athens and even less discovering her alone with Giuseppe. She should understand that because she wouldn't like the reverse either. Only she'd made him promise her fidelity. Perhaps he had his own insecurities. The idea was almost laughable, but the strangely intent expression in his eyes was not.

"I won't make a habit of being alone with other men and I will never be unfaithful to you." It was the best she could do, because she wasn't going to go running from a room if a man walked into it and she wasn't going to make a promise she couldn't keep.

He seemed satisfied and nodded. "We will marry in two weeks time."

CHAPTER EIGHT

"But why does he wish to see you before the ceremony? This is not normal." The older woman rang her hands. "*Ai, ai, ai.* American men, they are not rational."

Hope stifled a smile. Her future mother-in-law had very definite views of what constituted proper male and female behavior. Hope's grandfather had confounded her several times over the past two weeks, wanting to approve the wedding dress, insisting on consultation with the chef for the reception and a host of other equally odd, to her mind, requests.

She patted Claudia di Valerio's arm. "It's all right. He just wants to see. He won't touch anything."

Her grandfather had been ecstatic at the news of her upcoming marriage and had flown over immediately to take part in the preparations, much to Luciano's mother's dismay. She was not used to having a man around giving orders in the domestic arena, but Joshua Reynolds wanted to be involved on every level of planning the wedding.

Luciano might be bossy, but he wasn't quite the controller Joshua Reynolds was. When her grandfather was interested in a project, he wanted final say-so over every aspect. For some reason, he'd decided to take an interest in Hope's wedding. Assuming it was part of the strange change in his behavior since the heart attack, Hope dealt with his interference with more equanimity than her future mother-in-law.

Claudia rolled her eyes and crossed herself before opening the bedroom door. "Come in, then."

The old man came into the room, his expression as happy as Hope had ever seen it. He stopped in front of her. "You look beautiful, Hope. So much like your grandmother on our wedding day."

She'd never known her grandmother, but it pleased her for her grandfather to make the comparison.

His expression turned regretful. "I neglected her shamefully. Your mother too, but I've learned my lesson. I want better for you. I want you to be happy. Marrying Luciano makes you happy, doesn't it, child?"

"Yes." A little uncertain still about her future, but full of joy at the prospect of spending it with him. "Very happy."

At this both the old man and Claudia beamed with pleasure. For once, they were in one accord.

"Then it was worth it. I did the right thing."

Did he mean sending Luciano to visit her in Athens? She had to agree. "Yes."

He turned to Claudia. "I suppose you have a timetable for this shindig?"

Luciano's mother bristled with annoyance. "It will happen when it happens. I have planned the events, but a wedding cannot be rushed to fit a businessman's schedule."

Surprisingly, Joshua meekly agreed and left the room.

"I think you scared him, Mamma." Martina grinned from the other side of the room where she had been laying out Hope's going away outfit.

"*Ai, ai, ai.* That man. Nothing scares him, but at least he has left us in peace."

Only there was very little of that over the next hour as the final preparations were made for Hope's walk down the aisle.

It was to be a traditional Sicilian ceremony and celebration to follow. While she looked forward to becoming Luciano's wife, all the pomp and ceremony surrounding the event had numbed her emotions with fatigue. So, when her grandfather escorted her to the front of the church, she was in a haze of anesthetized exhaustion with no room in her foggy brain for fear or last-minute doubts.

And for that she was grateful.

When Joshua placed her hand in Luciano's, a look passed between the two men that she did not understand. There had been an indefinable tension between them since her grandfather's arrival in Italy. She wondered if they had had a business falling-out. She hadn't asked Luciano about it because although he had not gone back to treating her like the untouchable woman, he had made sure they were never alone together.

His hand was warm as it surrounded hers and she pushed her worries about his relationship with her grandfather to the back of her mind.

"So, the pill was not so bitter to swallow, was it?"

Luciano turned slowly at the sound of Joshua Reynolds' voice. The old man looked pleased with himself.

Would he be so happy when his business began to lose important contracts? Luciano did not think so, but he merely raised his brow. "Marriage is for life. It is in my own interests to make the best of taking Hope as my wife."

"You're a shark in business," Joshua said with satisfaction, "but traditional when it comes to family, aren't you?"

Luciano did not bother to reply. Joshua would have ample opportunity to learn for himself what a shark in business a Sicilian man blackmailed into marriage could be.

The other man did not seem bothered by Luciano's silence. "You won't make the same mistake I did and ignore her. She's a special woman, but I messed up my chance with her. We're not close and we could have been." Regret weighted his voice, making him sound old and tired. "She used to come into my office at home and sit on the rug by my feet playing with her dolls." A faraway look entered Joshua's pale eyes. "I guess she was about six. She'd ask me every night to tuck her in. I was too busy most of the time. She stopped asking."

The old man sighed. "She stopped coming into my office too. I wish I could say she had the love of my housekeeper or a nanny, but I hired for efficiency, not warmth."

The picture he was painting of Hope's childhood was chilling. Having been raised in the warmth of a typical Italian household, if a wealthy one, Luciano shuddered inwardly at the emotional wasteland Hope had been reared in.

"She is very giving." All things considered, that was pretty surprising.

"Takes after her grandmother and mother in that. They were like her. Soft. Caring." Joshua turned his gaze to Hope. "Beautiful too."

"As you say." Watching his new wife smile as she talked to Mamma, he wondered why Joshua had felt the need to blackmail him into marriage with Hope. "She is sweet and lovely. She would have landed her own husband soon enough. Your measures were not necessary."

Joshua shook his head. "You're wrong. There was only one thing Hope wanted and I got it for her."

Understanding came slowly. "Me."

Joshua turned and looked at Luciano, his expression almost harsh. "You. She wanted you and I was damned determined she was going to have you."

Had she known all along then? Had she told her grandfather she wanted to marry Luciano and then waited for the old man to procure her a husband? Remembering how difficult she had been to catch, he dismissed the idea.

He remembered too how Hope's gaze used to follow him at business dinners and how she had been on New Year's Eve. Luciano was positive that Joshua had witnessed more passion between Hope and Luciano on New Year's Eve than he had ever seen with her and another man. He had drawn his own conclusions about his granddaughter's behavior and acted accordingly.

Hope was not devious, not like her grandfather or her new husband. She was honest and giving as both men had agreed, too soft to be party to something as reprehensible as blackmail. She would be appalled by Joshua's ruthless actions in securing her a husband and equally devastated to know what Luciano planned in retaliation.

He would make sure she never found out.

He didn't want her hurt, but he did want her grandfather to realize the folly of blackmailing Luciano di Valerio.

Hope stood in the bathroom and brushed her hair and then fluffed it around her face for the tenth time. She'd tried pulling it up, but hadn't liked the severity of the effect, besides what woman wore her hair up to go to bed? It hardly seemed conducive to a passionate wedding night, but then neither did her hiding in the bathroom for an hour and a half.

Luciano was waiting out in the suite's bedroom. She'd come into the en suite to get ready on his suggestion. It had seemed like a good idea at the time, but now she was struggling with the courage it took to open that door and join the man she had married. It was the joining part that had her cowering like a ninny in the bathroom.

She should be ready.

They'd come close to making love twice. She'd been naked with him, for Heaven's sake.

None of that seemed to matter to the nerves shaking her

equilibrium until she felt like a soda bottle ready to fizz over the side in a bubbly mess.

She wanted Luciano. Desperately. But she was afraid. Afraid she would disappoint him. Afraid it would hurt. Afraid that once they had made love, he would lose interest in her. She was something different in his life, not one of the sophisticated jet-setters he was used to having affairs with. Not like Zia.

She was just Hope. A cultural anachronism. A twenty-three-year-old virgin. Could she maintain his interest once the newness wore off, the uniqueness of making love to a woman of no experience?

A hard tattoo sounded on the door. It had been gentle an hour ago and thirty minutes ago and even fifteen minutes ago, but the impatience he must be feeling was now coming out in the force with which he rapped on the door.

"Hope?" Definitely impatience in his voice.

"Yes?"

"Are you coming out, *cara?*"

She stared at the door as if it might explode into flame at any moment. If it did, she wouldn't have to go through it, she thought a bit hysterically. Of course it didn't and she forced herself to cover the few feet so she could unlock and open the door. She turned the handle and pulled the door toward her.

He stood on the other side, a pair of black silk pajama bottoms slung low on his hips. The rest of his magnificent body was naked.

She swallowed. "Hi." She was making Minnie Mouse impersonations again. That only happened around him.

"You are frightened."

What had been his first clue? The ninety-minute-long sojourn in the bathroom or the death grip she had on the door now? "Maybe a little."

"You have nothing to fear, *tesoro mio,*" he said with supreme confidence, "I will be gentle with you."

Easy for him to say. Not that she doubted his gentleness, but this was different than anything they had shared before. It was premeditated. She found that being overcome with passion was a very different animal to psyching herself up to making love completely for the first time.

If that weren't enough, what they were about to do would have permanent ramifications. The wedding was a ceremony, this was the reality of being married. She was about to become one with this man, a man who inspired both feelings of awe and love in her. But with love came trust, or so she had always believed.

"I'm not afraid of you." Just the situation.

He put one brown hand out toward her. "Then show me, little one. Come to me."

Luciano waited tensely for Hope to come to him. He did not know how much longer he could keep a rein on his desire.

The last few weeks had been interminable.

There at the last, when he had given her the ultimatum: marriage or go home to Boston, he had not even been thinking of making the marriage deal come off. He'd only been thinking of his need to possess her and his commitment not to do so outside the bonds of marriage. He had made a promise to her and the only way to keep that promise was to marry her or send her away.

That his ultimatum had led to the marriage he needed to regain control of the family company caused him satisfaction rather than guilt. He had not intentionally seduced her into marriage. He had kept his promise and courted her and he would be a good husband to her. He would keep his vow of fidelity and she would give him passion and children.

Joshua Reynolds had been right in that at least. The pill was not bitter to swallow, but the water it had gone down with had been rancid. The only way to rid his pride of the aftereffects of the blackmail was to plan a suitable measure of justice for the old man. Luciano did not want to ruin him completely. Joshua was now family, but he would learn a necessary lesson about Sicilian pride.

As Hope took the first step forward, all thoughts of vendettas and lessons faded from Luciano's mind. It filled with the primitive need to mate with his woman.

This woman.

Hope.

Her violet eyes were dark with conflicting emotions. It was the fear that kept him rooted, waiting for her to come to him. She was so beautiful in her cobalt blue silk gown. It swept the floor as she walked and it pleased him she had not opted for the traditional white for their wedding night.

He liked this indication of the fire within her. The hottest part of a flame was blue and when she was in his arms, she burned that hotly.

She stopped two feet away from him. "I'm nervous."

This he had not missed. "There is no need, *carina.*"

"What if I don't satisfy you?" Doubts swirled in her lovely eyes. "I'm not like Zia and the rest. I'm completely without experience."

She said it like she was admitting the gravest sin, but the words had a devastating affect on his libido.

He had to touch her or go mad.

Forcing himself to gentleness, he reached out and put his hands on her shoulders and brushed his thumbs over her collarbones. The fine bones felt fragile under his strength.

"Your innocence is a gift you give me, not a shortcoming you must apologize for." How could he erase the doubts? "I am honored to be your first lover, *cara.*"

She still looked painfully unconvinced.

"I do not want you to be like Zia. It will please me to teach you all I want you to know."

Her eyes widened at that. "Teach me?"

"*Sì.*"

Understanding warmed her eyes. "You like that. In some ways, you're a total throwback, aren't you? You really like the idea of being my first lover."

He didn't deny the charge. He felt primitive with her. "Your only lover."

She nodded. "My only lover." She swayed toward him, her lips soft and inviting. "Then teach me, *caro*. Make me yours."

Her words and the anticipation in her gaze splintered the final thread of his control. He pulled her into his body with less finesse than an oversexed teenager. She didn't seem to mind; her entire body melded to his and her arms came around him in a hold as fierce as his own.

Covering her mouth with his own, he demanded instant entrance. He got it, penetrating her sweet moistness with all the need tormenting him. In the back of his mind was a voice telling him to slow down, to savor her sweetness, but the primal yearning of his body did not listen.

Her tongue shyly dueled with his and small, feminine hands moved to cradle his face while she twisted her satin clad body into him.

Groaning, he swept her up into his arms and marveled at the passion exploding from her small body. She was frightened no longer. It was as if his first touch had dispelled her every concern.

He laid her on the bed and stepped back, his breath coming like an Olympic runner's after the triathlon. *Santo cielo!* She was perfect.

She leaned up on her elbows, the tight points of her nipples making shoals in the material. "Luciano?"

"If we do not slow down, I will hurt you." That knowledge was enough to temper the desire raging in his body.

He would not hurt her. She was too small. Delicate.

He had to be careful.

She sat up and stripped her nightgown down her arms, baring breasts flushed with arousal. Then she extended her hands to him. "Come to me, Luciano. Please."

Was this wild wanton his wife, the sweet little Hope that blushed when he spoke too frankly?

Her pansy eyes were dilated widely; her small body trembled. "I don't want to go slow."

"It is your first time."

"I *know*." She drawled out the word. "And I don't want the chance to get scared again. When you touch me, nothing exists for me but you."

He felt a smile come over his face and suddenly his need for satisfaction was almost wholly sublimated by his desire to show her what it felt to be made love to by a man who knew how to savor a woman.

"You will not be scared, *cara mia*. You will beg me for my possession and I will give it to you only when you want it more than the air that you breathe."

Hope shivered at Luciano's words, her tongue flicking out nervously to wet her lower lip. She was back to feeling fear despite his assurances, or maybe because of them. It was a sensual fear born from the heated expression in his dark brown eyes. Tonight, there would be no stopping.

He leaned down and tasted her lips. "You are sweet, *mi moglie*. Like candy."

His wife. She loved the sound of that and her lips clung to his, but he pulled back to sit at the end of the bed.

Her eyes had closed during the kiss, but opened again. He was looking at her feet. "Luciano?"

He lifted her right foot into his hand. "You are very small, Hope."

"And you aren't." His hand swallowed her.

His eyes dared her to imply that was a bad thing while his

fingers moved against the sole of her unexpectedly sensitive foot. She didn't feel like laughing though.

She wasn't feeling ticklish, she was feeling excited and more so by the second.

She moaned as he brushed his thumb over her arch. He smiled and did it again. And again. And again. Then lifted the foot to kiss the instep and she moaned again, this time several decibels higher. What was he doing to her?

Feet were not erogenous zones. Were they?

"You smell of wildflowers."

"Bath salts," she panted.

He rubbed his lips along her arch, not kissing so much as caressing. "You're soft like silk."

He flicked his tongue out and licked. Her toes curled and air hissed out of her lungs on a shattered gasp.

"There are over seven thousand nerve endings in your feet."

"R-really?" she asked breathlessly and then cried out as he pressed between two of her toes and she felt the reaction in a totally different part of her body.

He laughed softly. "*Sì*. Really." He touched her gently, but firmly. "If I caress you here, you feel it here."

He brushed the nest of curls between her legs through the slick material of her gown while his other hand massaged her foot. Oh, man, he was right.

She tilted her pelvis upward, desperate for more intimacy, confused by her body's reaction to his not-so-innocent massage. "Yes. Oh… I felt it."

"And do you feel this also, *carina?*"

She bowed completely off the bed as he touched her again. "I feel it! It's…" Her voice trailed off into a gasp of pleasure.

By the time he had given similar treatment to her other foot, she was incoherent with pleasure, having flopped back against the pillows, her body totally open to whatever he wanted to do to her.

Silk slid sensuously against her legs as he pushed her nightgown up inch by slow inch. He trailed his fingertips along her calves, pushing her nightgown up further until his mouth pressed against the skin behind her right knee. He tasted it and the dampness between her legs increased.

Whimpering, she squirmed against the bedspread as he continued his erotic tasting up her legs until he'd pushed her gown into a crumpled mass of blue silk around her waist.

Oh, Heavens. He wasn't going to do that. He couldn't. She couldn't let him. She tried to scoot backward. "You can't kiss me there!"

His response to her frantic efforts to get away was a sexy smile as two big hands clamped firmly to her thighs. Holding them apart when she instinctively tried to close them, he also held her securely in place. "I promise you will like it."

"I…"

Then his mouth was on her. There. She'd read about this, but it felt more intimate than any words could describe. His tongue did things to her that had her body arching toward him, not away. An unbearable pressure built and built inside her.

The pressure burst without warning and her entire body went taut, every single muscle convulsing in rigidity and she screamed. She couldn't hear her scream over the blood rushing in her head, but she could feel the rawness in her throat from the strain.

Luciano wanted to give Hope a surfeit of pleasure, finding vicarious satisfaction in her passion. He could feel each muscular contraction of her virginal body in his inner being. He had never experienced another woman's pleasure so fully as his own and the experience was its own kind of fulfillment.

She shuddered under his ministering mouth, the taste of her growing sweeter with each explosion in her flesh. He didn't stop, pushing her to one higher plateau of ecstasy after another.

Her breath was labored, but then so was his. He felt on the verge of exploding, but he couldn't make himself stop. The sounds of her enjoyment were addictive. Each cry made him feel like the conquering male. Each moan of rapture made his own sex throb with pleasure and desire.

"Luciano, it's too much. Please stop. Please… Please… Please…" She was sobbing with each breath, but still she pressed herself against his mouth.

Her lips said one thing, her body another.

Finally, she went completely limp, little whimpering noises interspersed with each breath and he pulled away, kissing her gently as he did so.

He knelt between her legs and surveyed the effect of the first level of their loving on her. Her small body was flushed with arousal all over, her purple eyes awash with tears, and her mouth parted on shallow pants. Hard, red berries, crested the swollen flesh of her breasts. He reached out and gently touched them.

A moan snaked from her throat.

Her nightgown was still bunched around her waist and he wanted her naked.

Disposing of the silk cloth was easy as she languidly allowed him to move her any way he wanted to. He pushed his own pajama bottoms down his hips, his body experiencing relief at the removal of the light restraint of the fabric.

He wanted to touch only one thing with his hardened shaft, the rich, swollen tissues of her inner woman.

"Are you ready for me, *carina?*"

"I want you to be part of me." The words were a soft whisper, but very certain.

"*Sì.*" He would hesitate no longer. He could hesitate no longer. He had to have her.

He covered her body with his in one movement, his hard flesh pressed to the most secret part of her. He had been this way once before, but tonight he would not stop. He would consummate their marriage and perhaps even give her their child. "Now, you become my wife."

CHAPTER NINE

"YES." It was a broken sound, a mere breath as she curled her fingers into the hair on his chest.

He pressed inward, but though he had brought her to completion many times, she was still tight. "You must relax for me, little one."

"You're so big."

"I am just right for you. Trust me." The urge to press forward without caution and bury himself in her wet heat was almost more than he could bear. "Give me yourself, *mi moglie.*"

"I don't know how," she whispered brokenly.

"Absorb me, sweetness. Open yourself to our joining."

She closed her eyes and took a deep breath and then let it out slowly. Inside, the tight clasp on his body loosened and he slid forward a bit more. He started a rocking motion that made her breath hitch and his body break out in sweat as he went deeper into her.

He felt the barrier of her innocence and would have paused, but she arched up toward him crying his name and suddenly he was sheathed in her softness completely. He stilled immediately.

"Are you all right?"

Her eyes slid open, their pansy depths warm with emotion that caught the breath in his chest.

He made love to her then, forcing himself to go slow, to

build the pleasure in her again until he felt the beginning tremors of her release.

"Now we share it," he cried and gave in to the rapture exploding through him.

Her pleasure prolonged his own until he shook with exhaustion from his release. Unable to hold himself above her any longer, he collapsed on top of her. She made a muffled sound and with the last bit of his strength, he rolled them both so she was on top of him, but they were still connected.

"Now you belong to me."

She rubbed her face against his chest, adjusting herself against his body with a movement that unbelievably teased his recently satisfied flesh. "And you belong to me."

He did not deny it. The bitter pill had turned out sweeter than nectar and he reveled in his possession of a woman so sweet, so passionate and so completely lacking in artifice. She was everything her grandfather was not.

Everything women like Zia could never hope to be.

Tenderness he had never known toward a lover washed over him and he caressed her back, wanting to soothe her to sleep in his arms.

A soft butterfly kiss landed near his left nipple. "I love you, Luciano," she whispered against his skin.

The words did strange things to his insides and he could almost thank Joshua Reynolds for giving him the gift of such a woman.

They spent their honeymoon in Naples. Luciano kept his promise to Hope and took her to Pompeii to visit the ruins of the ancient city. They did other touristy things together, Luciano never once growing impatient with her desire to see and experience new things. He made love to her every night, most mornings and frequently in the afternoon as well.

He was insatiable and she loved it. Shocked by her own

capacity for passion, she became a total wanton in his arms. It worried her a little bit, this lack of control she had over her body when he touched her, but his ardor made her feel better about her own.

Every day her love for him grew. Though while she told him frequently of her feelings, he said nothing of his own.

He was solicitous of her needs, tender when he loved her and gentle when she needed him to be. There were several times Hope almost convinced herself that Luciano loved her as she loved him. Although he never said the words, he seemed to like hearing her say them. And he made her feel so special, never letting his gaze slide to other women when they were out, using endearments when he spoke to her, and touching her frequently with affection.

When they returned to Palermo, she was so happy she was sick with it.

"It looks like your marriage to my brother is having a very good effect on you," Martina teased the evening following their return as Hope set up for a billiard shot. "You are positively luminescent with joy."

She grinned at her new sister-in-law. "I'm happy."

Martina laughed, the sound echoing in the cavernous game room. "You two were made for each other."

Hope was beginning to believe that was true both ways and the sense of elation she felt at finally finding her place in the heart of another person knew no bounds. "He's a really incredible guy."

Martina rolled her eyes. "To each her own, but I think you are biased. Luciano is no better. He couldn't keep his eyes off you all through dinner last night. Mamma had visions of babies dancing through her head. I could tell."

Hope placed her hand over her stomach. It had only been two weeks, but she couldn't help thinking that with all the physical attention she received from Luciano, the odds of pregnancy were good.

But she shrugged, refusing to expose her hidden hopes in case they proved futile. "Who knows?"

The phone rang in the other room and seconds later a maid came into the game room. "*Signora* di Valerio, your grandfather, he wishes to speak to you."

Martina laid down her cue stick. "Take the call in here. I'll go get dressed for dinner."

Hope picked up the phone. "Hello, Grandfather."

He returned her greeting and asked about the honeymoon. She told him about their visit to Pompeii and a garden she had found enchanting.

They had been talking about ten minutes when he asked, "Are you happy then, little Hope?"

"Fizzing with it," she admitted without hesitation.

"That's good to know."

His concern had come late in life, but it still felt nice. "Thank you."

"I finally managed to give you something you really wanted." He cleared his throat in a familiar way that made her realize she missed him even if he hadn't been a big part of her daily life in Boston. "I knew what you did with the coat and my housekeeper told me the car stayed in the garage."

"I never got around to learning to drive," she said somewhat sheepishly.

He chuckled. "So, that was it." The line went silent for a second. "I don't know you very well."

It was true. He hadn't wanted to, but maybe that had changed. "It's all right."

"Hell no, it's not, but now maybe that will change. I'm damn happy things are working out for you and Luciano. He's a good man. Proud and stubborn, but smart and understands the value of family." His satisfaction rang across the phone lines.

"Yes, he does."

"I trussed him up like a Thanksgiving turkey for you and I'm glad I did." More blatant satisfaction.

The comparison was unfortunate. She couldn't imagine Luciano in such a scenario at all, nor was she sure that a bit of matchmaking could be likened to trussing someone up, but she didn't argue with her grandfather. His matchmaking efforts had brought her and Luciano together.

For that, she could swallow a lot of male self-aggrandizement.

"I guess you did, Grandfather. Thank you," she said warmly.

"I'm just glad you're happy, girl."

"I am." Very, very happy.

"I called to talk to Luciano. Have him call when—"

Luciano's voice cut across her grandfather's. "That won't be necessary, I am here."

He must have picked up another extension.

"Consuella said you were on the phone talking to Hope while waiting for me to arrive," he explained his intrusion into the conversation.

"That's right," her grandfather replied, "wanted to talk to my granddaughter and see how you were treating her."

There was an odd note in her grandfather's voice.

"As she has said, she is happy." Luciano's tone was flat and emotionless.

She felt like an intruder on their conversation even though she and her grandfather had been talking first. "I'll let you two talk business," Hope interjected.

Her grandfather said goodbye, but Luciano said nothing and she hung up the phone.

Up in their bedroom, she undressed and took a quick shower before pulling on matching lace bra and panties. She was pulling a lavender sheath dress from the closet when Luciano walked into the room.

She laid it on the bed and went over to him, expecting a kiss of greeting, but he sidestepped her. "I need a shower."

"You look wonderful to me." She smiled.

He looked better than wonderful. In his tailored Italian suit that clung lovingly to the well-developed muscles of his thighs, he looked edible.

He didn't return her smile. "Like a Thanksgiving turkey all tied up?" he asked grimly.

"You heard that?"

"*Sì*. I heard." He looked totally unapproachable.

Heard and been seriously upset by it.

"Don't let Grandfather's analogies annoy you." She pulled her dress off the hanger and tossed the hanger back onto the bed. "It's just the way he is."

"He is blunt."

She smiled again, this time in relief at his understanding. "Right," she said as she pulled the dress over her head. "He's not very tactful, but I think he means well."

She straightened the dress over her hips.

"When it comes to you, his granddaughter, there is no doubt of this."

"You know, I think you're right." It was a novel concept, but one that unraveled some of the pain that had been caused by her grandfather's rejection throughout her growing-up years. "It feels good to be cared about, to tell you the truth."

"Regardless of what form that caring takes?" Luciano asked, his expression just this side of feral.

She didn't know what was wrong with him, but then there were still a lot of things about her husband she did not understand.

"We can't always choose how someone will love us." Or if they would love you at all, she thought. Her grandfather had certainly done a good job of hiding any affection he felt for her before.

"And you will take whatever form of love he gives, or is it that you are happy to reap the advantage of his desire to give it at all?"

Okay, her grandfather's comments had been less than flattering to Luciano, but surely he wasn't offended by the older man's claim at matchmaking. Perhaps his male ego was wounded by the thought of someone interfering in his life like that.

She stepped over to him and laid her hand on his chest. "How we came to be together is not as important as the fact that we are together, is it?"

"For you, I can see that it is not." He swung violently away and stormed into the bathroom.

The door shut with an audible click.

Shocked into immobility, she stared at it for the longest time. What in the world had just happened?

Luciano's reaction to the situation was totally over the top. His fury at the discovery that her grandfather's request he check on her in Athens had been an attempt at matchmaking was disproportionate to the circumstances. Even taking into account that it had been a successful attempt and he might feel somewhat manipulated, was it really so awful?

Luciano was a really smart guy. Hadn't he even suspected ulterior motives when Joshua Reynolds asked for such a personal favor? Especially after that kiss on New Year's Eve.

One thing became glaringly clear to her as she stood in transfixed stupefaction. If Luciano really had loved her, it would not have mattered. His pride would not find such offense in her grandfather's harmless machinations. After all, it wasn't as if Joshua had held a gun to Luciano's head and forced him to marry Hope.

He'd set them up to meet again, but Luciano had been the

one to pursue her. He had invited her to come to Palermo, so why was he acting like her grandfather's actions and her acceptance of them was so heinous? If anything was at fault for their marriage, it was Luciano's desire.

Feeling sick, she realized that was all it was. Desire.

And desire was not the soother of pride that love was.

She'd been so sure he was coming to love her, but his reaction tonight showed her how wrong she had been.

Luciano stood under the hot water and cursed until his throat was raw with it.

She had been in on it all along.

This woman he had trusted and believed would make the perfect mother for his children was in reality a scheming witch who did not care how she got what she wanted so long as she got it. Where he had seen innocence, there had been deviousness.

He now saw the initial reticence she had shown to his advances as the ruthlessly manipulative tactic that it was. The classic game of playing hard to get refined to the point of deviousness. She had known he had no choice but to pursue her. Yet, she had made the pursuit difficult, knowing his male instincts to hunt would be aroused. She had done her own part to make sure he was caught in her grandfather's trap.

He had been right to suspect such duplicity and a fool to dismiss the possibility so easily.

The knowledge he had been so used filled him with a desire to do violence. He hit the tiled wall of the shower with his fist, ignoring the pain that arced up his arm.

He had trusted her. He had believed she was unlike any woman he had ever known. And she was. She was a better liar. A better cheat. And better at entrapment. Many women had wanted marriage, but she had managed to secure his name on the other side of the marriage certificate. Had she begun making her plans before or after that kiss on New Year's Eve?

No matter what, he was furious at his own gullibility.

The pain of betrayal radiated through him and that made him even angrier. He could not feel betrayed if he had not trusted her and knowing he had trusted unwisely was a direct hit to his pride.

He had allowed himself to care for her, to believe in a future together and all the while she and her grandfather had no doubt been laughing over how easy he had been to dupe. Her feminine arrogance knew no bounds. Telling him that it did not matter how they had come together.

Perhaps that would have been true if she had been a woman worthy of his name and not a lying manipulator.

She wasn't and the fact she had colluded with her grandfather to blackmail him into marriage enraged Luciano.

No longer would he withhold his revenge from her. She would learn right alongside her grandfather that a Sicilian man would not lie down to coercion.

He was a man, not a fool, no matter that he'd been behaving like one for weeks.

Hope cuddled around the pillow in her lonely bed for the third night in a row. Luciano had gone from attentive and lover-like to cold and dismissive in a devastatingly quick and thorough transformation. And all because he was furious her grandfather had played matchmaker.

She'd tried to talk to him about it, but Luciano had refused to listen.

He'd spent the last three days working long hours and although he returned to the family villa before dinner, he did not come to bed until after Hope fell asleep.

Tonight, she was determined to wait up for him, to have it out. She wanted her marriage back. Things had been so good in Naples. She could not accept that something so unimportant could destroy it all.

She threw herself on her back and kicked the covers off. A minute later, she rolled onto her stomach. Thirty agonizing minutes later he had still not come up. Unable to wait another second in the silence of their huge bedroom, she got up. Where was it written that she had to wait meekly in bed for him to show up? She would go to him.

She went in search of her robe. Pulling it on, she left the room. He would probably be working in the study. Light filtering from the cracked doorway indicated she had been right.

She pushed the door open and found him sitting at his desk, papers spread before him.

"Luciano?"

His head lifted and he looked at her with eyes that sliced into her heart with their coldness. "What?"

"We need to talk."

"This is not so. We have nothing to talk about."

She glared at him, fed up with his stupid male ego. "How can you say that? You're being ridiculous about this thing with my grandfather. Can't you see that?"

In a second, he was towering over her, his big body vibrating with rage. "What are you saying to me?"

Okay, so she hadn't been tactful. Her grandfather's bluntness had rubbed off on her, but it was the truth. "We were happy together in Naples. Why do you want to throw that away over something that just doesn't matter?"

"To you it does not matter, but to me it is important."

She reached her hands out in appeal. "I love you, Luciano. Isn't that more important than an old man's machinations?"

His eyes burned her with a contempt she didn't understand, but that hurt her horribly.

"Do not speak to me of love again. I can do without the kind of love a woman like you feels."

"A woman like me?" What did he mean? "You told me you would treasure my love." Whatever kind of woman she was.

"A man will say anything when his libido is involved."

"I don't believe that." He couldn't mean it. "You wanted to marry me. You said you wanted me to be the mother of your children." He had to care a little, even if he didn't love her.

He scowled at her. "I have no choice about that, do I?"

Did he mean because like her, he thought she was already pregnant? "I don't know," she said honestly. Her menses weren't due for another week.

His laugh was harsh. "For a man with family pride, it is no choice."

"You feel like you have to get me pregnant?" She felt further and further out of her depth, while the pain of his rejection went deeper and deeper.

"Enough of this playacting. You know the alternative is untenable for me."

"I only know that three days ago I was happier than I have ever been in my life and now I'm miserable." Tears clogged the back of her throat and she couldn't go on.

Something twitched in his face, but he turned away from her. "Go back to bed, Hope."

"I don't want to go back without you." Her pride was in tatters around her, but she was desperate to get through to him.

"I'm not in the mood for sex right now."

For a hopelessly oversexed guy like her husband, that statement was the final blow to her rapidly toppling confidence.

"Neither am I," she whispered from a tight throat as she turned to leave the room. She had never wanted just sex with him and clearly even that wasn't on offer.

He let her go without a word.

* * *

The next day, Luciano took off for a business trip abroad and Hope did her best to hide her despair from his mother and sister. She wasn't entirely successful, but both women assumed her melancholy was due to Luciano's absence and she did not disabuse them of the notion. In a way it was the truth. She did miss him, but she had missed him before he left and had no faith his return would decrease that one iota.

On the third day of his absence he called to tell her he would be gone another week. While he had not been overly warm on the phone, the fact he had called at all led to a rise in her spirits. His rejection had not diminished her love or need for him any more than years of her grandfather's neglect had exorcised the old man from her heart.

Was she destined to spend her whole life loving, but never receiving love?

Luciano walked into the bedroom he shared with Hope without turning on a light. He had been gone for ten days and he'd missed his wife. He hated the knowledge. It made him crazy. He shouldn't miss a woman who had deceived him so ruthlessly, but he had.

He woke in the night, reaching for her body and she was not there. He had dreamed about her and ached for the release he found in her sweet flesh. That, at least, he would no longer deny himself.

He reasoned that he had to make her pregnant so his control of his family's company would be assured. Which meant he had to make love to her. Besides sleeping in separate beds was not an option. His mother and sister would notice and his pride would take another lashing.

He'd told himself that was why he called her so frequently when he was gone. It would look odd if he called his mother more frequently than his wife and he had no intention of telling his family how he had been blackmailed into marriage.

He stripped off his clothes and climbed into the bed. His wife's small body was wrapped around a pillow. She looked so damn innocent, completely incapable of the duplicity he knew she harbored within her. She also looked desirable like no other woman did to him now.

He caressed her in a way he had learned aroused her and she moaned his name in her sleep. A shaft of pain went through him. At least she had been honest about that.

She did want him.

He pulled the pillow from her arms and kissed her in one movement. Her lips responded even though her body remained limp from sleep. He tugged at her bottom lip with his teeth and she opened her mouth. She tasted so sweet, it was impossible to keep reminding himself that she was his enemy.

Right now, she was just his wife.

He slid the thin strap of her nightgown off her shoulder, exposing one pouting breast. Caressing the velvet flesh of her nipple with his palm, he nuzzled her neck, taking in the scent of wildflowers that he associated so completely with her.

The soft bud below his palm hardened and she moaned.

His body responded predictably.

It had been almost two weeks since he had lost himself in the sweetness of her body. Thirteen days too long. He ached with hunger for her, with the need to feel her naked skin against him.

She did not wake up as he carefully removed her gown. He laid down beside her again, pulling her body into full contact with his. He closed his eyes, allowing himself to revel in the sensation of holding her again. Something he could not have done if she was awake.

He let his hand trail down her body, brushing tender buds that taunted him with remembered sweetness.

He lightly touched the soft curls at the apex of her thighs and she stirred.

Her breathing changed and he knew she was waking up.

CHAPTER TEN

HOPE swirled to consciousness, unsure whether she was awake or still dreaming.

Luciano was kissing her, touching her.

She'd dreamed about it so much that she was sure at first it was just another realistic flight of her subconscious and she did not want to wake up to the reality of her marriage and Luciano's absence. She fought her return to consciousness, but it was as if his voice was whispering in her ear, telling her he wanted her.

Then his hand made a path between her legs, penetrating moist folds with intimate caresses and she realized she was awake; Luciano was with her; and they were making love.

"You're home," she whispered, her vocal cords thick with sleep.

"*Sì*. I am here, *cara*."

Had he said *cara*? Or was that part of the dream that had meshed with reality?

His mouth trailed down her neck, nibbling her skin and making her shiver.

She whispered his name, clutching at his shoulders. "I'm glad you're home."

His fingers did something magical to her feminine flesh.

"I missed you," she panted, her defenses obliterated by his touch and her disorientation in coming awake to it.

"I missed this also," he said in a husky voice that sent shivers of need rippling through her.

He wanted her again. Relief mixed with her growing passion in a volatile combination that had her moving restlessly under him, spreading her legs in an age-old invitation. "I want you."

He groaned his approval and took her nipple into his mouth, but he did not move to join their bodies together. He tortured her with bliss, touching her body in ways he knew drove her crazy with desire.

"Please, Luciano. Now." She arched toward him. "Be with me. Please."

He made a sound that sounded as tortured as she felt and joined their bodies with one passionate thrust.

Tender flesh stretched to capacity, but she did not murmur a complaint. She wanted this very thing. Needed it.

He cried out in Italian and then began to move, his body surrounding her, filling her, completing her.

Afterward, he rolled over so she was on top of him, but they were still connected. He was still partially aroused inside her and little jolts of pleasure shot through her every time he moved.

She nuzzled into his neck and kissed wherever her lips landed. "You're not mad at me anymore."

Instead of answering, he gripped her hips and started moving her on his rapidly hardening flesh. Soon, she lost all desire to talk as sensual hunger took over.

This time they reached the pinnacle of pleasure together and their cries of satisfaction mingled in the air around them. When they were finished, he pulled her into his body and fell asleep before she could get answers to the many questions roiling in her mind.

She snuggled closer to him, reveling in the physical contact, needing the affirmation of her place in his life. He'd been desperate for her, but did that mean anything more than he hadn't tired of her physically yet? She could not believe he could touch her so gently and take such care to insure her pleasure and still hate her.

The absence of hatred did not guarantee love, however.

And she needed his love, now more than ever.

She took the masculine hand resting on her hip and pulled it over her to press against her flat stomach. Her menses had not come. She wanted to take a pregnancy test, but she was sure deep inside that she carried Luciano's baby.

Would he be happy?

His mother would be ecstatic, but it wasn't her mother-in-law that Hope wanted to please. It was the man who had made such beautiful love to her, the man now holding her as if she meant something to him, as if he had missed having her in his bed as much as she had missed his presence in the night.

The last two weeks had been horrible and she had vacillated between certainty that marrying Luciano had been the biggest mistake of her life to an irrepressible hope that things could get better, that he would come to care more deeply for her. After that first phone call, he had called every day. She didn't know if it was because he wanted to put a good front on for his family, or if he'd discovered he needed the connection as much as she did. Did it really matter?

Those phone calls had been her lifeline.

They hadn't talked about personal issues, but he hadn't been curt with her either. He always asked how she was doing and showed interest in how she had spent her day. He'd answered her questions about his business, sharing his frustrations and satisfactions depending on how his day had gone.

Would a man who hated being married to her share that kind of meaningful communication with her?

It was a question she'd asked herself at least fifty times a day since he'd gone. No satisfactory answer was forth-coming.

Still, after their recent lovemaking, she had more peace than she'd experienced in days.

The next day, Luciano was gone before she woke up, but since he had woken her to make love around dawn, she wasn't too upset by that fact. The renewal of their physical relationship had gone a long way toward increasing her sense of security in their relationship. So, that evening when Luciano called and said he would not be home for dinner, she took the news with equanimity.

At least he had called.

She ate with Claudia and Martina and spent the rest of the evening teaching her mother-in-law how to play gin rummy after Martina had gone out with friends.

When Hope went to climb into bed, she was in a fairly good mood even though Luciano had still not returned to the villa. Claudia had assured Hope that this was not unusual for her son and had hinted heavily that he would work less when the *bambini* started coming.

She was dozing lightly when she sensed his presence in the bed and woke up. They made love again and just like the night before, Luciano fell asleep without giving her an op-portunity to talk about anything important. To be fair, she hadn't tried very hard. She didn't know if she wanted to tell him about her suspicion that she was pregnant. Having proof one way or the other would be better.

That day set the pattern for the ones to follow. If Luciano did return in time for dinner, the hours before sleep would be spent making love. Yet, no matter how many times they made love the night before, he always woke her around dawn to make love again. And just like the first day back, he was always gone to the office before she came awake for the day.

They didn't talk and sometimes she caught him looking at her with a bitterness that shocked her. The look never lasted long and the one time she'd brought it up, he had changed the subject very effectively by seducing her.

She stopped telling him she loved him, even in the throes of passion. Because although he had clearly not rejected her completely as his wife, she felt an important element of their relationship had been lost. His respect for her.

The longer she played the role of lover, but not true wife, the more she felt like nothing more than a body in his bed.

Even his exquisite lovemaking was taking on a bitter aftertaste when he refused to discuss the stalemate their marriage had become.

She couldn't quite get how he could blame her for her grandfather's matchmaking. It didn't jibe with the man she knew Luciano to be. He was ruthless in business, but fair. Taking out his anger over her grandfather's actions on her was anything but. Not to mention that those actions hardly warranted the fury they had sparked in her husband.

If she didn't talk it out soon, she was going to lose respect for herself. She'd been afraid to make waves, to risk another all-out rejection from her husband, but being a body in his bed and nonentity in his life was taking its toll on her sense of self-worth.

She wanted to find out if she really was pregnant before they talked. Perhaps knowledge that she carried his child would give her a better chance of getting through to him.

Using the excuse that she did not want the first time she met her doctor to be during a health crisis, Hope asked Claudia to make an appointment for her with the family doctor. She felt shy about sharing her suspicions with anyone before she talked about it with Luciano. Her mother-in-law appeared to accept Hope's excuse and made an appointment for her early that afternoon.

A couple of hours later, Hope left the doctor's surgery in a daze of emotions.

She was pregnant.

Thinking it was a possibility was very different from knowing it to be a reality, she discovered. She felt both terrified and elated at the prospect of motherhood. She knew she would love her baby with every fiber of her being, but she had never even held a toddler in her arms.

The prospect of living with Luciano's mother had never bothered her, but now Hope saw it as an absolute blessing. She wasn't alone. Claudia would help her learn the ropes of motherhood and Luciano would be there as well. Family was important to him.

Suddenly she couldn't wait to tell him. He was bound to be happy. He wanted children. She knew he did. This finally would stop him from acting like she only existed in the bedroom. A man could not dismiss the mother of his child so easily. Especially a traditional Italian male like Luciano.

She instructed the driver to take her to Luciano's office building.

When she got there, she took the elevator to the top floor without stopping at reception. She barely waited for his secretary to buzz through and tell Luciano she was there.

When Hope walked into his office, he stood up and came around to the front of his desk. "This is a surprise."

She nodded. She hadn't even ever called him at work. Showing up out of the blue was bound to shock him. "I had something I wanted to tell you."

"And it could not wait until I returned to the villa?" he asked with one sardonic brow raised.

"We don't talk when you're home," she said with a tinge of the pained frustration that caused her.

He didn't reply but led her to a chair by the huge plate-glass windows overlooking Palermo's wealthy business section.

He took the chair closest to her own. "Would you like something to eat or drink?"

She shook her head. "I want to talk."

He looked at his watch. "I have a meeting in ten minutes. Perhaps this can wait."

"No."

His expression was not encouraging. "Make it short."

Darn it. This should be special, but he made it impossible, or was that her timing? Maybe she should have waited to tell him at home, but she was here. She might as well finish it. For a second, the words simply would not come.

He moved impatiently and looked pointedly at his watch again.

"I'm pregnant."

He went completely still, the sculpted angles of his face moving into emotionless rigidity. "You are sure of this?"

"I went to see the doctor today."

"And he confirmed your suspicions?"

"Yes." Why wasn't he reacting? He was acting like they were discussing the details of a rather boring business deal.

"I am surprised you didn't do something to prevent conception so early." His black eyes mocked her in a way she did not understand. "I had the distinct impression you were enjoying our physical intimacy."

Did he think they couldn't make love now that she was pregnant? "The doctor said there would be no risk to the baby during normal intimacy."

"You asked. This surprises me. You are still shy about some things."

She blushed under his mocking scrutiny. "He offered the information."

He nodded. "That is a more believable scenario."

She waited for him to say something about how he felt knowing she was carrying his child, but he stood and looked at his watch again. "If that's all?"

She stood too. "Yes, but…"

"But what?"

"Are you glad about the baby?" she blurted out.

"You must know that I have every reason to be pleased that you have conceived so quickly."

Was this the man who had made love to her with such gentleness the night before that she had cried?

"I could do with you saying it." She could do with a lot more, but she would settle for that.

He smiled derisively. "I am happy about the baby. Are you now satisfied? May I return to my business?"

He had managed to say the words she most wanted to hear in a way that caused pain rather than pleasure. Tears burned the back of her eyes as pain radiated from her heart outward. Why her? What had she done to earn this kind of constant rejection from the people that were supposed to care about her?

She jumped to her feet and spun toward the door, not bothering to answer his hurtful question. Obviously his upcoming appointment was much more important to him than his wife or the knowledge he would be a father.

She stumbled toward the door, her vision blurred by tears spilling down her cheeks.

"Hope!"

She ignored him and made top speed for the elevator outside his office suite. Following a pattern set in early childhood, she wanted only to find someplace to be alone where it would be safe for her to grieve in private. That precluded going back to the villa.

She couldn't even stand the thought of getting in the di Valerio limousine and exposing her pain to the chauffeur. She hated the fact that Luciano's secretary had no doubt seen the tears.

She used her mobile phone to call and dismiss the driver, telling him she would find her own way home.

Anger warred with pain in Luciano. He wanted to go after Hope, to hold her and tell her he was thrilled about the baby. The thought of her pregnant with his child was sweet when it should be sour.

He wanted to wipe the look of misery off her face and he despised himself for his weakness.

She had lied to him.

But what was the lie and what was the truth? She had looked so lost, so vulnerable when she told him about the baby and he had forced himself to contain his response.

The woman who had colluded with Joshua Reynolds to trap herself a husband was not vulnerable.

But Hope *had* been vulnerable. And she had been hurting. Was it possible he had misunderstood what he had heard on the phone two weeks ago? His brain rejected the thought as the words replayed themselves in his mind. Yet, he could not reconcile those words with the woman who gave herself so completely when they made love.

She was too generous in her passion to be such a heartless schemer. And yet, what other explanation was there? Joshua Reynolds had blackmailed Luciano and Hope had known about it.

She had said she loved him.

The reminder caused more disquiet in the region of his heart. She hadn't repeated the words since he returned from his business trip abroad, but he could not forget the sweetness of them on her lips when their bodies were intimately joined.

He wanted to hear her say it again, which enraged him. What was the love of a deceitful woman worth?

Nothing.

Only if that were true, then why did the lack of those words weigh on him in the dark of the night? She slept in his arms, but felt separated from him in a way he could not define?

He was not used to feeling like this.

He did not like it.

He did not like the confusion, or the need she engendered in him.

He did not like the way he doubted the wisdom of including Hope in his revenge, his weak desire that she not find out what he had done to hurt her.

He did not like the feeling that his actions had been stupid rather than decisive.

A short buzz alerted him that his next appointment had arrived. Business was much more comfortable than wallowing in conflicting and destructive emotions, so he forced himself to focus on it.

Stepping out into the sunshine from the air-conditioned building, Hope asked herself where she could go. Looking up and down the busy street, she knew she wanted only to get away from the crush of people. An image of the grounds surrounding the di Valerio villa rose in her mind like Valhalla to her ravaged state. She would take a taxi to the grounds and then when she was ready, she could walk home.

Having a plan of action helped calm her churning emotions enough to wipe her tears away and wave down a cab.

She had the driver drop her on the outskirts of the di Valerio estate. Luckily, she remembered the code for the small gate in the far wall. She and Martina had used it once before on an afternoon walk.

Once inside the estate's walls, she walked only far enough to hide herself in the trees, then sank to the ground. Her back resting against the trunk of one of them, she let the tears fall freely. It hurt so much.

Not only had she made a huge mistake in marrying Luciano, but she was pregnant with his baby. No matter what she wanted from life, she was now inexorably linked to a man who had as much affection for her as the man on the moon. Less even.

The sobs came harder and she cried out her grief over the years of neglect in her grandfather's house followed by marriage to a man destined to treat her the same way.

A long while later, her mobile phone chirped. She had stopped crying, but had not moved from her place against the tree. She dug the phone from her purse. The display identified Valerio Industries as her caller.

Luciano.

She didn't want to talk to him.

She wanted to shoot him, which didn't say much for the gentle nature others were so convinced she possessed.

He had taken the joy of her discovery and turned it to ashes. His rotten attitude was tearing her apart and she knew that tonight there was no way she could lie with him in their bed and pretend nothing had happened.

She could not bear the thought of being just a body and their baby meaning nothing to him.

The phone stopped ringing.

Ten minutes later it rang again.

She refused to answer it.

He kept calling and finally, she turned off the volume on the ringer.

She stood up and dusted off her skirt before starting the walk toward the villa.

It took her twenty minutes because she didn't rush in any way.

A maid saw her approach and went running inside. Seconds later, both Martina and Claudia came rushing toward her.

Claudia was babbling at her in Italian, much too fast for her to understand, but Martina spoke English.

"Where have you been? Luciano is worried sick about you. We all were. What happened to your cell phone? Why didn't you answer? You'd better call him right away. He's ready to call in the authorities."

She couldn't understand why a man who treated her the way her husband had would worry. Surely if she disappeared, he would be off the hook for a marriage he clearly no longer wanted. Then she remembered the baby. Maybe he cared more about their child than he had let on.

"I'm sorry. I didn't mean to upset anyone. I wanted to take a walk." Which was true as far as it went. "And I turned off the ringer on my mobile." Which was also true, but she neglected to mention she had turned off the ringer after Luciano started calling.

"Why would you turn off your ringer?" Claudia demanded in heavily accented English.

Hope felt really badly for upsetting her mother-in-law so much, but she wasn't about to tell her the truth. Hope's problems with Luciano were private and she refused to visit them on the other women.

"You don't even carry a mobile," she said instead.

Claudia grimaced. "I also do not dismiss the driver and disappear for hours."

Hope looked at her watch and realized it had been three hours since she left Luciano's office and forty-five minutes since the first phone call. "Are you saying you never go shopping or for a walk where you can't be reached?"

Claudia's hands rose in the air. "*Ai, ai, ai.* I see there is no reasoning with you."

Hope said nothing. She didn't want to hurt the older woman, but she couldn't explain her actions without divulging her impasse with Luciano.

"It is nothing more than a storm in a teacup. She went for a walk and time got away from her. Mamma, there is no need for you to keep carrying on."

"Tell your brother this."

Martina grimaced. "No thank you."

"There you see." Claudia crossed her arms and gave both Hope and Martina a baleful look.

The maid came out at that moment, a cordless phone in her hand. "*Signor* di Valerio wishes to speak to his wife."

Hope looked at the phone with as much enthusiasm as she might feel for a plateful of spoiled fish.

"Hope?" Claudia asked, her expression now concerned.

Hope put her hand out for the offending phone.

Claudia stopped her from lifting it to her ear. "Every marriage goes through growing pains in the beginning, child. Do not be too hard on my son, whatever he has done. A woman must be strong enough to forgive."

Hope forced herself to smile and say, "Thank you."

Her mother-in-law and Martina showed a great deal of tact by leaving her to speak to Luciano in privacy.

She lifted the phone to her ear. "What?"

"That is no way to greet your husband."

The censure infuriated her. "Go to hell, Luciano."

His indrawn breath told her he hadn't liked hearing that.

She didn't care. Not anymore, she told herself. "I don't want to talk to you."

His sigh was audible through the phone lines. "The driver said you dismissed him. How did you get home?"

"What do you care?"

"You were upset when you left my office."

"And this surprises you?" she asked scathingly.

"No." He sounded odd. "How did you get home?" he repeated.

"I took a cab and I went for a walk. I turned the ringer volume down on my mobile after you called. Any more questions?"

"No."

"If that is all…" she said, reversing the roles they had played in his office.

Again the sigh. "I'm flying to Rome and will be gone overnight. I realize it is not the best time for me to leave, but it cannot be helped."

"Why are you bothering to tell me?" She stared across the swimming pool, her body aching from the pain filling her heart. "I'm just a body in your bed. I'm not your wife. You don't even want our baby." She was crying again and hated him for hearing the choking sobs she could not hide.

"Hope—"

She hung up the phone before he could say whatever it was he had meant to say. All his words hurt her and she was so tired of being hurt.

CHAPTER ELEVEN

LUCIANO called again that evening from Rome. She came to the phone, feeling subdued and just plain not up to arguing with his mother or sister about taking the call.

"Hello, Luciano. Was there something you wanted?" she asked in a voice that sounded dead to her own ears.

"*Sì*, Hope, I want many things, but I called to apologize for my behavior when you told me about the baby." He sounded tired. "I want our *bambino, cara*. I am sorry I was less than enthusiastic when you told me."

She dismissed the apology as too little, too late. Perhaps if he hadn't been treating her so hurtfully for days before-hand, it would have been enough. "Don't call me *cara*. It means beloved and you don't love me. I don't ever want you to use that word with me again."

"Hope, I…" He hesitated.

Strange to hear her super-confident husband hesitant.

"If that's all, I'm tired and want to go to bed."

"I want to go to bed also, but with you, not in solitude."

For once his sexy voice had no affect on her whatsoever. "I don't want to sleep with you anymore."

He said something low and forceful. "You are not leaving my bed."

"Really? How are you going to stop me?" she asked with

little more interest than she had felt for the rest of the conversation.

"*Santo cielo*. You are my wife. You sleep in my bed."

"I don't like you anymore, Luciano." She didn't say she didn't love him because it was not true. She did, more fool her. And it hurt.

"*Cara*—"

"Please, Luciano. I don't want to talk anymore. I don't know why you married me, but I can see now it was a huge mistake."

"You know why I married you."

For the sex?

He went on when she remained silent. "Even so, it was not a mistake. We can make our marriage work. We will talk when I return from Rome."

He wanted to make their marriage work now? "I can't deal with this. You just keep hurting me and I don't want it anymore."

"That is over. I will not hurt you again, *cara*."

Was there something significant about the fact that he kept calling her *beloved* even after she had asked him not to? It was such a tantalizing thought that she rejected it immediately.

She had believed too many times things would work out only to discover they would not.

"We'll talk when you get back," she said, repeating his words.

What form that discussion would take she did not know.

When the maid brought her the phone the next morning, she was in a stronger frame of mind and prepared to discuss her marriage with Luciano. He had said he wanted to make their marriage work and he had apologized for being such a toad when she told him about the baby. Men like Luciano didn't say sorry easily and if he was willing to work on their marriage, she was too.

Only her caller wasn't Luciano. It was her grandfather.

"What the hell is going on over there?" he demanded in a voice that had her pulling the phone a few inches from her ear.

"I'm not sure what you mean," she hedged, wondering if Luciano had called him after she'd hung up the night before.

"I've got two society columns in front of me. They've both got pictures of your husband eating dinner with a woman in a swank New York restaurant. That woman is not you."

Hope felt the words like multiple body blows. Luciano had promised. *No mistresses.* But he'd also promised to treasure her love and he'd broken that one. "I don't know what you're talking about," she answered truthfully.

"Could be his secretary I guess, but where were you when he was having these business dinners?"

"Here, in Palermo. Luciano flew to New York right after we returned from our honeymoon." And he'd been furious with her when he left.

Would that fury have translated into actions that would destroy their marriage?

Yet, the idea of a series of business dinners was not so far-fetched. She knew what his secretary looked like after visiting his office yesterday, but if she asked her grandfather to fax the articles he would know she was worried. Maybe it was stupid, but her pride forbore her airing her marital troubles to either her family or Luciano's.

"What else would it be besides a business dinner?" She forced a laugh. "Surely you aren't implying that Luciano would have sought other feminine companionship so soon after our marriage."

"Stranger things have happened, girl."

"Not with a man like Luciano." Until the last two weeks,

she would have sworn she could trust him with her life and everything in between.

"There are things you don't know."

Dread snaked through her at her grandfather's tone. "What do you mean?"

"That's not important. Ask Luciano about these pictures, Hope. Communication is important to a healthy marriage."

Coming from her grandfather, who considered asking if she wanted more wine at dinner a foray into personal conversation, that was laughable. Only she didn't feel like laughing.

She rang off and went in search of a computer with Internet access. She found one in Luciano's study. He didn't have a password on the Internet browser, so she was able to go right in. It took her less than thirty minutes to find the newspaper stories her grandfather had mentioned. They were both small articles in the society section of a New York paper.

They mentioned Luciano's name, but failed to identify his companion.

She didn't need the information supplied to her.

The dark, exotic beauty was very familiar to Hope. The woman in the photos was Zia Merone and she was not wearing the expression of a woman discussing business.

Hope barely made it to the bathroom before she was sick.

Fifteen minutes later, she was in their bedroom with the door shut and a copy of the articles clutched in one hand, dialing his mobile phone with the other. She needed to talk to Luciano, to hear a rational explanation for his dinner dates with Zia. Or to hear from his own mouth that he had broken this promise too. Could she trust him not to lie to her? She just didn't know.

It rang three times before being picked up.

"Ciao."

Zia? Zia had answered Luciano's cell phone.

Hope's stomach did another somersault. "Ms. Merone, I would like to speak to my husband."

"This is Hope?" Zia's voice rose in surprise.

"Yes. Where is Luciano?"

"He is in the shower."

Hope gasped, feeling ripped in two by the answer. "I'm surprised you aren't with him. He likes sex in the shower." The crude sarcasm just slipped out, but even if it wounded Zia, it hurt Hope more.

"I was not in the mood." Far from sounding wounded, Zia's voice was laced with innuendo.

The tacit agreement to her fears made Hope's knees give way and she sank onto the side of the bed. "Are you saying you spent the night with my husband?" Her voice trembled, but she couldn't help it. She wanted to die.

"Are you sure you want me to answer that question?"

"No," Hope whispered, her vocal cords too constricted for normal conversation, "but I need you to."

Zia hesitated. When she spoke, her voice had changed, become more tentative. "Perhaps you had better discuss this with Luciano."

Hope didn't answer. She just held the phone to her ear and stared at the far wall of the room she shared with Luciano. Was this what death felt like? Your whole body going numb and your emotions imploding until there was nothing left?

Another voice intruded on her blanked out mental state. "Hope? Is that you, *cara?*"

And she realized she wasn't numb.

"Don't call me that you bastard!" She'd gone from whispering to screaming so loud she strained her throat. "You lied to me." A sob snaked out and she covered the mouthpiece so he wouldn't hear it.

He started to speak, but she plowed over him. "You

p-promised. No mistresses. I *believed* you. What an idiot I am. Look how good you've been at keeping your promises. You said you would treasure my love too, but you stomped all over it. *I hate you.*" And at that moment she meant it.

"Hope, *mi moglie,* it is not what you are thinking!"

She would be a fool to believe the desperation that seemed to infuse his voice. She heard him ask Zia what she had said. Hope couldn't hear Zia's answer and she didn't want to. She did hear the Italian curses erupt from her husband's throat when Zia stopped speaking.

"Did you sleep with Zia?" she demanded in a voice raw from pain.

"No!"

"No, I don't suppose you did. I'm sure there was very little sleeping involved."

"Stop this. You are upsetting yourself for nothing."

He called adultery nothing? "Were your dinners with her in New York nothing too, Luciano?"

Silence greeted that.

"Maybe you didn't think I would find out?"

"How *did* you find out about them?"

"My grandfather."

"Damned interfering old man."

"Don't blame him for showing me what a lying swine you are." How dared he try to foist the culpability for this awful situation onto someone else? "If you hadn't broken your promise to me, there would have been nothing for him to interfere over."

"I have not lied to you. I have broken no promises either." He didn't deny being a swine.

She'd like to know how he justified that statement to himself. "You were in the shower when I called, Luciano."

"This is proof of nothing."

"It proves you're in a hotel room with another woman." Let him try to deny it.

"I am not."

Getting ready to blast him, she remembered his preference for not staying at hotels and she choked on a bitter laugh. "You brought her to the company apartment? How brazen, *Signor* di Valerio, but then I suppose she's been there before."

"No, Hope. It is not like that." He sounded like she felt, miserable. She couldn't trust what she heard in his voice though, not when his actions had already spoken so loudly.

"It is exactly like that. Zia said as much."

"What Zia said, it was a mistake."

"Our marriage was the real mistake."

"No! *Amore mia.* That was not an error. Our marriage was meant to be. You must listen."

"Why? So you can tell me more lies?" She was choking on her pain. "Your girlfriend was honest at least."

He said something to Zia and then the other woman came on the line. "Hope, I am sorry I implied I slept with your husband. *I did not,*" she said sounding distressed, *"you must believe me about this."*

"That's why you're there when he's taking a shower." Hope wasn't that gullible.

"I am truly sorry I made this sound like an intimacy. It was not. Luciano was still asleep when I arrived this morning to discuss some business."

"Oh, please…" He never slept late.

Zia made an impatient sound. "He was recovering from a hangover, I think. He looked terrible." She paused. "He does not look any better now."

Luciano drinking to excess? Not likely. "You expect me to believe he got drunk, passed out and didn't wake up until you got there this morning?"

"*Sì.* Believe, for it is the truth. Your husband cares for you. I am sorry for the part I have played, but it was only a part. Luciano wants no woman but you."

Hope didn't understand Zia's remarks about playing a part, but she no longer believed the fairy tale that Luciano wanted only her. "What kind of business do you have with my husband?"

Why was she bothering to ask? The answer was devastating to her self-awareness. *Because she wanted to believe. Idiot,* she castigated herself.

"He is investing money for me. A model's career is not a long one. It is nothing more. I promise you."

"You were with him in New York."

"No. I had a show. Our meeting was happenstance, nothing more."

"That nothing resulted in two dinner dates."

"Dinner between old friends. That is all. Not dates. Have you never had an evening with a man that consisted of innocent conversation only?"

All Hope's dates ended innocently, except those with Luciano. "I don't have your sophistication." Her voice should have frozen the phone lines, it was so arctic.

Zia sighed, proving it had not. "Nothing happened between Luciano and I. He does not even kiss my cheek in greeting now."

Hope wanted so desperately to believe the model's words, but would that be opening herself up for further heartache?

"Hope?" It was Luciano.

She opened her mouth to speak, but nothing came out.

"Are you there, *cara?*"

Beloved. She wasn't loved by him, but she was his wife. Presumably that fact had finally sunk in with some meaning. "I'm here."

"I will be home as soon as I can get a takeoff time at the airport for my jet."

"And?"

"We need to talk. Wait for me at the villa."

Was she willing to give him this chance?

"Please, *cara*."

The humble plea got to her.

"I'll be here."

Barefoot and wearing a pair of cotton crop pants and T-shirt, Hope flipped through the baby magazine she had picked up in the doctor's office the day before. Her clothes and lack of makeup were in defiance to her husband's ego and her own emotions. As promised, she was waiting for Luciano, but she refused to gild the lily for this confrontation.

She tucked her feet up on the small sofa in the outer room of her and Luciano's suite. At least they would have privacy here for their discussion. Living with his family necessitated eating most meals with company however, having the private *sala* meant there was a certain measure of independence within the confines of the household.

Hope needed that. Although she loved both Claudia and Martina, she had spent too much of her life alone to easily adjust to the continuous company of others.

"Hope…"

The magazine slid from her fingers and she barely caught it before it fell to the floor. So much for a cool reception at his arrival. Picking the periodical up, she laid it neatly on the small table in front her. She fiddled with it, attempting to get it perfectly perpendicular to the edge. She didn't want to look at her gorgeous husband. It would hurt.

To see him and experience the deepest sort of love imaginable and know it was not returned was beyond her emotional capabilities at the moment.

One brown hand covered hers where it fiddled with the corner of the magazine. "*Cara.*"

He was on his knees beside her, the warmth of his hand a seductive lure when she felt chilled to her soul.

Having no choice if she did not want to come off the coward, she lifted her head and took in the superficial details of his appearance. He had removed his suit jacket and tie and the top few buttons of his shirt were undone. His hair looked like he'd run his fingers through it…several times. And there was an intensity in the brown depths of his eyes she dared not trust.

"Your mother and Martina have gone shopping in Palermo. They invited me to go along, but I told you I would wait here." It was inane chatter, but safer than the questions screaming through her mind.

His jaw tightened. "I'm glad you stayed."

She nodded. "You said we needed to talk."

"*Sì*." He stood up and swung away from her. "I want our marriage to last."

"Why?" After all this, she needed concrete answers.

"I am Sicilian. I do not believe in divorce." He still hadn't turned around and she was glad.

His words were a death knell to the hopes she had tried so hard not to nurse.

"Why did you marry me if you don't love me?" She just could not believe he was so determined not to have an affair with a virgin that he had chosen to marry a woman he had so little feeling for.

He spun back to face her, his expression almost scary. "You know why. I have been unkind, I admit this, but you must also admit that you carry some of the blame for that."

"Because I was a virgin?"

"Do not play games." His hands clenched at his sides. "I heard you tell your grandfather thank-you for his manipulations on your behalf."

She stared at him, as at sea about this whole thing as she had been when he'd gone off the rails the first time. "I just don't understand why you're so upset about a little matchmaking. You didn't have to succumb."

"Is that what you call it, matchmaking? How innocent that sounds, but I call it blackmail."

There are things you don't know. Her grandfather's words echoed in her mind. "Are you saying my grandfather blackmailed you into marrying me?"

Impossible. That sort of thing just didn't happen in the twenty-first century. It was positively Machiavellian and that kind of business had gone out with the Middle Ages, at least when it came to marriage bargains and the like.

But Luciano's expression denied her naive certainty. "Are *you* attempting to convince me you did not know?"

She glared at him, anger and resentment boiling in a cauldron inside her that was ready to explode all over him. She jumped up and faced him, fury making her body rigid. "I don't have to convince you of anything." He was the one who'd been caught taking a shower while his former girlfriend lounged around answering his cell phone. "If you won't tell me, I'll call my grandfather and ask him."

She turned to do just that, but his words stopped her.

"Do not go. I will tell you." Luciano's olive complexion had gone gray. "You thought your grandfather tried to get us together, but you did not realize the methods he used?"

The methods had been pretty obvious, or at least she had thought so at the time. "He sent you to check on me in Athens."

"He sent me, *sì,* but not to check on you. I was under duress to convince you of marriage."

That explained so much.

Luciano looked sick and she could imagine why. A proud man like him would have been severely bothered by the fact that he was being manipulated by someone else. Her grandfather's weapon of blackmail must have been a good one.

"What did he use as leverage?" she asked.

"Di Valerio Shipping."

"Your great-grandfather's company?" Luciano had told her about the modest shipping company during one of their discussions at a business dinner.

She had thought he was sweetly sentimental for holding on to it when it was such a small concern compared to his other holdings. "I don't understand how my grandfather could threaten it. It's a family held company."

"It was, but my uncle gambles. He lost a lot of money and rather than swallow his pride and ask me for it, he sold his shares in the family company to your grandfather."

"So?" She still didn't get how that could impact her husband. He was the head of the company. Her grandfather could play pesky-fly-in-the-ointment, but that wouldn't be enough to force Luciano into doing something he didn't want to.

"Joshua also was able to secure enough shares and proxies from family members no longer close to the company to take control. He threatened to approve a merger with our chief competitor, a merger that would result in the disappearance of the di Valerio name."

And his Sicilian pride had found that untenable.

"What were the terms?" she asked, a little awed by her grandfather's ruthlessness.

As Luciano outlined the terms for their marriage arrangement, she went cold to the depths of her being.

"So you planned to make me pregnant and then ditch me."

It made sense. Once she had his baby, he had control of his company back and he didn't need her. Even if she divorced him, he retained control of the company through the child. It also explained his chilly reaction to her announcement of the pregnancy. He needed the baby, but Luciano couldn't work up any enthusiasm for having a child with her, the granddaughter of the man who had blackmailed him and so severely offended his Sicilian pride.

"That's why you made that crack about me not using

anything and getting pregnant so fast." She couldn't breathe, but she had to force the words out anyway. "You had no intention of returning to my bed after I conceived."

"It was not like that."

"It was just like that! You said so." She sank back onto the small couch, feeling drained.

Luciano came toward her, but something in her look must have gotten to him because he stopped before reaching her. "At first, I believed you did not know. I intended our marriage to be real and forever. You were innocent." He swung his hand out in an arc to punctuate the words. "To include you in a vendetta against your grandfather would have been wrong. This is what I told myself."

His eyes appealed to her, but her heart was bleeding and she couldn't offer the understanding he sought. "I believed you would make a good wife, an admirable mother," he said, his tone driven.

Two weeks ago those statements would have been compliments, but now they were testament to how lukewarm his feelings were for her. "You decided to make the best of a bad situation."

The muscles in his face clenched. *"Sì."*

"But then you overheard my grandfather and me talking and drew your own conclusions." She felt sick remembering what had been said and how it could have been interpreted.

Her grandfather had a lot to answer for and she intended to hold him accountable, just as soon as she wasn't doing her utmost to control her roiling stomach.

"Sì." Luciano did not look too good himself. "Can you not understand how I felt? Your grandfather used my uncle's weakness against me, against the di Valerio family. I could not let that go unchallenged."

"So, you decided to get your revenge by dumping me once I got pregnant."

CHAPTER TWELVE

IT WAS such a cold thing to do, definitely not something he would have contemplated if he loved her.

He shook his head, if anything looking more grim than he had a moment ago. "That was not my plan."

"What was your plan?" she asked, dreading the answer. Could anything be worse, though?

"I wanted you to believe I had taken a mistress. Zia agreed to help me with this. I intended to shame you into asking for a divorce. The baby did not come into it."

"But how would that have gotten you control back of the company?" Hadn't he said if she divorced him, he only got fifty percent of the shares in the settlement?

"I have purchased all outstanding stock, including that for which your grandfather held proxies. Getting back half of the shares would have fulfilled my pride more than my need. It was part of my vendetta."

"You never intended me to get pregnant." Her hand went in automatic protective gesture over her womb.

He looked haunted. "I did not think of it."

At her look of disbelief, he turned away again and spoke with his back to her. "I went *pazzesco*. Crazy. *Santo cielo!* I was only thinking of how you had played me for a fool. How stupid I had been to trust you."

And his pride, which had already been smarting from her grandfather's behavior would have been decimated by this turn of events.

"Your carrying my *bambino* did not enter my mind." His broad shoulders were tense with strain. "I wanted to hurt you. I admit this. I wanted to make Joshua pay."

"You succeeded. You should be proud of a job well done." Too well done. So much for bleeding, she felt like her heart was hemorrhaging from the pain.

He turned back, his face set in bleak lines. "I am not proud. I am ashamed and I am sorry."

Every straining line of his body spoke of sincerity, his brown eyes eloquent with his regret.

"I believe you." She sighed, trying to ease the tightness in her chest. She believed that he was sorry, but his apology could not undo the hurt. Repentant, or not, he had married her not because he wanted her, but because he'd been forced to do it. The rejection she felt was shattering.

"I thought you cared about me. I knew it wasn't love, but this thing between you and my grandfather—it's so demeaning. The knowledge that our marriage was the result of an arrangement between you and my grandfather so you could get your company back…" Words failed her for several seconds as she struggled to keep the tears at bay.

Finally, she swallowed. "I never would have suspected anything like that, but it explains so much."

He stepped toward her, his hand extended. "Hope, please, we can make this marriage of ours work."

She reared back, almost falling off the sofa. "Don't come near me. I don't want you touching me." When she remembered how he had blackmailed her into marriage, using his body as the bait, she shuddered.

His expression was that of a jaguar thwarted of its prey.

"I want some time to think. Alone."

He shook his head in sharp negative. "We have both spent enough time alone."

"Whose fault is that?" She slapped the hand away that came within touching distance. "I missed you so much, but you treated me like little more than a whore on tap."

"No!"

"Yes! Since you got back from your trip, you've refused to talk to me, but you've been more than willing to use my body. I have to assume that was part of the revenge plan. Make me feel like a tramp and I would hurt even more, right?"

He looked horror-stricken by her words. "That is not the way it was."

"From where I'm standing, it is. I don't know if I can stay married to you," she whispered painfully.

"I will not allow you to divorce me."

"Contrary to the way both you and my grandfather have been behaving, we are no longer in the Dark Ages. You can't dictate my life's terms to me."

He ran his fingers through his hair in agitation. "I made a mistake, I admit it, but I will rectify it. I promise you this."

"And you are so good at keeping your promises." She couldn't help the dig, but she felt no satisfaction when he winced.

"I did not have sex with Zia."

"The jury is still out on that one."

His revenge plot made sense, even down to only pretending to have an affair. Breaking his word would not sit well with Luciano, but she wasn't ready to let him off the hook on that one. He'd set himself up, he could squirm.

All that aside, how could he keep his latest promise without love? How could he make it better when his lack of love was what hurt the most?

"I need some time alone," she said again. The tears she'd

fought since first looking at him, washed into her eyes. "I want to call my grandfather. I don't understand how he could have done this to me."

Luciano's hand lifted and fell, as if he wanted to touch her but knew she would reject him again. "We will talk again after this?"

She didn't see how they could avoid it. "Yes."

He nodded his head jerkily, his normal confidence for once shaken. "I will leave you to make your call."

He turned to go and she had an insane urge to call him back, but she didn't.

She had meant what she said. She needed time to determine if their marriage could survive its conception.

Luciano walked from the room feeling like a dead man inside. His beautiful wife hated him. It had been in her eyes: hatred, disgust, disappointment. Soft pansy eyes that had once looked on him in love now despised him.

She would talk to her grandfather, discuss the sordid events surrounding their marriage. And what would that accomplish? He hoped that time apart would calm her down enough to discuss their future, but an equally strong possibility was that in speaking to the old man, she would lose whatever vestiges of faith she maintained in their marriage.

Luciano had screwed up so badly. He was not used to messing up and knew his apology had not gone off the way he wanted. He had left so much unsaid. Words he found it impossible to voice, words that expressed emotion he had a difficult time admitting he was even feeling. To admit his feelings made him vulnerable and that was the one thing he abhorred above all others. Vulnerability.

But he would say anything, do anything to keep his wife.

He could not even contemplate the empty black hole he would fall into if she left him.

* * *

Hope waited impatiently for her grandfather to answer the phone. It was early morning in Boston, but he was already at work.

His voice came on the line. "Hope?"

"Yes, Grandfather, it's me."

"Did you find out what was going on with Luciano and those dinners in New York?"

"Yes. I know everything now. *Everything,*" she reemphasized.

"He told you about the deal?"

"You mean about your blackmailing him into marrying me? Yes, Luciano told me."

Hope swallowed tears while her grandfather cursed.

"How could you do that to me?" she asked.

"I wasn't doing anything to you, girl. I was doing it for you. Only one thing you really wanted. I realized that on New Year's Eve. Luciano di Valerio. You've had a thing for him for years, but I didn't notice until then."

She didn't deny her grandfather's words.

"Figured after the way he kissed you that he wanted you too, but he was going to marry some traditional Sicilian girl and leave you in the cold."

"He was engaged to someone else?" she asked, horrified.

"No, but it was only a matter of time. I baited the trap and he fell into. With the passion between the two of you, I figured propinquity would do the rest."

"But he doesn't love me!"

"Bah! Men like Luciano don't admit to tender emotions. Just ask me. Only told your grandmother one time that I loved her. The day she had our baby girl. It's the way we're made."

Hope felt sorry for her unknown grandmother. Marriage to Joshua Reynolds could not have been easy. "Well, I wanted to marry a man who loved me and was capable of saying so."

"You wanted Luciano."

"Not trussed up like a Thanksgiving turkey! Do you have any idea how humiliated I'm feeling right now? I hurt, Grandfather, all the way to my toes."

"What's that boy done?"

Momentarily disconcerted at having her ultra-alpha husband referred to as a boy, she waited a second to answer. "It's not what he's done. It's what you did. You set me up."

"I set you up all right, I set you up with Luciano."

"You set me up to be rejected by a man whose pride had been stomped on by your ruthless arrangement. You can't force a man like Luciano to do something so personal as get married and expect it all to work out in the end."

"Don't see why not. He had to get married someday. Why not to you?" Joshua didn't even sound sorry.

"Because he doesn't love me," she fairly shouted across the phone lines.

"No reason to yell, missy. I may be old, but I hear just fine. The man wants you and for him, that's probably as close to love as any woman will ever get."

She curled her knees up to her chest and rested her chin on them. Could her grandfather be right?

"You should not have done it."

"Hope, you wouldn't take anything else from me."

"I didn't want anything, just your love." That was all she'd ever wanted from the two most important men in her life and the one thing she was destined not to get. "I've got to go."

"No, wait, child."

"What?" she asked with a lackluster voice.

"I do love you."

Four words she'd longed to hear since she was five years old and lost both parents. They touched her now, healed some things inside her, but could not soothe the pain from Luciano's rejection and her grandfather's part in it.

"I love you, too," she said nevertheless.

He cleared his throat, the sound harsh. "I never meant to hurt you."

"I can see that."

They hung up, her grandfather sounding not quite his normal confident, gruff self.

She decided to take a walk and slipped her feet into a pair of sandals. Once she was beyond the formal gardens surrounding the villa, she let her feet wander where they would.

So many things were tumbling through her mind, she couldn't hold a single thought for longer than a second.

Luciano had been blackmailed into marrying her. She had no right to hold him, even less chance at securing his love. How could he come to love a woman he associated with the pegging down of his pride?

He'd forgotten about getting her pregnant, but now that she was, he wanted to stay married. She'd been humiliated to realize her marriage was the result of little more than a business arrangement between two powerful men, but this made it worse. For him to stay with her, to want her only for the life she carried inside of her was a total denial of herself as a woman.

Luciano had believed she was part of the plot and felt made a fool of because of it. So he had hurt her. He was sorry now and both he and Zia denied having slept together. Hope believed them. She remembered how sexually hungry Luciano had been his first night back from New York. He was hopelessly oversexed anyway, but that night, he had been desperate for her. That was not the response of a man getting all the sex he wanted from his ex-girlfriend.

Where did Hope's love for him fit into all this? She was pregnant with his child, but was that enough to keep a marriage that was nothing more than an arrangement together?

No.

But her love and his sincerity might be.

He was right. They'd spent too much time alone lately. If he was serious about trying, she didn't see that she had much choice because to contemplate life without Luciano was to contemplate a pain she did not want to bear.

She headed back to the house, determined to find Luciano and finish their discussion.

She found him on a lounger by the pool. He hadn't changed clothes and his expression was bleak.

"Luciano."

He looked up.

"We need to talk."

He nodded. "Where?"

He was asking her? "Can we go back to our room? It's the only place we're sure not to be overheard by your mother or Martina when they get back from shopping."

He stood up and took her arm. She didn't fight his touch now and some tension drained from him, not all, but some.

When they reached their small *sala,* he led her to the sofa where he sat and pulled her down beside him.

"What have you decided?"

"Tell me again why you were with Zia."

"I wanted you to believe I was having an affair." He took her hands in his, his grip crushing. "But I swear this is not true. I want no other woman, have not since New Year's Eve."

Was he saying he'd been celibate for six months before his pursuit of her? "No other woman…at all…since then?"

"None," he confirmed.

That meant something, but she wasn't sure what yet.

"You wanted me to think you and Zia were back together because you wanted to get back at my grandfather and me?"

He shook his head. "I was devastated by the belief you had been part of the blackmail scheme. Hurt. When I hurt, I lash out. I did not think it through, I just did it. By the time I came back from New York, I knew I did not want you to believe I had broken my promise."

"But you neglected to tell Zia, so when I called and she answered, she played it up," Hope guessed.

Luciano nodded, his mouth twisting. "Much to my detriment."

"I want to believe you." She *ached* to believe him.

"But," he prompted.

"You broke your other promise. The one about treasuring my love." She tried to pull her hands away at the painful memory, but he would not let go.

"No, I did not. In my heart, I always treasured your love and when you stopped saying the words, it hurt more than I wanted to admit. I made love to you frequently to assure myself that if nothing else, the passion between us was real and honest. That you wanted me even if you did not love me."

The words sounded so like the way she'd been feeling that she choked on her next question. "So, I wasn't just a convenience you used to assuage your strong sexual appetite?"

Suddenly she found herself on his lap, his arms wrapped tightly around her, his face close to hers. "I never thought of you that way. I was hurting and the only place I could connect with you was in bed."

"We connected pretty often."

His sculpted cheekbones turned dusky. *"Sì."*

"Do you want me to stay only for the baby?"

His face contorted and he buried it in the hollow of her neck. "No. I want you to stay for me. I cannot live without you, *cara*. Do not go away from me." He punctuated the words with tiny kisses that made her shiver.

"But a marriage without love has little hope of surviving."

His hold was almost bruising now. "I know you have stopped loving me. I deserve it, but I love you, *amore mia*.

You are the air that I breathe. The only music my heart wants to hear. The other half of my soul. I will make you love me again. I can do it. You still want me," he said as one hand cupped her breast with its already tight peak.

She turned her head and cupped his face between her palms so she could see into his eyes. "You love me?"

"For a long time. Since before New Year's Eve I think, but to admit it would have been to admit the end of my independence. Fool that I was, I thought that mattered. Without you all the freedom in the world would be a tiny cell in a prison of loneliness."

Her jaw dropped open. She couldn't help it. Not only had he said he loved her, but he'd gotten positively poetic about it. "Those are pretty mushy sentiments."

He shrugged, his Italian nature showing stronger in that moment than she had seen before. Emotion warmed his eyes and his body radiated heat just for her. "I feel mushy about you." He kissed her softly until her lips clung and then gently pulled away. "Tell me you will stay and let me teach you to love me again."

"I'll stay, but I can't let you make me love you."

His expression was devastating and much too painful to witness for her to keep up her teasing.

"I already love you. I will always love you and therefore you cannot make me do something I already am…doing that is."

She wasn't sure that made sense, but she didn't care because he looked like dawn was rising in his eyes. "My beautiful Hope! I love you. I adore you." He went into a litany of Italian phrases as he divested both of them of their clothes.

They made love on their bed, both saying words of love and need they had held back before.

When it was over, she cuddled into his side. "So, I guess this means, you really are fabulously happy about the baby."

"I am." His smile would have melted the polar ice caps.

And just to show her how much, he made love to her again, this time touching her stomach with reverence with his hands and mouth and whispering words of love to the *bambino* growing inside her.

Some time later, she was lying on top of him sweaty and sated. "Luciano."

"Sì, amore mia?"

"You really do love me?"

He sprang up, tumbling her into his lap and grasping her chin so their eyes met. "How can you doubt it? I love you more than my own life."

"It just seems so unreal. You married me because my grandfather forced you into it." Would she always remember that?

"He played matchmaker in the most unconventional way, but had I not wanted to be caught, I would not have been."

She sighed and said nothing.

"It is true. You realize I do not wish to pursue revenge on him now? I am grateful for his interference even if I was too proud to acknowledge it before."

Could she believe him? Knowing what a shark her husband was capable of being, she shivered a little with relief on her grandfather's behalf. "I'm glad."

"To hurt him would hurt you and I will never again do that."

"Sicilian guilt is stronger than the vendetta."

He turned very serious. "Not guilt. Love. This Sicilian's love."

She so desperately wanted to have faith in his love, but perhaps that was why it was so hard to do so. He had been forced into the marriage. How could he love her like she loved him? "Grandfather didn't really leave you an out."

He shook his head. "You do not believe me, but it is true. I had repurchased most of the stock by the time of our marriage. I did not need half of your shares to control Valerio Shipping."

"But you said…"

"I told you a plan I hatched in hurt and anger, not the truth of my heart, *cara. I did not need the shares.*"

And that truth was burning in his sexy brown eyes.

"You wanted to marry me," she said with awe.

"*Sì.* So much, I was in despair you would not believe me about Zia and leave me. I was terrified of losing you."

The concept of him terrified seemed unbelievable, but the aftereffects lingered in his expression. "That was before you knew I wasn't part of the blackmail plan." Understanding washed over her in a wave and with it came unstoppable love and belief in his love. "You wanted to make our marriage work believing I had colluded with my grandfather to force you into it."

That fact had gotten lost in her pain and confusion, but no Sicilian male as strong as Luciano would have come to that point without being very much in love.

"I could not lose you." His hold tightened. "You are the other half of myself. Without you, I am not a man."

"I love you, Luciano."

His eyes closed and he breathed deeply as if savoring the words. "Say it again."

"*Ti amo,*" she said it in Italian.

His eyes opened, burning into hers with purpose. "Always."

"Yes."

"And I will love you forever. I am going to make you feel like the most loved woman that ever walked the face of the earth."

As goals went, it was a big one, but he could do it. All he had to do was keep looking at her like he was doing right now.

And she would love him like no other woman could.

Luciano looked into his wife's soft pansy gaze, his precious Hope. Her love was worth more than his pride, more than his company, more than anything else in the world to him and he would never let her forget it.

* * * * *

THE GREEK'S VIRGIN BRIDE

Julia James

PROLOGUE

"YOU want me to do what?" Nikos Vassilis stared at the old man seated at the desk.

Yiorgos Coustakis looked back with a level gaze. At seventy-eight he was still a formidable figure of a man. His eyes were still as piercing as they had been when he was young. They were the eyes of a man who knew the price of everything.

Especially human souls.

"You heard me." His voice was unemotional. "Marry my granddaughter and you can go ahead with the merger."

"Maybe," replied the younger man slowly. "I just didn't believe you."

A twisted smile pulled at Yiorgos Coustakis's mouth. "You should," he advised. "It's the only deal on the table. And a deal, after all," he said, "is what you've flown four thousand miles for, *ne*?"

His visitor kept his hard, handsome face expressionless. Revealing anything in front of Old Man Coustakis was a major error in any kind of negotiation with him. Certainly he did not reveal the exasperation he had felt when the head of the Coustakis empire had phoned him at three a.m. in his Manhattan apartment the night before last to tell him that if he wanted a deal he'd better be in Athens this morning to sign it.

If it had been any one else phoning him Nikos would have given him short shrift. He'd had Esme Vandersee with him in bed, and sleeping was not what they'd been doing. But Yiorgos Coustakis had attractions that even the spectacular Esme, queen of the catwalk, could not compete with.

The Coustakis empire was a prize worth forgoing any woman for.

But was it a prize worth marrying a woman for? Giving up his freedom? For a woman he'd never met? Never laid eyes on?

Nikos shifted his gaze past the penetrating dark eyes and out through the plate-glass window. Athens lay below—crowded, polluted, unique. One of the most ancient cities of Europe, the cradle of western civilisation. Nikos knew it as a child knew its parent—he had been raised on its streets, toughened in its alleyways, tempered in its unforgiving crucible.

He'd clawed his way up off the streets, fighting tooth and nail, pushing poverty behind him deal by nerve-racking deal, until now, at thirty-four, it was as if he had never been that unwanted, fatherless boy running wild in the alleyways.

The journey had been long, and tough, but he had made it—and the fruits of his triumph were sweet indeed.

Now he stood poised on the edge of his greatest triumph—getting hold of the mighty Coustakis Industries.

"I was thinking," he said, keeping his face blank, "of a share-swap."

He had it all planned. He would reverse Vassilis Inc into the far larger Coustakis empire, and take the lot in a cashless exchange of shares. Oh, Old Man Coustakis would need a lot of personal financial sweeteners, he knew that, but Nikos had that covered too. He knew the old man wanted out, that his health—deny it officially as he would—was not good. But he knew Yiorgos Coustakis would never cede control of his business without a top-dollar face-saving deal—he'd go out like a lion, with a final roar, not like an old wolf driven from the pack.

That didn't bother Nikos—when his time came to quit he'd drive a hard bargain too, just to keep his successor on his toes.

But what Coustakis had just thrown at him had winded him like a blow to the gut. Marry his granddaughter to get hold of the company? Nikos hadn't even known the old man *had* a granddaughter!

Inside, behind the mask that was the carefully schooled expression on his face, Nikos had to tip his hat to the old man. He could still catch his rivals out—even a rival who was posing as a friendly merger partner.

"You can have the share-swap—on your wedding day."

Yiorgos's reply was flat. Nikos kept his silence. Behind his composed appearance his mind was teeming. Racing.

"Well?" Yiorgos prompted him.

"I'll think about it," returned Nikos. His voice was cool. He turned to go.

"Walk out the door and the deal is off. Permanently."

Nikos stopped. He rested his eyes on the man seated at the desk. He wasn't bluffing. Nikos knew that. Everyone knew Old Man Coustakis never bluffed.

"You sign now, or not at all."

Nikos's slate-grey eyes—a legacy from his unknown father, as was his un-Greek height of well over six feet—met with Coustakis's black ones. For a long, timeless moment, they held. Then slowly, unflinchingly, Nikos Vassilis walked back to the desk, picked up the gold pen Yiorgos Coustakis silently handed him, and signed the document lying there.

Without a word, he set down the pen and walked out.

On his brief journey down to ground level in the plush executive lift in the Coustakis HQ, Nikos tried in vain to rein in his thoughts.

Exultation ran side by side with anger—exultation that his longed-for goal was now within his grasp, anger that he had been outmanoeuvred by the wiliest fox he knew.

He straightened his shoulders. Who cared if Coustakis had driven a bargain he hadn't even seen coming? No one could have. The man played his cards closer to his chest than anyone Nikos knew—himself included. And if he could suddenly produce a granddaughter out of thin air that no one had ever heard of till now, well, what did it matter to him, Nikos Vassilis, who was going to get what he'd wanted all his life—a safe, secure, glittering place at the very top of the greasy pole he'd been climbing all his life?

That the unknown granddaughter fated to be his wife was a complete stranger was an irrelevance compared with taking over the Coustakis empire.

He knew what mattered in his life. What had always mattered.

And Old Man Coustakis—and his granddaughter—held the key to his dreams.

Nikos was not about to turn it down.

CHAPTER ONE

ANDREA could hear her mother coughing wheezily in the kitchen as she made breakfast. Her face tensed. It was getting worse, that cough. Kim had been asthmatic all her life, Andrea knew, but for the last eighteen months the bronchitis she'd got the winter before had never been shaken off, and her lungs were weaker than ever.

The doctor had been sympathetic but, apart from keeping Kim on her medication, all he'd advised was spending the winter in a warmer, drier climate. Andrea had smiled with grim politeness, and not bothered to tell him that he might as well have said she should take her mother to the moon. They barely had enough to cover their living expenses as it was, let alone to go gallivanting off abroad.

A clunk through the letterbox of the council flat she'd lived in all her life told Andrea that the post had arrived. She hurried off to get it before her mother could get to the door. The post only brought bills, and every bill brought more worries. Already her mother was fretting about how they would be able to pay for heating in the coming winter.

Andrea glanced at the post as she scooped it off the worn carpet by the front door. Two bills, some junk mail, and a thick cream-coloured envelope with her name typed on it. She frowned. Now what? An eviction order? A debt reminder? Something unpleasant from the council? Or the bank?

She ripped her thumbnail down the back and yanked open the paper inside, unfolding it. She caught a glimpse of some ornate heading, and a neatly typed paragraph—"Dear Ms Fraser…."

As she read, Andrea's body slowly froze. Twice she re-read the brief missive. Then, with a contortion of blind rage on her face, she screwed the letter into a ball and hurled it with all her force at the door. It bounced, and lay on the carpet.

Andrea had heard the phrase "red-misting"—now she knew first-hand what it meant.

Bastard!

She felt her hands fist in anger at her side. Then, with a deep, controlling breath, she made herself open her palms, bend down, and pick up the letter. She must not let Kim find it.

All that day the contents of the letter, jammed into the bottom of her bag, burned at her, the terse paragraph it contained repeating itself over and over again in Andrea's head.

You are required to attend Mr Coustakis at the end of next week. Your airline ticket will be at Heathrow for you to collect on Friday morning. Consult the enclosed itinerary for your check-in time. You will be met at Athens airport. You should phone the number below to acknowledge receipt of this communication by five p.m. tomorrow.

It was simply signed "For Mr Coustakis".

Dark emotions flowed through Andrea. "Mr Coustakis's." Aka Yiorgos Coustakis. Founder and owner of Coustakis Industries, worth hundreds of millions of pounds. A man Andrea loathed with every atom of her being.

Her grandfather.

Not that Yiorgos Coustakis had ever acknowledged the relationship. Memory of another letter leapt in Andrea's mind. That one had been written directly to her mother. It had been brief, too, and to the point. It had informed Kim Fraser, in a single, damning sentence, that any further attempt to communicate with Mr Coustakis would result in legal action being taken against her. That had been ten years ago. Yiorgos Coustakis had made it damningly clear that his granddaughter simply didn't exist as far as he was concerned.

Now, out of the blue, she had been summoned to his presence.

Andrea's mouth tightened. Did he really think she would meekly pack her bags and check in for a flight to Athens next Friday? Darkness shadowed her eyes. Yiorgos Coustakis could drop dead before she showed up!

A second letter arrived the next day, again from the London office of Coustakis Industries. Its contents were even terser.

Dear Ms Fraser,
You failed to communicate your receipt of the letter dated two days ago. Please do so immediately.

Like the first letter, Andrea took it into work—Kim must definitely not see it. She had suffered far too much from the father of the man she had loved so desperately—so briefly. A sick feeling sloshed in Andrea's stomach. How could anyone have treated her gentle, sensitive mother so brutally? But Yiorgos Coustakis had—and had relished it.

Andrea typed a suitable reply, keeping it as barely civil as the letters she had received. She owed nothing to the sender. Not even civility. Nothing but hatred.

With reference to your recent correspondence, you should note that any further letters to me will continue to be ignored.

She printed it out and signed it with her bare name—hard and uncompromising.

Like the stock she came from.

Nikos Vassilis swirled the fine vintage wine consideringly in his glass.

"So, when will my bride arrive, Yiorgos?" he enquired of his host.

He was dining with his grandfather-in-law-to-be in the vast, over-decorated house on the outskirts of Athens that Yiorgos Coustakis considered suitable to his wealth and position.

"At the end of the week," his host answered tersely.

He didn't look well, Nikos noted. His colour was high, and there was a pinched look around his mouth.

"And the wedding?"

His host gave a harsh laugh. "So eager? You don't even know what she looks like!"

Nikos's mobile mouth curled cynically.

"Her looks, or lack of them, are not going to be a deal-breaker, Yiorgos," he observed sardonically.

Yiorgos gave another laugh. Less harsh this time. Coarser.

"Bed her in the dark, if you must! I had to do that with her grandmother!"

A sliver of distaste filtered through Nikos. Though no one would dare say it to his face, the world knew that Yiorgos Coustakis had won his richly dowered, well-born wife by dint of getting the poor girl so besotted with him that she'd agreed to meet him in his apartment one afternoon. Yiorgos, as ambitious as he was ruthless, had made sure the information leaked to Marina's father, who had arrived in time to prevent Yiorgos having to undergo the ordeal of sex with a plain, drab dab of a girl in daylight, but not in time to save her reputation. "Who will believe she left my apartment a virgin?" Yiorgos had challenged her father callously—and won his bride.

Nikos flicked his mind back to the present. Was he insane, going through with this? Marrying a woman he hadn't set eyes on just because she happened to have a quarter of Yiorgos Coustakis's DNA? Idly he found himself wondering if the girl felt the same way about marrying a complete stranger. Then he shrugged mentally—in the world of the very rich, dynastic marriages were commonplace. The Coustakis girl would have been reared from birth to know that she was destined to be a pawn in her grandfather's machinations. She would be pampered and doll-like, her primary skill that of spending money in huge amounts on clothes, jewellery and anything else she took a fancy to.

Well, Nick acknowledged silently, glancing around the opulent dining room, she would certainly have money to spare as his wife! Once he'd taken over Coustakis Industries his income would be ten times what it already was—she could squander it on anything she wanted! Spending money would keep her busy, and keep her happy.

He paused momentarily. With a wife in the background he would obviously have to keep his personal life more low-profile. He would not be one of those husbands, all too familiar in the circles he now moved in, who thought nothing of flaunting their mistresses in front of their families. Nevertheless, he had no intention of altering the very enjoyable private life he indulged himself in, even if he would have to be more discreet about it once he was married.

Oh, he was well aware that as a rich man he could have been as old as Methuselah and as ugly as sin and beautiful women

would still have fawned on him. Wealth was the most powerful
aphrodisiac to those kind of women. Of course even when he'd
been dirt-poor women had always come easily to him—
another legacy from his philandering father, no doubt. One of
Esme's many predecessors had said to his face, as she lay exhausted and sated beneath him, that if he ever ran out of money
he could make a fortune hiring himself out as a stud. Nikos
had laughed, his mouth widening wolfishly, and turned her
over...

He shifted in his uncomfortably ornate chair. Thinking
about sex was not a good idea right now. His razor-sharp
mind might not have objected to kow-towing to Old Man
Coustakis's summons that night, but his body was reminding him that it had been deprived of its customary satiation.
Even though he'd put in extra time these last few days at the
gym and on the squash courts in the exclusive health club he
belonged to, Nikos could feel a familiar tightening that
presaged sexual desire.

As soon as he decently could he'd take his leave tonight and
phone Xanthe Palloupis. She was an extremely complaisant
mistress—always welcoming, always responsive to his
physical needs. Even though it had been three months since
he'd last visited her—Esme Vandersee had replaced her over
two months ago—he knew she would greet him warmly at her
discreetly located but very expensive apartment, confident
that he would tell her in the morning she could go to her favourite jeweller's and order something to remember his visit
by.

Would he keep her on when he had married this
unknown granddaughter of Yiorgos Coustakis? She had
other lovers, he knew, and it did not trouble him. Esme, too,
right this moment was doubtless consoling her wounded—
and highly developed!—ego by letting another of her
crowded court do the honours by her. As a top model she

always had men slavering after her, but for all that Nikos knew perfectly well that he would only have to snap his fingers and she would come instantly to his heel—and other parts of his anatomy.

He shifted uncomfortably in his seat again. He definitely needed some energetic physical release before his wedding night! The Coustakis girl would be a virgin, of course, and bedding her would be more of a duty, not a pleasure, though he would be as careful with her as was possible. He'd never taken a virgin—he would have to make totally sure he was not sexually frustrated on his wedding night or she'd be the one to suffer from it, however plain she was.

Just how plain was she? Nikos wondered, his mind running on. He had a pretty shrewd idea that from the tinge of open malice in Yiorgos's expression when he'd made that coarse comment about bedding her in the dark she had no looks at all. The old man probably thought it amusing that a man who was never seen without a beautiful woman hanging on his arm should now be hog-tied to a female whose sole attraction was as the gateway to control and eventual ownership of Coustakis Industries.

Another thought flitted through his mind. Just who exactly was this unknown granddaughter of Yiorgos Coustakis? One of the main attractions of taking over Coustakis Industries was that Yiorgos had no offspring to fight him for control. His only son had been killed in a smash-up years ago. Marina Coustakis had had some kind of seizure, so the gossip went, and had become a permanent invalid—though not managing to die until a few years ago. That meant that Yiorgos had not been free to marry again and beget more heirs. But then, mused Nikos, if the son had indeed been married when he died, and the granddaughter already born, maybe that hadn't mattered too much to Yiorgos. The son's widow had presumably married again and was out of the picture, apart from having dutifully reared the Coustakis granddaughter to be a docile, well-behaved, well-bred Greek wife.

Her docility would certainly make things easier for him, Nikos thought. Oh, he wouldn't flaunt his sex-life in her face, but obviously her mother would have taught her that husbands strayed, that it was in their nature, and that her role was to be a dutiful spouse, immaculate social hostess and attentive mother.

Nikos's hand stilled a moment as he raised his wine glass to his mouth. Yiorgos was retelling the drama of some coup he'd pulled off years ago, clearly relishing the memory of having beaten off a rival, bankrupting him in the process, and Nikos was only paying attention with a quarter of his mind. Three-quarters of it was considering what it would be like to be a father.

Because that, he knew, was what all this was about. Yiorgos was approaching the end of his life—he wanted to know his DNA would continue. He wanted an heir.

And Nikos? Strange feelings pricked at him. What did he know about fatherhood? His own father didn't even know he existed—he'd impregnated his mother and sailed with the tide at dawn. He could even be alive somewhere, Nikos knew. It meant nothing to him. His mother had scarcely mentioned him—she'd worked in a bar, when she'd worked at all, and her maternal instincts had not been well developed. Her son's existence hadn't been important to her, and when he'd left home as a teenager she'd hardly noticed. As he had slowly, painfully, begun to make money, she'd accepted his handouts without question, let alone interest, and hadn't lived to see him make real money. She'd been knocked down by a taxi twelve years ago, when he was twenty-two. Nikos had given her an expensive funeral.

He lifted the wine glass to his mouth and drank. It was a rare, costly vintage, he knew—learning about wines and all

the other fine things of life was information he'd gathered
along the way. He relished all fine things, and once he ran
Coustakis Industries the finest things in the world would be
his for the taking. He would have taken his place not just
amongst the wealthy, as he now was, but amongst the super-
rich. And if Coustakis wanted him to impregnate his granddaughter and give him a great-grandson—well, he could do
that.

Whatever she looked like.

Andrea stood by the front door of the flat, staring at the
opened letter. It was not from Coustakis Industries. It was
from one of London's most prestigious department stores,
and informed her that enclosed was a gold store card with an
immediate credit limit of five thousand pounds. It further
stated her that all invoices incurred by her to that limit would
be forwarded to the private office of Yiorgos Coustakis for
payment. A second opened letter underlaid the one from the
store. That one *was* from Coustakis Industries, and it instructed her to make use of the store card that would be sent
under separate cover in order to provide herself with a
suitable wardrobe for when she attended Mr Coustakis at the
end of the following week. It finished with a reminder to
phone the London office to confirm receipt of these instructions.

Andrea's dark eyes narrowed dangerously. What the hell
was the old bastard playing at?

What did he want? What was going on? Her scalp prickled
with unease. She didn't like this—she didn't like it at all!

Her brain was in turmoil. What would happen if she did
what she wanted to do and cut the store card in half and sent
it back to her grandfather with orders to stick it where it hurt?
Would he get the message? Somehow she didn't think so.

Yiorgos Coustakis wanted something from her. He'd never

acknowledged her existence before. But he was a rich man—very rich. And rich men had power. And they used it to get their own way.

Her face set. What could Yiorgos Coustakis do to them if he wanted to? Kim had debts—Andrea hated to think of them, let alone the reason for those debts, but they were there, like a millstone round their necks. Both of them, mother and daughter, worked endlessly, repaying them little by little, and given another five years or so they finally would be clear. But that was a long way off.

And Kim's health was getting worse.

Anguish crushed Andrea's heart like a vice. Her mother had suffered so *much*—she'd had such a rotten life. A brief, tiny glimpse of happiness when she was twenty, a few golden weeks in her youth, and then it had been destroyed. Totally destroyed. And she'd spent the next twenty-four years of her life being the most devoted, caring, *loving* mother that anyone could ask for.

I just wish we could get out, Andrea thought for the millionth time. The high-rise block they lived in was overdue for repairs, though she could understand the council's reluctance to spend good money on doing up an estate when half its population would simply start to trash it the moment the paint was dry. The flats themselves had a list as long as your arm of repairs needed—the worst was that the damp in the kitchen and bathroom was dire, which did no good at all for Kim's asthma. The lift was usually broken, and anyway usually served as a late-night public convenience, not to mention a place for scoring drugs.

For a brief, fleeting second Andrea thought of the immense wealth of Yiorgos Coustakis.

Then put it behind her.

She would have nothing to do with such a man. *Nothing.* Whatever he planned for her.

CHAPTER TWO

NIKOS pushed the sleeve of his suit jacket back and glanced at the slim gold watch circling his lean wrist. What had Old Man Coustakis called him here for? He'd been cooling his heels on the shaded terrace for over ten minutes—and ten minutes was a long time for a man as busy as Nikos Vassilis. He did not like waiting patiently—he was a man in a hurry. Always had been.

The manservant approached again, from the large double doors leading into the opulent drawing room beyond, and deferentially asked him if he would like another drink. Curtly, Nikos shook his head, and asked—again—when Mr Coustakis would be ready to see him. The manservant replied that he would enquire, and padded off silently.

Irritated, Nikos turned and stared out over the gardens spread below. They were highly ornate, clearly designed to impress, not to provide a pleasant place to stroll around. Nikos had a sudden vision of a small boy trying to play out there and finding nothing but expensive specimen plants, and fussy paths and over-planted borders. His mouth tightened unconsciously. If he were to become a father he would need a decent place to raise his family...

His mind sheered away. The reality of what he was about to do—marry Yiorgos Coustakis's plain, pampered granddaughter, a female he'd never met—was starting to hit him. Could he really go through with it? Even to get hold of Coustakis Industries?

He shook the doubts from his mind. Of course he would go through with it! Anyway, it wasn't as if he were signing his life away. Old Man Coustakis would not live for ever. In half a dozen years he would probably be dead, and then Nikos and the unknown granddaughter could come to some sort of civilised divorce, go their separate ways, and that would be that.

And what about your son? What will he think about your "civilised divorce"?

He pushed that thought from his mind as well. Who knew? Maybe the granddaughter would turn out to be barren, as well as plain as sin.

A footfall behind him made him turn.

And freeze.

Nikos's eyes narrowed as he saw the unfamiliar woman step onto the wide sweeping terrace where he stood. The cloud of dark bronze hair rustled on her shoulders, making him take notice of her long, slender neck. Then, as if a brief glance were tribute enough for that particular feature, his eyes clamped back to her face.

Theos, but she was a stunner! Her skin was paler than a Greek's, but still tanned. She had a short, delicate nose, sculpted cheeks, and a wide, generous mouth. Her eyes were like rich chestnut, the lashes ridiculously long and smoky.

He felt his body kick with pleasure at looking at her. As of their own volition, his eyes wandered downwards again, past that slender neck framed by that glorious hair, down over full, swelling breasts, superbly moulded by the tight-fitting jacket she wore, nipping in to a deliciously spannable waist, and then ripening outwards to softly rounded hips, before descending down long, long legs.

He frowned. She was wearing trousers. The sight offended him. With legs that long she should be wearing a short, tight skirt that hugged those splendid thighs and clung lovingly to the lush, rounded bottom he felt sure a woman like that must have...

Who the hell was she?

His brain interrupted his body's visceral contemplation of the female's physical attributes. What was a woman this lush, this drop-dead gorgeous, this damn *sexy*, doing here in Yiorgos Coustakis's house?

The answer came like a blow to the gut. There was only one reason a woman who looked like this would be swanning around Old Man Coustakis's private residence, and that was because she was a private guest. Very private.

All of Athens knew that Yiorgos Coustakis liked to keep a stable of women. He was renowned for it, even from long before his wife became an invalid.

And they'd always been young women—even as he'd got older.

Even now, apparently.

Distaste filled Nikos's mouth. OK, so maybe the old man was still up for it, even at his age, but the idea of the man of seventy-eight keeping a woman who couldn't be more than twenty-five, if that, as his mistress was repugnant in the extreme.

Andrea blinked, momentarily blinded by the bright light after the dim shade of the interior of the huge house she had been deposited at barely five minutes ago by the lush limo that had met her at the airport.

Then, as her vision cleared, she saw someone was already on the terrace. She took in an impression of height, and darkness. Black hair, a sleek, powerful-looking business suit, an immaculately knotted tie—and a face that made her stop dead.

The skin tone was Mediterranean; there was no doubt about that. But what struck her incongruously was the pair of piercing steel-grey eyes that blazed at her. She felt her stomach lurch, and blinked again. She went on staring, taking in, once she could drag her eyes away from those penetrating grey ones, a strong, straight nose, high cheekbones and a wide, firm mouth.

She shook her head slightly, as if to make sure the man she was staring at was really there.

Suddenly Andrea saw the man's expression change. Harden with disapproval. And something more than disapproval. Disdain. Something flared inside her—and it was nothing to do with the unmistakable frisson that had sizzled through her like a jolt of electricity in the face of the blatant appraisal this startlingly breath-catching man had just subjected her to. She would have been blind not to have registered the look of outright sexual attraction in the man's face when he'd first set eyes on her a handful of seconds ago. She was used to that reaction in men. For the most part it was annoying more than anything, and over the years she had learnt to dress down, concealing the ripeness of her figure beneath loose, baggy clothes, confining her glowing hair into a subdued plait, and seldom bothering with make-up. Besides—a familiar shaft of bitterness stabbed at her—she knew all too well that any initial sexual attraction men showed in her would not last—not when they saw the rest of her…

She pulled her mind away, washing out bitterness with an even more familiar upsurge of raw, desperate gratitude—to her mother, to fate, to any providential power, to everyone who had helped her along her faltering way in the long, painful years until she had emerged to take her place as a functioning adult in the world. Considering what the alternatives might have been, she had no cause for bitterness—none at all.

And if she felt bitter about the man who was her father's father—well, that was not on her own behalf, only her mother's. For her mother's sake *only* she was here, now, standing on this terrace, over a thousand miles from home—being looked at disdainfully by a man she could not drag her eyes from.

It had been a hard decision to make. It had been her friends Tony and Linda who had helped her make it.

"But why is he *doing* this?" she'd asked them, for the dozenth time. "He's up to something and I don't know what—and that worries me!"

"Maybe he just wants to get to know you, Andy," said Linda peaceably. "Maybe he's old, and ill, and wants to make up for how he treated you."

"Oh, so that's why I've been getting letters just about ordering me to go and dance attendance on him! *And* not a dickey-bird about Mum, either! No, if he'd really wanted to make up he'd have written more politely—and to Mum, not me."

"If you want my advice I think you should go out there," said Linda's husband, Tony. "Like Linda said, he *might* be after a reconciliation, but even if he isn't, suppose he wants to use you for his own nefarious ends in some way? That, you know, puts you in a strong position. Have you thought of that?"

Andrea frowned.

Tony went on. "Look, if he does want you for something, then if he doesn't want you to refuse he's going to have to do something *you* want."

"Like what?" Andrea snorted. "He doesn't have a thing I want!"

"He's got money, Andy," Tony said quietly. "Shed-loads of it."

Andrea's eyes narrowed to angry slits. "He can choke on it for all I care! I don't want a penny from him!"

"But what about your mum, Andy?" said Tony, even more quietly.

Andrea stilled. Tony pressed on, leaning forward. "What if he forked out enough for her to clear her debts—and move to Spain?"

Andrea's breath seemed tight in her chest. As tight as her mother's breath was, day in, day out. Instantly in her mind she heard her mother's dry, asthmatic cough, saw her pause by the sink, breathing slowly and painfully, her frail body hunched.

"I can't," she answered faintly. "I can't take that man's money!"

"Think it through," urged Tony. "You wouldn't be taking his money for yourself, but for your mum. He owes her— you've always said that and it's true! She's raised you single-handed with nothing from him except insults and abuse! He lives in the lap of luxury, worth hundreds of millions, and his granddaughter lives in a council flat. Do it for her, Andy."

And that, in the end, had been the decider. Though every fibre of her being wanted never, ever to have anything to do with the man who had treated her mother so callously, the moment Tony had said "Spain" a vista had opened up in Andrea's mind so wonderful she knew she could not refuse. If she could just get her grandfather to buy her mother a small apartment somewhere it was warm and dry all year round...

It was for that very reason that Andrea was now standing on the terrace of her grandfather's palatial property in Athens.

She would get her mother the dues owed her.

She gave a smile as she looked again at the impressive man who stood before her. A small, tight, defiant—dismissive— smile. So, he knew who she was, did he, Mr Mega-Cool? He looked so sleek, screaming "money" in his superbly tailored suit, with his immaculately cut dark hair, the gleam of gold

at his wrist as he paused in the action of checking his watch—
oh, he must be one of her grandfather's entourage. No doubt.
One of his business associates, partners—whatever rich men
called each other in their gilded world where the price of electricity was an irrelevance and there was never green mould
on the bathroom walls…

So much, she thought with self-mocking acknowledgement, for the shopping spree she'd been on with Linda and
Tony in that ultra-posh London department store, courtesy of
its gold store card! She'd thought the outrageously priced
trouser suit she'd bought, shouting its designer label, would
do the trick—fool anyone who saw her that the last thing she
could possibly be was a common-as-muck London girl off a
housing estate! And Linda had even done her hair and make-
up that morning, before she'd set out for the airport, making
her look svelte and expensive to go with the fantastic new
outfit she'd travelled in. Obviously she need not have
bothered!

The man looking at her so disdainfully out of those cold steel-
grey eyes knew perfectly well what she was—who she was.
Yiorgos Coustakis's cheap-and-nasty bastard granddaughter!

Her chin went up. Well, what did she care? She had her
own opinions of Yiorgos Coustakis—and they were not
generous. So if this man standing here on her grandfather's
mile-long terrace, looking down his strong, straight nose at
her, his mouth tight with disdain, thought she wasn't fit for
a palatial place like this, what was it to her? Zilch. Just as
Yiorgos Coustakis was nothing to her—nothing except the
price of some small, modest reparation to the woman he had
treated like dirt…

Her eyes hardened. Nikos saw their expression change,
saw the derisive smile, the insolent tilt of the woman's chin.
Clearly the female was shameless about her trade! The
distaste he felt about Old Man Coustakis keeping a mistress

at his age filtered into distaste for the woman herself. It checked the stirring of his own body, busy responding the way nature liked it to do when in the presence of a sexually alluring female.

So when the woman strolled towards him, the smile on her face unable to compensate for the hardness in her eyes, he responded in kind.

Andrea saw the withdrawal in his eyes, and suddenly, like a cloud passing in front of the sun, she felt a chill emanate from him. Suddenly he wasn't just a breath-catchingly, heart-stoppingly handsome man, looking a million dollars, tall and lean—he was an icily formidable, hard-eyed, patrician-born captain of industry who looked on the rest of humanity as his inferior minions...

Well, tough! She tilted her head, almost coquettishly, letting her glorious hair riot over her shoulders. An intense desire to annoy him came over her.

"Hi," she breathed huskily. "We haven't met, have we? I'd remember, I know!" She let a gleam of appreciation enter her glowing eyes. That would annoy him even more; she instinctively knew.

She held her hand out. It was looking beautiful—Linda had given her a manicure the night before, smoothing the work-roughened skin and putting on nail extensions and a rich nail-varnish whose colour matched her hair.

Nikos ignored the hand. A revulsion against touching flesh that had caressed, for money, a rich old man, filled him. It didn't matter that half his body was registering renewed arousal at the sound of that breathy voice, the heady fragrance of her body as she approached him. He subdued it ruthlessly.

Besides, it had just registered with him that the woman was English. That would account for the auburn colouring. Presumably, he found himself thinking, for a woman of her profession hair that colour would command a premium in lands where dark hair was the norm.

The man's rejection of her outstretched hand made Andrea falter. She let her hand fall to her side. But still, despite the shut-out, she refused to be intimidated. After all, if she failed at the first test—being sneered at by a complete stranger for being the bastard Coustakis granddaughter—then she would be doomed to fail in her mission. Intimidation was, she knew from the painfully extracted reminiscences of her mother's abrupt expulsion from Greece twenty-four years ago, the forte of the man who had summoned her here like a servant. She must not, above all, be intimidated by Yiorgos Coustakis as her mother had been. She must stand up to him—give him as good as she got. Tony's words echoed in her mind—if he had summoned her here, he wanted something. And that made her position powerful.

She had to remember that. *Must* remember that.

She was in enemy territory. Confidence was everything.

So now, in the face of the obvious disdain of this stunning stranger, she refused to be cowed. Instead, she gave that derisive little smile again, deliberately tossed her head and, shooting him a mocking glance, strolled right past him to take in the view over the grounds. She leant her palms on the stone balustrade, taking some of the weight off her legs. They were aching slightly, probably tension more than anything, because she'd been sitting down most of the day—first in the luxurious airline seat and then in the luxurious chauffeur-driven car. Still, she must do her exercises tonight—right after she'd phoned Tony, as they'd arranged.

Her mind raced, thinking about all the safety nets that she and Tony had planned out. The man behind her was totally forgotten. However good-looking he was—however scornful of the Coustakis bastard granddaughter—he was not important. What was important was going through, for the thou-

sandth time, everything she and Tony had done to make sure
that her grandfather could not outmanoeuvre her. Had they
left any holes? Left anything uncovered?

Working on the premise that Yiorgos Coustakis was totally
ruthless in getting what he wanted, she and Tony had planned
elaborate measures to make sure that Andrea always had an
escape route if she needed one. The first was to ensure that
every evening of her stay in Greece she would phone Tony
on the mobile he had lent her. If he did not hear from her by
eleven p.m., he was to alert the British consul in Athens and
tell them a British citizen was being forcibly held against her
will. And if that did not do the trick—her mouth tightened—
then Tony's second phone call would be to a popular British
tabloid, spilling the whole story of how the granddaughter
of one of the richest men in Europe came to be living on a
council estate. Yiorgos Coustakis might be immune to bad
publicity, but she wondered whether his shareholders would
be as sanguine about the stink she could raise if she wanted…

And then, if her grandfather still didn't want to let her go,
she had left her passport, together with seven hundred euros,
plus her return ticket, in a secure locker at Athens airport—
the key to which was in her make-up bag. She had also, not
trusting her grandfather an inch, purchased a second, open-
dated ticket to London while she was still at Heathrow, which
she had not yet collected from the airline. She had paid for
that one herself.

Andrea smiled grimly as she stared out over the ornate,
fussily designed gardens. Though she hadn't been able to
afford to buy the full-price ticket from her own meagre funds,
she had come up with a brilliant idea for how to pay for it.
The day that she and Tony and Linda had gone into the West
End to buy her outfit, they had also visited the store's jewellery department. The balance from the five thousand pounds
after buying the trouser suit and accessories had purchased a

very nice pearl necklace—so nice that they had immediately taken it to another jewellery shop and sold it for cash. With the money they had bought the airline ticket, a wad of traveller's cheques, and split the rest into a combination of sterling, US dollars and euros. That, surely, she thought, her eyes quite unseeing of the view in front of her, should be enough to ensure that she could simply leave whenever she wanted.

Behind her, Nikos Vassilis had stiffened. The woman had simply walked past him as if he were no one! And that derisive little smile and mocking look of hers sent a shaft of anger through him! No woman did that to him! Certainly not one who stooped to earn her living in such a way. He stared after her, eyes narrowing.

Then a discreet cough a little way to his side caught his attention, as it was designed to do. The manservant was back, murmuring politely that Mr Coustakis would see him now, if he would care to come this way.

With a last, ireful glance at the woman now leaning carelessly on the balustrade, totally ignoring him, her hair a glorious sunset cloud around her shoulders, Nikos stalked off into the house.

CHAPTER THREE

AN HOUR later, as she was shown into the dim, shaded room, Andrea straightened her shoulders, ready for battle. At first it seemed the room was empty. Then a voice startled her.

"Come here."

The voice was harsh, speaking in English. Clearly issuing an order.

She walked forward. She seemed to be in a sort of library, judging from the shelves of books layering every wall. Her heels sounded loud on the parquet flooring. She could see, now, that a large desk was positioned at the far end of the room, and behind it a man was sitting.

It seemed to take a long time to reach him. One part of her brain realised why—it was a deliberate ploy to put anyone entering the room at a disadvantage to the man already sitting at the desk.

As she walked forward she glanced around her, quite deliberately letting her head crane around, taking in her surroundings, as if the man at the desk were of no interest to her. Her heels clicked loudly.

She reached the front of the desk, and only then did she deign to look at the man who had summoned her.

It was the eyes she noticed first. They were deepset, in sunken sockets. His whole face was craggy and wrinkled, very old, but the eyes were alight. They were dark, almost black in this dim light, but they scoured her face.

"So," said Yiorgos Coustakis to his granddaughter, whom he had never set eyes on till now, "you are that slut's brat." He nodded. "Well, no matter. You'll do. You'll have to."

His eyes went on scouring her face. Inside, as the frail bud of hope that maybe Yiorgos Coustakis had softened his hard heart died a swift, instant death, Andrea fought to quell the upsurge of blind rage as she heard him refer to her mother in such a way. With a struggle, she won the battle. Losing her temper and storming out now would get her nowhere except back to London empty-handed. Instead, she opted for silence.

She went on standing there, being inspected from head to toe.

"Turn around."

The order was harsh. She obeyed it.

"You walk perfectly well."

The brief sentence was an accusation. Andrea said nothing.

"Have you a tongue in your head?" Yiorgos Coustakis demanded.

She went on looking at him.

Was a man's soul in his eyes, as the proverb said? she wondered. If so, then Yiorgos Coustakis's soul was in dire condition. The black eyes that rested on her were the most terrifying she had ever seen. They seemed to bore right into her—and, search as she would, she could see nothing in them to reassure her. Not a glimmer of kindness, of affection, even of humour, showed in them. A feeling of profound sadness filled her, and she realised that, despite all the evidence, something inside her had been hoping against hope that the man she had grown up hating and despising was not such a man after all.

But he was proving exactly the callous monster she had always thought him.

"Why did you bring me here?"

The question fell from her lips without her thinking. But instinctively she knew she had done the right thing in taking the battle—for this was a battle, no doubt about that now, none at all—to her grandfather.

He saw it, and the dark eyes darkened even more.

"Do not speak to me in that tone," he snapped, throwing his head back.

Her chin lifted in response.

"I have come over a thousand miles at your bidding. I am entitled to know why." Her voice was as steady as she could make it, though in her breast she could feel her heart beating wildly.

His laugh came harsh, scornful.

"You are entitled to nothing! *Nothing!* Oh, I know why you came! The moment you caught a glimpse of the kind of money you could spend if you came here you changed your tune! Why do you think I sent you that store card? I knew that would flush you out!" He leant forward, his once-powerful arms leaning on the surface of the polished mahogany desk. "But understand this, and understand it well! You will be on the first plane back to London unless you do exactly, *exactly* what I want you to do! Understand me?"

His eyes flashed at her. She held his gaze, though it was like a heavy weight on her. So, she thought, Tony had been right—he *did* want something from her. But what? She needed to know. Only when she knew what the man sitting there, who by a vile accident of fate just happened to be her grandfather, wanted of her could she start to bargain for the money she wanted from him.

Play it cool, girl...play it cool...

She lifted an interrogative eyebrow.

"And what is it, *exactly*, that you want me to do?"

His brows snapped together at the sarcastic emphasis she gave to echo his.

"You'll find out—when I want you to." He held up a hand, silencing her. "I've had enough of you for now. You will go to your room and prepare yourself for dinner. We will have a guest. With your upbringing you obviously won't know how to comport yourself, so I shall tell you now that you had better change your attitude! In *this* country a woman knows how to behave—see that you do not shame me in my own house! Now, go!"

Andrea turned and left. The walk back to the door seemed much further than it had in the opposite direction. Her heart was pounding.

It went on pounding all the way back upstairs to her room. She shut the door and leant against it. So, that was her grandfather! That was the man whose son had had a brief, whirlwind romance with her mother, who had thrown her, pregnant and penniless, out of the country, and left her to bear and raise his grandchild in poverty, refusing to acknowledge her existence.

She owed such a man nothing. Nothing! Not duty, nor respect—and certainly not loyalty or affection.

What does he want of me?

The question went round and round, unanswered. Fretting at her.

In the end, to calm herself down and pass the time, she decided to make use of the opulent bathroom. Inside its lavish, overdone interior she could not but help revel in the luxury it offered.

The bath was vast, and it had, she discovered, sinking into its deep scented depths, whirling jets that massaged her body, easing the aching muscles in her tense legs. Blissfully, she gave herself to the wonderful sensation. Towering bubbles from the half a bottle of bath foam she'd emptied in veiled her whole body, from breasts to feet.

You walk perfectly well…

She heard the harsh accusation ring in her head again, and her mouth tightened.

When she emerged from the bathroom, entering her lavishly decorated bedroom suite, swathed in a floor-length towel, it was to see a maid at the open door of her closet, hanging up clothes. The girl turned, bobbing a brief curtsey, and hesitantly informed Andrea that she was here to help her dress.

"I don't need any help," said Andrea tersely.

The girl looked subdued, and Andrea immediately regretted her tone of voice.

"Please," she said temporisingly, "it's quite unnecessary."

She walked past the huge bed, covered in a heavy gold and white patterned bedspread, and across to the room-sized closet. Whatever Yiorgos Coustakis had imagined she'd bought with her gleaming gold store card, all she was going to appear for dinner wearing was a chainstore skirt and blouse. But suddenly she stopped dead.

The racks were full, weighed down with plastic-swathed clothes.

"What—?"

"Kyrios Coustakis ordered them to be purchased for you, *kyria*. They were delivered just now by a personal shopper. There are accessories and lingerie as well," said the maid's softly accented voice behind her. "Which dress would you like to wear tonight?"

"None of them," said Andrea tightly. She reached for the hanger carrying her own humble skirt and blouse.

The maid looked aghast. "But…but it is a formal dinner, tonight, *kyria*," she stammered. "Kyrios Coustakis would be very angry if you did not dress appropriately…"

Andrea looked at the maid. The expression on the girl's face made her pause. There was only one word for the expression, and it was fear.

She gave in. She could defy her grandfather's anger, but she was damned if he would get the chance to terrorise one of his own staff on her account.

"Very well. Choose something for me."

She went and sat back on the bed while the girl leafed through the clothes hanging from the rail. After a few moments she emerged with two, deftly removing the protective wrapping from them and laying them carefully across the foot of the bed. Andrea inspected them. Both were clearly very expensive, and although it was the short but high-necked cocktail length one that she preferred for style, she nodded at the other one, a full-length gown.

"That one," she said.

It was emerald-green, cut on the bias, with a soft, folding bodice and a long, slinky skirt. Andrea found her hand reaching out to touch the silky folds.

"It is very beautiful, *ne*?" said the maid, and sounded wistful as well as admiring.

"Very," agreed Andrea. She glanced at the girl. "I don't know your name," she said.

"Zoe, *kyria*," said the girl.

"Andrea," she replied. "And I don't believe in servants."

Some twenty minutes later, staring at herself in the long mirror set into the door of the closet, Andrea was stunned.

She looked—fantastic! That was the only word for it. The dress was a miracle of the couturier's art, its soft folds contrasting with the rich vividness of its colour. True, the bodice, held up by tiny shoestring straps, was draped dangerously low over her full breasts, encased in a fragile, strapless bra, but she had to admit the effect was very…well, *effective*! It gave the dress the finishing touch to the "wow" impact it made.

She had scooped her hair up into a knot on her head, with tendrils loosening around the nape of her neck and gracing her cheeks and forehead, and she'd redone her make-up to match the impact of the dress.

With a final look at her reflection, she turned and headed towards the door, where the manservant who had come to summon her stood waiting. Staff though he was, she could see the admiration in his eyes. For an instant, in her mind's eye, it was not one of the house staff who stood there, but the man she had encountered on the terrace that afternoon, looking at her with those powerful grey eyes, making her stomach give a little skip…

She bestowed a slight, polite smile on the manservant, and headed towards the curving marble staircase.

It was time to go into battle once more…

Nikos Vassilis stepped on the accelerator, changed gear and heard the powerful note of the engine of the Ferrari change pitch. He was not in a good mood. Twice in one day now he'd made the journey out of Athens at the behest of Yiorgos Coustakis. Tonight was not a good night to be dining with the old man. He'd planned a leisurely evening with Xanthe, whose petite, curvaceous body was, he had discovered, a pleasant alternative to Esme Vandersee's greyhound leanness. Xanthe was proving very attentive—she was clearly keen to take his mind off Esme Vandersee, and was now pulling out all the stops to renew Nikos's interest. Which meant, he mused, that she was coming up with some very interesting ideas indeed to do so…

A smile indented his mouth. Last night with Xanthe had been very enjoyable—she had seen to that. Ah, he thought pleasurably, there was nothing like a Greek woman for making a man feel good! Yes, Esme Vandersee might be eager for him, he was certainly a catch for her, but as an American she suffered that infernal affliction of thinking that a woman had a right to give a man a hard time if she chose! Usually, of course, any petulance that Esme displayed he disposed of very swiftly—she was as sexy as a cat and getting her horizontal soon improved her mood…

But even so, he mused, Xanthe understood what it was that a man wanted a woman to be. And she made it obvious that she was keen to be so very attentive to his every need….

His smile vanished. Well, he'd be kept waiting tonight before availing himself of Xanthe's rediscovered charms! Yiorgos Coustakis was obviously taking considerable pleasure in jerking his strings—just for the hell of it, it seemed. Their meeting that afternoon, ostensibly to discuss the technicalities of reversing Vassilis Inc into Coustakis Industries, had hardly been urgent, and could have been left to their respective finance directors to sort out. But obviously Old Man Coustakis had relished getting Nikos Vassilis to come traipsing out of Athens to that overblown villa of his whenever he snapped his fingers.

Thinking about the afternoon meeting brought another image vividly to mind—that of Yiorgos Coustakis's flame-haired mistress.

Nikos's mouth tightened. The woman had been so blatant, and so unashamed of what she was doing at the Coustakis villa. Not to mention eyeing him up and trying her wiles out on him to boot!

Mind you, Nikos thought, had the woman not been tainted by her distasteful association with a man old enough to be her grandfather, then her approach to him might well have got a warmer welcome.

Considerably warmer, in fact…

An image of her dark auburn hair floating around that perfect face, the way her breasts had thrust against the material of her jacket, played in his memory. Oh, yes, she was worth remembering, all right! Her beauty was so flamboyant, so eye-catching, that almost—almost he had been tempted to overlook just for whose benefit it had been paraded that afternoon. Not for him—for a seventy-eight-year-old man.

He thrust her memory from him. However alluring the woman, she was beyond the pale so far as he was concerned.

He revved the engine again, enjoying the superb handling of the extortionately expensive car beneath his hands. Driving a high-performance car like this was like having sex with a high-performance woman…they were both so extraordinarily responsive to his touch…

His mind snapped away from the analogy. For the next few hours, until the ordeal of a tedious, overlong dinner with Yiorgos Coustakis was done with, he had better keep his libido under control.

Think of your bride, Nikos!

That sobered him all right. It was about time Old Man Coustakis brought the girl out from wherever he had her stashed. She would know all about her intended bridegroom by now, no doubt, and she and her mother were probably already waist-deep in wedding plans. Presumably the girl wanted a lavish society wedding. Well, he didn't care one way or the other, and, since the whole purpose of marrying her was to seal his acquisition of Coustakis Industries, the more high-profile the better! After all, he had nothing against the girl—let her have her extravagant wedding if she wanted. Once she was his wife it would be *her* who would have to fit herself around what *he* wanted—that was what Greek wives did. Oh, he would be generous, of course, and considerate to her position—he had no intention of making a bad husband—but he did not envisage changing his life a great deal on account of the Coustakis heiress.

Pity she was obviously so plain… The thought of having a sexually desirable, docile and attentive wife had its attractions, now he came to think of it.

He braked the Ferrari in front of the security-guarded gates of the Coustakis villa, presented his credentials, and moved on down the drive at a speed greater than he would normally. He wanted this evening over and done with.

CHAPTER FOUR

NIKOS stood in the ornate salon, itching for dinner to be announced. His host seemed to be in no hurry. He was regaling his guest with a lengthy description of his latest toy—a one-hundred-and-fifty-foot yacht which he had just taken delivery of. It was, by all accounts, an opulent vessel, and Yiorgos was telling him in great detail about the splendour of the décor of its interior—and how much it had all cost. The telling seemed to be putting him in a good humour. His colour was high, but his eyes were snapping with satisfaction.

"And you, my friend," he said, slapping Nikos on the back with a still powerful hand, "will be the first to try her out! You will spend your honeymoon on it! What do you think of that, eh?"

Nikos smiled briefly. Again, a honeymoon spent on board Yiorgos Coustakis's new yacht would send just the message to the world he wanted.

"Good, good," said his grandfather-in-law-to-be, and slapped him once more on the back. Then his head snapped round. Automatically Nikos followed his gaze. A servant had opened the double doors to the salon.

A figure stepped through.

It was the flame-haired temptress!

Nikos felt a kick to his gut that was as powerful as it was unwelcome.

What the hell was she doing here?

The woman had paused for a moment in the doorway—*making sure all eyes were on her*, Nikos thought—and now started to glide forward towards them. Her head was held high—that glorious dark auburn hair twisted up into a topknot that revealed the perfect bone structure of her stunning face.

As for the rest of her…

Nikos felt his breath catch again. The dress was simply breathtaking on her, revealing the lushness of her figure even more generously than the close-fitting jacket had that afternoon. Now, instead of only being able to imagine the rich creaminess of her skin, he could see acres of it displayed for him, from her swan-like neck down across the sculpted beauty of her shoulders, the graceful curve of her bare arms and, best of all, towards the swell of her ripe breasts…

He felt himself ache to caress them…

Like a chill breath on the back of his neck, he felt Yiorgos Coustakis watching him. Watching him lust after his mistress.

Disgust flooded through him. Whatever the hell the old man was playing at, bringing his mistress to dinner, taking pleasure in seeing his guest responding to her lavish charms, he would have none of it! His face hardened.

For Andrea, walking in through the doors and then freezing to a stupefied halt at seeing the very man she had been trying not to think about all evening standing there beside her grandfather, it was like *déjà-vu* all over again. Just as the first sight of her had brought instant sexual appreciation into the man's eyes, so, an instant later, that had been replaced by disdain—all over again.

And, just as she had on the terrace, she reacted instinctively. Her chin went up; her eyes glinted dangerously.

She was glad of her anger—it took her mind off the fact that her heart was racing like a rocket and that her eyes were glued to his face.

She stopped, resting her hand on the back of an antique sofa beside her. Her eyes met those of the stranger, defiant and glittering.

"Well," said Yiorgos Coustakis to the man he had chosen to be his son-in-law, "what do you think of her?"

What the hell do I say? thought Nikos savagely. He said the only thing he could.

"As ever, Yiorgos, you have impeccable taste. She is…outstanding."

They were speaking Greek, Andrea registered. Well, of course they would be! Her eyes flew from one to another.

"You are to be envied," Nikos went on, with gritted politeness, wondering what the hell to say to the old man about the woman he was warming his bed with. Disgust was filling his veins. He wanted out of here—fast.

Yiorgos Coustakis smiled.

"I give her to you," he said. He made a gesture of presentation with his hand. The satisfaction in his voice was blatant.

Nikos froze. *What the hell was this? Was this supposed to be some kind of sweetener that the old man imagined he might want in order to bed his plain, sexless granddaughter?* If so, he had better extricate himself from the delusion.

"Your generosity is…overwhelming, Yiorgos," he managed to get out. "But I cannot accept."

A look of deliberate astonishment lit Yiorgos Coustakis's face. "How is this?" he demanded. "I thought…" He paused infinitesimally, milking the pleasure he was getting from the situation to its utmost, watching this arrogant, ambitious pup squirm for one moment longer. "That you *wanted* my granddaughter? That you were impatient to meet her…"

He gave a short laugh, his eyes snapping with malicious

pleasure as he watched Nikos's face change expression as the truth dawned.

"She is my granddaughter, Nikos—what did you imagine, eh?" he asked softly.

Only Nikos's years of self-discipline enabled him to keep his expression steady. Inside, it felt as if the floor had given way beneath him.

"This is your granddaughter?" he heard himself say, as if seeking confirmation of the unbelievable.

Yiorgos laughed again, still highly pleased with the joke he had played on the younger man. He knew perfectly well what conclusions he had jumped to when, just as Yiorgos had planned, he had first set eyes on the girl that afternoon, sublimely unaware that the plain-faced fiancée he had been led to expect was no such thing at all.

He glanced across at the girl and beckoned imperiously.

"Come here," he commanded in English.

Andrea walked forward. Her heart was pounding again. She could feel it thrilling in every vein. The man with the steel-grey eyes was looking at her full on, and she was all but knocked senseless by the way he was looking at her—either that or jolted by a million volts of electricity scorching through her.

If she'd thought he'd looked a knock-out that afternoon, in his hand-made business suit, the way he looked now, in his tuxedo, simply took her breath away! She swallowed. This was ridiculous! No man should have such an effect on her! She'd seen good-looking blokes before, been eyed up by them—even kissed some in her time—but never, *never* had any man made her feel like this.

Breathless, terrified—enthralled. *Excited!*

Beside the man, her grandfather ceased to exist. She took in a vague impression of a stockily built figure, shoulders bowing with age, and that craggy, heavy-featured face she had registered as he'd sat at his desk that afternoon.

But right now she had no eyes for him.

She was simply drinking in the man at his side—she wanted to stare and stare and stare.

"My granddaughter," said Yiorgos.

Nikos hardly heard him. The entire focus of his attention was on the woman in front of him. *Theos*, but she was fantastic! Was she really the Coustakis girl? It couldn't be possible. Then, with a fraction of his brain that worked, he realised that the old man had set him up deliberately—leading him on to think that he was going to be shackled to a plain wife, when all along...

He smiled. Oh, what the hell—so the old man had set him up! He didn't care! Hell, he could even share the joke! A sense of relief had flooded through him, he realised, and something more—exultation.

Yes! That woman, that fantastic flame-haired temptress, was *not* out of bounds after all. In fact—his smile deepened—she was very, very within bounds...

Andrea saw the smile, brilliant, wolfish, and felt her stomach lurch. Oh, good grief, but he was something all right! She felt the breath squeeze from her body.

Nikos reached and took the girl's hand. He lifted it to his mouth. Andrea watched the dark head bend as if in slow motion. She still couldn't breathe, her lungs frozen as she felt the long, strong fingers take hers.

Then even more sensation laced through her. He was brushing her fingers with his lips. Lightly, oh, so lightly! But oh, oh, so devastatingly. A million nerve endings fired within her, like the *whoosh* of a rocket cascading stars down upon her head.

As he raised his head he smiled down at her.

"Nikos Vassilis," he said, and looked right into her eyes.

His voice was low—the tone intimate.

She stared up at him, lips parted. She could say, or do, nothing.

"Andrea—"

The word breathed from her. She could hardly speak, she found.

"Andrea…" His voice echoed her name, deeper than her husky contralto. "It is good to meet you."

He let his eyes linger on her one last, endless moment, then, tucking her hand into the crook of his arm, he turned to his host.

"You're an old devil, Yiorgos," he said with grating acknowledgement. "But in this instance the joke was worth it."

Andrea's eyes flew between them—the language was back to Greek. What was going on? Then, suddenly, Nikos turned back to her.

"Come, let me take you through to dinner." His voice was warm, and the caress in it made her nerve-endings fire all over again. That and the over-powering closeness of him, her hand caught in his arm. She felt she ought to pull away from him—but for the life of her she could not.

As if in a dream she let herself be escorted from the room, across the vast entrance hall, and into a grandiose dining room.

With the utmost attentiveness this most devastating man, Nikos Vassilis—*Who is he?* she found herself wondering urgently—drew back her chair, waving away the manservant who came forward to perform the task, and settled her in her seat.

She wanted to glance up and smile her thanks politely, but she could not. Shyness suddenly overwhelmed her. This was like something out of a fairytale—she dressed like a princess, and he, oh, he like a dark prince!

Instead she mumbled a thank-you into her place-setting.

As he took his place opposite her—only one end of the long mahogany table was occupied, with Yiorgos taking the head and his granddaughter and her fiancé on either hand— Nikos felt a deep sense of well-being filling him.

He couldn't have asked for a more beautiful bride! Old Man Coustakis was doing him proud. Oh, he would never have been unkind, even to a plain wife, but having that flame-haired beauty at his side, in his bed, was going to make married life a whole, whole lot sweeter for him!

He glanced across at her. She was still staring at her place-setting as if it was the most interesting thing in the room, but she was aware of him all right. Every male instinct told him that. But if she were behaving as a well-brought-up young girl should—showing a proper shyness in the face of the man she was to marry—well, who was he to complain?

A memory of the way she had boldly walked up to him on the terrace, her voice husky as she sought to introduce herself, intruded, conflicting with the image of the meekly downturned head opposite him. A frown flickered in his eyes. Then it cleared. She must have seen the look he had given her then and been angered by it—and rightfully so! No gently reared female would care to be taken for such a one as he had first thought her. Well, now that misunderstanding was out of the way it would not trouble them again.

Another frown flickered in his eyes. The girl was English, that was obvious—both by her colouring and her use of the language, quite unaccented.

As the manservant drew forward to start serving dinner Nikos glanced at his host.

"You did not tell me that your granddaughter was half-English, Yiorgos," he opened. He spoke in Greek, and as he did he noticed Andrea's head lift, her eyes focus intently on him, concentrating.

Yiorgos leant back in his chair.

"A little surprise for you," he answered. His eyes gleamed.

Nikos let his mouth twist. "Another one," he acknowledged. Then he turned his attention to Andrea.

"You live in England? With your English mother?" he

asked politely, in Greek. That must be the reason she had addressed him in English this afternoon.

Andrea looked at him. She made as if to open her mouth, but her grandfather forestalled her.

"She does not speak Greek," he said bluntly. He spoke in English.

Nikos's eyes snapped together. "How is this?" he demanded, sticking with English.

"Let us say her mother had her own ideas about her upbringing," said Yiorgos.

Andrea stared at her grandfather—just stared. Then, as if knowing exactly why she was staring, he caught her eye. Dark, intent. Warning.

His words echoed in her mind from the afternoon. *You will be on the first plane back to London unless you do exactly, exactly, what I want you to do!*

She felt her blood chill. Was going along with some fairy story he wanted to tell this guest of his about her upbringing part of that imprecation? What do I do? she thought wildly. Open my mouth and set the record straight right away?

And achieve what, precisely?

She knew the answer. Get herself thrown out of her grandfather's house and sent back to London without a penny for her mother. And she wouldn't go home empty-handed; she *wouldn't*! She would get Kim the money she deserved, whatever it took. Even if it meant colluding with Yiorgos Coustakis's attempt to whitewash his behaviour.

So she buttoned her lip and stayed silent.

From across the table Nikos saw her expression, saw the mutinous gleam in those lustrous chestnut eyes. So, the girl had been brought up in England, by a mother who had her own ideas, had she? Ideas that included depriving the Coustakis heiress of her natural heritage—the language of her father, the household of her grandfather. What kind of mother had she been? he wondered. An image presented itself in his mind—one of those sharp-tongued, upper-class, arrogant Englishwomen, expensively dressed, enjoying a social round of polo and house-parties at one stately home after another. He frowned. Why had she married Andreas Coustakis in the first place? he wondered. Doubtless the marriage would not have lasted, even if Yiorgos's son had not been killed so young. He found himself wondering why Yiorgos had so uncharacteristically let the widow take his granddaughter back to England with her, instead of keeping her in his household. Well, his generosity had been ill-paid! Now he had a granddaughter who could not even speak his own language!

I could teach her...

Another image swept into his mind. That of this flame-haired beauty lying in his arms as he taught her some of the more essential things that a Greek bride needed to be able to tell her husband—such as her desire for him...

He let his imagination dwell pleasantly on the prospect as they began to dine.

Through his long lashes, Nikos watched with amusement as Andrea began to eat appreciatively. Though he was pleased to see her take evident sensuous delight in fine food—Esme's gruelling diet had always irritated him, and Xanthe was picky about what she ate as well—he would have to keep an eye on his bride's appetite. At the moment she could get away with hearty eating—her figure was lush and queenly, and she carried no surplus pounds at all, he could tell—but if she continued to put food away like that for the next twenty years she would be fat by forty! A thought struck him. How old was she, exactly? When he'd first set eyes on her he'd taken her for twenty-five or so, but surely Yiorgos would not have kept her unmarried for so long? She must be younger. Probably her English mother and that sophisticated aristocratic society she doubtless enjoyed had served to make her appear more mature than she really was.

Yet another thought struck him, less pleasant. If she'd been brought up in England just how sure could he be that she was coming to him unsullied? English girls were notoriously free with their favours—every Greek male knew that, and most of them took advantage of it if they got the chance! Upper-class English girls were no longer pure as the driven snow—some of them started their sexual lives at a shamefully early age. Could she still be a virgin? He thought of asking Yiorgos outright, but knew what the answer would be—*Do you care enough to walk away from Coustakis Industries, my friend?*

And he knew what his own answer to that would be.

Virgin or no, he would marry Andrea Coustakis and get Coustakis Industries as her dowry.

Eating the delicious dinner—there seemed to be an endless array of courses—served to take Andrea's mind a fraction off the man opposite her. But only by a minute amount. Then, just as she was beginning to calm, he started talking to her.

"What part of England do you live in, Andrea?" he asked her civilly, clearly making conversation.

"London," she replied, daring to glance across at him briefly.

"A favourite city of mine. Your life there must be pretty hectic, I guess?"

"Yes," said, thinking of the two jobs she held down, working weekends as well as evenings, putting aside every penny she could to help pay off those debts hanging over her mother. Kim worked too, in the local late-night-opening supermarket—neither of them got much time off.

"So what are the best clubs in London at the moment, do you think?" Nikos went on, naming a couple of fashionable hot-spots that Andrea vaguely recognised from glossy magazines.

"Clubbing really isn't my scene," she answered. Not only did she get little free time to go out, but the kind of nightlife available in her part of London was not the kind to feature in glossy magazines. Anyway, dancing was out for her, and Kim had brought her up to appreciate classical music best.

"Oh," replied Nikos, realising he felt pleased with her answer. Clubbing was strongly associated with sexual promiscuity, and he found himself reassured by her answer. "What is your 'scene', then, Andrea?"

She looked at him. Presumably he was just making polite conversation to his host's granddaughter.

"I like the theatre," she said. It was true—the biggest treat she could give Kim, and herself, was to see the Royal Shakespeare Company, visit the National Theatre, or go to any of the great wealth of other theatres London had to offer. But tickets were expensive, so it was something they did not indulge themselves in often.

Nikos named a couple of spectacular musicals running in the West End currently—obviously he was no stranger to London, Andrea thought. She shook her head. Tickets for such extravaganzas were even more expensive than for ordinary theatre.

"I prefer Shakespeare," she said.

She could tell, immediately, she had given the wrong answer. She glanced warily at her grandfather. His eyes had altered somehow, and she could sense his disapproval focussing on her. Now what? she wondered. Wasn't it OK for her to like Shakespeare, for heaven's sake?

She got her answer a moment later.

"No man likes a woman who is intellectually pretentious," the old man said brusquely.

Andrea blinked. Liking Shakespeare was intellectually pretentious?

"Shakespeare wrote popular plays for mass audiences," she pointed out mildly. "There's nothing intellectually élite about his work, if it isn't treated as such. Of course there are huge depths to his writing, which can keep academics happy for years dissecting it, but the plays can be enjoyed on many levels. They're very accessible, especially in modern productions which make every effort to draw in those who, like you, are put off by the aura surrounding Shakespeare."

Yiorgos set down his knife and fork. His eyes snapped with anger.

"Stop babbling like an imbecile, girl! Hold your tongue if you've nothing useful to say! No man likes a woman trying to show off!"

Astonishment was the emotion uppermost in Andrea's reaction. She simply couldn't believe that she was being criticised for defending her enjoyment of Shakespeare. Automatically, she found herself glancing across at Nikos Vassilis. Did he share her grandfather's antediluvian views on women and their "intellectual pretensions'?

To her relief, as she met his eye she realised that there was a distinct gleam of conspiratorial humour in it.

"So," said Nikos smoothly, coming to the girl's rescue after her grandfather's reprimand, "what is your favourite Shakespeare play?" He ignored the glare coming from his host at his continuing with a line of conversation he disapproved of.

Andrea ignored it too, glad to find her grandfather's dinner guest was more liberal in his expectations of female interests.

"*Much Ado About Nothing,*" she replied promptly. "Beatrice and Benedict are my favourite hero and heroine! I just love the verbal warfare between them—she always answers back to every jibe he puts on her, and never lets him put her down!"

The humour vanished from Nikos's eyes. A bride with a penchant for a heroine specialising in verbal warfare with her future husband was not his ideal. However stunning her auburn looks, he found himself wishing that the Coustakis heiress was all-Greek after all. A pure Greek bride would never dream of taking pleasure in answering her husband back!

Andrea saw his disapproval of her choice, and her mouth tightened. Nikos Vassilis might be a drop-dead smoothie, but scratch him and he was cut from the same metal as her grandfather, it seemed. Women were not there to be anything other than ornamental and docile.

She gave a mental shrug. Well, who cared what Nikos Vassilis thought women should be—let alone her grandfather? She wasn't here to win the approval of either.

She went back to eating her dinner. Across the table, Nikos was distracted from thinking further about the woman he had elected to marry by Yiorgos peremptorily asking his opinion on some aspect of global economic conditions. Clearly he had heard quite enough from his granddaughter. It was obviously time for her to revert to being ornamental and docile. And silent. Knowing nothing about global economic conditions, only a great deal about her straitened personal ones, Andrea tuned out.

Then, after the final course had been removed—and she felt as if she could never look another rich, luxurious dish in the face again—her grandfather abruptly pushed his chair back.

"We will take coffee in the salon, after I have checked the US markets," he announced. He looked meaningfully at Nikos as he stood up. "Join me in twenty minutes."

He left the dining room. Nikos glanced after him, then back at Andrea.

"Even at his age he does not relinquish his mastery, not for a moment," he said. He sounded, thought Andrea, almost approving.

"Surely he's got enough money," she said tartly.

Nikos, who had got to his feet as the older man had risen, looked down at her.

"Easy to say that," he observed evenly, "when you have lived in luxury all your life."

She stared at him. Again, astonishment was uppermost in her breast. Was this more of her grandfather's fairytale at work? She said nothing—Nikos Vassilis was the dinner guest of the man who was going to fund her mother's removal to Spain. Baring her family's unpleasant secrets to him was unnecessary.

He came around to her side of the table and held out his hand, a smile parting his lips. "Come," he said. "We have been given twenty minutes to ourselves. Let us make the most of them."

Thinking that the company of Nikos Vassilis was a good deal more bearable than that of her grandfather—even if he clearly didn't like her approving of Shakespeare's feisty heroine Beatrice!—Andrea went along with him. He escorted her, hand tucked into the crook of his arm again—a most disturbingly arousing sensation, she rediscovered—from the dining room, opening large French windows to emerge out on to the same terrace where she had first seen him that afternoon. After the brightness of the dining room the dim night outside made her blink until she got her night vision. She glanced up.

The night sky was ablaze with stars. Though it was early summer still, the air was much warmer than it would have been in England. She gave a little sigh of pleasure and walked forward, disengaging herself to place her hands on the balustrade and look out over the dim gardens.

All around in the darkness she could hear a soft chirruping noise.

"What's that?" she asked, puzzled.

"You would call them by their Spanish name, I think—cicadas," said Nikos behind her. He had come up to her and was, she realised, standing very close to her. It made her feel wary, and something more, too, that made her heart beat faster. "They are like grasshoppers, and live in bushes—they are the most characteristic sound of the Mediterranean at night." He gave a frown. "Surely you have heard them before?" he asked.

Whether or not she had been brought up in England, it was impossible to imagine that a girl from a background as wealthy as hers would not be well-travelled, especially in fashionable parts of the Mediterranean.

She shook her head, not really paying him much attention. Cicadas—so that was what they sounded like. She remembered how her mother, when Andrea was just a little girl, asking after the father she had never known, had sat on her bed and told her, her soft voice sad and happy at the same time, how she had walked along the sea's edge, so many years ago, hand in hand with the man she loved, heard the soft lapping of the Aegean, the murmurous sound of cicadas in the vegetation. Her heart squeezed—*Oh Mum, why did he have to die like that?*

"What are you thinking of?" Nikos asked in a low voice as his fingers drifted along the bare cusp of her shoulder.

That the touch of your fingers is like velvet electricity…

"Just someone I think about a lot," she answered, trying to make her voice sound normal when every nerve in her body was focussed on the sensations of his skin touching hers.

Why is he touching me? He shouldn't! He's only just met me!

She wanted to move away, but she couldn't.

"A man?" There was the slightest edge in his voice, but she didn't hear it. She was only aware of the drift of his fingers on her bare shoulder.

"Yes," she said dreamily.

His hand fell away.

"What is his name?" The question was a harsh demand. She turned, confused. Why was he angry? What on earth made him think he had any business being angry? Was it just because an unmarried Greek girl shouldn't think of men?

"Andreas," she answered tightly. As she spoke she found herself noticing that anger, though it shouldn't, seemed to have sharpened his features into bold relief. He looked, though she shouldn't think it, even more gorgeous.

"Andreas? Andreas who?"

She lifted her chin. Whatever right this complete stranger seemed to think he had subjecting her to an inquisition, she answered him straight.

"Andreas Coustakis," she bit out. "My father."

He was taken aback, she could see.

"Your father?" His voiced echoed hollowly. He nodded his head stiffly. "My apologies." He paused. "You knew him?"

She shook her head. Her throat felt tight. He must have walked on this very terrace, she suddenly thought. Known this house. Stormed from it the night he was killed…

"No. But my mother…tells me of him…"

Nikos heard the betraying husk in her voice. It struck a chord in him deeper than he had thought possible. He, too, had never known his father. Never even known who he was…

And his mother had never talked of him, except to say that he had been a sailor on shore leave. From a northern clime. Given his son's height, a Scandinavian, perhaps? She hadn't known. Hadn't cared.

Andrea's mother had cared. Cared enough to tell her daughter about the father she had never known.

A shaft of envy went through him.

"What does she tell you?" he heard himself asking.

Was it the soft Aegean night? Andrea wondered. The kind,

concealing blanket of the dark that made her feel, suddenly, that she could tell this man anything—that he would understand?

"She tells me how much she loved him," she answered, her eyes skimming out into the darkness of the gardens below, lit by the stars above. "How he loved her, so dearly. How he called her his sweet dove—how he would lay the world at her feet…"

Her voice broke.

"And then he died." The sob sounded deep in her throat. "And the dream ended."

Tears pricked in her eyes. Blinding her vision. Blinding her senses. So she did not feel his arms come around her, turning her into him, folding her head upon his chest so that the tears might come.

"Hush," he murmured. "Hush."

For a long, timeless moment she let herself be held by this man, this complete stranger, who had shown her so unexpectedly the kindness of strangers.

"I'm sorry," she mumbled. "I think it's being here, in the house he lived in, and realising how real he once was."

She pulled away from him, but he caught her elbows so she could not back away completely.

"Don't be ashamed to weep for him," he said to her quietly. "You honour him with your tears."

She lifted her face to his. The tears gleamed on her lashes like diamonds beneath the starry heavens. Her soft mouth quivered.

He could not help himself. Could not have stopped himself if an earthquake had rumbled beneath his feet.

His mouth lowered to hers. Caught her sweetness, her ripeness. His hands slipped from her elbows, around her slender back, pulling her in towards him.

She gave a soft gasp, and it was enough. His tongue

slipped between her parted lips, tasting the nectar within. He moved his mouth slowly, but, oh, so sensuously on hers, and he felt her tremble in his arms.

A rush of desire flooded through him. She was exactly how he wanted her to be. Her body ripe in his arms, her mouth tender beneath his.

He deepened his kiss, his hands as of their own volition sliding down her back to shape the rich roundness of her bottom.

Sensation whirled through Andrea. She felt as if she was melting against him, her body moulding to his, and her mouth—oh, her mouth was like a flower, dissolving in sweetness.

Warm shivers ran through her body. She couldn't think, couldn't focus on anything, anything at all, except the sensations flooding through her veins, liquid, honeyed, sweeping her away, drowning her in desire.

And then, with a rasp of reality, she surfaced, pulling away from him. She was shocked, trembling.

"No—" The denial breathed from her, eyes distended. Heart pounding.

What was she denying? she thought wildly. Denying his helping himself to her? Denying that a moment's brief human comfort had suddenly been transformed into a sensuousness so overwhelming she was reeling with it?

Or more? Denying—and her stomach clenched as she faced up to what she was really denying—denying that never, ever in her whole life had she ever dreamt it was possible to feel such sensations…

He had not let her go, she realised. Although she had pulled away, he was holding her still, his hands in the small of her back. She was arching back, away from him, totally unaware of how the gesture thrust her breasts towards him, making him ache to bend his head and touch his mouth to their swollen fullness, aroused, all against her knowledge, to crested peaks.

"No—" she breathed again. Her hands came up to the corded strength of his arms and tried to dislodge them.

He felt the pressure on them and released her immediately, though it went against every primal instinct, which was to keep her close against him, closer still, press her warm, ripe body against his, moulding her to him, feeling every rich curve, every soft, delicious inch of her...

Theos, but he wanted her! Wanted her with an urgent aching that was nothing, he realised, nothing at all like the controlled, detached sexual desire that he felt for Esme, or Xanthe—or any other woman he had ever bedded, he realised with a shock.

Was it because this woman here, now, was to be his bride, his wife? Was it the primeval emotion of bonding, cleaving, that had released something in him he had never known existed?

Until now?

A rush of fierce possessiveness surged through him. It was like a revelation. He had never felt possessive about his women before—had always known that for them he was just one more male, just better-looking, richer—or both—than most of the men they took to their beds. Exclusivity, on either side, was not a word applied to the relationships he had enjoyed. He knew perfectly well that Esme Vandersee had a whole court she picked her lovers from, depending on her whim and their availability in her hectic globe-trotting life. And Xanthe—well, he was not the only man keeping her in the luxury she enjoyed so much. Of course she was skilful enough, tactful enough, never to let her lovers catch a glimpse of each other, but Nikos could have named a handful of wealthy Athenians who enjoyed her carefully disposed favours.

It didn't bother him.

Not like the thought of Andrea Coustakis thinking about another man...

The rush of possessiveness intensified. It was as alien as it was heady, and he gave himself to it totally.

Then, as the rush consumed him, he realised that he was going too fast—much too fast. Too fast for him—and certainly too fast for her.

His eyes focussed on hers.

She was standing, backed against the balustrade, still close enough for him to reach and pull her to him, but he did not. The expression in her eyes stopped him.

They were shocked, staring.

For a moment exultation speared him. She felt the same way he did! As if a revelation had suddenly made her see the world in a completely different way. Then, with a sobering recognition, he realised that her reaction to what had just happened was more complex than his.

More fearful.

"Andrea," he said softly, "don't be alarmed. I'm sorry— I'm rushing things too much." A wry smile tugged at his mouth as she stared at him, half of her mind drinking in the male beauty of his face, the other still too shocked to take in anything at all. "You must blame your beauty," he told her. "It is too lovely to resist."

She shivered. He fancied her, and so, on the briefest acquaintance imaginable, he had pounced on her?

"Don't look at me like that," he said ruefully. "I will not touch you again until you want me to. But you must not blame me—" the tug of wry humour came again to his well-shaped mouth in a way that did strange things to her insides "—if I try very hard to make you want me to touch you again..."

He stepped back a pace, giving her more space.

"Come," he said and his breath was more ragged than he

preferred, "take my hand, if nothing else, and let us talk a while. We have, after all, much to talk about."

He took her hand, and she let its cool strength curl around her fingers and draw her away from the balustrade. They began to head down towards the far end of the terrace at a leisurely pace. The night air fanned Andrea's heated face and gave her a moment's breathing space.

But her mind was racing as fast as her heart!

What was she doing out here on a starlit terrace with a man who took her breath away, who had casually kissed her as she had never been kissed in her life?

A man she didn't even know.

But who had promised to make her want him touch her again...

What was it he had said? she wondered. *"We have, after all, much to talk about."*

Puzzlement suffused her. Was that some kind of Greek pick-up line? Or was he simply trying to take the pressure off her and make polite chit-chat again?

She looked up at him as they walked.

"Why have we got so much to talk about?" she asked. Her voice was still husky, even though she did not mean it to be. It was also puzzled.

He glanced down at her. His lashes were extraordinarily long, she found herself thinking irrelevantly. It made her completely miss what he said in answer.

Except for one word.

She stopped in her tracks.

"Say that again," she said. Her breathing seemed to have stopped.

Nikos smiled down again at her, his eyes warm.

"I said, my sweet bride-to-be, that perhaps we should start by talking about our wedding."

Andrea's breathing stopped totally.

CHAPTER FIVE

IT WAS as if, in front of his eyes, she had changed. Like some alien shape-shifting from a harmless creature into some terrifying monster.

She thrust her hand from him, backing away, freezing as she did so.

"Our *what*?"

"Our wedding," he repeated. His voice was tighter now, automatically responding to the visible rejection her whole body was projecting.

She was staring at him as if he had grown another head.

"Our *wedding*?" She could hardly get the word out. Then, as terror seized her, she found her voice. Only a frail one. "Oh, my God," she breathed, as the only possible truth dawned, "you're some kind of lunatic—"

She swirled around, catching at the narrow skirt of her dress, forcing her legs—weak, suddenly—to hurry back along the stone terrace towards the lights—the safety—of the open French windows at the other end.

He caught her wrist before she could even take a single frantic step.

"*What* did you call me?"

The circle of his strong fingers crushed her bones. She tugged to free herself, but to no avail.

"Let me go!" The fear was naked in her voice now, her eyes wide with panic.

His face darkened. "What the hell is going on?" he demanded. "I simply said we ought to discuss our wedding— I am quite prepared to give you as free a hand as possible, but I have to say," he went on, still at a loss to account for the bizarre reaction he was getting from her, "I would prefer to be married here in Greece."

"*Married?*" She echoed the word with total incredulity.

"Yes, married. Andrea, why on earth are you behaving like this?" There was impatience in his voice, as well as bewilderment.

"Married to *you*?"

His mouth thinned. It was the way she said that, as if it was the most outrageous idea in the world. He glared down at her.

He let her hand go abruptly. She rubbed her wrist, and would have tried to bolt to the doors leading inside, but he was blocking her back against the stone balustrade.

"We need to talk," he said abruptly.

Andrea shook her head violently. The only thing she needed to do was to get inside, away from this lunatic who had suddenly gone nuts and started talking about weddings and getting married...

"Answer me," he commanded. "Why did you let me kiss you just now if you did not believe that I would marry you?"

Her heart was plummeting around all over the place inside her. Panic was nipping at her, ready to explode again at any moment. Now it did.

"Oh my God, you are completely nuts!" She tried to push past him, but he was an immovable block.

Nikos, not moving an iota, gave a heavy, impatient sigh and tried hard to hold on to his patience. Why she was throwing this fit of hysterics was incomprehensible. Could it really be that she did not know about their marriage? How could that possibly be? Of course she knew! She *must* know! So why the hysterics now?

Did she not *want* to marry him?

The thought enraged him suddenly! How dared she lead him on as she had this evening, letting him taste the sweetness of her lips, inflaming his desire with the allure of her body, if she did not agree to their marriage? And why should she not agree? What, if you please, was so very wrong about the idea of being his wife?

Perhaps because you are the bastard son of a barmaid and an unknown sailor?

The poisonous root took hold and would not be shaken loose. His jaw tightened. If she had objected to their marriage on those grounds she had had time enough to make her opinions clear to her grandfather.

And was Yiorgos Coustakis the kind of man to listen to his granddaughter's objections about the social origins of her intended husband?

He thrust the thought from him. It was irrelevant. Right now he simply had to stop her throwing a full-scale fit of hysterics.

"Be still. You are not going anywhere until you have calmed down—"

His words were cut off by a sharp expletive as he registered pain in his shins. Then, as he was caught off-balance, Andrea thrust him back with all her strength and hurtled as fast as her evening dress would allow towards the open doors at the end of the terrace.

Pain forgotten, Nikos surged after her and intercepted her at the threshold to the dining room.

"Enough!" He was angry now. His hands closed over her shoulders and he gave her a brusque shake. "Behave yourself! There is no need for such a ludicrous reaction to what I have said!"

As he spoke, it dawned on Nikos that that was what was angering him most of all—her instant and total rejection of the notion of marrying him! He found it intolerable! Here he was, having steeled himself for the past couple of weeks to doing the unthinkable—marrying at all, and to a complete stranger—and then finally, tonight, to have all his worries so deliciously and unexpectedly set aside by seeing just what a peach the Coustakis heiress actually was…and here she was having a fit of hysterics over it! As if the prospect of marrying Nikos Vassilis was the most repellent in the world!

Andrea arrowed her hands and forearms up between his and jerked them sideways with a violent movement to free herself. Her heart was pounding now—panic, disbelief and above all hot, boiling anger was pouring through her.

She could not believe what she had just heard—couldn't *believe* it! It couldn't be true! It just couldn't!

Her face twisted. "This is some kind of joke, yes? Talking about me marrying you! Some idiotic, warped idea of a joke, right?"

Nikos bristled. A joke, the idea of marrying him? A fatherless bastard raised on the streets of Athens? His face darkened. He looked scary suddenly, she realised.

"You are the Coustakis heiress," he said coldly. "I am the man who will take over the company when your grandfather retires. What else but we should marry?"

"The Coustakis heiress?" Andrea echoed in a strange voice. A laugh escaped her. High-pitched. Distorted. She took a deep, shuddering breath. "Let me get this right. You, Mr Vassilis, want to marry me because I am Yiorgos Coustakis's granddaughter and you want to run his company for him—is that it?"

He assented with a brief, glancing nod of his dark head. "That is so. I am glad you understand."

Completely missing the ironic tone of his voice, she took

another breath—a tight one this time. "Well, sorry to disappoint you, chum, but it's no go. You'll have to find yourself another heiress to marry!"

She made to turn away. She felt in urgent need of escape, not just into the villa, but up to the sanctuary of her own room.

An arm barred her way in.

"You are offensive."

The voice was soft, but it raised the hairs on the back of Andrea's neck.

She turned back slowly. Nikos Vassilis was very close. Far too close.

"*I* am offensive? Mr Vassilis, you are a guest in my grandfather's house and I suggest you start remembering your responsibilities in that role." She spoke in as forbearing a manner as possible, which was extremely taxing in the circumstances. "I make due allowance for the different customs in Greece, but if you imagine that kissing me on a terrace somehow converts instantly into a proposal of marriage you are living in the Middle Ages! You have *not*, I do assure you, compromised me into marrying you! So you can just forget all about blackmailing my grandfather into marrying me off to you just because I was stupid enough to fall into your arms like a…like an *idiot*!"

Her anger was with herself as much as him. This was what came of letting herself be swept away by a drop-dead gorgeous stranger on a starlit terrace! He suddenly got ideas of catching himself a rich wife. A sudden, inexplicable stab of pain went through her as she realised that that was all the kiss had meant to him—it had been nothing to do with *her*, just a cheap way to entrap the girl he thought was Yiorgos Coustakis's heir!

The Coustakis heiress he had called her! Hysterical laughter threatened in her throat. God, it might almost be worth indulging his insane pretensions just for the joy of seeing her grandfather's reaction when he demanded marriage to save the "honour" of the offspring of a woman he'd called a slut to her face—and her daughter's!

"Blackmail?" The word ground out. Furious outrage seared in Nikos's voice. To have his behaviour likened to that of Yiorgos Coustakis when he had forced his father-in-law's hand to get his daughter and her dowry was insupportable. "How dare you make such an accusation!"

Andrea threw back her head. "What else should I call it? Sliming around after me like a dog sniffing out a bone! Well, let me tell you something, Mr Vassilis—my grandfather will laugh in your face at the idea of your marrying me to get hold of Coustakis Industries!"

The scorn in her voice enraged him.

"You are mistaken." His voice was icy. "It was his idea in the first place."

She stilled.

"Are you saying—" her voice was choked "—that my grandfather is in on this?" Her insides were hollowing out all over again. "My *grandfather* wants me to marry you?"

"What else?" Could it really be that she did not know? That Old Man Coustakis had not bothered to tell his granddaughter what his plans were? Another of his "little jokes", Nikos thought grimly to himself.

"Let me get this straight." Andrea's voice was controlled. "My grandfather wants *me* to marry *you*—"

"In exchange for my taking over Coustakis Industries when he retires, which will be shortly after our marriage. It is all agreed between us," Nikos elucidated. He felt in no mood to spare the girl's feelings any more. Her reaction to the discovery of their betrothal was insult enough to warrant his spelling out the financial grounds of their marriage very, very clearly.

"How very convenient." Her voice was flat. And still very, very controlled.

"Is it not?" agreed Nikos. The irony was back in his voice.

Disbelief washed over Andrea, wave after wave. Total disbelief at what she had heard. She felt quite faint with it. Then, deep, deep inside, she felt the waves break upon some hard, immovable bedrock.

"Excuse me—"

She moved past Nikos Vassilis. The man who had just told her that her grandfather—her dear, kind grandfather, who had ignored her existence all her life—had plans for her. Marriage plans.

Marriage!

She had thought Nikos Vassilis insane, and assumed he was just chancing it. But his assumptions were based on something much, much more solid than a soft, seductive kiss…

As she walked across the dining room she could feel the rage mounting. Misting over her eyes like a red miasma. She marched through the double doors into the wide, marble-floored hallway and strode across, flinging open the doors to the library.

At her entrance her grandfather looked up from the bank of computer screens flickering on the console drawn up beside his mahogany desk.

"Out!"

The order was given imperiously. She ignored it. She surged forward.

"This man," she burst out, gesturing wildly behind her to where Nikos had paused in the doorway, following her dramatic entrance, "has announced that he will be marrying me! I want you to tell him *right now* that it's not going to happen!"

Her grandfather's face had hardened.

"You heard him correctly. Why else would I send for you? Now, leave—you are disturbing me."

The sick hollowness caverned in Andrea's stomach.

"Are you completely out of your mind?" Her voice was hard—hard, and trembling with fury. "Are you completely insane—to bring me here, spring this on me and think I'd go along with it? What the *hell* do you think you're playing at?"

Yiorgos Coustakis got to his feet. He was no taller than his granddaughter, but his bulk was considerable.

And suddenly very, very formidable.

Almost she faltered. Almost she quailed beneath the look of excoriation on his lined, powerful face. But rage carried her forward.

"You must be *mad* to think you can do this! You must be completely ma—"

Her denunciation was cut short. A look of blinding fury flashed across Yiorgos Coustakis's face.

"Be silent!" he snarled. "You will not speak in such a fashion! Go to your room! I will deal with you in the morning!"

She stopped dead.

"Excuse me?" Her eyes were wide with disbelief. "You think you can give me orders? I am not one of your hapless lackeys!"

"No, you are my granddaughter, and as such I demand obedience!"

Andrea's mouth fell open.

"Demand away," she told him scornfully. "Obedience isn't a word in my vocabulary."

Behind her, Nikos's eyes narrowed. He was witnessing, he knew, something that very few people had ever seen—someone standing up to the vicious, domineering and totally ruthless head of Coustakis Industries.

For a brief, fleeting second Andrea could see by the expression in her grandfather's heavy hooded eyes that he had *never* been spoken to in such a fashion. Then, swiftly, his face hardened into implacable fury at her defiance of him.

"You will leave this room now or I will have you removed!
Do you understand?"

He jabbed his finger at an intercom button on his desk and
snarled something into the speaker in Greek. Then he turned
his attention back to Andrea.

She was in front of the wide desk now, adrenaline running
in every vein. She was simply too furious to be frightened.
Besides, deep down in her consciousness she knew that if for
a moment she gave in to her grandfather, let herself be cowed
by him, it would all be over. He would have won and she
would have been reduced to a terrified, intimidated wreck.
Just the way he had terrified and intimated her mother. Well,
he was not going to do the same to her! No way! It was essential, absolutely essential, that she outface him.

And she had every right to be angry—every right! The
very idea that he had been discussing marriage…*marriage!*…at all, let alone behind her back like this, was so appalling she could hardly believe it to be true. It couldn't be
true! It just couldn't!

"I'll go when I'm ready!" she bit at him. "When you tell
me that this lunatic you invited here is out of his mind!"

She had enraged her grandfather all over again.

"Silence! You will not shame me in my own home, you
mannerless brat! And you will not speak of your betrothed
husband like that!" The flat of his hand slammed on the
surface of his desk to emphasise his anger.

Andrea's eyes widened with shock. "You don't mean that,"
she said. "You don't seriously mean that. You can't! Tell me
this is some kind of idiotic joke the two of you are playing!"

Yiorgos Coustakis's face was like stone.

"How dare you raise your voice to me? Why do you think
you are here? You are betrothed to Nikos Vassilis and will
marry him next week. Anything else is not your concern!
That is an end to it! Now, go to your room!"

Faintness drummed at her. This was unreal. It had to be. It just had to be…

"You can't *possibly* have brought me here for such an outrageous idea," she said. Her breathing was heavy, heart pounding in her chest. "It's the most insane thing I've ever heard in my life! And *you* must be insane to think I'd go along with it!"

Somewhere, behind her, she could hear a sharp intake of breath. She didn't care. A whole lot of anger was coming out now—twenty-five years worth of anger against the man who had behaved so unforgivably to her mother. She owed him nothing—nothing at all.

And as for this insane idea of his…

Her grandfather was standing up, coming out from behind his desk. His face was almost purple with anger.

The blow to the side of her head sent her reeling. She gasped with the pain and the shock, unable to believe that she had just been struck. Automatically she stepped back, almost tripping in her long tight skirt, raising her right forearm into a blocking gesture.

"Go to your room! This instant!" snarled Yiorgos Coustakis again. His eyes cut into her like knives.

Lowering her guard by merely a fraction, Andrea thrust her head forward. "If you ever hit me again I'll send you flying, so help me! You're a vile, callous *bastard*, and you don't push me around, not *ever*, so get that through your head right now!"

"Get out of here!" A stream of vituperative Greek poured out of Yiorgos Coustakis's mouth.

She took a deep, shuddering breath. "I'm going. Don't worry! But before I go," she said, her jaw tight with controlled rage, "you had better understand something! I am *not* some pawn, some patsy for your vile machinations! The very *idea* that you seriously thought you could marry me off like some *chattel* is so ludicrous I can't *believe* you even entertained it for a second! So go take a hike, Yiorgos Coustakis!"

She saw his hand lift again and threw her arm back up to block him just in time. The blow landed on her arm-bone, jarring it painfully, but it had shielded her face.

She screamed, in shock, rage, pain and horror, and then suddenly her left arm was being taken in a grip she could not shake off, her right arm forcibly lowered from its blocking position.

"Enough—"

Nikos's voice was harsh and imperative. It was directed at both of them.

Yiorgos's face was contorted, eyes alight with a viciousness that would have scared her had she not been so overwhelmed. Then his eyes shot past her, towards the door. Two men were standing there, deferentially awaiting further orders. Nikos's head swivelled around to look at them. Security guards.

"Get her out of here," Yiorgos Coustakis instructed them curtly. His breathing was heavy, his colour dangerously high. The two men started towards Andrea.

"Stop." Nikos's voice held the note of command and it stopped the men in their tracks.

Andrea twisted in Nikos's unshakeable grip, taking in the uniformed men. Her eyes had widened yet again, in even greater disbelief.

"This is not necessary, Yiorgos," said Nikos tightly.

"Then *you* get her out," growled his host. "And you had best take a whip to her to control her! She needs a good beating!" He raised his hand again, as if he would start the process himself, and willingly.

"You *bastard*!" spat Andrea at her grandfather.

Nikos jerked her backwards, turning her around to get her out of the room.

She went. Getting away from that vile, ugly scene was suddenly the most urgent thing in the world. As she was frogmarched out she tried to shake herself free.

"Let me go! I'm getting out of here!"

As they entered the hallway, the two security guards stepping smartly aside to let them pass, Nikos released her.

"You little savage! What were you thinking of, behaving like that? Do you run so wild you can't have a civil discussion without yelling your head off?"

Her eyes flared.

"He hit me! He *hit* me and you defend him?"

Nikos, exasperated, gave a sharp intake of breath. "No, of course I do not defend him, but—"

The two security staff walked by, heading back to their own quarters. Nikos waited till they were out of earshot. He knew the type. Utterly professional, utterly incurious. They would do the bidding of their employer, whatever orders they were given. Manhandling a young woman upstairs to her bedroom would have been a piece of cake for them.

A thought struck him and he called out after the men as they were about to disappear. Old Man Coustakis had looked fit to have a seizure—him dropping dead right now would be highly inconvenient.

"Send Kyrios Coustakis's valet to him—he may need attention."

One of the men paused and nodded, then went off with his companion. Nikos glanced back at the woman he had agreed to marry for the sake of Coustakis Industries. His mouth tightened.

Andrea was holding the back of her hand to her reddened cheek. Her own colour was high, irrespective of the blow she had taken. *Theos*, she had obviously inherited the old man's temper, thought Nikos. What a termagant!

An immense sense of exasperation overcame him. What

the hell was he doing here, stuck in the middle of a battle between Old Man Coustakis and his spitting she-wolf of a granddaughter? Why the hell couldn't the old man have sorted it out first with the girl, telling her about the husband he had chosen for her instead of letting him get caught in the cross-fire like this?

He needed a drink. A strong one. Perhaps that would calm the girl down as well.

She was still trembling with anger. His frown deepened. Her ear and cheek were still red where Yiorgos's hand had impacted.

He tilted her face into the light. "Let me see."

She brushed his arm aside, and jerked free. "Don't touch me!" she spat.

She was still in complete meltdown, chest heaving, stomach churning, adrenaline going crazy inside her.

"You need a drink—it will calm you down." He spoke grimly.

He took her elbow again, and this time Andrea let herself be led back into the drawing room. She collapsed down on a silk-upholstered sofa while Nikos went to raid the antique inlaid drinks cabinet. He returned with two generous measures of brandy.

"Drink," he ordered, handing Andrea one of the glasses.

She took a sip, finding her hands were shaking. The fiery liquid seemed to steady her, and she took another sip. Across the room Nikos was standing, his expression closed and moody, one hand pushing back his tuxedo jacket, resting on the waistband of his trousers. Absently she noticed the way the white lawn shirt showed the darker shading of chest hair, the way the material stretched across toned pecs and abs.

She dragged her eyes away and rubbed again at her stinging cheek. She was in shock, as well as everything else, she knew.

I've got to get out of here, she thought wildly. She would leave, first thing in the morning, and head back to London. To home, to sanity.

It was the only thing to do.

She still couldn't take it in. Couldn't believe it.

"Is it true? Tell me?" She heard the question burst from her.

Nikos frowned.

"That you and he have hatched some idea of me…me marrying…marrying you?" She could hardly get the words out.

"Yes." Nikos's voice was terse. Dear God, what an unholy mess! "I had thought," he went on, openly sarcastic, "that you had just obtained irrefutable corroboration from your grandfather?"

Her face hardened.

"That bastard!"

Nikos's expression iced. He had no love for Coustakis— he doubted if anyone in the world did, now that his poor besotted wife was dead!—and certainly he should not have hit her, but Andrea must be stupid indeed if she did not realise that her grandfather would not tolerate her shouting defiance at him, let alone in front of another male, and her selected husband to boot! Yiorgos Coustakis would never permit himself to lose face in front of the man he had accepted would run the empire he had amassed. Moreover, whatever his faults, Andrea should be mindful of the fact that it was Yirogos's money that kept her in her luxurious lifestyle, and that she owed him courtesy, if nothing else.

"You will not use such language."

"Or what?" she spat. "You'll take a whip to me like he told you to?"

Nikos swore. He wanted out, right now. He wanted to be miles from here, away from this madhouse! The thought of

Xanthe Palloupis hovered tantalisingly in his mind. She would be soft, and warm, and soothing, and cosseting. She would sit him down and make him comfortable, and relaxed, and speak only when he wanted her to speak, and never say a word otherwise, would know instinctively, from long practice, what he wanted, what he did not want...

But he wasn't with Xanthe; he was listening to this redheaded hot-head spitting venom.

"You certainly need *something* to stop you behaving like a foul-mouthed spoilt brat!" he barked back at her.

She got to her feet. "I suggest you leave, Mr Vassilis," she said. "And I also suggest, next time you get around to thinking of marrying someone, you have the courtesy to ask her first before announcing a done deal! However much you want to get your greedy hands on Coustakis Industries, I'm not available—especially not to some pretty-boy fortune-hunter like you!"

She slammed the brandy glass down on the sideboard, not caring that the liquid slopped on to the marquetry surface, spun on her heel and stormed out of the room, clattering up the marble staircase to get to her room as soon as she could.

Behind her, Nikos's face was rigid with fury. Ten seconds later he was out of the house and gunning his Ferrari down the driveway as if possessed by demons.

Andrea's fingers were trembling as she punched the buttons on the mobile phone Tony had leant her. Reaction had set in with a vengeance, and she felt as weak as a kitten.

The conversation was brief and to the point—if for no other reason than she did not want to run up Tony's phone bill more than she had to.

"Tony—it hasn't worked out. I'm going to have to come home. Tomorrow. Don't worry." She swallowed, not daring to let herself start on what had happened. "It's nothing drastic, but I'm just going to come home anyway. OK?" She paused fractionally. "Look, if you don't hear from me from Athens airport tomorrow, go on yellow alert, will you? And if I don't show up at Heathrow—or, worse, don't phone tomorrow evening—go to red, OK? I've met my beloved grandfather and he's—" she swallowed "—running to type."

After she'd hung up, desperately grateful not only to have heard Tony's familiar calming voice, but also just to have been reminded that a sane, reasonable world existed outside the confines of this palatial madhouse, Andrea realised her hands were still trembling.

How she managed to get any sleep at all that night she didn't know. She awoke late in the morning, with a jolt, woken by Zoe gently shaking her shoulder. Her grandfather, it seemed, wished to see her. Immediately.

Oh, does he? Well, as it happens, I want to see him as well! To order a car to take me to the airport!

He was in his bedchamber, Andrea discovered as, grim-faced, hastily dressed in a cheap blouse and cotton trousers of her own, she followed the maid along the corridor. With clammy hands she walked into the room.

Her grandfather was sitting up, propped on an array of pillows, ensconced in a huge tester bed that would not have looked out of place in Versailles. He did not look well, Andrea registered, and for the first time she realised that he was an old man not in the best of health.

I'll do this civilly, she thought. *I can manage that if I try.*

She approached the foot of the bed. Dark, hooded eyes bored into her. Yiorgos Coustakis might be confined to his bed, but the power he could wield had not lessened an iota.

"So," he said heavily, "you are worse than I ever feared. Insolent beyond belief! I should have taken you from your slut of a mother and raised you myself! You would have learned proper respect from the back of my hand!"

Every good intention vanished from Andrea's breast instantly. She felt the fury surge in her veins. But this time she would not lose control.

Instead she simply stood there, looking at the man who had fathered her father. It seemed unbelievable that they should be related in any way.

"Silent at last! A pity you could not have held that hellish tongue of yours last night, instead of showing yourself up so abominably in front of your husband!"

"Nikos Vassilis is not my husband, and he never will be," replied Andrea. Her anger was like ice running in her blood.

Yiorgos Coustakis made a rasping sound in his throat.

"And you could whistle for him now! No man would touch you after witnessing your despicable display last night! But then—" his dark eyes filled with contempt "—without Coustakis Industries as your dowry you would be fit only to warm a man's bed for hard cash, like your whore of a mother!"

"This conversation," said Andrea, her voice as tight as a drawn bowstring as she tamped down the fury that filled her as she heard this vile man speak so of her mother, "is pointless. I am leaving for London. Be so good as to order a car to take me to the airport."

Yiorgos Coustakis's dark face suffused with colour.

"You are going nowhere! You will stay in your room until the morning of your wedding if you take that attitude with me! I will be master in my own house!" His fist slammed down on to the bedcovering. "And if it takes something more than incarceration to bring you to heel, then so be it! A good beating will turn you docile!"

Andrea paled. A memory of those two expressionless security staff sprang into her mind. Fear stabbed at her. He saw it, and smiled. Her blood chilled as she saw him.

"Hah! Do you think I wouldn't? I thrashed your father

with my belt often enough! He soon learnt obedience!" His face darkened. "Until he met the whore who gave you birth! Then he defied me! I sent him packing! He would have got not a penny from me—if he hadn't smashed himself to pieces in his hurry to get back between the slut's legs!"

She felt the horror of it as if it had been yesterday. Her father, terrorised and abused by this foul man who had caused such misery, and then, just when happiness was at last within his reach, to have it all snatched from him—even his life.

"You vile, vile man..." she whispered. "You're not fit to live."

The dark, soulless eyes scorched through her. "Get out, before I take my belt to you myself! I will not be defied by you—or anyone!"

"Oh, I'm going," said Andrea. "If I have to walk into Athens on foot, I'm going!"

His face contorted.

"You will not be allowed to step foot outside this house until Nikos Vassilis takes you off my hands!"

She shook her head. "You are mistaken. I am leaving— today."

"From inside a locked room? I think not!"

Andrea looked at him steadily. Now was the time to make things clear to him.

"That," she said, her eyes like stones, "would be unwise. You see, if I don't make a certain phone call every night, the British embassy in Athens will be alerted that I am being held against my will. You will not, I am sure, wish to be charged with imprisoning me! Let alone invite the feast the press will make of it!"

The effect of her words was visible. He spat something at her in Greek. She smiled scornfully.

His face contorted. "And if I *make* you make that phone call?"

The threat was open—and quite plain to understand.

"Oh, that would be unwise too. You see—" she smiled unpleasantly, hiding the shudder that had gone through her at his words "—if that should happen then I might give the wrong code word during the conversation…"

As if a shutter had dropped, her grandfather's face suddenly became completely unreadable. There was nothing there—none of the fury and temper that had been blazing from him a moment ago.

"Tell me," he said suddenly, "if you please, just why is it that you are so averse to the prospect of marrying Nikos Vassilis?"

His change of tack took her aback. Then she rallied. "Is that a serious question? It's too absurd to be worth asking!"

"Why? Is he not a fine man to look at? He would make a handsome husband, *ne*? His reputation with your sex, I understand—" his voice became sly "—is spectacular! Women flock to him, and not just because of his money!"

"Money?" Andrea caught at the word. "He's a fortune-hunter! He admitted as much."

Yiorgos Coustakis gave a harsh laugh. "He seeks to net a greater fortune, that is all! Do you imagine I would entrust my empire to someone untried and untested? Nikos Vassilis has his own fortune—he will not waste mine by incompetence and mismanagement!"

She frowned, trying to take in this turnabout. Her grandfather went on. "Vassilis Inc is capitalised at over five hundred million euros! He's been after a merger with Coustakis Industries for the last eighteen months—he's an ambitious man, and now, finally, I have decided to let him realise his ambitions." His voice hardened. "But I've driven the price higher—he has to marry you before I sign the deal."

Andrea's brain was racing, trying to make sense of what she was hearing.

"Why?" she said bluntly. "You've denied my existence for twenty-five years, ever since your goons forced my mother to the airport and shoved her on a plane back to England!"

Nothing showed in his face, not a trace of regret or shame, as she related the way Yiorgos Coustakis had disposed of the woman who had dared to tell him she was pregnant by his dead son.

"Why?" Yiorgos Coustakis echoed. "Because you carry my blood. You and no one else. I have no choice but to use you, tainted though your blood is. When you marry Nikos Vassilis he will guard my fortune, and my blood will pass through you to your son. He will be my heir. I have had to wait two generations, but I shall have my heir!"

There was a fierceness of possession in his eyes that even his inscrutable expression could not disguise.

So, thought Andrea, as his words sank in, this is what it's all about. I am the vessel for his posterity. Revulsion filled her. Yiorgos Coustakis was nearing the end of his misbegotten life and he wanted the only immortality he could find.

She looked at him. He had everything money could buy, but as a human being he was worthless. He had no kindness in him, no compassion, no gentleness, no feeling for anyone except himself. He had treated his own son like a possession to be beaten into obedience, and her mother had been instantly condemned as a gold-digger trying to get at his precious money!

And now, twenty-five years later, she was standing in front of him, knowing that she was the only person in the world who could give him what he wanted. The final thing he wanted.

The memory of Tony's voice echoed in her mind. *Look, if he does want you for something, then if he doesn't want you to refuse he's going to have to do something* you *want.*

And there *was* something she wanted. Something she had

travelled over a thousand miles to get—the money for her mother that was not just her escape to the sun but her reparation as well. Justice. Finally.

Her grandfather's eyes were resting on her. Seeing her as a tool to be used. Nothing more. Her heart hardened. Well, tools had to be paid for.

Five minutes ago she had wanted nothing except to shake the dust of her grandfather's house from her feet. Now she wanted to get what she came for.

Money.

His shoulders relaxed into the pillow as he read her mind.

"So," he said, "tell me—what price do you set on opening your legs to Nikos Vassilis with a ring on your finger to keep you respectable?"

The sneer in his voice was irrelevant. So was the insult and the crudity. Everything about him was irrelevant—except the money he would pay her. Her heart was hard, like stone all the way through. Somewhere in the back of her mind a memory was flickering—the memory of being held in strong arms, her body on fire with soft, seductive flame…

She thrust it away. That kiss had been nothing to do with her. Nikos Vassilis had kissed her because she was the gateway to Coustakis Industries. No other reason. She just hadn't realised it at the time. Now that she did she must not read anything more into it. Nothing.

"Five hundred thousand pounds," she announced crisply. "Sterling. Paid into a bank account in London of my choosing, in my name—Andrea Fraser."

She gave her mother's surname—her name—deliberately. She was no Coustakis. Never had been. Never would be.

His laugh was derisive. "You set a high price on yourself for the daughter of a penniless slut!"

Nothing showed in her face. She would not allow it.

"You need me. So you'll pay for me. That's all."

A flash of fury showed in his eyes. "Do you think that as the wife of Nikos Vassilis you will live the life of a pauper? You will live in a luxury you can hardly dream of! You should be grateful, *grateful*—on your knees that I have plucked you out of your slum to live such a life as I am offering you!"

"Five hundred thousand." Her voice was implacable. She needed that much to clear the last of Kim's debts, buy her a decent apartment in Spain, and have enough left over to invest safely for an income for her mother to live on, albeit modestly, for the rest of her life. "Or I go back to London today."

Dark eyes bored into hers. She could see the hatred in them. The loathing that this tool he wanted to use was daring to defy him. But defy him she would—she had something he wanted, and he would have to pay for it. Just as Tony had said.

But he would not go down easily.

"You get not a penny until you are married."

She laughed scornfully. "There will be no marriage," she said as her eyes narrowed, "unless I am paid."

Even as she spoke her mind was splintering in two. What was she doing here? What was she thinking of, selling herself like this? She must be mad! Quite mad!

But then the other side of her mind slammed back. This was no time for scruples, no time for doubts! It was now or never—this was her one and only chance to get reparation for Kim. She would do whatever it took! And agreeing to marry a total stranger was what it was going to take.

A stranger who can melt your bones in a single embrace? Oh, be careful—be careful of what you are doing!

Compunction flashed at her. She was standing here, negotiating a price to marry Nikos Vassilis as if she were doing nothing more than haggling over a CD at a car-boot sale! How low was she stooping?

Then her heart hardened again. And hadn't Nikos Vassilis stood in front of Yiorgos Coustakis and negotiated a price to get hold of Coustakis Industries? A price that included marriage to a woman he'd never set eyes on? What kind of man did that?

No, she need feel no shame, no compunction. The man who had kissed her last night deserved no more regard than did her grandfather!

For one long, last moment she held her grandfather's eyes, refusing to back down. It was too important to even think of giving in. At last, after what seemed like an eternity of challenge, he suddenly snarled, "On your wedding morning—and not till then! Now, get out!"

CHAPTER SIX

NIKOS sat in his boardroom, lounging back in his leather chair at the head of the table, listening to his directors droning on about the impact of the merger with Coustakis Industries. He wasn't listening. Wasn't paying the slightest attention. His heart was stormy.

What the hell kind of woman had he agreed to marry? A raging hell-cat! A spoilt brat of a pampered princess! An ill-mannered, ill-tempered, badly behaved harpy who threw tantrums and hysterics at the drop of a hat! A true Coustakis!

His jaw tightened. The last thing on earth he needed was a wife who took after Yiorgos Coustakis!

A splinter of grudging admiration stabbed him. The girl hadn't flinched from confronting Old Man Coustakis. She'd just stormed in there and laid in to him!

A smile almost curved his mouth at the recollection. *Theos*, but it had been a sight to see. Someone giving as good as they got from that vicious brute whose ugly reputation made most people walk on tiptoes around him, from house servants to business associates. Even he trod carefully around the old barracuda! At least until Coustakis Industries was his to run.

The smile turned to a frown. For all that, however, it was not behaviour to condone. Certainly not in the woman who would be Mrs Nikos Vassilis. It was unthinkable that his wife should behave like that—for whatever reason!

The frown deepened—but from a different cause this time. Had the girl truly not known of her grandfather's marriage plans for her? It was typical of Yiorgos Coustakis not to bother himself with trivial details such as telling his granddaughter what husband he had chosen for her. In which case, Nikos knew he had to acknowledge, the girl had a right to object to having been kept in the dark about such an important matter. True, her reaction had been wildly over the top, but in the first immediate shock of the news it was understandable that she should be affronted at her grandfather's typically high-handed behaviour in keeping her ignorant of her future.

An image flashed in his mind. Yiorgos Coustakis slashing his hand down across Andrea's cheek. Nikos straightened suddenly in his chair. Anger clenched at him. *Theos*, but the old man was a brute! Who cared if he was from a generation that thought nothing of beating children? Who cared if his granddaughter had provoked him by yelling like a harridan in front of the man he had chosen for her husband? No man ever hit a woman. Ever.

Revulsion filled him. Whilst he would never dream of raising his fist to a man of Yiorgos's age, the memory of him hitting his granddaughter burned.

I've got to get her out of there!

A surge of emotion swept through him—not anger with that brute of an old man. Something he had never felt about any woman before. A fierce, urgent burst of protectiveness.

Abruptly he lifted a hand, cutting off whatever his sales director was saying.

"Gentlemen, my apologies, but I must leave you. Please continue with the meeting."

Ten minutes later he was in his Ferrari and nosing through the impossibly jammed streets of Athens. Heading out of town.

Andrea sat out on the terrace overlooking the ornate gardens that spread like an embroidered skirt around her grandfather's opulent villa. Her heart was heavy—but resolved. The final scene with her grandfather replayed itself over and over again in her head. Was she insane, even to contemplate going along with what he wanted? This wasn't just some kind of trivial business contract she had agreed to—this was *marriage*!

The enormity of what she committed herself to overwhelmed her, making it seem almost unreal. So much had happened so quickly! Less than two days ago she had been at home, in her own drab but familiar world. Now she was sitting on a sun-drenched terrace beneath a Mediterranean sun—about to marry a complete stranger!

Panic rose in her throat and she fought it down.

It's not a real marriage! It's just a wedding ceremony. That's all. The day after the wedding I'll be on a plane to London! My "husband" will be glad to see the back of me!

And I'll have half a million pounds waiting for me in the bank!

She and Kim could be in Spain, house-hunting, in a month!

The warm sun poured down on her, bathing her legs stretched out in front of her. They had been aching since last night—wearing high heels was never a good idea—and the strain and tension of the past day and a half was telling. Gently she stretched and eased them, rubbing her hands lightly along her thighs in a careful massage.

The warmth did them good, she knew. Living in Spain would help. She would get work there, enough to keep Kim and herself, so that Kim could take life easy at last. Spain was full of Brits now; she was bound to be able to get some kind of job, even if she didn't speak Spanish yet.

I'll invite Tony and Linda for a holiday she thought happily. They'd been so good to her; it would be great to give something back. She'd had to phone Tony from her room, just a short while ago, telling him she was staying after all. It had taken quite a lot to convince him she really meant it, that one of her grandfather's bully-boys hadn't been twisting her arm to say so!

Cold filled her. Her grandfather was unspeakable—her every worst fear about him was deserved! He really would have thought it perfectly acceptable to keep her a prisoner here and force her into marrying that man!

That man—

Memory leapt in her throat. It was here, on this terrace, that she had first laid eyes on him, not twenty-four hours ago. Here, beneath the beguiling stars, that he had slid her into his arms and kissed her…

I'm going to marry him…

A shaft of pure excitement sliced through her. She felt a quickening inside herself. That man, that drop-dead, fabulous-looking, breathtaking man, whose touch had set fire to her, melting her very being into him, Nikos Vassilis, was going to be her husband…

Reality hit like a cold douche. Of course he wasn't going to be her husband! Not for more than a day! All he was to her was her passport to Spain with her mother, nothing more!

And all I am to him is his passport to my grandfather's money!

Her lips pressed together. What kind of man was he that would even think of marrying a woman he'd never laid eyes on just to get hold of an even bigger fortune than he yet had? That he wasn't even a fortune-hunter somehow made it worse! Being poor herself, she knew how tempting it must be to think that you could claw your way out of poverty the easy way. But if Nikos Vassilis was already rich, had already made his pile, then why did he want even more? If his company really was worth five hundred million euros then a fraction of what he already possessed would have kept her and Kim in luxury by their standards!

Well, it was none of her business. She didn't care about Nikos Vassilis. He was using her to get what he wanted—and she was simply returning the favour! And she wasn't even cheating him. Even after she'd been packed off home he'd still have got what he wanted—Coustakis Industries—courtesy of his brand-new and totally unwanted wife! He'd be perfectly happy if the bride didn't stick around like glue! A grim smile played about her mouth. In fact, the only person who would end up with a bad bargain would be her beloved grandfather! He'd have handed over his company to Nikos Vassilis, along with his despised grand-daughter, but he'd be waiting a long time for his precious heir!

The throaty roar of a high-powered car approaching the house along the long drive that was hidden from the front gardens interrupted her bitter reveries. She tensed. It did not sound like the purr of the huge limousine her grandfather had taken his leave in some half-hour ago—heading, she assumed for his office in Athens. This was a much more aggressive engine indeed—and it didn't take a genius to guess whose it was.

Some few minutes later her assumption was confirmed. Nikos Vassilis strode out on to the terrace. He came to where she was sitting.

Andrea felt her body tense. Something leapt inside her. He was looking spectacular again. A pale grey immaculately cut business suit, gleaming white shirt, grey silk tie, made him look taller and more svelte than ever. His expression was un-readable, made more so by the dark glasses covering his eyes, and as she looked at his face she felt her stomach hollow out.

Oh, dear God, he's just gorgeous! she felt herself thinking.

He sat himself down opposite her, stretching out his long legs, his feet almost touching hers. Automatically she drew her legs back, the sudden movement causing a jolt of mild pain to go through them.

He caught the expression on her face and frowned slightly. "Are you all right?"

The rich timbre of his voice, so seductively accented, made her feel weak. She nodded briefly to answer his query, unable to speak.

"How is your cheek?"

The frown had deepened, and before she could stop him he had reached across the table and touched the side of her face with his fingers. They felt cool, but where they made a thousand sensations quiver through her. He tilted her head slightly, so that he could see where he touched.

There was a bruise, definitely, even if only faintly visible. She had made no attempt to cover it with make-up, though she had let her hair fall loose, so that it covered her right ear which was still red from having caught the main thrust of her grandfather's blow.

"Fine," she said quickly, brushing his hand aside. She did not want his concern—the last words she had flung at him had been an atrocious insult, and his evident concern for her now put her off kilter. So did the echoing resonance of his light velvet touch just now…

The soft-footed approach of a servant carrying a tray of coffee for two was a welcome interruption. It gave Andrea precious moments to collect herself.

Nikos lifted off his dark glasses and slid them into his breast pocket. Andrea wished he hadn't. Although it was disturbing to address a man whose eyes she could not see, it was far, far worse to have those keen slate-grey eyes visible to her.

The eyes searched her face.

"You are upset still," he said quietly. "Last night was very distressing for you. I apologise—it should not have happened that way." He paused, feeling carefully for his words. "Your grandfather is a...difficult...man, Andrea, as you must surely already appreciate from all your years of knowing him. He is used to commanding others, to giving orders—and to getting his own way by the swiftest means possible. However brutal." There was a frown in his eyes. "Hitting you was insupportable. But—" he held up a hand to ward off what her reply must be "—understandable. That is not to excuse him, Andrea—merely to point out that there was no way he was going to be outfaced by his own granddaughter in front of me, and that he comes from a generation which did not believe in sparing the rod."

Andrea stilled. She thought of her father, brought up here, a vulnerable boy, bullied by his father from the day he was born—thrashed into obedience...

The only bright hope of his life had been Kim, the girl he'd met on a beach and fallen in love with on the spot, their young romance an idyll out of *Romeo and Juliet*. And just as doomed.

I'm not just doing this for you, Mum—I'm doing it for my father too. Looking after you the way he was never able to...

Nikos Vassilis was talking again. She forced herself to listen.

"You must believe me when I tell you that last night I naturally assumed you knew of your grandfather's marriage plans for you—and agreed to them."

She reached forward to the coffee pot—filter coffee, she noticed gratefully, not the treacly Greek brew—and started to pour them both a cup.

"But I do agree to them," she announced. "I've had a talk with my grandfather this morning and it's all settled, Mr Vassilis. You can continue with your merger plans."

Her voice was remarkably calm, she thought. But then that was the way to play it—cool, calm and collected. This was not a real marriage they were talking about; it was part of a business contract that would benefit them both. She must remember that and not think about anything else.

Certainly not about the way the sensual line of his mouth contrasted with the tough, cleanly defined edge of his jaw, or the way his dark silky hair made her long to reach her fingers to it...

She pushed the cup towards him.

"Milk and sugar?" she asked politely.

He shook his head briefly, a frown creasing between his eyes.

"Did he bully you again?" he demanded openly.

Her eyes widened in surprise.

"Certainly not," she answered, economising on the truth to cut to the chase. "We struck an excellent deal that I'm perfectly satisfied with."

She poured milk into her coffee and took a reflective sip.

"Deal?" There was an edge in Nikos's voice that Andrea would have had to have been deaf not to hear. "What deal?"

She smiled. It was an artificial smile, but for all that she could not stop a curl of satisfaction indenting her mouth. Satisfaction that at last, after a quarter of a century, her mother would get reparation from Yiorgos Coustakis. Devastated, heartbroken and pregnant, Kim had asked nothing from Andreas's father, had wanted only to offer him and Andreas's mother the comfort of knowing that, although their son had died so tragically, a grandchild had been conceived. She had not asked for money—she had offered comfort and consolation.

But Yiorgos Coustakis had treated her like a gold-digging whore...

"Finally, Mr Vassilis, I get money of my own."

"Money?" There was a chill in his voice now that raised the hairs on her neck, but she kept the tight, artificial smile pasted to her lips.

"Yes, money, Mr Vassilis. You know—the crisp folding stuff, the bright shiny stuff, the silent, electronic stuff that wings its way into bank accounts and makes the world go round."

Her eyes were bright and hard.

"Explain."

That was an order, just as if Nikos Vassilis had been speaking to one of his underlings. And if he owned a company worth five hundred million euros, Andrea reminded herself deliberately, that meant he had one hell of a lot of underlings!

"Explain? Well, it's an extremely simple contract, Mr Vassilis. Just between me and my grandfather—it will have no impact on your own contract with him, I promise. My grandfather undertakes to make a certain amount of money over to me upon my marriage to you." She smiled again, bright and hard. "Unlike you, I prefer Coustakis cash, not shares."

Nikos's face had frozen.

"He is *paying* you to marry me?"

Andrea could have laughed. Laughed right in his handsome face. He was angry! He actually had the nerve to be angry! God, what a hypocrite! But she couldn't laugh. Her throat felt very tight suddenly, as if there was a cord around her neck. Choking at her. All she could do was give a careless, acknowledging nod and take another mouthful of coffee.

She set her cup down with a click.

"Just as he is paying *you*," she pointed out, "to marry *me*."

"That is different! Completely different!"

Refutation was in every syllable. Andrea busied herself topping up her coffee. She felt very calm now. Extremely calm.

"I don't see why. You would hardly hitch yourself to an unknown woman if there weren't something in it for you, would you? I just happen to come with enough Coustakis shares to make it worth your while." She replaced the coffee pot and looked straight across the table at the man she was going to marry. For half a million pounds.

"Mr Vassilis, let us be completely up-front about this. You did me the courtesy last night—" she did not trouble to hide the sarcasm in her voice "—of pointing out that our marriage was predicated upon your taking control of Coustakis Industries. You can't do that without a majority shareholding. Even I, with my tiny business brain, know that!"

Nikos looked at her. His grey eyes were like cold slate. "I am *buying* Coustakis shares! Not in cash, but in paper—exchanging them for Vassilis shares at a hefty premium, I assure you! Your grandfather will do very well out of the deal! I'm undertaking a reverse takeover, whereby the much smaller Vassilis Inc can acquire the much larger Coustakis holding with a minimum of debt purchase or rights issues to fund it."

She waved her hand impatiently. "Spare me the technicalities! The salient point, so far as I am concerned, is that my grandfather will not agree to the merger—reverse take-over, acquisition, whatever you call it—unless you marry me. That means you're marrying me to get Coustakis Industries. Owning the majority of Coustakis shares will make you even richer than you are—i.e. you're being *paid* to marry me. End of story."

Tony would be proud of my cool, clear logic, she thought defiantly.

Every good resolution that Nikos had entertained since brooding on Andrea Coustakis in his boardroom vanished. Every last shred of sympathy. Sympathy for her being kept in ignorance by Old Man Coustakis, sympathy for her having a brute like him for a grandfather—all went totally. He had come to make his peace with her, to start over again, begin his wooing of her as a man should woo his bride…

That hysterical harpy he had seen last night would never come back—there would be no need for her. Instead only the soft, yielding, sensual woman he had held in his arms so tantalisingly would be the bride he took for his wife.

But what did he find now? A woman sitting and talking about marriage and money in the same breath. A woman with a mind like a cash-box.

Conscience pricked at him, but he pushed it away. No, of course he would not have dreamt of marrying an unknown woman without the chance to take over Coustakis Industries! But dynastic marriages of convenience were commonplace in the world of the very rich—that did not mean they had to be sordid. And since setting eyes on Andrea Coustakis he had known straight away that marriage to her would be anything but a marriage of convenience—it would be a marriage of mutual pleasure…

Andrea sat across the table and studied him dispassionately. He was offended. Offended by her frankness. She no longer wanted to laugh. Nor did her throat feel tight any more. Instead, a sort of dull, hard, unemotional carapace had descended on her, covering every inch of her.

As he looked back at her Nikos felt his gaze hardening. *Theos*, but she was a cool piece. Coustakis blood ran in her veins, no doubt about that!

Revulsion shimmered through him. The woman he had held trembling in his arms last night seemed a thousand miles away, as if she had never been. This was the true Andrea Coustakis now. Like her grandfather—knowing the price of everything, the value of nothing.

And she knew her own price, that was for sure. He smiled grimly. Well, he knew her price too. And he would treat her accordingly.

He got to his feet.

"Well—" his voice was abrupt "—since we now both know where we stand, we can begin."

She looked up at him, uncertain suddenly.

"Begin what?"

He flashed a smile. It had no humour in it.

"Our official betrothal."

He reached down and took her hand, drawing her to her feet.

"And, though you might wish to seal such an event with a chequebook, I prefer a more traditional method—"

She had a fraction of a second to read his intent. It was utterly inadequate to allow her to react in time and pull away.

His kiss was deep and sensuous. Slow and possessive.

Very, very possessive.

His mouth moved over hers, lazily, exploringly, tastingly...

Making absolutely free with her.

She felt her stomach plummet to the floor, felt adrenaline flood through her veins, felt weakness debilitate her totally.

Felt her hand lift of its own accord and curl around his neck, splaying its fingers into his silky hair. Felt herself moan softly, helplessly, as he played with her mouth.

He let her go, casually unwinding her hand and letting it drop nervelessly to her side. Then he took her chin in his fingers and tilted it up. Her mouth was bee-stung, lips red and swollen. Aroused.

Her eyes were lustrous, wide and staring at him, her lashes thick and lush.

"You are an acquisition, Andrea Coustakis, that I shall very much enjoy making," he said softly, gazing down at her with gleaming possession in his eyes. His voice dropped, making her heart stop. "I look forward, very much to our personal merger..."

His meaning made perfectly clear, he stroked her cheek and stood back. Then he glanced at his watch.

"Come—we shall lunch, and show the world that Vassilis Inc has plans for Coustakis Industries."

He tucked her hand into his arm and led her off.

Andrea went with him helplessly. She hadn't a bone left in her body to resist.

The restaurant was plush and crowded. It was clearly excruciatingly expensive. Andrea didn't have to glance at the menu prices to know that.

As they'd walked in, she stiff and wary, concealing her nervousness at being in such a place, she'd felt every eye upon her. A covert glance around showed her that just about everyone here was male—the place was awash with suits. Very expensive suits. This was a place, she knew immediately, where the most successful businessmen in Athens took their lunch and cut their deals, made their contacts and their money.

The maître d' who advanced upon them at their entrance knew her escort, that was obvious. His manner was oh-so-attentive, oh-so-deferential. Though the place looked packed, he did not seem in the least dismayed by the prospect of having to find a table for his latest arrivals.

Nikos knew he'd sort something. For a start he was too curious about the female at his side not to want to find out more. Athens was a city that liked to gossip, and Nikos had made sure that it liked to gossip about him. Having a reputation as a connoisseur of fine women did him no harm at all in the business world. Men envied him—envied his success, his ability to have a beautiful woman on his arm, envied the fact that, unlike most of them, he did not need his money to keep them there—he could do it on his looks alone.

"Kyrios Vassilis," smiled the greeter. "How delightful to

have you as our guest today. And your lovely companion, of course…"

His voice trailed away expectantly.

With an acknowledging half-smile, Nikos accommodated him.

"Thespiris Coustakis," he obliged.

The man's face was a picture. Nikos almost laughed. Then, revealing nothing but the excited gleam in his eyes, the man immediately bowed to Andrea and murmured, in breathless tones, how greatly honoured he was to have her grace his establishment.

"No fuss, if you please," said Nikos, and began to head for the bar area. "We'll have a drink until our table is ready." He caught the man's eye and made his message clear. "Something as private as you can manage."

"Of course." The man bowed again, eyes gleaming even more, and clicked his fingers imperiously for a pair of minions, who were there immediately and then despatched variously at his bidding. Then, bowing yet again, he ostentatiously ushered Nikos and Andrea towards the bar.

"This way, if you please, Thespiris Coustakis," he said, in a voice that was intentionally louder than before. Andrea could see a couple of men seated nearby, also waiting for their table, look up sharply, subjecting her to penetrating stares. Then one of them promptly got up and moved across to one of the tables in the dining area, bending low to speak into the man's ear. The man looked up abruptly and followed his line of gaze towards Nikos Vassilis and his companion.

As she took her seat—a huge, soft leather chair into which she sank almost completely—she said through clenched teeth, "What the hell is this circus? Have I got two heads or something?"

Nikos gave a brief laugh, his teeth gleaming wolfishly.

"Oh, the show has begun, Andrea, *agape mou*. The show has most very definitely begun."

It was not the most comfortable meal Andrea had eaten in her life, but it was certainly the most expensive. Not even dinner last night could match lunch today. For a start they were drinking vintage Krug champagne. Andrea did not even want to think what that must have cost. Then there were black truffles, caviar, exotic seafood she couldn't even identify served in a delicate sauce with exquisitely presented vegetables. As well as the champagne Nikos ordered wine as well, and by the reverence with which it was served—from displaying the label for his approval and the sommelier tasting some in his little silver cup, to Nikos's final approving nod as he sampled first the bouquet and then the wine itself—she could see it must be as expensive as the champagne, if not more so.

She wished desperately, as she ate her way through a lunch that it would have taken her six months to pay for herself, that she could enjoy it more. It seemed dreadful to have such expensive food in front of her and yet feel as if she had to force down every mouthful. Tension knotted in her stomach like rope.

It wasn't just that she could see she was being looked over by every person in the restaurant, from the humblest waiter to the richest patron, it was that she was lunching, in public, with Nikos Vassilis.

Who was making it very, very clear just who he was keeping company.

The Coustakis heiress.

It clearly, she thought, her lips tight, gave him one hell of a kick!

He said as much at one point. Leaning closer, as though to whisper some intimacy to her, he murmured, "They are all

agog, Andrea *mou*—your name has gone round like wildfire
and they are desperate to know who you are! Strange as it
seems, no one in Athens knew Yiorgos Coustakis had a
granddaughter—you have been kept as a card up his sleeve!
And now—" satisfaction—the satisfaction of a hunger sated,
a long hunger born many years ago in the streets of the city—
gleamed in his slate eyes "—they can see exactly how the old
man has decided to play you! There isn't a man here who
does not realise the significance of your being here with
me!"

"Is it public knowledge yet that you will be taking over
Coustakis Industries?" Andrea asked. She kept her voice cool
and businesslike, though it was an effort to do so. Since he had
kissed her with such confident possession, sealing their
bargain, it had been an effort to do anything except drown her
memory of the recalled sensation of his lips tasting her
mouth...

He took a mouthful of wine, clearly savouring it, then set
down the glass.

"There have been rumours—there are always rumours.
After all, Yiorgos is getting older—something must happen to
the company. Up till now no one realised he had any heir at
all—let alone a hide-away heiress! But now—well, I think
they will draw their own conclusions, do you not, *agape mou*?"

"Don't use endearments to me!" she responded sharply.
She didn't like the sound of the liquid syllables in his low,
intimate voice.

He raised a mocking eyebrow. "My dear Andrea, we are
to be married. We must, as I have just told you, put on an appropriate show. And, speaking of marriage, what are your
wedding plans? I tell you frankly I would hope above all that
they are speedy. But other than that you can have free rein.
I assume your mother will fly out for it?"

Andrea's face froze. "No," she said shortly.

Kim mustn't even know about the wedding. Andrea would have to get Tony to say she was just staying on here for a few weeks, that was all. The last thing she wanted was Kim finding out just what she was planning to do!

"She dislikes your grandfather so much?" There was an edge in Nikos's voice as he remembered Yiorgos saying that Andrea's mother had had very different views on upbringing from him. Well, given Yiorgos's demonstration of grandfatherly chastisement last night, he could hardly be surprised.

"I don't want to talk about it," said Andrea tightly.

Nikos's eyes narrowed, studying her closed face. There was something wrong here, he thought suddenly. Her eyes were a little too bright, her soft mouth almost trembling beneath the hardened line of her lips. The memory of her standing on the terrace, talking about her father and her mother's memory of him, came back to him. He cursed himself for an insensitive fool.

"I'm sorry," he said suddenly. "Of course she would find it distressing to revisit the place where she was so happy with your father."

"Yes," said Andrea, swallowing, "that's it."

"Then perhaps a private wedding would be best, *ne*?"

"Definitely," she agreed. "And as speedily as it can be arranged."

She reached for her wine glass. She had drunk more than she had meant to, but her nerves, beneath the unemotional carapace that had descended on her, were shaky, she realised. As she moved forward his hand stayed her wrist, closing around it loosely.

"You are so eager to be my wife, Andrea?"

His voice had lowered again, taking on that intimate timbre that made her go shivery. Her eyes flew to his. In her wrist, as his thumb rubbed casually along the delicate skin over her veins, a pulse throbbed.

"I meant," she said, as brusquely as she could, "that you must be keen to get the merger underway as soon as possible."

She drew her hand away and picked up her wine glass, drinking deeply.

For a moment Nikos hovered between indignation and amusement. Amusement won out. Mocking amusement. She was responsive to him—he had proved that twice already—and he knew perfectly well that he would dissolve any last resistance to him. Knowing now that she was only interested in marrying him for money, he would take particular pleasure in revealing to her just how sexually vulnerable to him he could make her—when he chose. She would leave their marriage bed in no doubt whatsoever that he could turn her into a willing, purring sexual partner, eager to do in bed whatever he wanted her to…

He frowned. A moment ago he had been feeling sorry for her—mourning, with her mother, her lost father. The girl with the cash-box mentality had been completely absent then.

Now she was back with a vengeance.

"As eager to get on with your merger as I am to get my grandfather to release my capital," she announced crisply.

The phrase sounded good in her ears. Made it sound the sort of thing that heiresses said—the sort of thing that went down well, with approving nods, in places like this. People were still looking at her, she knew. Word had gone round—the Coustakis heiress was in town.

And she was lunching with Nikos Vassilis.

Marriages or corporate mergers—they were all the same thing to people like these.

There was a sour taste in her throat, despite the wine.

CHAPTER SEVEN

LUNCH seemed endless, and it was well into the afternoon before Andrea could finally escape. And even then she could not escape Nikos.

He had phoned his office on his mobile, cancelling all his appointments. That alone, he knew, would accelerate the rumours. Nikos Vassilis never cancelled appointments—he was assiduous in his pursuit of business and profit.

He smiled down at his bride-to-be, an intimate smile that Andrea knew was for the benefit of the remaining diners, as they took their leave from the restaurant. "I thought that you might like to go shopping. I'm sure you will wish for a spectacular trousseau!"

"I've got all the clothes I need," she replied sharply. She didn't want any more clothes—the closets in her room at her grandfather's house were groaning. Today, having made the momentous decision to marry Nikos Vassilis, she had changed into one of the outfits Zoe had shown her—a pair of beautifully cut taupe trousers and a shaped appliquéd top. There were more than enough remaining to see her through to her wedding day.

He gave a disbelieving laugh. "No woman has all the clothes she needs," he commented dryly.

"I'm not interested in clothes," she said carelessly.

He laughed again. "Then you are unique amongst your sex! Besides…" his voice took on a caressing note "…even if you are not interested in clothes, Andrea, they most definitely are interested in you…"

His eyes worked over her torso, blatantly taking in how the jersey material of her top stretched across her full breasts, outlining their generous swell.

Unconsciously she tugged at the hem of her top, as if that would instantly conceal her figure.

"You only reveal yourself more to me," he said softly, his breath warm on her throat. Fleetingly he ran the back of his hand down her cheek, making her breath catch. "I would like to choose some clothes for you, Andrea—please allow me that privilege."

"I told you I had enough!" She pulled away from him, wishing her heart-rate had not suddenly started to race at his touch.

"Something special," he went on, as if she hadn't spoken, "for our wedding night."

She stilled. Then, with a curious twist to her lips, she nodded.

"If you insist."

He smiled with satisfaction. "Oh, but I do, *pethi mou*, I do."

He took her to an exclusive lingerie boutique in the chic Kolonaki shopping area of Athens. It was the kind of place, Andrea thought, where if you asked for a cotton bra and panties they would throw you out! It was also the kind of place, she realised, the moment the attentive assistant started to fawn all over her escort, where Nikos Vassilis was clearly an extremely valued customer indeed.

And it didn't take a genius for Andrea to guess just what kind of woman he bought lingerie here for!

Oh, the assistant was polite enough to her, that was for

sure, but it was obvious that she regarded her actual customer as Nikos Vassilis. Andrea knew she had been labelled a passing floozy with a single glance! She let the woman take her measurements and whisk out one gauzy confection after another, but declined the offer to try anything on.

She wouldn't be wearing any of it anyway. Her wedding night would be short—and very far from sweet.

Well satisfied with his purchases, Nikos was all set to keep going.

"Come," he said persuasively, "we are surrounded by designer shops—take your pick!"

"No, thanks," she returned indifferently. "I keep telling you I've got enough."

"Then do me one favour, *ne*?" He caught her arm. "Let me buy you a single skirt, now, to change into. You have worn trousers two days running. I far prefer women to wear skirts."

"How surprising," she said with a wry smile. "Unfortunately for you, I don't wear skirts."

He frowned. "What do you mean, you don't wear skirts?"

"Exactly that," she replied.

"You wore an evening dress last night!"

"That was long," she said briefly. She wanted to change the subject—fast.

Enlightenment dawned on him—and relief. For a moment he had feared that she was the type of female who made some kind of nonsensical stand about insisting on wearing trousers on principle. Nikos saw no sense in such an attitude. He was no chauvinist—Vassilis Inc was unusual, he knew, in taking a proactive stance on hiring and promoting women—but he saw no reason why a woman should think she became demeaned as a sex object just for wearing a skirt!

Now he realised this was not Andrea's attitude.

"I'm sure your legs are beautiful," he reassured her. "They are long and elegant and shapely—I can see that even now."

She glanced up at him. The curious twist was on her mouth again.

"Can you? You must have X-ray vision."

He smiled indulgently. "Even if they are not your best point, *agape mou*, I can make allowances."

The twist to her mouth deepened, but she said nothing.

"So," he said, "let us buy you a skirt—and I will set your fears at rest."

Her face went blank.

"I've done enough shopping for today. I'm bored."

His eyebrow rose. He knew of no woman who was bored by shopping—especially when it was his money they were spending. Esme, naturally, was obsessed by clothes and her own appearance—it was her profession, after all. And Xanthe adored being taken by him to her favourite jewellers' shops. She was like a magpie for jewellery, and decked herself in glitter whenever she could. For her, Nikos knew with a cynical tightening of his jaw, it was an insurance policy for her old age, when she could no longer hold her rich lovers to her side.

Perhaps Andrea, born to expectations of vast wealth from birth, saw things in a different light.

"Well, I would hate you to be bored, so how can I amuse you?"

Andrea didn't like the note in his voice, hinting at meanings she would rather ignore. Didn't like it at all. She started walking along the pavement.

"I want to go sightseeing," she said suddenly. After all, she would never come to Athens again. She might as well go sightseeing now, while she could.

A pang hit her, hard and painful. This was her father's city. He had been raised here. His blood sang in her veins. She was as Greek as she was English—and this was the first time in her life she was setting foot on Greek soil. And the last.

Sadness swept through her—sadness and bitterness.

"Sightseeing?" Nikos queried. "But you will have seen all the sights a hundred times!"

She stared at him. "I've never been to Athens before—never been to Greece before."

Nikos looked at her, disapproval in his expression. It was one thing for Andrea's English mother to be worried about her father-in-law's views on disciplining children, or unwilling to revisit her dead husband's country herself, quite another to forbid her daughter to visit at all. It was bad enough Andrea did not speak Greek, let alone that she had never been here! He'd assumed that although Yiorgos Coustakis had not paraded his granddaughter to the world, she had, of course, been out here for holidays and so forth.

"Then it is high time," he said decisively, "that I show you Athens."

And he did. They spent the afternoon doing what all first-time tourists in the city did—climbing the Acropolis to pay homage to the glory of the first flowering of Western civilisation, the Parthenon.

Andrea was enthralled, refusing to acknowledge the wave of desolation that swept over her at the thought that soon, all too soon, she would never see Nikos again.

It didn't matter how much her eyes were drawn to him; it didn't matter how much she revelled in drinking in, as secretly as she could, the bounty that was this paean to manhood at her side. All of this, heady and intoxicating as she increasingly found his company, was nothing more than a temporary interlude in her life. Nikos Vassilis, though he could send a shiver of electricity through her with a single glance, the barest brush of his sleeve on her arm, was nothing more than a temporary interlude.

It was a phrase Andrea forced herself to remember day after day as, for the next two weeks, Nikos Vassilis made it very

clear to the rest of the world that he had snapped up the
Coustakis heiress as his forthcoming bride and that his sights
were set, very firmly, on Coustakis Industries.

Andrea wished she could get used to him squiring her
around—lunching in fashionable restaurants, dining in fashionable nightspots, always at her side, attentive, possessive,
ramming home to all who saw them, time after time, that he
was the favoured choice of Yiorgos Coustakis for the rich
prize of Coustakis Industries—but she could not. Every time
he picked her up in his gleaming, purring, powerful Ferrari
she felt a kick go through her like an electric shock.

She did her best to hide it. Did her best to maintain the
stony façade that she knew, instinctively, annoyed him.

Almost as much as it amused him.

"My English ice-maiden," he said to her softly one
evening, as she deliberately turned her face away from his
greeting so that his lips could only brush her cheek, "how I
will enjoy melting you."

She might think she was only marrying him to extract her
capital from the covetous claws of Old Man Coustakis—but
he would prove otherwise.

And take great relish in it!

"You're mussing my hair, Nikos," she replied snappily.

"It will get a lot more mussed than that soon," he replied,
eyes gleaming with mocking amusement—and promise.
"Tonight," he went on, "we shall go dancing." He leant
forward. "I long to hold you in my arms again, Andrea *mou*."

She backed away, almost tripping.

"I don't dance," she said abruptly.

He laughed. The sound of it made her feel irritated.
Among other things she didn't want to put a name to.

With every passing day her feet were getting colder and
colder. She would wake in the middle of the night and the sheer
disbelief of what she was doing would wash over and over her.

Only one thought kept her going—money. Money at last. She had to hold out—hold out until the money was in the bank.

Then she could cut and run—and run and run...

From demons she refused to give a name to.

"I wasn't suggesting we go hot-clubbing till dawn," he assured her. "Since it isn't your scene anyway, I recall, I was thinking of something a little more...sophisticated. I think you will enjoy it. I know I will..."

She compressed her mouth. "I said I don't dance. I mean it."

He smiled lazily down at her, his mockery at her refusal glittering in his eyes like gold glinting in a sheet of slate, "I can see I shall have to persuade you otherwise."

He let the tips of his fingers brush lightly along her arm, amused at the way she jerked away again. He knew just how to handle her now, baiting her with her own responsiveness to him. She didn't like being that responsive, she was fighting against it, but it would be a losing battle, he knew.

And the victory would be his.

A sweet victory—reduced to abject pleading for his love-making this woman who made it totally, shamelessly clear that the only reason she was marrying him was to gain control of the capital her grandfather held for her. That would be a victory he would savour to the full.

As for Andrea, all she could do was put her mask in place and try and get through the evening.

Despite her protestations Nikos took her out later that night, and though it was not some packed and heaving strobe-lit club, there was no way she was going to let him lead her out onto the small, intimate floor in the rooftop restaurant he took her to.

"I said I don't dance and I meant it!" she repeated.

"Try," he said. There was a glint in his eye, and it was not entirely predatory. There was determination in it as well.

Andrea gave in.

He led her out—she as stiff as a board—onto the dance floor. A love song was playing, and though with one part of her mind she was grateful, with the rest of it she felt her terror only increased, for reasons which had nothing to do with her habitual refusal to dance.

Nikos slid his arms around her, resting on the curve of her hips at either side. They burned through the thin fabric of her long peacock-blue dress with a warmth that made the pulse in her neck beat faster. She stood immobile. Her legs began to ache with the tension.

"Put your arms around my neck, *pethi mou*."

The warmth of his breath on her ear made her shiver. He was too close. Much, much too close. The long, lean line of his body pressed against her, hip to hip, thigh to thigh.

Don't think! Don't feel! she adjured herself desperately.

Gingerly, very gingerly, she lifted her arms and placed one palm on either shoulder.

He was in evening dress, and the dark fabric felt smooth and rich to the touch. Beneath the jacket she could feel the hardness of his shoulders. She tensed even more.

"Relax," he murmured, and with the slightest of pressures on her hip started to move her around with him.

For a brief moment she went with him, her right foot moving jerkily in the direction he was urging her. Her legs were like wood, unbending.

"Relax," he said again.

She moved her left leg, catching up with him, and they repeated the movement—him smoothly, she with a jerkiness that she could not control. Her spine was beginning to hurt with the effort.

She lasted another ten seconds, her face rigid, willing herself to keep going. Then, with a little cry, she stumbled away from him.

"I can't! I can't do this!"

She broke across the little dance floor, desperate to sit down, and collapsed back on her chair. Nikos was there in an instant beside her.

"What the hell was that about?" he demanded.

She could hear the annoyance in his voice. Only the annoyance.

"I told you, I don't dance!" she bit at him.

"Don't? Or won't?" he asked thinly, and sat down himself. He seized at the neck of the champagne bottle nestling in its ice bucket and refilled his glass. Hers was almost untouched.

"When we are married," he said, setting down his glass with a snap, "I shall give you lessons."

"You do that," she replied, and took a gulp of her champagne.

Nikos Vassilis would never teach her to dance.

Or anything else.

Surreptitiously, under the table, she slowly rubbed at her thighs. The ache went right through to her bones. And beyond.

Andrea clenched the phone to her ear.

"You're sure? You're absolutely sure?"

"Yes, Miss Fraser, completely sure. The sum of five hundred thousand pounds has been credited to your account."

"And it can't be removed without my permission?" Her question was sharp.

"Certainly not!" The voice of the bank official, a thousand miles away in London, sounded deeply shocked as he replied.

It was the morning of Andrea's wedding.

The happiest day of my life! The day I finally, finally wave a wand over Mum and start our new lives!

As she terminated the call, with repeated assurances from her bank that the money deposited in her account first thing that day was totally and irrevocably hers to dispose of as she would, deep, deep relief flooded through her. She had done it! She had got what she had come for—the promise of freedom from poverty, from ill-health, from the grind and drab penury her mother had put up with for twenty-five years.

Now all she had to do was endure the next twenty-four hours and she would be on her way home.

I can do it! I've done it so far and I can do this last thing!

"*Kyria*, may I start to dress you, please?" Zoe's voice sounded anxiously from the doorway. "Kyrios Coustakis would like you to go downstairs as soon as possible."

Andrea nodded, and the lengthy process of dressing Yiorgos Coustakis's illegitimate granddaughter for her wedding to the man who would run his company and give him the heir he craved got underway.

Andrea felt the relief drain out of her, replaced by a tightness that started to wind around her lungs like biting cord. As she sat in front of the looking glass, Zoe skilfully pinning up her hair, she stared at her reflection. Her eyes seemed too big, her skin too pale. She clenched her hands together in her lap. The reality of what she was about to do hit her, over and over again, like repeated blows.

For all that it was a small, private wedding, it seemed to go on for ever, Andrea thought bleakly. She stood beside her bridegroom, unsmiling, her throat so tight she could hardly say the words that bound her to the tall, straight figure at her side. Sickness churned in her stomach.

She was marrying him! She was actually marrying Nikos Vassilis. Here. Now. Right now. Faintness drummed at her. Her legs and spine ached with the tension wiring her whole body taut.

There was a ring on her finger. She could see it glinting in the sunlight.

It doesn't mean anything! This time tomorrow he'll have

*packed me off back to London and wished me good
riddance. He'll have what he wanted—my grandfather's
company. He'll be glad to see the back of me. He never
wanted me in the first place.*

And he doesn't even intend to be faithful…

Her lips compressed. Three nights ago her grandfather had
summoned her again. Nikos had returned her from yet
another night out, this time a concert, where the combination
of Dvorak and Rachmaninov, plus the thrill of hearing one
of the world's greatest soloists give the Dvorak cello
concerto, had conspired to weaken her façade. As they left
the concert hall she had turned impulsively to Nikos.

"That was wonderful! Thank you!"

Her eyes were shining, her face radiant.

Nikos paused and looked down at her. "I'm glad to have
given you pleasure."

For once there was no double meaning in his words, no
sensual glint in his eyes. For a moment they just looked at
each other. Andrea's ears rang with the echo of the tumultuous finale of the Rachmaninov symphony. Her heart was
almost as tumultuous.

Her eyes entwined with his and something flowed
between them. She could not tell what it was, but it was
something that made her want the moment to last for ever.

She was almost regretful that in fact she never was going
to be his wife in anything but briefest name.

It was a regret that had been destroyed in the two-minute
conversation with her grandfather on her return to his villa.

"There are things to make clear to you," he began in his
harsh, condemning voice, as she stood unspeaking in front of
him to receive her lecture. "From the moment you become
Nikos Vassilis's wife you will behave as a Greek wife should.
He will teach you the obedience you so sorely lack!" His
soulless eyes rested on her like a basilisk, "You will under-

stand that you will gain no privileges from your connection with me. Nor should you imagine that you will gain any privileges from the fact that you are handsome enough for your husband to find you, for the moment, sexually desirable."

He saw the expression on her face and gave a short laugh. "I said 'for the moment' and that is what I meant! Understand this, girl—" his eyes bored into hers "—in Greece a man who is a husband is still a man. And his wife must know her place. Which is to be *silent*! Nikos Vassilis has two mistresses currently—an American model, a tramp who sleeps with any man who passes, and a woman of Athens who is a professional whore. He will discard neither for your sake." His voice dropped menacingly. "If I hear any whining from you, any screeching tantrums because of this, you will regret it! Do you understand?"

She understood all right and she felt revulsion shimmer through her.

Be grateful you're not marrying him for real!

But marrying him she was—if she wanted money for Kim then she must go through this farce of a wedding ceremony.

Not one mistress but two! Her mouth twisted. My, my, what a busy lad Nikos Vassilis was! And still intended to be, so it seemed! Well, that might be the way Greek males saw the world, but she would be having none of it!

The pop of a champagne bottle made her jump, exacerbating her jittery nerves. One of the servants was pouring out foaming liquid into tall glasses. Andrea sipped at hers and looked around her.

All this money, all this wealth, all this opulence and luxury, she thought. I've been drowning in it for two weeks, nearly three.

I want to go home!

The thought caught at her, making her want to cry out with it. She wanted to go home, back to Kim, back to the poky, damp flat that Nikos Vassilis would be appalled to know she had grown up in! He thought he was marrying the Coustakis heiress. What a joke! What a ludicrous, ridiculous joke!

Well, the joke would be on him before the night was out. But she didn't feel like laughing.

Andrea sat in the Louis Quinze armchair, her eyes shut. The champagne had been drunk, she had endured the painfully polite congratulations of the household staff, and now she was waiting for her brand-new husband to emerge out of the library, where her grandfather was finally allowing him to sign the merger contracts. A bevy of men in suits had arrived on the doorstep an hour ago, all with aides and briefcases, and disappeared into the inner sanctum of Yiorgos Coustakis to conduct the real business of the day.

Her legs ached. Carefully she rubbed them through the material of her trousers. Zoe had helped her change out of the long ivory satin gown she had worn for the ceremony, and now she was back in the clothes she had arrived in. Although the staff had emptied just about the whole of the closet into half a dozen suitcases to see her through her honeymoon, Andrea had insisted on her own small case—the one she had brought with her—being handed to her personally. She had packed it the night before, with all her own clothes and the make-up bag containing the key to the airport locker holding her money and passport, right after phoning Tony and telling him that she was coming home in forty-eight hours, and asking him, as always, to give her love to Kim. She hadn't spoken to her mother since arriving here. Hadn't been able to bring herself to. She knew Kim would understand, would make do with having her love passed on every day by Tony.

The ormolu clock on the gilded mantelpiece ticked quietly. The room was silent. The only sound in it was Andrea's heavy heartbeat.

Let me just get through tonight, and then I can be gone!

There was the click of a door opening across the marbled hall, and the sound of voices. She opened her eyes. She could hear the besuited visitors taking their leave, their business done.

Time for Nikos to move on to the next item on his agenda—taking his bride on honeymoon, thought Andrea viciously. Being angry seemed like a good idea right now.

Safer.

She heard Nikos's voice in the hallway, and her grandfather answering shortly. Then footsteps as her grandfather trod heavily back to his own affairs. It must have been a good day's work for him, Andrea thought, selling his company and his bastard granddaughter at the same time.

Something flickered in the corner of her eye, and she twisted her head. It was just a drape, fluttering in the breeze from the open window. The day was warm, the sun inviting. Something caught at her heart, an echo from very long ago, from long before she was born.

Out of nowhere a memory came. A memory of something that had never happened but that she had so often, as a child, wished so ardently were real, and not a mere hopeless longing. The memory of her father, kind and smiling, calling her his princess, her mother his queen, crowning them both with happiness...

But it had never happened. Never. Instead he had died before she was born.

It shouldn't have been like this!

The silent cry came from deep inside her.

But it *is* like this, and there's nothing more I can do about it than I have already done.

"Are you ready?"

Nikos's voice was harsh, cutting through her sombre thoughts. He sounded tense.

She got to her feet.

"Yes," she answered, and walked towards him where he stood in the doorway.

They took their places in the back of her grandfather's vast limousine, Andrea sinking back so far into the seat that she felt she would disappear. Nikos threw himself into the other corner. The car moved forward smoothly.

They did not talk, and Andrea was glad. She had nothing to say to this man now. After tomorrow morning she would never see him again. He was a passing stranger, nothing more.

"Would you like a drink?"

She blinked. Nikos was pulling out a concealed drinks compartment, revealing an array of crystal decanters. She shook her head. He lifted one of the decanters and poured a measure of its contents into a glass. Andrea could smell whisky. He knocked it back in one shot, then replaced the glass and slid shut the cabinet.

"How are you feeling?"

The abrupt question took her by surprise. She shrugged.

"OK," she said indifferently.

He made a sound in his throat that sounded to her ears like an impatient sigh, and then, with a swift movement, he loosened the tie at his throat and undid his collar. Andrea couldn't help looking across at him.

Immediately she wished she hadn't. She didn't know what it was about loosened ties and opened shirt collars, but the kick to her guts was immediate. Nikos ran a hand roughly through his hair, ruffling its satin smoothness. Another kick went straight through her guts.

To her relief, he wasn't paying her any attention, simply staring moodily out through the smoked glass window. Then, abruptly, he spoke.

"*Theos*, but I'm glad that's over!"

The kick in Andrea's guts vanished instantly. He was glad it was over. Fine. So was she. Very glad. Very glad indeed. Couldn't have been gladder. Her lips pressed together.

She looked away, staring out of her own window, and heard Nikos shift in his seat.

"Don't sulk, Andrea," he told her tersely. "You enjoyed that ordeal as little as I did! But it's over now. Thank God!" Then, on an even terser note, he said, "Did you get your money?"

There was condemnation in his voice. Andrea thought of the merger contracts, signed not half an hour ago. Making Nikos Vassilis one of the richest men in Europe.

"Of course," she answered.

"You won't need it," said the man she had married. "I will give you everything you want."

She didn't reply.

He gave another, heavier sigh.

"Andrea, this is a time for plain speaking. We are married. And there is absolutely no reason to suppose things will not work out between us! Your grandfather is out of the picture now. He does not concern us. It is up to us to make this marriage work, and I believe it can—very successfully. If we both just make an effort to make it work! I am prepared to do so—and I ask that you are too. As soon as our honeymoon is over we shall fly to England to meet your mother, and mend bridges there. However much she disapproved of your grandfather, I hope she will think more kindly of me."

She'll never lay eyes on you, thought Andrea, never even know you exist.

Nikos was talking still.

"For now you must put your mind to where we shall live. For the moment I propose my apartment in Athens, but I would prefer, I admit, a more permanent property. We can have a house in London, of course, for when you want to be with your English relatives, and I suggest we buy a villa on one of the islands as well, where we can relax in private."

"Fine," said Andrea. The issue was academic; it didn't matter what she said.

Tonight, she thought, over dinner, or perhaps, better still, in the hotel suite, where I don't have to worry about waiters hovering or other diners looking us over, I can tell him the truth about me. That will put an end to this farce.

Nikos gave up. He had done his best to be civil, but enough was enough. He felt rough. He had been working like crazy ever since Old Man Coustakis had dangled the prospect of a takeover in front of him. Mergers and acquisitions didn't happen overnight—the planning and preparation involved was immense. On top of that he still had to keep Vassilis Inc rolling along, even while he was gearing it up to ingest the much larger Coustakis Industries. It had not, he thought grimly, been the best time to have to go off wooing a bride! Nevertheless he had found the time to squire Andrea around, knowing that being seen prominently in public with her was all part of convincing the Athens business community—and beyond—of the reality of his intentions towards Coustakis Industries.

But for all the evenings spent taking Andrea out he was still no closer to seeing anything more of her than the closed, controlled surface she presented to him. There was certainly a deal of English blood in her, all right, he thought, exasperated. All that cool, calm, collected front she insisted on—polite, but distant. The only time he'd seen any trace of enthusiasm in her had been the other evening at the concert—then her eyes had shone like glossy chestnuts in autumn, and a vitality had filled her usually deadpan expression, catching at him. For a moment, he recalled, as he had looked down at her something had moved in her eyes….

But that had been the only moment. Maybe he had just

imagined it anyway. Certainly the only way he was guaranteed to get a reaction from her was by reminding her, as he took such satisfaction in doing, of just how fragile that English sang-froid of hers really was! Of how a single touch could set her thrumming with sexual awareness of him. *That* was the only currency she responded to! However much she tried to suppress her responsiveness to him.

He looked across at her. She was still staring out of the window, ignoring him. Well, let her! It gave him the opportunity to look her over. Catalogue, in his discerning mind, all her sensual charms—from the generous fullness of her mouth to the richness of her breasts, the long line of her legs...

He felt himself relax for the first time that day. It was done. Today had set the seal on his long, long ascent from the rough streets of Athens to the pinnacle of his achievements.

And he knew exactly how to celebrate.

He closed his eyes and gave himself to the pleasure of contemplating just how good it would be to have the woman beside him beneath him.

"Where the hell are we?"

Andrea's voice was sharp.

"Piraeus," replied Nikos. "The port of Athens."

"The *what*?"

"The port of Athens," Nikos repeated. "Where we embark."

"*Embark?*"

Nikos looked across at her. Now what was she making a fuss about?

Andrea gazed wildly out of the window. She had been paying no attention to their journey from her grandfather's villa, deliberately diverting her mind from what she had just done by thinking about what would be involved in moving Kim out to Spain as soon as possible. But instead of drawing up outside some five-star hotel in the middle of Athens, whence she could easily take a taxi to the airport the following morning, the car had stopped on what she could now see was a quayside, alongside what seemed to be a huge, gleaming vessel.

The chauffeur opened her door and stood back to let her get out. Stiffly, aware that her legs had suddenly started to ache again with unexpected tension, Andrea climbed out and looked around her.

There was a vessel moored at the quayside all right. Absolutely huge. Vast. Stretching like a gleaming monster from bow to stern. A wide gangplank faced her.

"Come," said Nikos.

He took her arm.

"I'm not going aboard that! What the hell is it?"

His mouth tightened. Hadn't Yiorgos even bothered to tell his granddaughter about his latest spending spree?

"It's your grandfather's new toy," he told her. "He's lent it to us for our honeymoon."

Andrea stared. "I thought we were going to spend the night in Athens. At a hotel."

"What for?" countered Nikos. "We might as well set sail as soon as possible."

"I'm not going on that thing!"

Her face was set. Aware, as she was blissfully not, of the highly interested if superficially indifferent attention not only of the chauffeur but of the crewmen at the foot of the gangplank, Nikos impelled her forward. He was not about to have his brand-new bride balk him.

She stumbled slightly, and with a sudden gesture Nikos swept her up into his arms. She gave a small shriek, but Nikos only gave a victor's laugh.

"I'm carrying you over the threshold." He grinned down at her, as much for the sake of his audience as himself, and plunged up the gangplank.

Short of screaming blue murder, Andrea had no option but to let herself be carried aboard the monstrous vessel. She was too terrified to struggle in case they both landed in the murky water lapping beneath the gangplank.

Nikos set her down on the deck and said something in Greek to the man standing there. Hurriedly she smoothed down her jacket and tried to regain her composure. Then Nikos was introducing her.

"This is Captain Petrachos, Andrea *mou*," he said smoothly.

Andrea took in a smartly dressed middle-aged man in an immaculate white naval uniform, with a lot of rings around his cuffs and gold epaulettes, sporting a trim, nautical beard.

"Welcome aboard, Kyria Vassilis. I hope you have a very enjoyable voyage."

"Thank you," she murmured in a strangled voice. It wouldn't be an enjoyable voyage, she thought wildly, it would be a very short one!

"If you're both ready, I'll get her underway."

"Thank you," said Nikos. He held out a hand to Andrea. "Come, let us explore."

His fingers closed around hers, tighter than was strictly necessary. Meekly, Andrea went off with him. She was rearranging her thoughts as quickly as possible. OK, so she had assumed—rashly so, it seemed!—that they would spend the first night of their honeymoon at some luxury hotel in the middle of Athens. Instead they were launching out on this floating private liner! Well, she thought grimly, so what? Her ludicrous marriage could come to a speedy and ignominious end here as well as anywhere else! They'd be docked right back here again before tomorrow morning.

Despite her best intentions to remain indifferent to her oh-so-temporary accommodation, Andrea found her eyes widening automatically as Nikos conducted her around the boat.

It was opulent beyond belief! Everywhere she looked there was rare wood panelling, silk, velvet and leather upholstery, gold and silver fittings, cashmere, suede and skins on floors and walls, inlays and gilding all around. A fortune must have been paid to fit out the interior, let alone the cost of the massive yacht itself, thought Andrea.

As they were shown round by an oh-so-attentive chief steward, Andrea felt increasingly oppressed. What had Nikos called it? Her grandfather's latest toy…

On the upper deck, she watched the mainland of Greece slip away behind them as the yacht nosed out towards the open sea. Meanwhile Nikos watched the wind billow through Andrea's exquisite hair. Her face was set. Clearly she was still in a mood.

Nikos's expression hardened. Just how spoilt was this woman? he thought. Here she was, aboard a yacht that was the last word in extravagance, and she still wasn't happy! He thought back to the days of his childhood, so long ago, when he had been a no-hope street kid. No pampered upbringing for him! He had got here, to the deck of a luxury yacht, as head of one of Europe's largest companies, Coustakis Industries, by his own efforts.

And now he was married to Yiorgos Coustakis's granddaughter.

Well, he had better make the most of it…

CHAPTER EIGHT

CHAMPAGNE beaded in Andrea's glass, fizzing gently. She took another sip. Across the table from her, Nikos did likewise. They were in the dining room—a vast expanse dominated by a huge ebony table, lavishly set with crystal and gold. A suffocating smell of lilies permeated the atmosphere, emanating from the banks of bouquets all around the room. Above their heads a vast chandelier shed its light upon them. Four uniformed stewards stood in a line to one side, ready to do the slightest thing that the honeymoon couple required of them. Deep below the steady thrum of the vessel's motor was the only indication that they were actually on board a boat—the windows were obliterated by vast swathes of black velvet, tasselled in gold, reflecting the gold and black patterning in the deep, soft carpet under Andrea's feet.

She picked at her food. It had probably cost a fortune, just like everything else around her.

"You would prefer something else?" Nikos broke the oppressive silence.

"No, thank you. I'm simply not hungry." Andrea's voice sounded more clipped than she intended, but civility was hard to project right now. Her whole body felt as if it had been tied into an excruciatingly tight knot.

You've got to tell him! End this farce right now! Then you

*can go to bed—alone!—and the yacht can start heading
back to port.*

She wished she had managed to talk to Nikos earlier. She
should have stopped him leaving her alone on the deck, when
he, with nothing more than a brief, "There are a few matters
I must attend to—excuse me," disappeared into the interior.
But he had not reappeared until a short while ago. In the
meantime a stewardess had politely enquired when she would
like dinner served, and when she would like to change for it.
Helplessly, Andrea had gone along with her, telling her to
refer to Mr Vassilis re the timing of dinner.

My, what a good little Greek wife I sound! she had thought.
Deferring to my husband right from the start!

Husband—the word echoed in her brain.

I'm in shock, she thought, as her fork lifted mechanically
to her mouth. I never really believed this would happen. I
blanked it out, focussed only on the money for Kim. But it's
real; it happened. I married Nikos Vassilis today and he's
sitting opposite me, and I *still* haven't told him that this is
going to be the shortest marriage in history!

So tell him now!

I should send away the crew, she thought—get rid of them
all. Then simply open my mouth and tell him I'm leaving in
the morning.

Instead, she found her mind wandering off. What on earth
did all those stewards think? she wondered. A pair of newly-
weds eating in stony silence? Did they think anything? Did
they care? Were they even human? Their faces were totally
expressionless. She had a sudden vision of them being
androids, like something out of science fiction, and had to
suppress a hysterical laugh. Quickly she snapped her mind
onto something else.

Like who on earth had been in charge of the interior design
of this place? They should be taken out and shot, she thought

viciously. To spend such money for such atrocious results seemed like a criminal offence. The décor was hideous, just hideous!

Nikos looked across at her. Her eyes were working around the room disdainfully. Was she picking out flaws, signs of cheapness? he wondered sourly. He glanced down at her plate. She had stopped eating.

With sudden decision Nikos pushed his plate away from him. He was in no mood to eat. No mood to go on sitting here, with a row of statues like a silent Greek chorus witnessing his bride display her feelings about marrying him.

He got to his feet. Andrea started, and looked up at him.

"Come."

He held out a hand to her. His mouth was a thin line.

She hesitated a fraction. There was something about him that unnerved her, but at the same time she, too, felt an over-powering urge to get out of this oppressive room. And after all she needed to speak privately with him, so she might as well go with him.

As he headed towards the door one of the stewards was there before him, attentively opening it. Andrea hurried after Nikos in the same tight green evening dress she'd worn her first night in Greece as he strode along the wide, thickly carpeted corridor. He flung open a door at the end and held it for her.

She went inside.

It was their bedroom.

Mahogany panelled the room from floor to ceiling, and in the middle a gigantic bed, swathed in gold silk, held centre stage. Ornate gold light fittings marched around the room. She dragged her eyes away.

Do it—do it now!

"I've got something to tell you."

Andrea's voice sounded high-pitched and clipped.

"How remarkable. My silent bride deigns to speak."

His sarcasm cut at her. She lifted her chin.

"You might as well know," she said, "I'm going back to England tomorrow. I'm filing for divorce."

Nikos stared at her, completely stilled. The grey of his eyes was like cold, hard slate. Andrea felt her hands clench at her sides. Her legs had started to ache, sensing the tension in the rest of her body.

"You are mistaken."

The brief, bald sentence was quietly spoken, but the nape of Andrea's neck crawled.

"I'm not staying with you!" The pitch of her voice had risen.

"And may I be permitted to ask—" the icy softness cut slivers of flesh from her "—what has led you to make this…unexpected announcement?"

Somehow she managed to stand her ground.

"I should have thought it was obvious! Your sole purpose in marrying me was to clear the way to get hold of my grandfather's company. Now you've done that you don't need to stay married to me for a second longer!"

"An interesting analysis, but fatally flawed," he returned.

"Why?" she demanded.

"Because," said Nikos in that same soft voice which now, instead of cutting slivers from her, had somehow, she did not know how, started to send shivers of a quite different nature quivering down her arms, "you happen to possess charms beyond your possession of Yiorgos Coustakis's DNA. Charms," he went on—and now the shivers spread from her arms across her breasts, her flanks, "that I fully intend to enjoy."

He took a step towards her, the expression in his eyes making it totally, absolutely clear just what charms he had in mind.

She jerked backwards.

"Stay away!"

He stopped again. "Don't give me orders, *pethi mou*. You'll find I don't respond well to them!"

The edge in his voice, steel beneath the velvet, was a warning.

It was also a trip point.

"If you're after sex go and phone for one of your mistresses!" she flung at him.

He stopped dead.

"My what?"

"You heard me—your mistresses! You're running two that the whole world knows about and God knows how many more besides! Go and phone for one of them if you're feeling horny. But don't damn well come near me!"

His eyes were like splinters.

"And just how, may I ask, did you come by this information?"

"Oh, I got a full briefing from my grandfather! It was part of his pre-wedding lecture to me not to kick up a fuss about you still having sex with other women. An obedient Greek wife—" she let the sarcasm flow into her voice "—doesn't make a scene over such trifles as her husband's mistresses!"

Comprehension flooded Nikos's expression, masked by anger. Not at Andrea, but at her wretched grandfather. So that was why the girl had done nothing but sulk all day! Thanks, Yiorgos, for another big favour you've done me! Screwing up my marriage before I even get started on it!

"Right," he began, "we'll get a few things clear, I think. Firstly, yes, of course I have had liaisons with other women—I was free to do so and I did! But—" he held up his hand "—I have not set eyes on another woman since the day I met you."

His assurance left Andrea less than impressed.

"So you just dumped them, did you? Charming!"

Nikos shut his eyes briefly, then opened them. "My relationships with both women are—were—what you might call 'open'," he said. "Xanthe Palloupis has several other rich lovers who help keep her in the style she fully intends to hold on to for as long as her looks last, and Esme Vandersee—"

"Esme Vandersee? The supermodel?" Andrea's voice cut in incredulously. "She's one of the world's most beautiful women!"

There was a note in her voice that Nikos did not miss, and it sent a shaft of satisfaction through him which, right now, he badly needed. It had been something between dismay and jealousy.

"She is also," he said, "quite happy to reward a large assortment of her chosen admirers with a hands-on tour of her spectacular body. I'm confident she found it extremely easy to replace me," he finished dryly.

But Andrea didn't want to hear about Esme Vandersee and her spectacular body. In fact if the supermodel had suddenly beamed aboard right in front of her she would have got a dusty reception from her lover's bride. Extremely dusty.

She quelled the stab of pure possessiveness that darted through her at the thought of Esme Vandersee or Xanthe Whatever-her-name-was making moves on Nikos Vassilis. It was utterly inappropriate.

And totally irrelevant.

Why am I discussing Nikos's mistresses? she thought. They've got nothing to do with why I'm going home tomorrow!

"So," Nikos continued smoothly, "now I understand the reason for your ill-temper all day, Andrea *mou*—"

"I'm still leaving tomorrow morning! And it's got nothing to do with any of the women you put out for! I have absolutely no intention of staying married to you!"

The glitter was back in Nikos's eyes.

"And what objection, may I ask again, are you going to put forward now?"

Her eyes flicked to the opulence all around them. Kim's entire flat would just about fit into the space of this single stateroom! *Tell him the truth about yourself now—he'll send you packing the moment he hears!*

"For heaven's sake, how could I possibly even *think* of being married to you? We come from totally different worlds—"

She broke off. Something was in his face that made her feel frightened suddenly.

Different world? Oh, yes, different worlds indeed. A fatherless street boy and a pampered heiress...

"Nevertheless..." the softness was back in his voice, and it was slicing at her flesh again "...you are my wife, Andrea Vassilis, and if you understand nothing about what it means to be Greek, understand this—no husband lets his bride make a laughing stock of him by walking out on him straight after their wedding! And never, ever—" his eyes slid over her face, her body "—before their wedding night..."

He came towards her. She could not move. Slate eyes fixed her where she was. Slate eyes with only one purpose in them.

The fear dissolved. For a brief moment desire flooded through her, powerful and irresistible. She crushed it aside. There was no place for it. There could not be. There must not be. In its place came a flat, dull resolve. So it was going to be like this, was it? Very well, so be it. She'd see it through to the bitter end—and be on a plane home tomorrow.

She stood there motionless. In her mind she searched for the impenetrable mask she had donned every time she was in his company. It was time to wear it again.

He stopped in front of her. She was very still. Like a

statue. He reached a hand towards her. The back of his fingers brushed her cheek, trailing down over the column of her neck, turning to close over the cusp of her shoulder, bared except for the narrow straps of her dress.

"The last time you wore this you melted into my arms like honey on a warm spoon."

The thumb of his other hand came up to ease along the trembling line of her lips.

She stiffened, clutching the carapace to her.

She was holding out on him. Denying her response to him. He smiled. This and this alone was the way to communicate with the woman who today had been joined in matrimony to him. And when, eventually, she lay beneath him, and throbbed in his embrace, then—oh, then—let her think of the "different worlds" they came from. Let her think of the "release of capital" she'd gained today. Let her think of walking out of their brand-new marriage. Let her think of anything she liked—if she could.

But all she would be capable of thinking about, he knew, with every fibre of his being, would be him and him alone.

He let his hands fall to his sides. She was resisting him— she would do so no longer. Swiftly he crossed to the banks of wardrobes lining the side of the room, throwing open one door after another until he found what he was looking for. Then, grasping delicate folds, he tossed it at her.

"Go and change!"

He nodded towards the *en suite* bathroom. Andrea looked at the garment he had thrown her. She knew what it was— the negligee he had bought her in the shop that had treated her like a rich man's floozy.

She turned and walked into the bathroom. Well, in a few minutes now she would be a rich man's unwanted wife.

The knowledge stabbed at her. It hurt—it hurt more than she had ever dreamt it could. Knowing what was coming.

Knowing that she was to be Nikos Vassilis's oh-so-unwanted wife.

But it was inevitable. Had been from the moment he had looked across her grandfather's terrace at her and she had seen the flare of sexual interest in his eyes—felt it set light in her an answering flame.

Time to douse the fires.

Permanently.

She hugged the carapace to her more tightly than ever.

As the bathroom door clicked behind her Nikos got busy. Ringing for a steward, he had the scarcely touched bottle of champagne brought to him, and let the man turn down the bed. Then, retiring to the matching *en suite* bathroom he prepared himself. He had already shaved before dinner, and now it was a matter of moments to strip off and don a bathrobe.

He was already aroused. His celibacy of the last few weeks was obviously being felt—protestingly—by his body. He found himself thinking back to when he'd first thought through the implications of marrying Yiorgos Coustakis's unknown granddaughter. He had worried about her lack of looks, her virginity, the fact that he would have to steel himself to get through his wedding night while making it as physically painless as possible for his dutiful bride.

His mouth twisted. Well, that was one word he didn't have to apply to Andrea! Dutiful she was not!

Would you want her to be? came the immediate ironic question, and the answer was immediate. No way! What he wanted her to be was…passionate, ardent, melting, molten, sensual, arousing, scorching, purring…

The litany went on inside his head, each word an image that burned with increasing fire in his guts. *Theos*, he wanted her! Wanted her as he wanted no other woman!

As an academic exercise he tried to make himself

remember what Xanthe looked like, Esme—but he could not do it. There was only one face, one body that he could see.

Andrea's.

My wife.

Possession surged through him. He was about to make her his in very truth, physically merging their bodies into one.

Desire kicked at him again, more urgent than ever.

With a tug he opened a shallow drawer in the vanity unit and drew out a handful of the small silvery packets that nestled within. He gave a wolfish grin. Oh, he'd get through the lot of them tonight, he thought.

He felt his body tighten. Sexual anticipation flooded him.

He strode out of the bathroom.

She was there, waiting for him. His breath caught.

Beautiful! His body jerked in salute of the image she made.

She stood in the centre of the room like a flame-haired queen. Her glorious locks were loose, tumbling down over her shoulders. The white, almost transparent silk of her negligee outlined her body, her full breasts thrust forward, straining against the taut material.

Desire kicked in him, hard and insistent.

"You're so beautiful—"

His voice was husky.

Andrea heard it, heard the note of raw desire in it. Her breath caught, and a shot of pure adrenaline surged through her. Then the words he had uttered penetrated, and the rush died, draining away like dirty oil from the sump of a wrecked car.

You're so beautiful...

Her mouth made a tight twist, and her eyes took on a strange brightness.

"Am I? Am I beautiful?"

Her voice was as strange as the twist to her mouth, the

brightness of her eyes. She spoke to him, spoke to the man who stood waiting for her, stripped and ready for action.

A man who made her feel weak all over, inside and out, who made her heart clench and her breath catch just with looking at him.

But now it was him looking at her. She let him look. Wanted him to look.

That was the only way she could play this now—nothing else had worked. This must. It could not fail.

She went on speaking in that low, strange voice.

"This is what you want, isn't it, Nikos? A beautiful woman in your bed. Am I beautiful enough, Nikos? Am I?"

Her hands slid around the nape of her neck, lifting up her hair. She moved her head so that the glorious tumble flamed like fire. Then her hands slid down to the bodice of her negligee, fingers sliding beneath the delicate expensive material. She slipped it back, baring her shoulders, her hands grazing her breasts.

And all the time her eyes held his, never letting them go for a second.

"Am I beautiful, Nikos? Your beautiful bride?"

He couldn't answer her. His breath was frozen in his throat, though in his veins the blood roared.

She smiled. A fey, taunting smile.

Inside her head, behind the mask of her face, she was filled with flat, cold desolation. She was being cruel, she knew, but it was the only way. The only way.

She moved towards the bed, gliding softly, and lay down upon it, one hand loosely gathering the half-discarded material of her negligee to her breasts, the other smoothing the silk along the line of her legs.

"Am I your beautiful bride, Nikos? Beautiful enough for your bed?"

He came towards her. Purpose, desire, arousal—all in his eyes, his face—his ready, hungry body.

308 THE GREEK'S VIRGIN BRIDE

He could not resist her! Not for a second longer! Tumult consumed him. Who was this woman? One moment a cold, sulking ice-maiden, denouncing him for his sexual appetites, icily demanding a divorce before the ink was dry on the marriage certificate, sneering at him for his lowly origins. And now—now she was lying here, eternal Eve, displaying her body for him, lush and beautiful, oh, so beautiful, tempting him, arousing him—inviting him.

He looked down at her, caught in a pool of light, her body on show for him, veiled only by the sheerest of fabrics.

"Show me your body, Andrea—"

It was a rasp, a husk—a command, a plea.

There was a brightness in her eyes, a strangeness to her lips. He did not see it, saw only the soft outline of her limbs, her breasts, her belly...

"Show me..."

Her hand moved on her thigh, sliding the silk away, letting it slither from her thighs to the bedclothes on either side.

She looked at him. There was no expression in her eyes. None at all.

There was silence. A silence so profound Nikos knew he could hear his own heart beating.

Oh, dear God, dear God...

He stared down, the twisted, pitted surface of her legs scarring into his retinas as deeply as the scars that gouged and knotted her limbs from hip to ankle, runnelling through her wasted muscles, winding around her legs like some hideous net.

Horror drowned through him. She saw it in his face, his eyes. The brightness in her own eyes burned like acid. The tightness in her throat was like a drawn wire. Then deliberately, jerkily, she covered her legs again and stood up.

He stood aside to let her get to her feet. She yanked the negligee back into place over her shoulders, tugging at the belt to make it tighter—hugging her carapace into place. She must not lose it now. She must not.

"The comedy is ended," she announced. Her voice was flat. "I'll sleep in another room tonight. If you could be so good as to ensure we dock back at Piraeus tomorrow, I'll make my own way to the airport."

She turned to go.

He caught her arm.

She looked down to where his fingers closed around her flesh.

"Let me go, Nikos. There's no need to say anything. Not a thing. I'm—sorry—it came to this. I thought it wouldn't be necessary. That you would accept the dissolution of our ridiculous marriage without any need to get this far. But in the end—" her voice tightened yet another unbearable notch "—it seemed the quickest way to convince you. Now, please let me go. I'll get my things and find another room…cabin… whatever they're called on a boat like this."

He let her go, but only to slide his hand past her wrist and take her hand.

It was strange, thought Andrea, with the part of her mind where her act did not seem to work. The feel of his fingers wrapping hers was making her feel very strange. Very strange indeed.

He sat down on the edge of the bed, drawing her down beside him. His hand did not let go of hers.

"What happened, Andrea?" he asked.

There was something in his voice that made her eyes blink. The acid was burning them and she couldn't see properly. Something was misting her vision.

"What happened?" he asked again. His voice was very quiet.

She stared down at the carpet. There was a gold swirling in the pattern. It shifted in and out of focus. It seemed very important that it stay in focus. She stared at it again.

After a while, she spoke.

"It was a car crash, when I was fifteen. The older brother of one of my classmates was driving. He was driving us home—we'd been to the movies. I—I don't remember much. We swerved suddenly—a tyre burst, apparently—glass on the road, a broken bottle or something—and hit a wall. I was in the passenger seat. I was knocked out. I got trapped. The firemen had to cut me out. My legs were all smashed up. In hospital…in hospital…the doctors wanted…wanted…" Her voice was dry. "They wanted to amputate—they said they were so smashed up they couldn't save them."

She didn't hear the indrawn breath from the man sitting beside her. Nor did she feel the sudden tightening of his grip on her hand.

She went on staring at the carpet.

"My mother wouldn't let them. She said they had to save them. Had to. So—so they did. It…it took a long time. I was in hospital for months. Everything got pinned together somehow, and then, eventually, I was allowed into a wheelchair. They said I'd never walk. So much had gone. But Mum said I was going to walk. She said I had to. Had to. So…so I learned to walk again. I got sent to a special place where they help you learn to use your body again. It took a long time. Then they sent me for more operations, and that set me back, but Mum said it didn't matter, because I was going to walk again. I had to. And I did."

The pattern in the carpet was going out of focus again. She swallowed.

"The only thing is, I can't do things like…like dance, and so on. It…it hurts. And I get frightened I'll damage them somehow. And though I can swim—it was part of my physio and still is, because the water helps to take the weight off my legs as I exercise them—I do it very early in the morning, when no one can…no one can see me."

She blinked. "I'm very lucky. Incredibly lucky. I learnt that in hospital, and in the physio place. There were others much worse off than me. Now the only thing wrong with me is that I have to be careful and not overdo things. And never marrying—" Her voice shook, but she steeled it to be still, and carried on. "Never marrying won't be so bad. I've accepted that. I know no man can want me, not when they know, not when they've seen—"

Her voice broke.

Quietly, Nikos slid his hand out of hers. Then, just as quietly, he slipped to his knees on the floor at her feet. The dark of his head gleamed like black satin. He put his hands on her thighs. Beneath the flawless silk of the negligee he could feel the surface of her legs, uneven and knotted. Slowly he pushed the material aside.

She tried to stop him, tried to jerk her legs away from him, but his hands pressed on the sides of her thighs. His head bowed.

Slowly, infinitely slowly, Nikos let his hands move with absolute gentleness over the scarred, runnelled tissue of her legs, across the twisted muscles of her thighs, down over the knife-cut knees, along the warped, lumpen line of her calves, to circle her ankles. Then slowly, infinitely slowly, with the same absolute gentleness, he moved his hands back up, to rest once more on the sides of her thighs.

Then he lowered his mouth to her legs and kissed them— each thigh, each knee.

She sat still, so utterly still. All that moved within her body was her heart. She could not breathe; she could not think. Could not understand.

How can he touch them? How can he not be revolted? Disgusted?

A cruel memory surfaced in her thoughts. His name had been Dave, and he'd had a reputation with the girls. He'd made a play for her the moment he'd set eyes on her, and her refusal to go out with him had only made him more determined. She'd been twenty-two, and by then she had known just how ugly her legs were going to be all her life. She'd been chary of men. But Dave had gone on at her and on at her, and he was good-looking, with winning ways, and she couldn't help but fancy him, and in the end she'd given in to temptation and gone out with him. She'd wanted so much to be normal again—have boyfriends, discover sex. Fall in love. They'd dated quite a while, and he hadn't seemed to mind that she couldn't go clubbing, and she'd even, after a few weeks, told him about her accident. He hadn't seemed to mind.

Until the night she'd finally decided that twenty-two was no age to be a virgin still, and Dave had wanted her, so very, very much...

She could remember the look on his face as if it was yesterday. The strangled noise in his throat as she took her jeans off in his flat, the undisguised expletive that exploded from him. The word he'd called her.

Freak.

Crippled freak.

It's what I am. What every man will think me...

"Nikos—"

She caught his head with her hands. His hair was like black silk to her touch.

"Nikos—don't, please—"

He raised his mouth, lifting his face to her.

"Hush, *agape mou*, hush." His voice was low.

He slipped his forearms underneath her thighs, and with the lightest exertion swung her legs round and on to the bed, following them himself to lie beside her. He leaned over her as she lay there, eyes wide and confused.

"Nikos—" Her voice was faint.

He laid a finger over her mouth.

"This is not a time for talking," he told her.

Then slowly, sensually, he began to make love to her.

It was like walking along the blade of a knife. Every move, every gesture, every touch was crucial. Control beaded in every nerve.

This is for her, not for you—

Carefully, incredibly carefully, Nikos kissed her. His mouth was light, as light as swansdown, his lips feathering hers, his tongue flickering at the corners of her mouth until it opened to him, and then slowly, delicately, he explored within.

Her eyes had shut. He hadn't noticed when, but it didn't matter. He knew she could not help it. Knew that the only way she could accept what was happening to her was by closing herself to everything but sensation—pure, blissful sensation.

And it was the same for him. He too knew that he must focus only and absolutely on what was happening now. Not just because of the utter physical control he had to impose on himself, but because somewhere, deep down inside, emotions were running so deep he could not name them. All but one.

Anger. Anger at a universe where such things happened. Anger at himself for being such a boor, a fool. Anger, most of all, at the men who had looked at her and let her feel that she was repulsive to them...

His mouth glided down the smooth, flawless column of her throat, seeking the hollow at its base where her pulse throbbed. With the skill of all his years he parted her robe, shaping delicately, sensuously, the sweet richness of her breasts. His mouth moved to their reddened tips and his tongue flickered over the hardening peaks.

Her heard her gasp, low in her throat, felt her head roll back as she savoured the sensations he aroused in her.

His body surged, and he quelled it urgently. He wanted—*Theos* how he wanted—to take her swollen nipple into his mouth, to suck and take his fill, move his body over hers at once, fill her with his, and feed and sate his appetite on her.

This is for her, not you—

With extreme control he held back, focussing only on her response, compressing her ripe breasts together so that his tongue could move from one peak to the other, endlessly keeping both in straining engorgement while little moans pulsed in her throat.

He felt her fingers come around his shoulders, beneath the towelling of his robe, pushing it back, sliding it from him, seeking the broad swathe of his shoulderblade to press into the smooth, flawless flesh of his back. He eased the robe from him to let her access him, never for a moment lifting his mouth away from her, only letting it drift down, over the swell of her breast, to lave the suddenly tautened plane of her belly.

And soon beyond.

As his fingers began to thread, tantalisingly, oh, so tantalisingly, in the tight curls that nested above the vee of her legs, Andrea thought she could stand no more. The sensation overload of her whole body was so intense, so exquisite she could not bear it.

But she could not escape it. It was like being sucked into a dark, breathless whirlpool, circling with infinite slowness, infinite power. She knew she ought to open her eyes, but she could not. Knew she ought to stop this, now, right now, push away those hands, that mouth...

But she could not. She was drowning in sensation, lost to all reason. There was nothing, nothing in the universe except what she was feeling now—as if her whole body were one whole, sweet mesh of soft, liquid pleasure that suffused every cell, every fibre of her being.

A pleasure that was growing with a mute, remorseless crescendo, spreading out in one sweet wave after another, quivering down all her nerves, washing through and through her as the slow, dark whirlpool took her with it.

His mouth was where his fingertips had been, and now his fingertips had moved on, brushing down the tender flesh on either side of the tightly curling nest of hair, seeking the parting of her legs.

Almost she tensed. Almost she thrust him back—away. Almost the knowledge of her disfigurement triumphed. But then, with a breathless sigh of pleasure, she felt her thighs loosen, fall open.

The whorls of pleasure intensified. She was weightless, floating in some sea of bliss that took everything away but the flickering of his tongue, the soft easing of his fingertip through folds made satin with a dew that his touch drew out of her.

The sensation was all there was.

Nothing had felt like this. Nothing in all her life. She had not known such sensation could exist.

A long, sweet moan escaped her. Her head rolled back, shoulders almost lifting from the bedclothes. The flickering intensified, the stroking fingertip easing her lips apart, exposing new, sweet feminine flesh to his skilled, exquisite touch.

Her hands clenched in the bedcover and she moaned again. Sensation broke over her again, wave after wave. And yet, with an instinct she did not know existed, she knew she was not yet sated. These were just the shallows of sensation.

She felt her hips lift and strain towards him, seeking more—more.

He answered her supplication. His fingertip drew back,

gliding delicately in the flooding dew, circling slowly, rhyth-
mically, like the vortex of a whirlpool, at the entrance to her
body. Her fingers clenched again into the heavy folds of the
bedspread, and her hips called to him again.

His tongue hovered minutely, and then, as the most
drowning sensation yet broke through her, its very tip touched
at the part that had swollen, all unbeknownst to her, past the
protective furrow which had sheltered it.

Her breath caught, lips parting. What she had felt till now
had been an echo, a shadow. Now, *now* was the true flame to
her body lit. It burned beneath his touch, like a sweet, intense
fire, making her whole body molten, focussing her entire
being, as through a burning lens, on that single point of heat.
It grew, and grew. She did not know how, or why—could feel
nothing now, not the closeness of his body, nor the ministra-
tions of his fingertip circling steadily, steadily, as her body
opened to him, nor even the controlled, oh, so controlled
accuracy of the flickering of his tongue, just there, just *there*,
until the heat there, just *there*, was all there was, all there
could ever be.

She was molten, molten, the warmth welling from the
only centre of her body that could exist now, until it ascended
through every vein, higher, ever higher, as the whirlpool
sucked at her and sucked, and she could hear, from far, far
away, a long, slow, rising cry that came from somewhere so
deep inside she had never known its existence, reaching out,
reaching out to exhale through her lifted, opening mouth…

Heat flooded through her, a huge, overwhelming sheet of
flame that simply raced to encompass her whole body. It
flooded again and again—a surge of flame, lifting her body,
arching her spine, her neck, a surge of pleasure so intense,
so absolute, it filled her with incredulity and awe that her
body could feel so much…so much.

And go on feeling. It came, wave after wave, one more

blissful than the next, and the cry from the heart of her being went on, and on, and on...

She could feel the internal muscles of her body rippling inside her, feel the blood surging, feel the pulsing of every fold, the rush of moisture releasing.

Time lost all meaning as she gave herself, consumed, to the molten overflow flooding and flooding again through her. And still it came. Until, singing its ecstasy, her ecstasy, her body began, finally to ebb, exhausted, sated, the vast, encompassing whirlpool slowly, slowly stilling...

Arms were holding her. There was the alien scent of maleness, the strong hardness of masculine muscles, the brush of body hair against the new softness of her breasts. She was folded into it. Folded against him.

Slowly reality came back to her, and she realised what had happened.

Andrea lay in his arms as motionless as a rag doll. Her entire body was limp. He was not surprised. When she had peaked it had been like an endless outpouring of her whole body, the flush of ecstasy suffusing the paleness of her skin, her eyes fluttering beneath her long, long lashes, her breath exhaling in a long, slow susurration of bliss.

And now she lay in the sheltering circle of his arms.

Nikos held her quietly, not moving, not stirring, knowing his own body was at peace as well.

And more than his body.

He had done the right thing, he knew. Followed his unconscious instinct—knowing, somehow, that he must take her on a journey she needed to make. A journey that must be an exorcism of all her fears, a healing of the wounds that had been laid upon her.

He felt the inert length of her legs beside him and coldness iced through him. He heard her words again—*The doctors wanted to amputate...*

Inside his head he heard his answering cry of negation of such a fate.

"*Andrea mou...*" He did not know if he said the words aloud or not. But they echoed in him all the same.

His eyes were heavy. At his side, in the cradle of his arms, he felt her body slacken imperceptibly, saw her face slide into repose, her breath shallowing into sleep. He felt its call, his eyelids too heavy to hold apart, and as his own breathing slowed his muscles relaxed, like hers, into the sweet embrace of sleep as well.

CHAPTER NINE

THERE was sunlight in the room, bright and pouring, flooding in from the wide-set windows. Andrea stirred, surfacing unwillingly from sleep. There was some reason she didn't want to wake up, but she didn't want to think about what that might be.

But wake she must. Someone was shaking her shoulder. Not roughly, but insistently.

"Andrea, *mou*, we are wasting a glorious day! Come, breakfast awaits."

Nikos's voice was a mix of chiding and encouraging, his tone deliberately light. It would be the best way to play it, he knew. For the moment at least. She didn't want to move, didn't want to acknowledge his existence, but she must—this was not something she could run away from or deny any longer. He would not hurry her, he would be as gentle as she needed, but her denial must end. He desired her and she desired him—and the trifle of her scarred legs must not get in the way of her acceptance of that inalienable truth.

He dropped a kiss on her exposed cheek.

"What do you say in English? Lazybones?" He stood up. "There is a pot of tea for you here to wake you up—the chef poured all his genius into making you the perfect English 'cuppa'—you must not offend him by rejecting it! He will sulk for days and we shall starve! So, drink your tea like a good girl, and come and join me on deck in fifteen minutes." He stooped briefly, to brush her cheek very softly with his fingers. "It will be all right, Andrea—trust me."

Then he was gone.

She needed every one of those fifteen minutes he had allowed her. As she showered and dressed a single thought drummed through her brain—*Don't think about it! Just don't think about it!*

But the moment she emerged onto the sunlit deck, where a breakfast table was set up, and laid eyes on Nikos sitting there it was all for nothing. Memory, in total, absolute detail, came flooding back to her.

He could see it in her face, her eyes, and acted immediately. He got up and came across to her swiftly, taking her hands.

"Come—breakfast," he said. "What would you like to have?" He swept an arm to indicate a sideboard groaning with enough food to feed an army, with everything on it from fresh fruit to devilled kidneys.

Grateful, as he had intended, for the banality of choosing something to eat, she let him help her to lightly scrambled eggs, toast, and a plate of highly scented freshly cut pineapple. She felt surprisingly hungry.

*If I don't think about it, it never happened...*she told herself, sitting herself down at the table.

There were no crew in sight, and she was grateful for that too. Whether it was Nikos being tactful she didn't know, but she simply couldn't have borne to have that mute chorus in attendance.

Instead, she looked about her. The deck they were seated on faced the stern, and all Andrea could see all around was a glorious expanse of sparkling blue water. The sight lifted her spirits of its own accord. A tiny breeze whisked around her cheeks, fanning the tendrils of her hair. It was a bright, fresh, brand-new day.

From nowhere, absolutely nowhere, a sense of wellbeing filled her. It was illogical, impossible, but it was there. She felt her spirits lighten. Who could be otherwise on a morning like this?

She set to, demolishing her breakfast swiftly. She'd only picked at her food over that excruciating dinner last night, and now she was making up for it. There was something so incredibly comforting about scrambled eggs on toast...

Nikos said nothing, just busied himself leafing through a newspaper as he worked steadily through a surprisingly hearty breakfast. As they ate, with him paying her no more attention than from time to time checking if she would like more tea, more toast, more butter, little by little she found herself capable of lifting her eyes from her food, and instead of sliding them immediately to the sparkling horizon let them pass, in focus, over the man sitting opposite her.

Don't think about it! she reminded herself, and to her surprise the technique seemed to work.

Maybe it was because Nikos seemed so totally relaxed. He sat there, a man at peace with the world, eating his breakfast beneath an Aegean sky. Maybe too, Andrea realised, it was because for the first time she was seeing him in informal clothes. Instead of the habitual business suit or evening dress this morning he was wearing a beautifully cut but informally tailored short-sleeved, open-necked fawn-coloured shirt and tan-coloured chinos.

He still looked devastating, of course, but the air of command was absent—or, if not absent, definitely off-duty.

As he swallowed the last of his coffee, folded up his newspaper and glanced towards her some twenty minutes later she realised she was just sitting there, her own breakfast finished, content to feel the warm sun on her face, the air ruffling her hair occasionally, and watch the stern flag flap in the breeze.

It dawned on her that they were not moving.

"Where are we?" she asked, puzzled. "Why have we stopped?"

"We are on the approach to Heraklion. If you wish, we can make landfall."

"Heraklion?" queried Andrea. "Isn't that on Crete?"

"Yes. The island is visible from the aft. Shall we go and look?"

There didn't seem to be a particularly good reason not to, and Andrea found herself standing up as Nikos moved to draw back her chair. She walked beside him along the side of the vessel, and as they drew clear onto the foredeck she could see the long east-west land mass of Greece's largest island lying to the south of them. Mountains rose in the interior, almost all along the spine of the island, and Nikos pointed to the town of Heraklion on the coast in front of them.

"Knossos is only a few kilometres inland. Would you like to go and visit the Minotaur?" he asked genially.

The prospect tugged at her. Then, sinkingly, she realised she must ask for the yacht to put about and return to Piraeus. She had a plane to catch.

As if reading her thoughts, Nikos touched her arm lightly. Though it was only the briefest gesture, she felt her skin tingle.

"Stay a little, Andrea *mou*. What harm will it do, after all?"

His voice was light, but there was a cajoling beneath the lightness. "Today we could just play tourists. It's been a strain, these last weeks—let us relax a little, *ne*?"

She tried to answer, but couldn't. If she answered him she would have to open that door that she had banged tightly shut this morning as she got out of bed. And she couldn't face that.

The alternative was to go on along this path she was on now. It would be temptingly easy to do so.

She had never seen Knossos, and was unlikely ever to get the opportunity to do so again. Just as she had wanted to see Athens while she was there, now she wanted to see the famous site of the very first civilisation Europe could boast, the Minoans, whose vast, labyrinthine Bronze Age palace at Knossos made the Parthenon look modern.

And see it she did, joining the throng of tourists who poured over the massive remains of the excavated and partially restored site, amazed at the sheer size of a palace first built over four thousand years ago and destroyed so cataclysmically. She was both fascinated and awestruck—and saddened. The exquisite murals, even if restored, caught at a world where militarism and armaments seemed quite absent—a world where nature and fertility were more valued than war and conquest.

"They did not need military might—all the Minoan palace sites lack ramparts," Nikos reminded her when she found herself remarking on it. "Theirs was a maritime trading empire, a thalassocracy, linking Egypt, the Levant, Asia Minor and Greece. And, of course, the legend of the annual tribute of seven youths and seven maidens to feed to the Minotaur, so central to the story of the gallant Theseus, more likely represents the tribute the ancient mainland Greeks, the Myceneans, were required to pay the Minoans. It was more likely commercial rivalry that brought down the Minoan empire, not the death of a monster!"

"And the earthquakes and tidal waves," added Andrea. "How terrible it must have been!" She shuddered, remembering a television programme she had once watched which had recreated, with computer simulation, the terrifying volcanic explosion of the island of Thera, modern Santorini, which had blasted the atmosphere with dark, choking, poisonous dust and sent a wall of water hurtling south to crash devastatingly upon the low, defenceless Cretan shore.

She looked around her. All about had once been walls and rooms, stairs and chambers, courtyards and gardens, storerooms and towers, bustling with people carrying on their ordinary, everyday lives. All gone now. All silenced.

They were once as alive as you are now. Felt the warmth of the same sun upon their faces, felt the same earth beneath their feet as you do now.

As if he could read her thoughts on her face, she heard Nikos say quietly at her side, "We must live while we can, Andrea. We have no other choice except to make the most of what is given to us. Our minds, our hearts—our bodies and our passions."

For a moment, the briefest moment, she met his eyes and read what was in them. Then, his message sent, he lightened his expression.

"Are you hungry? Let us eat."

They lunched, at Andrea's instigation, at a small tourist restaurant close to the palace of Knossos, which, though clearly catering for the masses, appealed to her with its vine-dappled terrace set back, overlooking the road. It was pretty, and quite unpretentious, and they both ate a typical tourist salad of feta cheese and tomatoes drizzled in olive oil, followed by the ultimate Greek tourist dish of lamb kebabs.

If Nikos was taken aback by her choice, he hid it. Maybe after a lifetime of eating only in the most expensive restaurants it was amusing for her to eat such humble fare and mingle with ordinary folk whose grandfathers were not multimillionaires.

She looked quite natural in such a place, he suddenly realised. Her hair was drawn back into a simple plait, and if he did not know better he'd have said that her clothes—jeans and a simple white T-shirt—could easily have come out of a chainstore. She must be favouring a designer who charged a fortune to achieve that very effect.

Nor did she balk in the slightest at the taste of the robust but rough Domestica wine she drank. To Nikos it brought back memories from his early years, before his palate had become exposed only to the finest vintages. He wondered when it was that he had last drunk such table wine as now filled his glass.

Too long. The words echoed inside his head, and he put them aside with a frown.

"Where would you like to go this afternoon?" he asked, to change his thoughts. "Shall we drive to a beach and sun ourselves?"

Immediately he cursed himself. In his head he heard her low words, filled with quiet, unemotional anguish, saying how she only swam very early in the morning, when no one could see her legs...

"Or perhaps you would like to see Heraklion?" he hurried on. "Or we could drive further into the interior, perhaps? There is Mount Ida to see, where the god Zeus is said to have been born, in a cavern there."

"I'd like that," Andrea replied. "I...I'm not sure I'm up to much more walking, I'm afraid. I'm rather feeling it in my legs after tramping around Knossos. Not that I'd have missed it for the world!" she added, lest she sound whining.

"I'll phone for the car," said Nikos, and got out his mobile phone to summon the large, chauffeur-driven hire car that had brought them here from the yacht and which was now parked in the palace car park.

"Nikos—" She stayed his hand and he stopped, surprised. "I—I don't suppose," she found herself saying wistfully, "it would be possible—if not today, then perhaps tomorrow—if we are still here, of course," she burbled, feeling awkward suddenly, "to have a car like that one there to drive around in, would it?"

She pointed down to where one of the legion of open-sided

four-by-fours, favoured by tourists as hire cars, was making its way along the road.

"They look such fun," she said.

They *were* fun, she discovered shortly. For the first time it dawned on her that being the wife of a rich man—however fraudulently, to her mind, and certainly however temporarily—had its compensations. A swift phone conversation with the chauffeur and the luxury limo had been traded for a self-drive bouncing Jeep.

She had to hang on tight, especially as they started to climb into the central Cretan mountains. The hairpin bends were tight, and got tighter, but as they did the views got more and more stupendous. The mildness of the lowland air crispened into a clarity that cleansed the lungs.

"This is wonderful! Thank you!"

They had stopped at a viewpoint and were looking down over the island, towards the sea beyond. Forested slopes spread out like skirts around them.

"I am glad you are enjoying yourself, *agape mou*."

He smiled down at her. Again, as in the aftermath of the concert, there was nothing in Nikos's reply except open appreciation of her gratitude for showing her Crete.

She smiled back up at him, her eyes warm, and in that moment she saw his expression change, as if her smile had done something to him.

Hurriedly she looked away, saying the first thing that came into her head.

"For a Greek island, Crete is very forested," she observed.

"It was not always so," he answered, accepting her gambit. He must go slowly—oh, so slowly—with this wounded deer, lest she flee him and wound herself even more in the process. "When the Venetians ruled Crete, and then the Turks, much of the forest was cut down for timber for ships. In those days public enemy number one for trees were mountain goats, who ate the saplings before they could mature. So a decree went out offering a bounty for every dead goat brought down from the mountains." His voice became very dry. "It is perhaps predictable to relate that an active goat-breeding programme was soon well underway amongst the impoverished but financially astute mountain-dwelling peasants…"

She laughed, as he had intended.

"The best-laid plans of bureaucrats," she commented, equally dryly.

He slipped his hand into hers, making the movement very casual. "Indeed. Come—back on the road again. Finding a café would be very welcome, *ne*?"

They stopped for coffee at a little *cafeneion* perched precariously, so it seemed to Andrea, over the side of a precipitous slope. The view, however, more than made up for it. They sat in silence, absorbing the peace and serenity around them, but it was a silence a world away from the silence at dinner the night before, Andrea found herself thinking. Then it had all been strain and horribleness. Now—now it was… companionable.

The thought was odd. Almost unbelievable.

As she sat there, sipping her western filter coffee while Nikos drank the undrinkable treacly brew of the native, she decided she did not want to think about it.

She just wanted to enjoy the moment. For now, it was enough.

It was early evening by the time they got back to the coast. They did not arrive back at Heraklion, but further west, at Rethimnon.

"Just in time for us to make our *volta*," said Nikos.

"*Volta?*"

"In the early evening, after work and before dinner, we take our stroll around the town—to see and be seen," explained Nikos.

With the westering sun turning the azure sea to turquoise, and yellowing the limestone buildings around the pretty Venetian harbour of the town, it was a pleasant thing to do, discovered Andrea. They strolled around the quayside. And if at some point Nikos slipped his arm around Andrea's shoulders, to shield her from a group of lively tourists heading in the opposite direction, she found, when he did not remove it, that she did not mind. Indeed, the opposite was true. The warmth of his casual embrace was comforting. And when, as they took their places at a table set out on the quayside to have a drink, he let go of her, she felt, she realised, strangely bereft.

Nikos took a beer, Andrea a tall glass of fruit juice, and they watched the world go by. It was very easy, very relaxed. They talked about Crete—its long struggle for independence, its ordeals under Nazi occupation, and its modern Renaissance as a tourist destination. Neutral subjects. Safe subjects.

"Do you know the island well?" she asked.

He shook his head. "I'm afraid my visits have mostly been brief, and in respect of business. I've seen more of Crete today than ever before." He paused, then said with deliberate casualness, "Shall we stay a few days longer?"

She stilled. "I—I..."

He covered her hand with his. "You do not need to decide now, Andrea *mou*. Let us take things as they come, *ne*?"

There was meaning in his words, but she could not challenge him. Instead she looked out over the gilded water, streaming with the setting sun.

"Shouldn't we start heading back to Heraklion? Won't they be wondering where we are?"

He gave a laugh. "Captain Petrachos sailed the yacht along the coast—he's anchored off the shore now. We'll take a launch back to it whenever we want. There's no hurry."

"Oh," said Andrea. Once again she realised how very, very easy being a holidaymaker was if you had a luxury yacht trailing around after you.

"Shall we dine ashore?" enquired Nikos, calling for another beer.

"Can we?"

He laughed again. "Andrea, this is our hon—" He caught himself, and amended his words. "Our holiday—we can do anything we like!"

Andrea looked around. Everywhere were open-fronted restaurants, tables spilling out onto the quayside and the pavements, happy holidaymakers enjoying their escape from humdrum lives. It was livening up now, and she could hear the throb of bazouki music emanating from the bars.

"Let's eat here!" she enthused. She could not face returning to that opulent monstrosity of a yacht, whose garish luxury appalled her so. Besides, she felt safe here, amongst so many people....

And Nikos was being so *nice*...

She sipped her orange juice, nibbling moist, succulent olives out of the dish placed in front of them, staring out over the harbour. Carefully, tremulously, she opened her mind and let herself face up to what had happened.

Nikos had made love to her. He had taken her naked body and brought it to ecstasy. Initiated her into the realm of sensual experience. Changed her from an unknowing, virginal maiden into a woman who knew the power of the senses. The overwhelming, irresistible power that took away all reason, all logic, and swept her away, to let her do things, experience things that she had never, ever thought to experience.

It happened. It was real. I let it happen.

She could have stopped him—*should* have stopped him—but she hadn't. She hadn't found the strength to stop him.

Even though she knew exactly why he had done what he had.

She said the words to herself, spelling them out. Letting there be no mistake about it. Refusing to deceive herself.

He made love to me. Last night Nikos made love to me because he felt sorry for me.

That was the truth of it.

It tore at her, pulling her in two. Part of her was filled with mortification that this most perfect paean to masculine perfection should have had to force himself to make love to her scarred, disfigured body. But part of her was filled with wonder—wonder that a man who had married her for no other reason than to get her grandfather's business empire should have had the compassion, the kindness, to feel sorry for her...

Emotions stirred in her heart, welling up, but she knew they were dangerous. Very dangerous.

Nikos Vassilis, who had married the splendid Coustakis heiress, not the humble, ordinary Andrea Fraser, would have no use for such emotions—and neither must she.

It was late before they returned to the yacht. They had eaten in one of the harbourside restaurants, filled with chattering, cheerful tourists. It had been fun, and had distracted Andrea from her deeper thoughts. But now, as the motor launch creamed its way across the dark sea towards the string of lights that edged the massive bulk of her grandfather's latest toy, those thoughts surfaced.

Nikos could tell. As he helped her up the lowered steps to gain the safety of the deck he knew, by the way she immediately pulled her hand free of his, that she was filled with nervous self-consciousness.

Keep playing it easy, he adjured himself.

Dismissing the crewman with a smile, he turned to Andrea. "Come, let us watch the night."

He led her up to the uppermost deck, towards the stern. They would not be overlooked there. The bridge crew were out of sight, and he had given orders that the rest of the staff could stand down.

Glad for a reprieve from having to go to bed, and not having the faintest idea what on earth Nikos was going to do about sleeping arrangements now, Andrea followed him. It was, she had to admit, a glorious sight. The twinkling line of lights along the Cretan coast echoed the blaze of stars in the celestial oceans above their heads.

They stood side by side, leaning on the railings, trying to identify constellations.

"I only know the Plough and Orion in winter," admitted Andrea. "London isn't very good for star-gazing."

"We should sleep in a goat hut on the top of Mount Ida to have the clearest view on the island!" teased Nikos, and she smiled.

"Crete was wonderful," she said wistfully. "Thank you for taking me there today."

Lightly, very lightly, he slipped his hand underneath the plait of her hair at the back of her neck.

"As I said, *pethi mou*, we can spend as long as we like here. Shall we do that?"

His fingers were brushing her nape. Very lightly.

It set every nerve in her body quivering.

Danger!

You've got to stop this—now!

"Nikos—"

"Hmm?" His fingertips were playing with loose strands of hair. She felt ripples of sensation down her spine.

"Nikos—"

She paused again, trying to concentrate, trying to focus on what she had to tell him. *Must* tell him. Right now.

"I—I have to talk to you!" The words came out in a rush.

It did not stop his fingers gentling at the tender skin beneath her ear, nor did it stop the shivers of pleasure vibrating in her.

"What about?" he asked idly. His other hand had come around her spine to rest on her hip. It felt large, and heavy, and warm. And dangerous.

Still he went on feathering the loosening tendrils of her hair, brushing the velvet of her skin.

She forced herself to concentrate.

"About…about…what happened."

"When?" asked Nikos, in that same lazy tone, as his thumb moved to brush along the line of her jaw.

"Last…last night…."

"Ahh," breathed Nikos. "That."

"*Yes! That!*" echoed Andrea. It was supposed to come out forcefully, but as his thumb grazed the cleft of her chin it only came out as a sigh.

"This?" queried Nikos. His fingertips still stroked her cheek lightly, oh, so lightly, but now his thumb pressed lightly, oh, so lightly, on her full lower lip.

"No!"

"Ahh. Then *this*, perhaps…"

His hand smoothed over her hip languorously, shaping its feminine contour with lazy ease.

She felt her muscles clench spasmodically, unable to control them. She could feel how close he was behind her now, his body almost encircling hers. How had he got so close suddenly?

She had no time to think of an answer.

"Oh," he murmured, "then it must be *this, ne*?"

His thumb pressed on her lower lip and slid into the moistness within, gliding along the tender inner surface.

Sensation shimmered at his velvet touch, vibrating through her like a siren call she could not resist—could not.

She moaned, and softly bit the fleshy pad, drawing it into her mouth to do so.

She could not help herself. She simply could not help herself.

She heard herself moan again, a little whimper in her throat, and now his hand was cupping her jaw, and his thumbpad was grazing the edge of her teeth.

She bit again, laving it with her tongue longingly, help-lessly.

He turned her in his arms and kissed her properly.

She yielded without a word, her eyelids fluttering shut as she gave herself to the bliss of having Nikos kiss her.

It was a deep, sensual kiss. A kiss filled with all the hunger he had suppressed. A kiss for himself as well as her.

His arms slid around her, holding her tight against him, his hand spearing her hair, holding her head steady for him as he plundered the sweetness of her mouth, tongues mating and writhing.

Hunger flooded through her. Her body leapt in recognition of what was happening. This was no seduction. It was redis-covery. Glorious, potent rediscovery. Her hands wound around his neck, holding him to her, unable to let go—not while the hunger that suddenly seared within her was feeding on him, mouth to mouth, shaping and touching, wanting and needing…

Needing so much more… Wanting so much more…

Wanting everything. Wanting possession.

His possession. Nikos Vassilis. Only his.

Now—oh, right now…now…

Reality douched through her. She yanked away from him, breathless, horrified.

"Nikos! No!"

Her rejection was a gasp of disbelief that she had actually got to this point. She twisted free, backing away.

"No?" The tone was quizzically ironic. She did not see the control he had to use to maintain so light a voice.

"No," she said again, more firmly now, swallowing, trying to still the frantic beating of her racing heart. Trying to find reason, logic, hard sense. "You don't have to do this. I...I said we had to talk about...about last night, and we do—but it's just to say I understand. I know why you...why you did what you did. I accept that. You felt sorry for me. You felt sorry for me because you saw me as an object of pity. But it's OK—" she held her hand up "—it's OK. I understand." She swallowed again. "You don't have to feel you must give a repeat performance. I understand."

As she spoke Nikos had leant back against the rails, resting his elbows on the guard rail.

"I'm glad you understand," he said lightly. "It was certainly the worst night of my life, I can tell you!"

He looked at her, watching her face change as she took in what he had just said. There was a stricken look on it, but he ignored it.

"Yes," he said again, "certainly the worst night of my life."

Andrea could feel her nails digging into her palms. Did he have to be so brutal about it? Did he have to ram home just how repugnant he had found the ordeal of making love to a freak? Her throat had tightened, wire pulling on it. Agonising. He was talking again. She could hardly bear to hear what he was saying. But the words penetrated all the same.

"I've never done what I had to do last night," he told her. "It was excruciating."

The expression on her face was devastated, but he ploughed on. "And I never, ever want to go through it again. I tell you—" he eyed her straight, and said what he had to say "—having to hold myself back like that was absolute

agony. I was aching for you—totally bloody *aching* for you."
A long, shuddering sigh escaped him. "*Theos*, you've no
idea what it was like, Andrea *mou*—having your fantastic,
gorgeous body stripped naked and pulsing for me and not
being able to possess you totally. God, it was hell—sheer
hell!" He shook his head. "Never again, I promise you—
never again!"

He straightened suddenly, and rested his hand on either
shoulder. "But you needed your space, and I knew I owed you
that. So…" He looked down at her, starlight in his eyes. "Last
night was your night, Andrea *mou*. But tonight—oh,
tonight—" his voice had changed, husky suddenly "—tonight
is *mine*…"

He pulled her into him, jerking her, and closed his mouth
over hers. Then, with a rough, urgent motion, he swept her
up into his arms and strode off with her, to make her his wife.

It was, she realised some eternity later, the rawness of his
hunger, the voracity of his appetite that convinced her. As he
tumbled her down upon their vast bed, coming down beside
her and pinioning her hands either side of her head as he
lowered his mouth to hers again to feed and feed upon her,
she felt rush up from the depths of her being such a gladness,
such a glory, she was breathless with it.

His mouth ravished hers, allowing her no quarter, no
defence, and he overpowered her effortlessly, easily. She was
a willing traitor, oh, so willing! His body arched over hers and
her hands ran over the smoothness of his shirt, fumbling with
buttons as, overcome with a desperate urge she had never felt
before, never known existed, she longed frantically to feel his
skin, his flesh, his muscle and sinew beneath her seeking
hands.

He helped her—shucking off his shirt, peeling off her
T-shirt while he did so, slipping the clasp on the back of her

bra in one unseen skilful movement. Her breasts spilled free and she heard his throat rasp with pleasure at the sight before he buried his face in their ripeness, his questing mouth homing in on what he sought.

She gasped with pleasure as he suckled her, thrusting her breasts up, bearing down upon the bed with her hips, her shoulders. He fed voraciously, licking and sucking until her nipples were as solid as steel, radiating fiery points of pleasure fiercely through her body. Her hands roamed over the smooth steel of his back, glorying in the power of his perfect musculature, revelling in the feel of his body over hers.

He swept on, mouth racing down the flat, taut plane of her belly, tongue whirling within the secret of her navel even as he was urgently undoing the fastening of her jeans, sliding her zip open and then in the same movement sliding his hand inside. She gasped and roiled as a thousand fires lit where he touched.

Her heart was racing, thundering. There was no light in the room and she could not see its garish, tasteless opulence. She could feel only the satin of the bedclothes beneath her naked back, her naked bottom and thighs, for her jeans were gone and her panties too were tossed aside. Now Nikos was moving over her, and she realised that somehow, somehow, he was as naked as she.

She gloried in the feel of him, revelled in it, racing her hands all over his body. Flesh to flesh, skin to skin, mouth to mouth, hip to hip. She felt him straining at her, felt his engorged length against the softness of her belly, and the realisation, searing through her, sent a shockwave of exultation through her. He wanted her! Nikos wanted her! She knew it—knew it absolutely. Men could not fake it. Their desire, their lust, surged in their bodies, signalling the urgency of their passions.

Like an outgrown cloak her fears fell away from her, cast aside in the revelation, and in their place, released like a tiger from its cage, she was filled suddenly, desperately, with a longing so intense, a hunger so searing that her hand slid from gripping his shoulder as his mouth consumed hers down between their bodies to grasp him.

She wanted to feel him, strong and potent in her hand, his surging masculinity inflaming her with a hunger that only he could fulfil. She clasped him greedily, feeling the strength of him.

She heard him gasp with pleasure, sending a power-pulse of desire through her. She wanted to please him, wanted to give him pleasure now, right now, just as he was filling her with feelings, sensations that stormed within her, roiled and rocked her. She wanted him—wanted him to pierce and fill and stretch her, flood her with his seed, his very being.

"Nikos!" Her voice was a cry, a plea, an exultation.

He reared over her. "*Theos*, but I must have you!" His voice was a rasp of hunger, intensity. His hand caressed her belly, her thighs, then parted her legs for him. She guided him to her, heart pounding, blood surging in her veins, her body afire. She was flooding for him, her body straining to his, hips twisting and lifting to him, reaching for him, and then she felt, with a thrill that went through her whole body, that he was poised above her, ready to thrust and pierce her to the very core, her very heart.

"I must have you—"

The words grated from him and he took each of her hands, lifting and placing them each side of her head, pinioning them with his, holding her body still for him, spread for him, hips lifting to receive him.

She could feel the urgency of his need for her. Power surged through her. The power of her sex, flowering in a glorious, heady welling of sensation that fused her body to her mind, fused her aroused, throbbing flesh to the incandescence lighting her whole being.

She raised her mouth to his and bit softly, deliberately at his.

"Then take me," she answered. "Take me."

He waited no longer. With slow descent he lowered his body into hers.

His control, his purpose was absolute. Her dew-drenched readied body parted for him, accepting him within her as a needed, hungered-for presence. She stretched around him, and as pain fluttered briefly, fleetingly, it was swept away by the drowning tide of exultation that consumed her as he made her his.

He filled her absolutely, and she gasped with the realisation that their bodies had fused, become one, pulsing, beating to the same single heartbeat that throbbed between them, sex to sex, thigh to thigh, palm to palm, pressing and joining.

Her mouth opened in a wondrous, wordless cry, neck arching back, hips lifting higher to meld their flesh together.

He was reared over her, fused within her, and she gloried in it. Around his manhood's strength her muscles clenched, holding him tightly, dearly, and the pressure of his body in hers thickened him in answer to her. It was all she needed. Like a long, slow wave her body detonated around his, sending a tidal pulse through all her flesh.

She buckled around him, every muscle straining, and the detonation came again, surging out like a shockwave.

She cried out, gasping, spine arching like a bow.

It was liquid pressure, liquid pleasure, so intense, so absolute that it shocked her even as it convulsed her. It flooded through her, reaching through every vein, every overloaded nerve-fibre, rushing out to fill her fingertips, her toes, flushing her body with its tide.

And behind it surged another tide, and yet another, and

with one, wondering, stunned part of her mind she realised her body was resonating with another's. Nikos was gasping, surging, pulsing into her, and she was drawing him in, the tide convulsing her sucking him into her, possessing him utterly.

She heard him gasp, cry out in triumph, and the triumph was hers too, and his, and theirs, and still their bodies surged to the tidal wave carrying them on its endless bounty.

Her fingers clutched his, squeezing so tightly she could feel the slick between their joined palms seal them unbreakably, just as their bodies were joined—unbreakably.

Slowly, oh, so slowly, the tidal pulse began to ebb, draining deep away, back into the core, the heart of her body, where it had come from. Slowly, oh, so slowly, he lowered himself to her, to rest his exhausted, sated weight upon her, crush the slackening tissues of her breasts.

They were both panting, breathless with exertion, hearts thundering in their chests. His body covered hers, slick with sweat. Her hands slid free and came around his back, wrapping him to her. She could feel, against her own, his heartbeat slamming, then slowly, slowly, as the torpor of inertia took them over, it began to ease and lessen.

How long they lay like that, their bodies fast entwined, motionless with satiation and exhaustion, she did not know, could not tell. Time had no meaning any more. She had discovered eternity.

After a while, a long, endless while, he stirred. The sweat had dried on his back, and where her arms did not enfold him his skin was cold.

Heavily, he lifted his head from her shoulder.

She felt the movement of muscles in his back and instinctively tightened her grip around him.

He gave a laugh. A low, brief laugh.

"No, I, too, do not wish to move, Andrea *mou*, but yet we must."

He managed to lever himself up to his elbows, making her slacken her grip on him so that only her hands could touch either side his spine.

"Come—I must tend to you."

Carefully, he eased from her.

She felt bereft, empty, desolate. He slipped away from her in the dark and she heard him cross the carpeted floor. Then a door opened, and a light flooded briefly, before closing to dimness. She shut her eyes. Her heart was in tumult. But she could not think, could not reason. Could only lie and let the dimness close her round.

Exhaustion claimed her.

His footsteps crossing towards the bed roused her from the slumber she had sunk into. As she surfaced she could hear, she realised, the sound of water running. Before she realised what he was intending he scooped his hands underneath her and folded her up into his arms.

"I don't want you to feel sore, *pethi mou*," he murmured, and took her through into the bathroom, lowering her gently into the swirling water in the huge, circular bath, foaming high with bubbles.

It was bliss of a different kind. She gave a sigh, and gave herself up to the warmth, pausing only to reach and twist her hair into a precarious self-fastened knot on top of her head. She closed her eyes and let the water swirl around her.

There seemed to be fine jets of water shushing out at her from all around, and she realised the huge bath must be some kind of Jacuzzi. As the tumult in her heart subsided, washed away by the warm, relaxing water, she felt for the first time the physical effects of what had happened to her. She eased her thighs, letting the water swirl gently, soothingly, around her ravished body.

"Are you in pain?"

Nikos's voice was concerned. She opened her eyes. He had not put on the central light in the bathroom, only the light above the mirror, so the brightness was mellow, not glaring. He had put on a bathrobe and was looking down at her, his hands plunged into its pockets.

She could not quite meet his eyes. Not yet.

"No, not pain, but…I feel…exercised."

She caught his eye then, and suddenly there was an answering gleam in his.

"Oh, yes," he answered softly. "As do I, I assure you…"

He held her gaze, and the knowledge in his eyes flooded her. For a moment the mutual acknowledgement of what had happened flowed between them.

"Nikos, I—" she began—because she had to say *something*, she must.

He shook his head, silencing her. "No. Say nothing. We will take this slowly, Andrea *mou*. As slowly as we need. Now—" he held up a hand "—I shall leave you in privacy a while. Relax and recover. Don't move until I come and get you."

He left her in peace, the silence broken only by the occasional popping of a bubble. She felt—*fulfilled*, she realised, and a quiet wonder went through her to lie like a fine, rare sheen over her heart.

The warmth and the water, the silence and the solitude eased her, lapping her spent body. With a light tap to the door Nikos returned after a little while and helped her out of the bath, enveloping her in a huge fleecy bathtowel. She was almost asleep, and he could see that all she would do now was rest for the remainder of the night.

He gave a private rueful smile. He could have kept going all night, but for now he must let her set the pace. She had entered a new kingdom—he must give her time to take possession of it, to know its ways and passions.

So he simply lifted her off her feet, carrying her back to the bed like a swaddled baby, and set her down between smooth satin sheets, gently drawing the towel off her. The satin felt cold to her skin, and when he returned from the bathroom a moment later, and turned off the night, she welcomed the warmth of his encircling embrace.

"Nikos," she breathed, as his arms wrapped around her from behind and her spine warmed itself against his hair-roughened chest.

"Hush," he said. "Go to sleep."

He soothed his hand over her rough thigh and for a moment she went rigid in his arms, and then, with a little sigh, she relaxed again.

Slowly, soothingly, he smoothed the scarred and runnelled skin, as if it were lustrous marble.

CHAPTER TEN

HIS hand was still covering her thigh when she awoke. Sunlight pressed against the heavy drapes, dimly illuminating the oppressively decorated bedroom. She felt the bed swaying slightly, she thought, and remembered that this was no ground-based dwelling, but that they were afloat upon the bosom of the sea.

When she stirred, Nikos did too. And as he moved she realised, with a little gasp, that as she lay spoon-like, back against him, his body was taking notice of the fact.

He felt it too, the moment he surfaced into consciousness. The same sense of ruefulness he had felt last night filled him. Whatever his leap of appetite right now, he must not risk hurting her.

Besides, he thought encouragingly, abstinence now would bring its own rewards later.

So he stretched backwards and away from her, languorously extending his limbs before lithely jack-knifing and getting out of bed.

"This morning," he announced, "we shall have breakfast in bed. And then more sightseeing!"

He certainly needed something, Nikos thought, throwing

on his bathrobe before striding to the phone to order breakfast, to divert him from what he really wanted to do right now.

Sightseeing would do as well as anything.

In fact, he acknowledged later, it had its own compensations.
It was another glorious day, fresh and sweet in the early
summer. Setting off in the four-by-four, Nikos at the wheel,
they merged into the general throng of holidaymakers.

They headed for Samaria and the famous gorge. Andrea
had read about it in the guidebook Nikos had bought for her
before they left Rethimnon.

"I know I can't walk it," she said, "but at least I can see
it."

Nikos took her as close as he could, driving deep into the
heart of the White Mountains of western Crete. They drank
coffee on the terrace of the little *cafeneion* near the start of
the walk, the Xiloskala, wooden stairs that led into the gorge.
Above them towered the bare, bleak heights of the Gingalos
peak, skirted by rock and scree.

"Tomorrow we'll sail round to the mouth of the gorge,
Agia Roumeli, and cruise along the southern coast," said
Nikos. "In fact—" he glanced at his watch "—we have time
to drive down to Sougia today, if you wish."

Andrea nodded, happy to go anywhere with him. "What
does *agia* mean?" she asked. "There are so many places
called 'Agia' something or other."

Nikos laughed. "Saint—a female saint. Male saints are
agios." He looked at her a moment. "You must learn the
language of your forefathers, Andrea *mou*. Now that you are
to live here."

She was silent. Emotions racketed around inside her.
Nikos was opening doors she must keep shut.

"What about *mou*?" she asked. She did not want to think
about what he had said. "You keep saying, 'Andrea *mou*'."

"*Mine*," he said softly. The grey eyes held hers. "My Andrea."

She looked away, her face troubled.

She felt the brush of his fingers on her hand.

"I have made you mine, have I not, Andrea *mou*?" he murmured.

Colour stole into her cheeks, feeding the tumult in her heart.

I can't think about this! I can't think about anything!

She swallowed. "Where are we heading next?" she said brightly. "I'm starting to get hungry!"

His fingers closed around hers, his thumb lazily smoothing her skin. "So am I, *agape mou*, so am I…"

But it was a hunger he was to be prevented from sating for many hours to come. Even so, he consented to be her holiday companion, her fellow-explorer, willingly enough. She was a different person, it seemed to him, here on Crete. The reserved, composed, controlled Englishwoman who was such hard work to entertain, whom he had got used to squiring around Athens, had transformed into a vibrant, open personality who was a delight to be with. Was it just because the appalling tensions of the last weeks had finally resolved themselves? Or was it because he had made her his own?

For she was his own now; he knew that. No other man would ever touch her. She was his wife. Already he cherished her. A surge not just of possession but of protectiveness speared through him whenever he looked at her. No man would hurt her again, for she would need no other man now. Only him.

The future looked bright. Brighter than ever he had dared hope.

All that panic-generated talk she had spouted at him on their wedding night about leaving him in the morning was nothing.

It had been her fears speaking; that was all. And those fears he had shown to be nothing more than phantasms haunting her.

He had exorcised her ghosts, he knew, and from now on their path was clear and thornless.

This rushed arranged marriage would work out for them—he was sure of that now. Together they would move on through the years ahead.

Well-being filled him, and the future was bright with promise.

At his side, as they zig-zagged down the winding road through the lovely Agia Irini gorge towards the southern coast, Andrea could not stop herself from looking at him.

Her breath caught every time she did so. It was everything about him—everything! From the satin sheen of his dark hair, the impossible glamour of his sunglasses, the firm, sensual line of his mouth, the vee of his open collar, the flexible strength of his hands curving around the wheel of the car, the tanned sinews of his bare forearms—all, all made her want to drink him in, feast her eyes on him more and more.

And yet while her senses feasted her emotions swirled within her. His words at the *cafeneion*, about learning Greek, had filled her with dismay.

How could she live here, in Greece? How could she be truly married to Nikos Vassilis?

It was unthinkable!

And yet, and yet...

Too much pulled at her. Too many emotions.

I can't think about it! I just can't!

She knew she would have to, eventually. Knew that the future was looming over her like a dark, overpowering wall. But for now she would turn her back on it.

She had a few days' grace, she knew. The quick staccato phone call she had made to Tony from the bedroom, before they had set off for Knossos yesterday, had simply communicated an unforeseen change of plan. He had been worried, she could tell, for all she had said was that she was fine, but would not be coming home quite yet; she would let him know when.

"I'm not at my grandfather's house," she had reassured him rapidly. "I'm...I'm...somewhere else...with someone else."

Tony had been alarmed, despite her use of the code word they had agreed.

"Where else?" he demanded.

"I'm on my grandfather's yacht," she had admitted. "But he's not here. I'm OK, truly. I have to go; someone's coming! Give my love to Mum. I'll be home soon—promise."

But would she be home soon? She stared out of the windscreen, out over the alien landscape of Crete.

What am I doing? What am I doing?

She had no answer. She was adrift on a new ocean, carried by an unstoppable tide.

At her side, Nikos slipped his left hand from the wheel and took her hand, sensing her troubled frame of mind.

"All will be well, Andrea *mou*. Trust me."

For now there was nothing else for her to do.

For now it was enough.

They had lunch in the little town of Sougia, at a tourist taverna overlooking the shingle beach.

"It is a pity you are not up to walking," remarked Nikos. "There is, so I have just been told, a very popular walk to a place called Ancient Lissos—it is a Roman site, small, but very pretty. Perhaps we can land there from the yacht, another day. You cannot get there by road, I understand."

"Is it a long walk?" Andrea asked.

"About an hour, the waiter told me, but it could be rough, and I don't want to risk it."

"I'm sorry to be such a drag on you," Andrea said quietly.

He took her hand. "You are not a drag. You have done your best against great odds. I cannot begin to think what you must have gone through."

His kindness nearly undid her. She felt tears misting her eyes. He saw them, and patted her hand encouragingly.

"No, do not cry, Andrea. As you said to me yourself, there are others so much worse off!" His gentling smile took any reproof from the words. "And think too how much worse it would have been, what you went through, had you not been cushioned by your grandfather's wealth. I know that money cannot buy health, but it can buy comfort, and freedom from financial stress, in ways you cannot, perhaps, imagine. Your mother could afford the best treatment for you, the best doctors, the best care—it is something to be grateful for, *ne*?"

Cold drenched through Andrea. Cushioned by her grandfather's wealth? She saw again, vivid in her mind, the letter from his office, replying, finally, to the desperate pleadings of her mother after Kim had sent Yiorgos Coustakis all the medical reports on his granddaughter, detailing all the injuries she had suffered, recommending operations and physiotherapy that were so extensive, so expensive, that only private health care could provide for the years it would take to complete the treatment. The reports had been returned, accompanied by a terse letter to the effect that they were obviously gross exaggerations, and it was clearly nothing more than a ploy by a mercenary gold-digger to extort money from a man she had no claim on whatsoever.

And then Andrea chilled even more at the recollection of the final letter that had come, not from her grandfather, but from his lawyers, informing Kim that any further attempt at communicating with Yiorgos Coustakis would result in legal action.

Nikos watched her face shadowing. He had not meant to be harsh, but it was true, what he had said. Like so many born to wealth, Andrea seemed to take it all for granted. Oh, she was polite to servants, waiters and so on, but she never seemed to appreciate just how privileged her upbringing had been. In fact, he mused, she seemed to take more pleasure in something like a simple meal at a cheap taverna than in the lavish delicacies of a five-star restaurant…

If she'd had to work for her money, as he had done, she might appreciate the finer things of life more, he thought.

And do you appreciate anything else any more? Or will only the finest do for you now?

The quizzing voice sounded unwelcome in his mind, and he put it aside. He deserved his wealth—he had worked day and night to get where he was now. And Coustakis Industries was his rightful prize.

And the Coustakis heiress….

His mood lightened, and he lifted her imprisoned hand to his lips, grazing it lightly.

"I long for tonight, my sweet, passionate Andrea. I long for it—and you."

Colour stained her cheekbones as she read the message in his eyes, and he sat back, well pleased.

Right now life was good. Very good.

And the night was even better. All the rest of the day Andrea found her awareness of Nikos mounting and mounting—during the drive back to the north of the island, during dinner eaten by the harbour in Chania, this time, not Rethimnon, and the drive back across the isthmus of the Akritori peninsula to the deep water of Souda Bay, where the yacht was moored. That night she hardly noticed the garish décor of the state-rooms, hardly noticed the polite greetings of the crew, only noticed the way Nikos's eyes looked at her, wanting her, wanting her.

Desire swept through her, and the moment they gained the privacy of their bedroom she turned to him, and he to her. That night their coming together was even more incendiary— she knew now, so well, just what passion and desire, unleashed, could bring, and she revelled in it.

She felt wild and wanton, desirable and daring.

"I do believe," Nikos murmured to her, his eyes glinting wickedly as she climbed astride him at his urging, eager to find more and more ways of showing her desire for him and sating her own, "that you are making up for lost time."

He slid his hands helpfully under her smooth, round bottom, lifting her up and positioning her exactly where he wanted her to be. Then he relaxed back.

"Take me." The eyes glinted even more wickedly, making her feel weak with desire. "I'm yours…"

She looked down at him, her red hair streaming like a banner down her naked back.

And slowly, tasting every moment of the experience, she came down on him. Possessing him.

It was the first of numberless possessions, each giving and taking as much as the other, their appetites feeding on each other, inflaming each other, sating each other, long into the following day. They did not go ashore that morning, letting Captain Petrachos take the yacht westwards, to round the island into the Libyan Sea and nose along the southern coast. Though the day was warm, and fine, Andrea and Nikos found a strange reluctance to take the fresh air.

"We should get up," murmured Andrea, nestled against Nikos's hard-muscled chest.

"It's our honeymoon, Andrea *mou*. There is no hurry. We have all the time in the world." He began to nuzzle at her tender earlobe, and she felt—extraordinary though it was, considering how short a time ago they had come together this latest time—her body beginning to respond to his caressing. "On the other hand," he considered, "perhaps we should get up. Of course…" his teeth nipped gently, arousingly at her lobe "…we would need to have a bath first…"

Making love in a Jacuzzi was, Andrea discovered, a breathtaking experience, and one that lasted a long, long time. It was after noon before they finally emerged on to the deck, to take a long, leisurely lunch under an awning as the mountainous coastline of southern Crete slipped slowly past them. After lunch the launch was lowered, and Nikos took her first, as he had promised, to the tiny cove of Ancient Lissos, to explore the remains of the *asklepieion*—healing centre—and then sailing onwards, past the pretty white-washed village of Loutro, along the piratical Sfakiot coastline until they made landfall at a beach marked on the map as "Sweetwater Beach".

"What a strange name," said Andrea, and marvelled when she was shown the reason. Tiny freshwater springs pearled from beneath the pebbles. Andrea scooped some of the water to her lips.

"It *is* fresh!" she exclaimed in wonder.

It was such a beautiful afternoon, and the beach—unreachable by road—so relatively uncrowded, that they stayed to enjoy it. As Andrea started to relax, Nikos produced a swimsuit from amongst the towels.

"No one will look at your legs, Andrea," he told her. "They will all be too busy looking at your glorious figure." He leant and kissed her softly. "You are so beautiful. Your legs do not matter. Not to me. You must know that by now—you must!" He smiled cajolingly. "Do it for me, my beautiful bride."

How can I refuse? she thought. How can I refuse him anything?

Handing her a vast towelling changing tent, he helped her

slip on the plain black one-piece he had acquired for her. As she stepped free she felt overcome with self-consciousness, but after a while she realised it was true—the others on the beach, scattered as they were, were not looking at her.

"Come," said Nikos. "That sea looks too tempting!"

He was stripping off before she could reply, baring everything down to a pair of trunks under his trousers, and then he was taking her hand and leading her into the clear water.

This early in the year the water had a bite to it that made her gasp, but Nikos only laughed. He drew her in relentlessly, and then, letting go, dived into the turquoise water, surfacing to shake a shower of diamonds from his head.

"Come on! You'll thank me!"

And she did. When they finally emerged, some fifteen minutes later, she felt glorious, reborn. He swathed a towel around her and sat her down, pausing only to run a towel over his back before joining her.

He grinned at her. She grinned back. The water on his long eyelashes caught the sun, his damp, towel-dried hair made her ache to touch it, and the expression in his eyes as he looked at her made her weak.

All that marred her pleasure was the prospect of having to go back on board her grandfather's yacht. It oppressed her more and more. Not just because of the tasteless extravagance of its opulent décor, but because it reminded her, as she did not want to be reminded, of just why she had come to Greece at all.

And she did not want to think of that.

"Nikos?" She sat up, looking at him questioningly. "Do we have to stay on the yacht?"

"You don't want to?" He sounded surprised. He didn't know a woman who wouldn't have adored to luxuriate on board such a floating palace!

But then Andrea, he was beginning to realise, was like no woman he had ever known…

For so many reasons.

She shook her head.

"Can't we stay here, on Crete?"

He smiled indulgently. "Of course. I will phone the yacht and book a suitable hotel. Or would you prefer a private villa?"

"Can't we just take our chances? Wander around, stay where we want? There are rooms to let everywhere, and we've passed many little hotels in the Jeep."

He looked at her. "You'd like that?"

"Oh, yes! They look such fun. I've never done anything like that—"

Her voice was full of longing. How ironic, thought Nikos, that for someone raised in luxury, the commonplace was exotic!

He smiled lazily at her. "Your wish, my most lovely bride, is my command!"

For five, wonderful, unforgettable days Andrea toured the island with Nikos. For five searing, incandescent nights she flamed with passion in his arms. All cares were left behind. This was a special time, she thought—all she would have. She must make the most of it. Make the most of Nikos.

She knew, with a terrible clenching of her heart, that it would be all she would have of him. The realisation struck like a cold knife at her.

She heard his words at Knossos echo in her heart—*"We must live while we can, Andrea. We have no other choice except to make the most of what is given to us. Our minds, our hearts—our bodies and our passions."*

And she *would* make the most of it—draw every bead of

happiness, every pulse of pleasure and desire, every moment of calm, quiet bliss.

And make it last her all her life.

But I want it to last for ever!

That was impossible, she knew. This time with Nikos was nothing more than a brief, magical sliver of time. It shimmered with radiance, but it could not last.

Reality had to return, and she must accept that. Not willingly, but with a heavy, heavy heart. She knew, more than any, just how brief a portion of happiness life could hold. Her mother was testament to that. And yet she knew, for she had asked her once, that her mother would never have forgone the brief, fleeting bliss she had had with the man she loved, however long the empty years since then.

And I will be the same…

As they drove into Souda on their last evening on Crete, the setting sun turning the sea to gold, and saw the yacht moored there, Andrea's spirits became heavy. Her happiness was coming to an end and would never come again.

She looked across at Nikos, etching every line of his face into her memory.

I love him, she thought. I love him.

As the words formed in her mind she knew them for a truth she could never deny. Never abandon.

And never tell.

Andrea paced the deck of the yacht as it headed steadily, remorselessly, north in the starlight towards Piraeus. To the east the sky was beginning to lighten. It must be near dawn, she thought. Inside, Nikos lay asleep, exhausted by passion.

Our last time together, she thought in anguish.

She had slipped noiselessly away, needing—oh, needing solitude to think. To agonise.

This wasn't supposed to happen! This was never in the plan! I never meant to fall in love with him!

She stared blindly out over the sea, feeling the deck swell with the waves beneath the hull. The hull of a luxury Greek yacht.

This wasn't real—none of it was real! It was nothing more than a dream, a chimera. Reality was at home, in that drab council flat where she had lived all her life, bowed down by the debts that hung around Kim's neck—the money she had borrowed at ruinous interest, unsecured as it had to be, since they owned nothing of value, to pay for the private treatment Andrea had needed to make her walk again.

That's what I came to Greece for—to free her from that burden at last. To set her free from the cage and let her have some happiness in life at last, some comfort and ease.

And there was nothing stopping her—the money her grandfather had paid her to marry Nikos Vassilis was in her bank account. All she had to do was go home and spend it.

Leaving Nikos behind.

You'll never see him again! Never make love with him! Never hold him in your arms!

A cold wind gusted over her, and she shivered in the fine silk negligee.

So what? So what if you've fallen in love with Nikos Vassilis? He doesn't love you. He married you to get your grandfather's company. And if he seduced you, took you to his bed, made you his wife in deed as well as name, well, that is what a Greek husband would do with his bride—even one with crippled legs! Oh, he's been kind to you! Released you from your fears and made a woman of you! But he doesn't love you—and he doesn't want your love.

That was not in his plan. Don't think it was.

She hugged the negligee to her, but it could not keep out the cold that was seeping into her heart.

And how thrilled do you think he'll be when he discovers, as he must, that you are no more the precious Coustakis heiress than the Queen of Sheba? That you're nothing but the spurned, unwanted, bastard granddaughter of Yiorgos Coustakis, who's used you because he's got no one else to use to make a final stab at his own posterity! Do you think a man as rich as Nikos Vassilis wants a wife from a council flat?

She didn't even have to answer.

Desolation washed through her. Cold and empty.

At breakfast, taken indoors this time, as they made their way through the busy shipping lanes approaching Piraeus, Nikos, too, was not in the best of moods. The week away from Athens had made him forget the pressures that would await him on his return. Tonight, and for the foreseeable future, he would be burning the midnight oil with a vengeance, as the process of merging Vassilis Inc and Coustakis Industries got underway. Already, before breakfast, he had been on the phone to his secretary, his directors, setting wheels in motion. But for the first time in his life he had no appetite for work.

Only for Andrea...

He felt his body stir, and crushed it ruthlessly. It would be at least late tonight before he was free to enjoy his passionate bride again. His jaw tightened. He would have to explain to her that their time together would be at a premium now. At least until he had completed his takeover of her grandfather's company.

Did she realise that already? She was not looking happy, he thought, studying her across the table. In fact, she looked different altogether. She had lost the casual, easygoing look she had had for the last week. Now she looked stiff, and tense, picking at her food.

"I'm sorry we couldn't have stayed away longer," he said. "But doing an M&A takes a lot of work."

Andrea looked at him. He was wearing a business suit again, and it made him look formal. Distant. The man she had spent the most blissful week of her life with had vanished. In his place was the man who had married her to get hold of Coustakis Industries. And for no other reason.

She must remember that.

"I'm sure it does," she said impersonally.

Nikos's mouth tightened. She was ready enough to accept the lavish lifestyle her family wealth afforded—but balked at how it had been earned in the first place.

"A corporate merger is not a trivial thing to accomplish, Andrea…"

He paused suddenly. There was a bleakness in her eyes he could not account for.

No, she thought, a corporate merger was not a trivial thing at all—it was something you could marry a stranger for!

And then make love to her until she fell in love with you— hopelessly, helplessly!

But he hadn't asked her to fall in love with him, she thought. He had asked for nothing more than a passionate companion for a week—a pleasant, relaxing interlude before resuming his real life. Making money.

Well, I made money out of it too, she thought defiantly. And now I'm going home to spend it. It's what I came for, and it's what I'm going home with.

Falling for Nikos was an aberration, a mistake. I'll go home and forget all about him.

I have to!

A steward came into the room and walked up to Nikos, saying something to him in Greek. Nikos nodded curtly, and the man hurried off.

Nikos got to his feet. He looked so tall, Andrea thought.

And so devastating. Just the way he'd looked the first time she'd set eyes on him. It seemed a lifetime ago, not just a few short weeks.

Weeks that had changed her life for ever.

"Excuse me—but I have to take a phone call." He sounded remote. Preoccupied.

She nodded. There seemed to be an immovable lump in her throat suddenly.

"Of course."

Later, she stood on deck beside him, watching the yacht slide into its moorings. Then, later still, she sat beside him in the chauffeured limo driving them back to Athens. There was a third passenger, a young man introduced as Nikos's PA, and the moment the doors were closed the PA extracted a sheaf of papers and documents. In a moment he and Nikos were deep in business talk. Andrea looked out of the window.

She felt bleak, and sick, cold all the way through.

I'm leaving him, she thought. *I'm leaving him right now…*

The car made its slow way into Athens's business quarter, and as it finally pulled up outside Vassilis Inc she felt even bleaker, and sicker.

Nikos turned to her briefly.

"Yannis will drive you to the apartment. You must make yourself at home. I am sorry not to be able to accompany you myself, but something has come up—hence Demetrios's reception committee. I am sorry, but I could not avoid it. I will escape from the office as quickly as I can and we will have the evening together. Until then—"

He bent forward to kiss her.

She could not bear it. She jerked her head sideways, conscious, if nothing else, of the PA's presence. Nikos's kiss landed on her cold cheek.

* * *

Can you feel your heart break? thought Andrea, as Nikos climbed out of the car after his PA. Because mine broke, I know, just then.

She shut her eyes, leaning back into the seat. The car moved off.

Tears misted over her eyes.

After a while, she realised she would have to give the driver new instructions. He seemed surprised when she asked him to drive her to the airport, but did it dutifully enough.

On the way there she wrote a note. Every word drew blood from her heart.

> *Dear Nikos*
>
> *I am going back to England. We have both got what we wanted out of this marriage. You got Coustakis Industries. I got my money. Thank you for our time together in Crete—you were a wonderful first lover. I'm sure you'll make a huge success of running Coustakis Industries. Please ask your lawyers to sort out our divorce as soon as possible. Thank you.*
>
> *Andrea.*

It was all she could manage. And it cost her more than she could bear to pay.

She left it with the chauffeur to deliver it to Nikos.

CHAPTER ELEVEN

"WHAT do you think, Mum? Down on the coast or further up in the hills? Where do you want to live?"

Andrea's voice was bright and relentlessly cheerful, just as it had been since she had arrived back two weeks ago, bursting with the wonderful, glorious news that her grandfather, so she had told her mother, had given them enough money to settle their debts and allow them to move to Spain.

But, for all her determined high spirits, Andrea could see her mother was worried about her. Oh, she had been bowled over by the fantastic news about the money, which had settled their debts with a single cheque, and she had commented on how well Andrea looked with her sun-bronzed skin and burnished hair, and how she was walking, it seemed, with much greater confidence and assurance, but even so Andrea could sense Kim's concern.

She didn't want her mother worrying. Not about anything—least of all her. So she chattered away brightly as she prepared their evening meal, talking about Spain and the imminent prospect of living there. She was desperate to move as soon as possible. Perhaps, in Spain, starting her new life, she could start to forget Nikos…

Nikos—

Pain clenched at her heart. No—she mustn't think, mustn't

remember. It was gone, over, finished. She was starting a new life now—that was the only important thing to think about. That and making Kim happy. She mustn't, mustn't let Kim suspect anything…

She mustn't see your heart is broken…

She smiled determinedly at Kim.

"It's going to be all right, Mum. Everything's going to be just wonderful from now on! Just wonderful!"

Kim smiled and took her daughter's hand. "You are the best daughter a mother could have—always know that, my darling girl," she said softly, her eyes searching her daughter's face.

"I love you so much," Andrea choked, realising it had been worth everything just to know that she could at last repay her mother for her years of devotion. What did a broken heart matter?

The sudden imperative knocking on the front door made them both start.

Kim immediately looked nervous, and Andrea pugnacious.

"Ignore it, Mum. They'll try somewhere else."

Increasingly wild and aggressive kids often did the rounds at this time of day, the early evening, knocking on doors to see if they could cadge money from anyone inside.

Thank God we're getting out of here, thought Andrea feelingly.

They would be in Malaga in forty-eight hours—not for good, just for a fortnight's flat-hunting—and Andrea could hardly wait. Searching for an apartment would occupy her mind. Stop her thinking, remembering…aching…

The knocking came again, even more imperative.

"Right," said Andrea, "I've had enough of this."

She marched out of the kitchen and to the front door, ready to confront them, but the dark outline showing behind the strengthened frosted glass panel revealed a tall, masculine frame.

The demanding knocking came again, and Andrea heard the futile buzz of the broken doorbell being sounded. Like so much else on the estate, it was still waiting for the council to mend it.

As she yanked the door open to find steel-grey eyes blazing down at her, her heart stopped.

Nikos Vassilis stepped inside, forcing her to stumble backwards on numb, frozen legs.

"Don't ever," he said in a voice that made her spine chill, "walk out on me again."

Shock drenched through Andrea, wave after cold wave. But beneath the disbelieving horror another emotion had seared like flame through her.

"How—how…?" she floundered.

"How did I track you down? With great difficulty, I assure you!" His voice grated the words. He glanced around disparagingly at the shabby, narrow hallway, its smell of damp quite perceptible. "And with such a bolt-hole as this I am not surprised it took the investigators so long to find you! What is this dump?" His mouth twisted disdainfully at the evident poverty of her surroundings.

"This dump," said a quiet voice from the kitchen doorway, "is my home, Mr—?"

Andrea whirled. Kim was standing there, her expression wary and questioning.

"Vassilis," supplied Nikos curtly. "Nikos Vassilis. I have come for Andrea."

"I'm not going with you!" Andrea cried out. She couldn't believe what was happening—couldn't believe it was really Nikos standing there, his svelte, expensive presence shrieking money, looking as out of place in the hallway of a tower block council flat as if he were an alien from another planet.

"What's going on?" asked Kim anxiously, coming forward.

"Nothing! Nothing at all," Andrea replied instantly. "Mr Vassilis," she gritted, "has made a mistake! He's leaving right now! Without me!"

"Wrong." Nikos's voice was deadly. His eyes narrowed. "Get your things—and make sure your passport is among them!"

"I'm not going anywhere!"

"You are going," he ground out, "back to Athens! You were somewhat premature in your departure, I must point out. You might have got the money you wanted from your grandfather—your main interest, was it not—?" his voice was scathing "—but your precipitate departure has made him feel…cheated. He wants you back in Athens to fulfil your… obligations. Otherwise," he spelt out, "he will not proceed with the merger!"

It was her turn for her face to harden.

"Oh, well, we mustn't get in the way of the precious merger, must we?" she flared. "That was, after all, your main interest, was it not?" Deliberately she echoed his words, confronting him with the truth of why he had ever looked twice at her!

It did not hit its mark.

"There were other…interests…as I recall… Ones that I fully intend to resume when you return to Athens to fulfil your…obligations. *Ne?*" His voice trailed off, but his eyes washed over her. Weakness flooded through her—and memory—hot, humid memory.

He saw it in her eyes, and smiled. A blighting smile that had no humour in it. "You see, I too, Andrea *mou*, feel cheated by your precipitate and so unexpected departure."

She heard the anger in his voice—suppressed, restrained, but savage beneath the words. There was something more than anger in it too, she realised. Something raw, and painful.

Then he had snapped his gaze past her, the tight, controlled mask back on his face, and rested it where Kim was hovering, a puzzled, anxious look on her face.

"I need to speak to Andrea. Privately. If you would be so kind—?"

"I've got nothing to say to you!" Andrea flashed back at him.

Steel eyes, flecked with gold, rested on her. "But I," he said with a softness that raised the hairs at the nape of her neck, "have a great deal to say to you, Andrea *mou*."

She felt faint, hearing him say her name, that had once been an endearment, now edged with scorn. Behind her, Kim stepped forward and closed her hand protectively around Andrea's arm.

"Mr Vassilis, if my daughter does not wish to speak to you—"

The rest of her words were cut off by a rasp sounding in Nikos's throat. Shock etched across his face, and his eyes flashed back to Andrea.

"This woman is your mother?" Disbelief was in every word.

It was Kim who answered. "Yes, I am Andrea's mother, Mr Vassilis. And perhaps…" she took a faltering breath "…you would explain what is going on?"

Nikos's eyes were scanning from face to face, his eyes narrowed, comparing the two women. Andrea knew what he would see—she and Kim did not look much alike. Kim was slighter in build, and her hair was fair, greying now at the temples, her faded eyes blue. All that she had got from her mother was her bone structure and her fine skin. Her red hair had come from Kim's grandmother, she knew, and her chestnut eyes were a legacy from her father.

But whatever he saw must have convinced him. "Mrs Coustakis—" he began. His voice sounded shaken, but determined none the less.

Kim shook her head. "I'm Kim Fraser, Mr Vassilis. Andreas and I never married."

Her words were quietly spoken, and not ashamed. She had, her daughter knew, nothing—nothing—to be ashamed of.

Shock etched across Nikos's face again. It stabbed at Andrea. Telling her everything she needed to know. Bitter, bitter though that knowledge was.

"You see—" she twisted the words out of her mouth "—I'm not the woman you thought I was! Look around you!" Her arm swept the narrow hallway. "Do I look like an heiress? Living here?"

Her words were a bitter, defiant challenge.

"This isn't possible." Nikos's voice was flat. His denial total.

She gave a mocking, angry laugh. She had known, always known, that he would be horrified to discover her humble origins—to discover she did not come from his rich, sophisticated world. After all, what would a man as rich as Nikos Vassilis want with a wife from a council flat?

He moved suddenly, a hand flattening on the door beside him that led into the living room, pushing it open. He walked in. The room was clean and tidy, but the carpet was cheap and worn, the chairs and sofa-bed where Andrea slept shabby and frayed.

"You live here?"

His voice was still flat. Andrea followed him in.

"Yes. All my life."

"Why?"

The word exploded from him. Andrea gave a high, short laugh.

"Why? Because it's all Mum could afford, that's why! She lived on benefits until I was old enough to start school, and the council housed us here—she was lucky to get it, a flat of her own, a single, teenaged mother as she was! When I started school she got a part-time job, but it's hard work to put aside enough money to try and buy a place of your own when you've a child to bring up single-handed."

"Single-handed? When your grandfather is Yiorgos Coustakis?" His voice was a sneer.

Her eyes flashed. "Yiorgos Coustakis—" she ground out her grandfather's name with contempt "—told my mother she had no claim on my father's estate. She's brought me up on her own—totally."

As she spoke, his lips compressed. He scanned the room again, taking in every last detail. His gaze hardened.

"Are you telling me," he demanded, and his face was set, tight as a bow, "that your grandfather does not support you?"

"That's right," she said evenly. "I told you—I'm not a Coustakis at all."

Kim's voice intervened, sounding confused and distressed.

"Andrea, what about the money? You told me Yiorgos had given you all that money of his own free will! If you extorted it from in any way then you must give it back! You must!"

"No!" she cried, appalled. "No! The money's yours, it's yours totally—to buy you an apartment in Spain, to pay your debts, to—"

"Debts?" Nikos pounced on the word. His face was still carved from stone.

"Yes," said Kim, turning to him. "I'm afraid, Mr Vassilis, I owe rather a lot of money. You see, when she was younger, Andrea had a very bad road accident. The therapy needed to enable her to walk again was only available privately, so I had to borrow money to pay for it. We're still paying it back— Andrea helps all she can. She has two jobs, and every penny she can spare goes towards it!"

Nikos looked numb, then he recovered.

"You never asked Yiorgos Coustakis to help you?" The question grated from him.

A harsh laugh escaped Andrea. "Oh, Mum asked, all right! She went down on her knees to ask him to help her! She sent him all the doctors' reports on me—every last one of them! She begged him to help for the sake of his son—she promised she would repay the money as soon as she could."

"And?" Nikos's voice was chill.

"He refused. He said she was trying to get money out of him by false pretences! His lawyers wrote telling Mum that if she tried to contact him again for any reason they'd take legal action against her for harassment." She took a steadying breath, and went on. "That's why I won't give the money back to him! Whatever Mum says! I've cleared her debts and I'm going to buy her a flat in Spain. There'll be enough change from the five hundred thousand pounds to invest safely for her and give her an income to live on, and a pension, and all that stuff, and—"

Nikos's face had stilled again. "Five hundred thousand pounds?" His voice was hollow. "Are you telling me that's what Yiorgos Coustakis paid out to you?"

She lifted her chin defiantly. "I know it's a huge amount, but it's what I needed to get Mum sorted and settled."

"Five hundred thousand," he echoed. "Half a million pounds." His eyes blazed again suddenly. "Do you have any idea how much your grandfather is worth?" He took a step forward and his hands closed around her forearms. He was close, much too close to her. "Half a million is a pittance to him! A pittance!"

She jerked away.

"I don't care what he's worth! I don't care anything about him! He treated Mum like dirt and I loathe him for it! I don't want more of his filthy money—I just wanted enough to get Mum out of here to somewhere safe and warm, with enough to live on without worrying the whole time! She's got asthma, and the damp in the flat makes her really ill…"

Her voice trailed off. He was not listening. He was staring around him, taking in every shabby detail.

That's right, thought Andrea viciously, pain stabbing at her as he looked round so disdainfully at the place she lived in. Take a good look! This is where I come from! This is my home! Now you will despise me for it!

Now, into the silence, Kim spoke.

"Mr Vassilis, I can see this has been an unwelcome shock to you, and I am sorry for that. But…" She hesitated, then went on. "I would be grateful if you would please explain what the purpose of your being here is—"

His eyes flicked to her. "My purpose? My purpose, Ms…Fraser—" he said her maiden name as if it pained him "—has just changed."

Andrea's throat tightened. I'll just bet it's changed! You came here to take me home with you and now you probably can't wait to get out of here as fast as you can…

His attention suddenly swivelled to her. Her breath caught. His eyes were like slate, his face closed and shuttered.

And yet it was the face of the man she loved. Loved so much, so unbearably much!

I never thought I'd see him again! Thought I'd live the rest of my life without him! But he's here, now—

A vice crushed her heart.

Yes, and he's just about to walk out—for ever now he knows the truth about you.

A shaft of self-accusation hit her.

I should have been honest—right from the start. I deceived him—no wonder he is angry!

She took a deep, shuddering breath.

"Look, Nikos—I'm sorry. Truly. I didn't realise that my coming home would jeopardise your merger!"

A grim expression crossed his face. "There is no merger. Nor will there be."

No—how could there be? thought Andrea bleakly. Nikos Vassilis had thought he was marrying the Coustakis heiress—not the unacknowledged bastard of a woman Yiorgos Coustakis thought a gold-digging slut! Nikos had thought he was getting a wife who came from his world—not a girl who'd been born and bred in a decaying council flat.

"I should have told you," she said heavily.

His eyes rested on her like unbearable weights. "Yes, you should have told me, Andrea. You should have told me."

"I'm sorry," she said again. It seemed the only thing she could say.

"Are you?" There was something very strange in his voice. "So am I."

Well, of course he was. Andrea knew. Of course he wished he'd known from the start just how tainted she was! As if it wasn't bad enough to discover she was crippled—she was common as well...

Nikos's eyes had slid past her, lingering briefly on the tense, anxious figure of her mother, and then out, out through the window.

He wants to get out of here, Andrea thought. Get back to his own world. Where she had no place. Nor ever could have.

Through the window Nikos saw the other tower blocks of the estate and, far below, the world beneath. The sun was setting, starting to turn everything to gold. He stared down. All the kingdoms of the world spread before him.

He thought of the journey he had made—the long, hard journey from the streets of Athens—with only one focus, only one goal. Making money. More and more of it. Acquiring Coustakis Industries would have been the pinnacle of his achievement.

And he was a young man still. Who knew what kingdoms he could buy and sell before his time was up? Who knew what souls he could buy and sell with all his riches?

A face stole into his mind's eye. An old man's face, whose eyes knew well the price of a man's soul.

What is mine worth? thought Nikos. And the answer came clear. Clarion-clear.

Too much for Yiorgos Coustakis to pay.

He stepped away from the window and looked back at the two women in the shabby room. The kingdoms of the earth disappeared from view.

His hand slipped inside his jacket, taking out his mobile. He punched in a number. His voice, when he spoke, was curt. "This is Nikos Vassilis. I have a message for Yiorgos Coustakis. Tell him I am standing in front of Kim Fraser and her daughter in their home—the merger is off."

Then he disconnected.

As he slipped the phone back in his pocket his eyes met Andrea's.

She reeled.

The blaze of emotion in them was like a flash-flame.

"I will make him pay," he said softly. "If it takes me the rest of my life I will make him pay for what he has done to you."

Andrea stared. His mouth twisted at her expression and he forged on. "I knew the man was ruthless—all the world knew that! But that he would stoop so low… *Christos*, he has behaved like an animal!"

She couldn't speak—couldn't do anything but stare at him, disbelieving.

Nikos's eyes raced around the room again. "To make you live like this," he grated. "To turn his back on his own flesh and blood—to leave you to struggle on your own all these years. Not even—" His voice hardened like the edge of a knife. "Not even to lift a finger when his own granddaughter faced a lifetime in a wheelchair…" He shut his eyes. "Dear God in heaven, what kind of scum is he?"

His eyes snapped open. They glinted like steel. He reached for his phone again. "Well," he said grimly, "the world will soon know."

Before Andrea's very eyes she saw him speak in English again. "Demetrios? Prepare a press-release. The Coustakis merger is off. Yes, you heard me. And I shall be making my reasons for pulling out very, very clear. The stink will reach heaven, I assure you! I'll phone again in an hour, when you've had time to contact the board."

He snapped the phone off again.

"Mr Vassilis." Kim spoke, her voice agitated and perturbed. "Please—I don't understand any of this! What is happening?"

"What is happening…" Nikos's voice softened as he saw how disturbed Kim was "…is that I have decided not to take over Coustakis Industries. I refuse, absolutely—" his voice hardened again "—to have anything to do with a man who could behave in such a way to you and your daughter! I refuse, absolutely," he finished, "to do business of any kind with him!"

"But—but…" stammered Andrea. "But the merger means so much to you—"

A hand slashed through the air. "No. Only one thing means anything to me, Andrea." His voice changed. "Only one thing."

He took a step towards her. She wanted to step back, but she couldn't. She was rooted to the spot.

"Don't you know what it is, Andrea *mou*?" His voice had softened. "Surely you must know?" His hand reached out to touch the flaming aureole of her hair. Her breath caught. "Surely?"

He looked down at her, his eyes flecked with gold. "When you left me it was as if you had stabbed me to the quick. To the heart. I bled, Andrea *mou*. I bled."

His fingers brushed her cheek, and she felt faint. "Come back to me, *pethi mou*, come back to me—"

Her throat was tight, but she tore the words out. "What for? If there's to be no merger then you don't have the slightest need of me!"

He smiled. Her heart turned over.

"Need? Oh, my Andrea, I need you to breathe. Without you I cannot live. Do you not know that?"

His hand cupped her cheek. "I need you to light my way, to walk at my side all my life. I need you to be with me, every day and night." His other hand closed around her other cheek, cupping her face, lifting it to his.

It was odd, Andrea thought. His face had gone out of focus; the flecks of gold in his eyes were misting. Something must be in her eyes—some mote of dust.

"But—" she swallowed "—but I don't see why you need me…"

He smiled, and it filled a gaping hole in her heart.

"Didn't I show you every night, every day we spent together? Didn't you show me?"

"Show you what?" she breathed. Her eyes were brimming now; she could not stop it.

He lowered his head and kissed her softly.

"That we were falling in love, Andrea *mou*."

"Love?" It was a whisper, a breath.

"Oh, yes. Love—quite definitely love." There was no doubt in his voice. None at all. "There can be no other word for it. How else could the wound you dealt me when you left me have been so mortal to me? How else—" a finger lifted to her lashes and let the tears beading there spill onto him "—could these tears be making diamonds of your eyes?"

"But you don't love me—you can't—you don't have to! It was only because of the merger that you married me—"

The gasp from Kim went unheard.

"Our marriage, my sweet, most beloved Andrea, is the only good thing to come of that cursed merger! I always meant to make you a good husband, even when I thought ours was to be nothing more than a mutually beneficial arranged marriage. Once I would have been content with that. But on Crete—ah, then it became much, much more! And when I discovered you had left me, oh, I realised just how much more! The pain of losing you was agony—and I knew then that something had happened to me that I did not ever dream of. I had fallen in love with you—fathoms deep." He looked down at her tenderly, possessively—lovingly.

"You can't love me…" Her voice was a whisper, a thread. "We come from such different worlds. Look—"

She gestured helplessly with her hand at the shabby apartment.

He followed her gesture with his eyes, knowing now why she had said the same words to him on the night of their wedding. To think he had thought it was because she had been born to a wealth he'd had to fight all his life to acquire!

"When you return to Athens with me," he said in a low voice—and there was a strangeness in it Andrea had never heard, "I will show you were I was born—where I lived until I crawled from the gutter as a young man. A man, Andrea, who never knew his father, whose mother did not care whether he lived or died. A man, Andrea, who vowed—vowed he would make something of his life! I was determined to achieve the success and recognition I craved!"

He took a deep, shuddering breath, and Andrea stared at him, wordless, as suddenly—totally—she saw the man Nikos really was—not the gilded scion of a wealthy patrimony, but someone with the guts, the determination, the courage, to make something of himself out of the nothing he had been born with.

"But I have learnt…" his voice had softened, taken on a

sense of wonder "…that true riches are not in gold and silver. True riches…" his eyes melted her, and she felt her heart turn over "…are here—inside us. I envy you so much, Andrea." His eyes glanced across to where Kim stood staring, bemused and wondering. "To have had the love of your mother—and I envy even more—" his voice, she thought, almost cracked "—your love for her. And so I ask you—beg you—" as he spoke her throat tightened to an unbearable tightness "—to accept my love for you—and to give me yours."

He paused, looking down at her, gathering her hands against his heart.

"Come back to me, Andrea, and be the wife of my heart, for I love you more than I can bear."

The tears were spilling down her cheeks now.

"Yes!" she uttered as he kissed her tears away, and then his mouth closed over hers, and what was the gentle, soft touch of homage became a salutation to the future they would have together.

He released her, and turned to face Kim. Andrea could see the tears shining in her mother's eyes.

"Have we your blessing?" Nikos asked her quietly.

For a moment her mother could not speak. And then, with a broken cry, she answered.

"Oh, yes! Oh, yes!"

EPILOGUE

"IF IT is a boy, then Andreas. If a girl, then Kim."

Andrea smiled. "Kim isn't very Greek."

Her husband brushed this unimportant objection inside. His hand moved over the rounded contour of her belly.

"He kicked!" Nikos's voice was full of wonder—and astonishment.

"Or she," pointed out Andrea. Her hand closed over Nikos's. She leant her head back against his shoulder, her gaze stretching out over the azure Aegean that spread all around them, feeling the familiar swell of the sea beneath the hull. "How can I be so happy?" she asked.

With his free hand Nikos stroked her hair.

"Because you deserve it," he said.

Andrea reached up to kiss him. "And you do too."

It seemed to her still such a miracle—to be so happy together. Since that magical, miraculous evening, when Nikos had come to claim her heart for his own, her life had turned upside down all over again. And she rejoiced in it totally!

Nikos had whisked them both off to Greece, sweeping Kim with them as well, and settled them in a hired villa on a private island.

"I don't want you exposed to what will happen now," he had told Andrea. "It will be very ugly."

Then he had gone to Athens, to face Yiorgos Coustakis. His denouncement had been merciless—and so had the press coverage that had ensued. The scandal of the way one of the richest men in Greece had behaved to his own granddaughter had shocked the nation. That, and the cancellation of the expected merger with Vassilis Inc, had caused a steep plunge in the Coustakis share price, had precipitated the normally cowed board of Coustakis Industries into drastic action. Yiorgos had been deposed as chairman, forced to retire, a social pariah.

The seizure that had killed him a month later had moved few to pity a man who had had no pity in him for anyone else, no kindness in his hard, selfish heart.

His entire fortune had passed to his despised granddaughter, for in his rage at his new son-in-law he had destroyed the will that had left his wealth to his future great-grandson, and Andrea had become, by default, the Coustakis heiress after all.

It was a troubling inheritance.

"Nikos—are you sure, very sure, about what you want me to do?" Her voice was anxious as she stood in the circle of his arms, looking out over the shining Aegean sea.

He turned her round to face him.

"Completely sure." His answer came unhesitatingly. "The Andreas Coustakis Foundation will be a fine and fitting monument to your father—and your mother is in agreement as well. After all," he went on, "all three of us know what it is to be poor, Andrea *mou*. The foundation will give a chance to so many children blighted by their families' poverty."

Her eyes were still troubled. "But we could keep the Coustakis shares, and you could run the company as you always intended…"

He shook his head decisively. "No. We have more than enough money, Andrea—we will never be poor. To me,

Yiorgos's wealth is tainted. His neglect of you proves it. Let it be put to good use now." His mouth twisted. "Perhaps if we use his wealth to some good end, people might have something pleasant to remember him by."

"He was so vile to Mum, so needlessly cruel and offensive, and yet…" her voice sounded strained "…it was a miserable end for him—collapsing and dying alone, with not a soul to care about him."

"But then, he did not care for anyone except himself," Nikos answered soberly. "You and your mother were not the only ones he injured—there were many victims of Yiorgos Coustakis. When the newspapers ran the story of his shameful treatment of you and your mother other stories came out too, showing his brutality, his ruthlessness, his absolute disregard for anyone else."

He took her hand. "And now the Coustakis fortune is yours. Let it do some good for others, for a change—as Yiorgos Coustakis never did. Come," he said, starting to stroll down the deck with her, "we might as well make the most of our farewell cruise on this floating monument to execrable interior yacht design!"

Andrea laughed. "I'm sure some billionaire somewhere will love it—and that hideously gilded house he lived in as well! The sale of both will boost the coffers of the foundation handsomely!"

"Indeed. However," Nikos mused, "I think perhaps we ought to see if we can persuade Captain Petrachos not to leave us—I'm sure we can find some way of tempting him to stay. He was saying over dinner last night that he would be happy to help with the seamanship aspects of the youth training programme for the foundation."

Andrea exchanged glances with him. "Funnily enough," she commented dryly, "that was the very thing Mum said she was keenest on helping to set up. A striking coincidence, wouldn't you say?" Her voice changed. "Oh, I do so hope that something might come of them being together! I always dreamed of Mum meeting someone else—I know she was so in love with my father, but if she could find companionship, at least, it would be so wonderful for her!"

Nikos smiled. "Let us wish them well—for we have happiness and enough to spare, *ne*, Andrea *mou*?"

She wound her arm around him.

"I do love you, Nikos," she said, "so very much."

He stopped, and turned her in his arms, and kissed her.

"And I love you, Andrea *mou*. Through all the years we have."

The future, as bright and golden as the sun pouring over the Aegean sea, beckoned to them, and they walked towards it together.

* * * * *

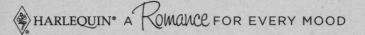
HARLEQUIN® A *Romance* FOR EVERY MOOD

If you enjoyed these passionate reads, then you will love other stories from

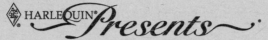
HARLEQUIN® *Presents*

Glamorous international settings...
unforgettable men...passionate romances—
Harlequin Presents promises you the world!

HARLEQUIN® *Blaze*

Fun, flirtatious and steamy books that tell it
like it is, inside and outside the bedroom.

Silhouette **Desire**

Always Powerful, Passionate and Provocative

Six new titles are available every month from each of these lines

Available wherever books are sold

HARLEQUIN *Presents*

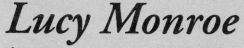

HIS PENNILESS BEAUTY

by

Julia James

Nikos Kazandros is outraged to see *his*
Sophie Granton, a woman he thought
he knew, offering her services as
a professional date! To stop her
he'll have to pay for her time…
something he is *more* than willing to do!

Available July 2010!

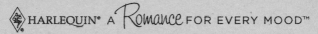

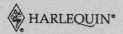

HARLEQUIN®

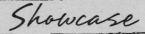

Showcase

On sale May 11, 2010

Reader favorites from the most talented voices in romance

Save $1.00 on the purchase of 1 or more Harlequin® Showcase books.

SAVE
$1.00

on the purchase of 1 or more Harlequin® Showcase books.

Coupon expires Oct 31, 2010. Redeemable at participating retail outlets.
Limit one coupon per purchase. Valid in the U.S.A. and Canada only.

52609015

Canadian Retailers: Harlequin Enterprises Limited will pay the face value of this coupon plus 10.25¢ if submitted by customer for this product only. Any other use constitutes fraud. Coupon is nonassignable. Void if taxed, prohibited or restricted by law. Consumer must pay any government taxes. Void if copied. Nielsen Clearing House ("NCH") customers submit coupons and proof of sales to Harlequin Enterprises Limited, P.O. Box 3000, Saint John, NB E2L 4L3, Canada. Non-NCH retailer—for reimbursement submit coupons and proof of sales directly to Harlequin Enterprises Limited, Retail Marketing Department, 225 Duncan Mill Rd., Don Mills, ON M3B 3K9, Canada.

U.S. Retailers: Harlequin Enterprises Limited will pay the face value of this coupon plus 8¢ if submitted by customer for this product only. Any other use constitutes fraud. Coupon is nonassignable. Void if taxed, prohibited or restricted by law. Consumer must pay any government taxes. Void if copied. For reimbursement submit coupons and proof of sales directly to Harlequin Enterprises Limited, P.O. Box 880478, El Paso, TX 88588-0478, U.S.A. Cash value 1/100 cents.

5 65373 00076 2 (8100)0 11651

HSCCOUP0410